I0822190

# SOLAR ASHES

BIRTH OF A HERO

## BIRTH OF A HERO

JASON BRADFORD

*SOLAR ASHES: Birth of a Hero*

This is a work of fiction. Names, characters, places, and incidents either are the product of the author's imagination or are used fictitiously. Any resemblance to actual persons, living or dead, events, or locales is entirely coincidental.



For information about this title or to order other books and/or electronic media, contact the publisher:

Jason Bradford
Lone Palm Publishing
Arizona, United States
www.bradfordbooks.com
www.solarashes.com

ISBNs:
979-8-9853736-2-2 (hardcover)
979-8-9853736-0-8 (softcover)
979-8-9853736-1-5 (eBook)

Printed in the United States of America

Interior design: 1106 Design
Cover Art and design by Leraynne

First paperback edition 2022

*This book is dedicated to my mother who taught me the value of storytelling as a child while waiting for our restaurant entrees. (A time before cell phones could distract us from the magic of imagination.) Thank you for encouraging and inspiring creativity throughout the decades.*

# ACKNOWLEDGMENTS

First and foremost, I need to thank my family for helping me bring this story out into the hands of readers: My parents, who provided endless encouragement, much-appreciated constructive criticism, and truckloads of developmental ideas. My children, who dedicated heaps of inspiration and distraction just to add a little more challenge along the way.

Thank you to Michele DeFilippo and her amazing team at 1106 Design, who took a chunky stone and polished it into a gem. Thank you to Belle Manuel for her insightful edit, and, of course, to Frank Kresen, my premier editor who examined each line of text to ensure you enjoy reading every paragraph without scratching your head. Ronda Rawlins, thank you for tossing the lasso around my waist and dragging me along the path to publishing. Leraynne is the talented artist whose cover art brings the characters to life and inspired you to pick up or click on this book in the first place.

And last but not least, I thank you, the reader, for embarking on this journey into the Vesputi Galaxy with me. I've worked to create an experience for you. Experiences create great stories, and great stories can turn humble writers into storytellers.

# CHAPTER 1

**Milky Way Galaxy**
**Odyssey Control Room**
**Year 2098**

Titan raced forward and dove under the captain's chair, causing it to spin in a full circle. The man still seated in the chair reached out to the control console in front of him and steadied himself. He continued to study the monitors around him, barely noticing the massive puppy underneath him still scrambling for the rubber ball. He reached downward and fished the ball from under his feet. He then flung it backward over his shoulder without paying attention to where it might land. Titan quickly changed course and, once again, dashed for her prize. This exchange had taken place so often that each player knew their expected part, and both performed as expected.

Norman remained fixated on the stellar charts. Their current projected course should steer them way clear of the asteroid field that CARIE just displayed. Computer Assisted Research Intelligence for (Deep Space) Exploration, or CARIE for short. The artificial intelligence was just as much a part of the crew as anyone else and proved to play quite a critical role on the ship. Besides, CARIE earned the name because she had a northern American accent that could be quite endearing if he hadn't already grown sick of listening to her chime in on something—anything—every 30 seconds. Sometimes it felt as if Norman had two wives on board barking orders at him. Never mind that he was supposedly the captain.

"So, Captain, how do we look?" Norman glanced over to his left to acknowledge the presence of the slender, raven-haired female who'd just entered the command room. He then turned right back to the monitor and entered in a few keystrokes before answering.

"Well, CARIE spotted what looks to be an asteroid field, but based on distance and our present trajectory, it shouldn't be a problem. Other than the fact that we've charted a course for oblivion, we should be just fine for quite some time."

"Aren't you just brimming with positivity today?" Melina asked, resting a warm hand on her husband's shoulder before settling into the chair next to him. She propped her bare feet up on the console, flipped a tress of long hair behind her shoulder, and leaned back as she sipped from a warm mug. "I've prepped our meal. It's waiting for us in the kitchen. Or at least what one could call a kitchen."

"Galley," Norman responded without looking over at her. He tapped the corner of the screen and brought up another star chart. He manipulated the graphics on the screen with his finger and punched in some additional data to update it with their current flight status. He integrated the charted course with the current fuel, oxygen, and food supply in order to estimate how far they could feasibly venture into the galaxy.

"It's just like home. I'm taking care of the family while you're stuck at the computer, effectively ignoring me." She awaited a response as she watched her husband, still fixated on the controls in front of him. "Norman . . ."

"Galley. It's called a 'galley' where we eat."

"I don't really care what it's called. It's a tight little room with a bolted-down table and chairs." She put down her cup and spun to face him. She saw the worry etched in his countenance. The past two years of desperate planning, preparation, and construction had maliciously stolen a dozen years of youth from his forty-year-old face. He was wearing the black uniform of a deep space explorer, and it fit his athletic frame well; but no matter how well he looked the part, there was no mistaking that this former pilot was overmatched for the task at hand. "We'll find a new home. There'll be something out there."

"Only time will tell."

"Actually, sir, *I* can tell you," CARIE chimed in. "You have charted a course for Sectors 12-27. There has been no discovered sign of life or hospitable planetary spheres in that region."

"Thanks, Dear. Good thing I wasn't asking you," Norman blurted as he turned to Melina and rolled his eyes. He lowered his voice to a whisper and spoke to Melina. "She's been on my nerves today. I'm deeply regretting that they never installed a mute button."

"If you would prefer, I can disable my system and leave the sector searches to you, Captain," CARIE responded in her usual dry tone.

"No need for sarcasm," Melina interjected. "We appreciate all you do for us, CARIE. Just keep scanning for atmospheric compatibility."

"I will. It is a primary function of my design."

"We understand. Thank you. Don't mind the captain; he just gets irritable when he's hungry. We will be retiring to the kitchen . . . er . . . galley, so, alert us if we're needed."

"Copy. You won't be needed. We have just traversed Sector 4 with negative results. Sector 5 will yield the same result."

"Okay," Melina said as she pulled her husband from his chair. Norman climbed out of its soft confines and walked beside her to the exit. Titan was already standing at his heels, ball in mouth and tail wagging.

They stepped into the corridor and moved toward the galley. It wouldn't be a long walk. The ship was designed for preliminary scouting. Normally, it would be found docked on the larger mobile space station and deployed on exploration missions that would typically last no more than a few months. It was built for speed and transatmospheric flight, so it could insert into a planet's atmosphere and survey much of the terrain, resources, and conditions in a relatively short period of time. Its design was derived from the image of a diving bird, and the starboard thrusters ensured that it moved with the same relative speed and grace.

Norman stopped and looked through the framed window into the cosmos. Historically, space had been referred to as "empty," but he knew this was not the case. Its cold silence and eternal vastness understandably influenced this notion, but his experience as a deep-space pilot had opened his eyes to the majesty of the universe—a universe that held innumerable possibilities. He clung to the hope of those possibilities. The desperate notion that a new home could be found out there. Somewhere.

In his previous mission, they had discovered life, albeit microbial, in Sector 10. But Norman knew they would have to venture out farther than ever to get to a truly hospitable planet. There would need to be a supernova capable of providing the warmth and life synthesis to inspire and sustain existence. This meant going beyond charted territory. The idea was nerve-wracking and ran its fair share of risk. The alternative meant certain death through oxygen depletion and starvation.

Day 56 since the sun failed and darkness fell.

They knew it would happen, but the process had accelerated unnaturally. The sun—the fiery ball of light and warmth—just went dark and cold, defying all scientific explanation.

He should feel relieved to be here now, having escaped their doomed world months before the collapse, but the horror of the event still hung fresh in his mind. How many survived? What had become of home? In a single moment, the whole planet had been extinguished like a snuffed flame. What had happened?

Day 18 since the launch from the space station. They were forced to deploy earlier than expected. Four months early. Way too early. But the station could no longer sustain so many refugees.

The sound of laughter spilling from the galley yanked him back to the present. Norman turned from the window and stepped into the next room. The galley wasn't anything to brag about. The cabinets and countertops were crafted of brushed aluminum. The table and round stools were bolted to the floor and weren't necessarily designed for comfort. Melina was sitting at the head of the table, divvying up noodles and rice among three different plates. As Norman stepped forward, she half-spun a plate toward him. He sat down between her and the empty chair to his left. He leaned over and kissed her cheek before sipping from the Bosa water in front of him.

"Where is he?"

"He's putting the pup away. He'll be back in a minute," Melina replied.

"He'd better hurry. This meal is notorious for going cold before we can finish." Norman spun the noodles on his fork and ate. His eyes grew wide. "Yum. Sweetheart, you truly have outdone yourself this time. This is even better than yesterday's."

"Shut up," she said with a smirk. "You say that every time."

"And I mean it every time." Norman patted her hand and snuck another kiss.

"Sure, you do."

A boy suddenly came running into the room. Before he reached the table, he dropped to his knees and slid several feet, practically striking the stool. He popped up and plopped himself down in front of his noodles. "Titan's put away. Though she still wanted to play some more. Dad made her hyper."

Melina shot Norman a look of disapproval. "Hey, don't blame me," he said, defending himself. "She almost killed me in the control room. I just tossed her ball, and I'm not taking the blame."

"Did you wash your hands, Conor?" Melina asked.

"Yep."

"How's Grayson doing?" Norman asked.

Melina finished swallowing a scoop of rice. "The baby has been asleep for about an hour. So, let's be quiet, or else I'm going to make you two take care of him."

The three ate in silence for a few minutes as the spacecraft traveled noiselessly toward the outreaches of space. The ship was large enough to normally outfit a crew of about 50 trained explorers. Unfortunately, in the desperation of the hasty launch, they couldn't gather more than 14 people. Their mission into the void didn't attract many volunteers. Fortunately, CARIE took care of most of the flight responsibilities, although a larger crew would be optimal for adequate planetary exploration.

Norman glanced to his left and spotted a smudge of black running down Conor's right arm. "How's the hot chamber?"

The slender boy looked up at him in surprise. "I wasn't . . ." Norman slightly shook his head. "How did you know?" Norman didn't answer. He simply pointed to Conor's right arm. The boy rubbed the grease smear from his forearm.

Melina blurted out, "What were you doing?"

"Titan ran inside, and I chased her. That's all."

"It's not safe. I know I've told you a hundred times not to go down there!"

"I didn't touch anything this time. Promise."

"The last time Charlie caught you in there, you almost died. I mean, do you want to have your skin melt off your bones like tree sap? Because it sounds like you won't be happy until you do," Melina said with a mother's anxiety-laced irritation.

"What's Charlie up to?" Norman interjected. Little did he know, but this seemingly innocent question aptly redirected his wife's indignation against him in an instant.

"That's all you're going to say?! You let me be the gruff bad guy and then ask about Charlie? Do something about your son, Norman." She was now staring at him with her mouth slightly parted and with eyes of fire. If she could have shot beams of hot light from those mystical eyes, Norman knew he would have been seared right through his chest. Good thing she didn't have superpowers.

Norman began to correct his oversight. "Your mother is absolutely right. The last time you fooled around in the rear power chamber, you almost blew the ship in half. The cores are highly volatile and unstable if they're disturbed, even in the slightest. I've already explained this to you, and I'm not going to let you blame the dog."

The commander looked at the steaming woman for an instant. Those fierce eyes were still aimed at him. The fire in them hadn't dissipated. He canted his body away from his accuser and directed his attention back to his son. "You are grounded." He risked a glance over his shoulder. The eyes were still piercing him. Still not good enough. "And by that, I mean" (Norman conjured up thoughts of some chore he didn't want to save for himself) "you're on latrine duty. Right after dinner, in fact."

"What? I have to clean the toilets?"

"Yep, indeed."

"How many? Not *all* of them."

"Nooo," Norman chuckled. He threw a sideways glance at his wife. How could such beauty hold such fiery contempt at times? "Yes, *all* of them."

"There's no way I'm doing the one in the mechanic bay. Forget it! That is just too nasty."

Melina couldn't resist any longer. "Your father and I have told you time and again not to wander around the ship and just go where you please. We can't afford to have you playing around and getting in the way all the time. This is not a playground. You need to be more responsible and act like you're twelve years old instead of five. Are you listening?"

Conor was still sitting with his head down and eyes fixated on his bowl of noodles. He continued to spin them around on his fork, waiting for the scolding to end. He could still hear his mother's voice sounding nearby, but he had since tuned her out. He was just feeling lucky right now that at least they hadn't found out about the mining equipment. How was he supposed to know one little button press on The Piercer could carve such a giant hole in the belly of the Land Hopper? Hopefully, it still worked. Otherwise, his punishment would be even worse, and his father might actually get angry this time. But for now, no one knew about the little mistake, and he still had some time to think of a good excuse.

Suddenly, the lights went out. Melina cut off her speech to Conor in midsentence and gave a startled gasp. Everything had gone black. Norman remained still, willing the lights to revive, as if any sudden movement might thwart his pretend ability to wish for light to return. He turned to reason. "Everyone, relax. The emergency lights will turn on any . . ."

Just then, dim emergency lights flickered on, and they were able to see again. The room was now thrust in shadow broken by scattered light, but it was much better than the heavy darkness that had fallen just moments before.

"See? I told you everything would be fine," Norman offered. "It's probably just a glitch in the power core conduit. I would bet Marshall is on top of it already." Conor and Melina settled down under Norman's calming words. If anyone knew this ship, it was Norman. And CARIE.

Melina breathed in deeply before calling out, "CARIE."

No response.

"CARIE. Please respond. CARIE." Melina's voice cracked a bit, as uncertainty began to seep in again. "CARIE! Respond!"

Norman also began to sense something wasn't right. "CARIE! Command for response."

"CARIE! CAR—" Melina yelled again.

"Yessss. I am here," the unseen computer finally responded.

"Give me a sitrep," Norman blurted out, still perturbed but relieved that the mother system was still functional and responsive.

"I've been running diagnostics. I'm unable to detect a system failure."

"Have you checked the power conduit switchback modules?"

"Of course, I have. We do not have a system failure."

"Well, something must be wrong."

"There is nothing wrong with the ship, Captain. We are fully functional and operating at predicted capacity," CARIE stated.

"Perhaps she just can't locate the issue," Norman said to Melina. "I'll have to head back to the control room and look into it myself."

"Negative, Captain," CARIE interrupted. "I am not mistaken. I repeat, the ship is fully functional. Do not seek to undermine my operational function."

"Then why has the power failed?"

"Sir?" CARIE started.

"Yes? Report," Norman commanded, as his frustration brimmed.

"Sir. . . . You are not alone."

Suddenly, the emergency power shut off, engulfing the ship in complete darkness.

Conor reached out and gripped the table tightly. He couldn't see anything. Not even a crack of light pierced the blackness. He began to hear breathing coming from his parents. Sounds were amplified, and it seemed as if he were sitting next to a winded dragon who'd just run the 50-yard dash.

Everyone sat completely still—shocked immobile and silent. The sensation of such deep dark was paralyzing. It seemed like hours before someone finally spoke. Conor's mother was first. She started calling for the computer again, shouting "CARIE" over and over.

Finally, Norman interrupted her. "She's not there. We've lost all power. That includes the computer assistance node. Just remain calm."

Suddenly a loud crash erupted from the front of the ship. Norman gasped, and Melina screamed. The terrified woman gripped the table and felt around to her left. She groped her husband's arm and moved her hands up and across his shoulders. She moved farther, seeking out her boy. She quickly found him and rested her chin against his neck. Conor reached up and clung to his mother. He felt better now under her touch, though he still couldn't see her.

Three more tremendous bangs echoed through the ship. The spacecraft teetered as if being rocked on a dark ocean. Reasonable explanations for the loss of power and the crashes began to circulate through Norman's mind. He calculated the possibilities—seeking out the cause and the solution.

"We need a light," Melina whispered. Her words brought Norman to the current predicament. First things first. He needed to be able to see in order to do anything. He was in the galley. There wouldn't be a portable light in here. The closest light device would be back in the control room. He'd have to retrace his steps, stumbling through the dark to get back to the helm.

"I need to get to the control room," he said. "There are lights there. I'll go and bring them back to you. You two just stay here, and don't move."

Conor reached out and gripped his father's arm. “Don't leave.”

“I need to get to the control room. The ship could be badly damaged. I'd wager we found some sort of light asteroid field or some type of floating debris. Our imaginations are having us think it's much worse than it really is.”

Conor squeezed his father's arm again. “I don't think so.”

Norman agreed, but he wouldn't tell his son that. The power had failed before the crash. That was odd. In all his travels through space, he hadn't dealt with a similar occurrence. Regardless, he had to move. He felt for his son's face and held it between his hands. “Conor, don't fear the dark. Just go find the light. And that's exactly what I'm going to do.” He tussled the boy's hair and then felt for his wife. His fingers wove through her soft, curly hair and found the back of her head. “Take care of our boy. I'll get us a light so you can go check on the baby. I'll be back.” Norman bent forward and kissed her lips. “I love you.”

“I love you. Please hurry,” she whispered. She felt him pull away. She listened intently as her husband moved in the direction of the forward door that would take him back to the control room. She heard his shuffled footsteps and the amplified noise of his hands brushing against the wall for support.

Then he moved through the open doorway, and she couldn't hear any more. She sat and waited for more explosive sounds, but nothing came. It was worse not to hear anything. Then Conor broke the silence with a soft whisper just below her face.

“Mother?”

Melina answered with a soft Hmmm?”

“What did CARIE mean?”

“About what?” She knew what Conor was asking. Since those words had been uttered, she'd been holding the deep fears in the back of her mind.

"About us not being alone."

Before Melina could muster an answer, heavy footsteps echoed from the starboard exit hallway. They approached at a hurried pace, and she could feel each thudding footfall in her chest.

*We're about to find out.*

Two blinding streams of white light pierced the room and carved through the heavy darkness like blazing swords. She held her breath.

"Hey! Glad we found you," said the first figure through the door. Melina felt her anxiety wash out of her like a tidal wave.

"Charlie!" she gasped. "I'm so relieved to see you. You guys scared the crap out of us."

"We came to find you as soon as we could," Charlie said, "but don't get too relieved just yet."

"Where's the captain?" the second figure asked. Melina recognized Rhonda's voice before she could make out her face.

"He went to the control room. It's just Conor and I here. I need to get to my baby."

"Of course," Charlie said as he pulled two small flashlights from his pocket and handed them to Conor and Melina. "Take these, and get your family together in the rear deck. Rhonda's going to try to get everyone together in the atrium since it's the largest space."

"The computer system is unresponsive," Rhonda added as she leaned forward toward Conor. She inhaled deep. "Mmm. Smells good." Conor could see her better now that she was closer and sharing her light with him. When she leaned forward, Conor could smell a sweet botanical aroma. He always liked the way Rhonda smelled. It also helped that she was a young, attractive brunette of twenty-something years. He could never remember how old she actually was, but it didn't matter. With only a few men left around, he assumed that he might have a chance one day to make her his girlfriend.

Her standard-issue explorer flight jumpsuit brushed up against his shoulder. "You gonna finish that?" she asked him in her usual gentle tone. Conor looked up at the soft contours of her face and noticed her staring down at his noodles. He slowly pushed it toward her.

"Nope. I was saving it for you," Conor replied in his coolest voice possible. At least he thought he was being cool by suggesting that he'd been thinking of her. His reward came when she brushed her fingers through his thick brown hair. Of course, he had to push it back behind his ears as she pulled the bowl toward her, but he didn't mind at all.

Rhonda began to slurp down the noodles as Charlie spoke up. "I'm still trying to get a handle on the power supply. I'll leave the control room and the computer issue to the captain."

"Sounds good," Melina added. "But what about those crashes?"

"Jose, Vlad, Beth, and a few others headed that way to investigate it."

"And the rest of the crew?"

Charlie looked at Rhonda. She set down her bowl and shook her head. Melina observed their little non-verbal communication and felt her anxiety mounting again. "What? What aren't you telling us?"

The room hung in silence.

"Tell me," Melina insisted.

"The commander needs to get the computer back online," Rhonda answered. She knew the lieutenant would never accept that kind of response, but she didn't have another answer she wanted to give.

Melina's irritation grew and came out in her words. "I'm not asking as Melina the Space Mom. I'm now asking as your superior officer. Tell me what is happening . . . to the best of your knowledge."

Charlie took over for Rhonda in an effort to deflect the lieutenant's ire. "With comms down, we don't know. We haven't had contact with them since the power went down."

"Since the explosions," Rhonda added.

"Explosions!" Conor blurted out.

His mother shared his shock. "Explosions?! We heard crashes but didn't know about any explosions. Is there a fire? Is the area contained?"

Charlie swallowed hard and responded, "As far as we know, the airlocks activated to seal off that portion of the ship. No fires have been reported, but . . ."

"We lost communication," Rhonda added.

"I understand that. We need to determine the extent and the cause." Melina slipped into her leadership role with ease. There was work to be done.

"Ma'am," Charlie started, "that is precisely why we sent Jose and the others to investigate. It's being taken care of. As for the rest of the missing crew, they were localized in the suspected area of the explosions."

Melina rubbed her brow and closed her eyes. "Oh, I see." She exhaled deeply and then took a steady drink of water. She methodically set down her cup. "What do you need?"

Charlie felt the tension leaving the conversation as he realized he wasn't going to be reprimanded for anything. At least not yet. "I would recommend that you get your baby and head to the atrium. You will be able to gauge and address any safety issues on the other side of the mid-ship airlock. No one has been back there yet, and we need a status."

"I copy. That's where I'll go."

Conor stood up in the midst of the three capable flight crewmembers. "I'll go with Rhonda. She might need help."

"No." All three adults answered in unison.

Conor wanted to help rather than go sit in a garden and wait while everyone else did important work. "Fine, I'll go with Charlie to the hot room."

"Negative," Melina said. The answer came without much required thought. "There is no way you will be going back to that area of the ship any time soon. We've already had one explosion—we certainly don't need a cataclysmic meltdown. You're staying with me."

Conor wasn't surprised. He knew there was no chance his mother would let him out of her sight right now. But it was still worth a shot. Rhonda nudged his shoulder and then moved toward the northern doorway. "I'll be back to you guys as soon as I can find the others," she said.

Charlie turned toward the south exit. He opened the door and paused. "Get your family," he turned and said before stepping into the darkness.

Conor held tight to the small flashlight in his hand. It illuminated enough of the room for him to see comfortably the shadowed shapes of familiar objects. More than anything, it gave him comfort to be able to see things. Hopefully it would keep any demons at bay. He also drew comfort from the strength and courage of the woman beside him.

"Okay. We need to get to the baby and then the atrium," Conor's mother whispered. "Are you ready?" Conor nodded. "Turn off your light." The boy shot her a look of bewilderment. *She must be crazy if she thinks I would ever turn this light off.* Melina calmly placed her hand against his cheek. "We should conserve their limited power. If they both go out at once, then we are back in the dark. We'll use my light for now."

Conor turned off the light and slid it into his pocket. The darkness seemed to creep closer now that they were employing only one of the flashlights. He took in a deep breath and stood up from the table. "We need to get Titan, too."

"We will. You can grab her when we get Grayson."

"She'll be scared," Conor said.

"No way, sweetheart. Not Titan. She's brave, like you are. Besides, did you know that she can see better than we can in the dark?"

"Yeah."

"Of course. But did you also know that she doesn't even need to see that well? Titan will be able to smell us coming long before we even see her. Now let's get moving before the lights come back on and we feel silly for all this trouble."

"You think dad will get power back?"

"If I know your father, he'll get this ship back on track. There isn't anything he can't fix. Now be brave. There's nothing that you and I can't handle."

Melina took her boy's hand and led him to the rear exit. They stepped through the door and into the long hallway. The light pierced the dark about 20 feet in front of them. As they moved forward, it swept back the dark edges. They moved with purpose—a mother determined to get to her child.

The hallway ended with a compression door. That's not where they needed to go. Prior to the door, another hall opened to the left. She hugged the corner and pushed the light down the secondary hall. Everything seemed in order. But it was eerily quiet. No cries from the baby or movement from crew members.

They were now in the sleeping quarters. Her room would be down the far end on the right—the largest of the rooms. The captain's quarters. One of the perks of being married to the commander. Although it wasn't really much to brag about, and they did share it with the newborn. At ten weeks old and born on the space station, Grayson was a true miracle. It didn't hurt that Dr. Hilbert had also made the voyage. While she wasn't an OBGYN by trade, she had known more than enough to care for Melina and the baby during the delivery.

As they neared her quarters, she felt Conor slip from her grasp. He moved away from her to the left and flicked on his light. His room was just across the hall from hers. That's where Titan would be.

Conor lifted the handle and pushed the door inward. His light painted the room back and forth. There was no sign of the puppy. Normally, she waited for him at the door just far enough for it to miss her nose when it swung open. She was fiercely loyal and protective of Conor. The boy bonded almost immediately with the charcoal-gray Cane Corso breed, and their union blossomed on this voyage as the rest of their world fell into ruin.

Conor's breathing became shallower as his heart thumped faster. Where was his dog? Forgetting about his mother and the black abyss enveloping the ship, Conor darted into the room. Nothing seemed out of place. "Titan," he called out in a harsh whisper. "Titan, come here." There was still no response.

His head jerked from left to right and back again. She had to be there. It's exactly where he'd left her just before dinner. Had someone let her out? Who would do that? It didn't make any sense. No. She had to be here.

"Titan," Conor called out in a raised voice, forgetting fear and any cautionary need for keeping quiet. To him, it didn't matter anymore. He moved to the closet but found it empty except for a few hanging shirts. Under the bed? Conor dropped to his stomach and swept the light under the metal frame suspended from the wall. Nothing.

He sat up and rested his hands on his knees, letting the light drop to the floor and roll away. Fear and worry began to creep back in.

Then a scream echoed nearby. It was his mother.

Conor jolted and grabbed the portable light on the floor nearby. He tried to jump to his feet but fell forward to his hands and knees. His head cracked into the long footlocker with a resounding thud. He shook it off and tried to regain his balance, but, suddenly, the chest that held several pairs of boots and miscellaneous clothes made another thud. At first, he thought it was from something tumbling inside, but it bumped again and again.

Without giving much thought to what horrors could be banging around inside with his socks and underwear, Conor lifted the latch and flung up the top. Before he could focus the light on the box's interior, he came under attack. The light caught a set of fangs and large white eyes just as the creature pounced on him, knocking him back on his butt and sending the flashlight skidding across the floor. With the light now focusing behind him, he couldn't see what had struck him. But once the beast ferociously licked his face, he knew he'd been attacked by nothing less than a titan. His Titan.

Conor gave the enthusiastic puppy a great squeeze as he allowed her to continue the kisses. He felt a shower of relief to find his friend hiding out and free from harm, but this joyful reunion couldn't linger long. The scream from across the hall still resounded in his memory.

Conor grabbed the flashlight and jolted upright. He flashed the light on Titan just to confirm she really was okay. "Come on, girl. Let's go," he said as he moved to the door. He stepped over the threshold and dashed into his mother's chambers. He found her standing with her back to the door. At first glance, she looked perfectly fine, and he couldn't determine what was up.

"What's wrong?" he asked as he moved toward her. Melina didn't answer him. She continued to trace her hands on the object in front of her. The baby's crib. It stood in the back corner and appeared to be undisturbed until he stepped closer. The entire front of the metal crib had been ripped away and tossed aside.

Grayson was gone.

# CHAPTER 2

**Odyssey**
**Sleeping Quarters**

At first, he hoped that perhaps Grayson had left the crib and climbed into a chest, like Titan had. But that was a ridiculous thought—impossible. Wait. How did his dog manage to do that? Conor looked down at the puppy seated next to him. Had someone put her there, or had she done it herself? That would have to be an investigation for another time. He grabbed his mother's arm and remembered to turn off his light. She stood riveted in shock. Had she even noticed he was standing there? Though standing right next to his mother, in that moment Conor felt an odd sensation of loneliness. He had to snap her out of it.

"Mom? What happened to Grayson?"

Melina didn't make a sound. She tossed the small mattress over as if the baby were hiding underneath, or to find some clue as to what happened. Suddenly, Titan pushed through them and began sniffing the mattress, the crib and all around the floor. Her eyes narrowed and a snarl curled across her lips, baring sharp teeth. Then without warning, she turned and ran to the hallway. Conor instinctively followed, yanking his mother along with him. Quickly noticing that he couldn't see anything in front of him, Conor reached behind and pried the flashlight from his mother's tenuous grip.

Mother and son trailed behind the determined puppy. She would sniff, pause, and then press forward—moving as if drawn by some unseen presence. Conor hadn't seen his dog behave this way before, acting so determined and disturbed.

They came upon a secured door. Titan sat beside it, waiting for her master to open it and facilitate the rest of the search. This particular door would lead them past the engine room and gravitational controls. The atrium was positioned at the other end of the corridor through an airlocked transition chamber. This chamber essentially divided the ship into two independent compartments, the front and rear of the spacecraft, each capable of sustainability absent the other.

The team of intrepid explorers ventured quickly through the hall with Titan still moving purposefully. She didn't stop and sniff much, as it appeared nothing of significant interest existed there. The engine-room door was still secure, and a quick flash from Conor's light through the small window in the upper center of the door revealed no one inside. They moved onward.

Titan suddenly stopped beside the gravitational control hatch. Her lips curled back, and she uttered a low, guttural growl. She then paced back and forth around the room's exterior threshold but refused to enter through the open door. Conor and Melina caught up to her. As he illuminated the doorway, they stood in shock.

Thick crimson blood was pooled around the entryway.

Melina quickly gained her resolve and snatched the light away from her son. "Wait here," she said as she moved beyond the threshold. She feared the worst but decided to hope that someone had merely bumped their head in the dark hard enough to cause bleeding. She swept the light along the room's interior. The control panels and computer systems sat lifeless due to the power outage. However, like the air-supply system, the gravitational controls could run independently on a backup generator in the event of an outage such as this.

Everything appeared in order other than the pooled blood outside and some smeared streaks along the door. Under closer inspection, she observed the door was broken—crumpled inside the threshold. Its aluminum carbonate had badly bent back on itself. Something powerful appeared to have twisted it. A flutter of movement caught her eye. Something loose was dangling from one of the sharp pieces jutting outward.

She held the light up closer as she reached out. It was soft and flimsy to the touch. When she peeled it away from the metal and flipped it over in her hand, she noticed the fabric. A piece of the flight uniform had been torn away from someone's upper sleeve. It held the patch of the Deep Space Flight Program.

Melina let the patch fall from her fingers as she moved out of the room to meet her son. She peered down at him and met his eyes with her own. She couldn't find the right words. "Grayson's not here, and someone's hurt. Let's keep moving." That's all she could manage.

Conor didn't question her. If he had needed to know something, then she would have told him. He figured she still didn't know what was happening on their ship. He just felt glad to have his mother back. She now moved and acted as a Space Force Lieutenant rather than the desperate and distraught mother from a few minutes before.

Melina shined the light around the hallway, seeking more clues. Streaks of blood carried down the corridor, leaving a ghastly trail on the floor toward the rear airlock. The smeared blood suggested someone had been dragged away. Her brimming fear urged her to turn back and move away from the potential danger ahead, but her instincts as a leader and a mother pressed her forward.

They arrived at the hatch. More blood was pooled around the entry and decorated the right side of the threshold. She reached out and slid the latch to the left. Compressed air hissed as the lock released, and the door cracked open. "Stay close to me," she whispered to the boy at her side. Conor reached down and stroked the head of his loyal pet waiting at his side.

The chamber wasn't more than a narrow space serving as the physical barrier between the fore and aft portions of the spacecraft. The design served to separate the ship into two parts in the event a separation became necessary during planetary exploration. With the rear section detached, the ship could perform planetary navigation more efficiently as a smaller craft. To Melina's knowledge, her husband had never found the need to cause a separation. This could be done only in the rear cockpit, the command room, or automatically in the event of a significant event that compromised the integrity of either section.

Regardless, she wanted to move as quickly as she could out of the transition chamber. If something were to happen while inside what she called "no man's land," they would be abandoned to empty space. Conor pulled the hatch closed behind him once Titan passed through. Hearing the door close and secure, Melina reached for the opposing door and opened it. Another hiss sounded as they gained entry to the rear deck.

A shroud of darkness covered this area as well. Titan moved past them and sniffed around the immediate area. She moved toward the atrium but then stopped. She snarled, sensing danger nearby. Melina and Conor sensed it, too. The area felt heavy, like gravity had doubled its force and compressed them from all sides. Melina covered the light with her hand to cut down on its brilliance. If an enemy were out there, she didn't want to give away their position.

They moved forward with caution and delicate precision in an effort to suppress the noise from their footsteps. They soon came up to the atrium. She recognized the half-walls encircling it. Inside would be benches, some exercise equipment, and live vegetation. But there was something else inside. Something that didn't belong there. She heard it shuffling around.

Melina instinctively crouched down and pulled Conor behind the half-wall. Even in the complete dark, she couldn't risk a premature discovery. She pressed her lips to her son's ear. "Someone is in there, and something tells me in my gut we don't want them to find us." Conor nodded without uttering a word. "Stay down behind this wall. We'll move around to the sleeping chamber," she whispered, her voice shaky. "There's a weapons cabinet inside. I'd feel better with a rifle in my hand."

Conor moved his head so he could put his mouth close to his mother's ear. "I would feel better, too. We'll follow you." He then pleaded for Titan to stay quiet. It was a long shot, but hopefully, she instinctively knew when to listen.

Melina extinguished the light and continued moving silently around the atrium's outer perimeter. She stopped suddenly when they heard a guttural noise from inside the room. The sound wasn't human.

Then she heard a hiss. And another. More than one thing was stalking around inside here with them. They seemed to be communicating with each other.

Now something moved. Several crashes sounded inside the atrium just on the other side of the wall. Melina recognized the sound of dumbbells being dropped to the floor. The intruder moved heavily, indicative of a large person or creature. Melina struggled to piece together all the information at her disposal. The deep darkness stifled her ability to resolve the threat or understand it. Part of her wanted to stand up and flash her light inside the atrium. Perhaps if she could see, then she would comprehend what was happening. Simple fear might have been fueling her imagination.

Nevertheless, she ruled against it. She wouldn't expose herself until her child was safe and she had armed herself. Then she could better handle the situation and figure out what the hell had happened to her baby boy.

She peeled off the atrium and moved to the back wall while pulling Conor behind her. The dog followed suit, clearly not wanting to have anything to do with what else was moving inside the room. Melina found the door to the cryogenic slumber chamber. Unfortunately, it was closed. Her heart sank because she knew it would make noise no matter how gingerly she pulled on the handle. The door would swoosh as she unlatched it and pulled it to the left. This would definitely alert whoever or whatever was lingering in the atrium. They would also be away from cover and concealment—stuck in the open.

More hissing pierced the silence. They moved again. She had to act fast.

Melina pulled Conor around her and posted him opposite her at the door. "Once I tell you to, I need you to open this door. They will know we are here, so I'll blind them with the light," she whispered. "You need to run inside. Move fast and get out of my way. I need to lock the door and get to the weapon cabinet. Understand?"

Conor simply nodded as he pulled Titan beside him. He then gripped the door latch with sweaty fingers, waiting for his mother's command. Melina took a deep breath and then whispered, "Now!" Conor pulled the latch out and jerked it to the left. The door made a *click* sound and a *whoosh* as it cracked its seal from the threshold and began to slide.

Deep growls sounded from the atrium. Something metallic dropped to the ground before heavy steps echoed through the chamber. Melina sprung to her feet and flashed the light in their direction in hopes to blind them for an instant. She wasn't prepared for what the light exposed.

Three hulking black masses were moving through the atrium, coming toward her position. They looked like giants draped in black armor from head to foot. She fixated on the closest threat as its red eyes stared directly at her. Its face was as dark as midnight with skin like weathered asphalt. Its lower jaw opened, baring jagged teeth as black as cauldrons. The two other creatures moved left and right. She recognized their effort to flank her position.

She didn't linger. Her hand moved to Conor's back, and she shoved him inside the room. As soon as they got inside the sleep chamber, Melina slammed the door shut and latched the locking mechanism. She moved with extreme urgency now. Her light brushed around the room, taking in as much of the setting as she could.

The weapon cabinet was affixed to the far wall. They moved quickly, no longer needing stealth or silence. She thrust her right palm against the panel on the upper right corner. Fortunately, it was battery powered and greeted her with two sweet-sounding beeps indicating that her prints had been analyzed and approved. The lever moved down with ease as the door opened, exposing three rifles, two hand pistols, and ample ammunition. She grabbed an assault rifle and a cartridge loaded with 30 high-powered rounds. The cartridge greeted the rifle with ease as it slid home. The spring-loaded lever on the side charged the weapon, sending a round into the chamber.

Although she didn't quite understand what she had just witnessed, or what she was now up against, she nevertheless felt a surge of power bestowed just by holding such a capable force in her hands. She stuffed the flashlight in her pocket along with two additional loaded magazines. She loaded a .45 caliber sidearm and tucked it at the small of her back.

The rifle was equipped with its own mounted light and a Seamus reticle optic. Top-of-the-line sweet firepower. She draped the weapon's sling over her shoulder and switched on the light.

The door handle clicked, followed by a loud crash as the invaders applied brute force to the door. Conor jumped. Whatever was outside wanted in, and he doubted the door would hold against it.

Melina suddenly grabbed his shoulder, guiding him toward the nearest sleeping pod. "Get inside, honey." The hatch opened upward, and the lights flickered to life. Apparently, the cryosleep pods maintained reserve power as well. It made sense, since they were life-sustaining, long-term independent chambers complete with feeding tubes and oxygen-intake nozzles.

Conor climbed inside as his mother began to close the hatch. "What about Titan?" he asked as he pushed back on the closing door.

"She'll go in the pod next to yours," Melina said as she accessed the neighboring pod and lifted Titan inside. She pressed several buttons inside it before closing it on the brave puppy. The chamber immediately began to function as a gaseous sleeping agent filled the interior.

"I'm going to activate Titan's pod," Melina advised as she slowly lowered the hatch over her son. "You be brave and stay quiet. If something happens, I want you to activate your pod. You remember how?"

"Yes," Conor replied, "but where are you going?"

"I've got to deal with a nightmare right now. Then I need to find your father and brother. But first I need to know you're safe. Are you safe?"

"Yes," her son said with a quick nod of his head. He knew his mother was in warrior mode and needed him out of her way. He remembered seeing her like this one time before—when the world fell.

"Good." Melina began to close the hatch. It latched in place, and she rested her palm lightly against its surface. She stared down at her son's worried face and choked back her brewing sadness. "I love you, Conor."

A solid bang sounded against the locked door protecting them from the horror outside. Melina quickly scanned the room, flicked off the weapon-mounted light, and dashed to the corner nearest the door. Another *bang* signaled the enemy's intention to make entry. The door wouldn't hold much longer against the destructive mass of whatever wanted to come inside.

She gripped the cold security of the polycarbonate-and-steel weapon in her hands. Those monsters were in for a treat when they came for her and her son. Nevertheless, she couldn't risk a gunfight in this room. She needed to lead them away from Conor.

The door blew open with a loud crash that sent a shudder through her bones. She gasped and moved backward from her kneeling position, causing her to bump into the aluminum cabinet door behind her.

The beasts slowly squeezed past the blown-out door and stepped into the chamber one by one. Melina could hear their steps and feel the enormous weight of their presence. One of the three made a guttural sound and moved past her position toward the far end of the room. The sleep pods, twenty of them in this particular chamber, were lined up, side by side, and joined head-to-head in the center of the room. All three of the creatures moved toward the far pods, where a frightened boy and dog waited defenseless.

She pictured their unseen forms moving away from her—toward Conor. She needed to draw away their attention and get them out of the room. Perhaps she could divert them and get them to follow her. Melina pushed lightly on the cabinet door to move out of the safe confines of her concealed position.

She slid out onto the cold floor and crawled to her right. The door would be to the right and behind her. She found the wall with her palm and eased to her feet. A few more soft steps to her right brought her to the corner.

She still couldn't see anything but deep blackness in front of her, but she knew the layout well enough to sense she was now facing the pods with her back to the ruptured door. The beasts were still moving away from her. She heard the crack and escape of air as they popped the hoods to the pods, seeking their prey. She refused to be their prey.

Melina raised the rifle to her shoulder and rested her trigger finger along the weapon's frame. Her left thumb twitched as it hovered over the switch to the light. She looked through the optic, a bright red reticle seeking its target pinned against the dark like a crimson beacon bouncing on the waves of an endless ocean.

She flicked the switch and lit up the room. Three massive shapes appeared. Their arms appeared like tree trunks; their bodies clad in midnight armor. Was it armor? It looked like blackened reptile skin, its own genetic armor. Each one stood hunched over a bit as they nearly scraped their helmets on the ceiling. They turned to face her, exposing jagged black teeth and reddened eyes that projected murderous purpose. The farthest one let out a growl as it raised a long staff.

She'd seen enough. Her finger found the trigger and she pulled it, sending a flurry of bullets toward the closest enemy. The rifle was set for a three-round burst. She sent three bursts as her optical gunsight marked its torso. The nine bullets found their mark, peppering the beast's chest and sending it stumbling backward. The monster next to it, holding the staff, suddenly pulled an object from its waist and flung it toward her. Melina sidestepped to the right to avoid being struck, but the object froze in midflight, hanging weightless. A sphere of swirling gray and white smoke spun at an immeasurable speed until it exploded outward.

Melina felt a heavy wave of the material strike her like a hammer. Yet she didn't fall from the blow. Instead, she felt immobile, as if she were buried in invisible, wet cement. Her mind still raced as the paralysis took hold. She watched as the beast she had shot with enough rounds to destroy a charging bull slowly raised itself up. It snarled and stepped toward her. Although the round sphere's blast had expanded outward in all directions, the beasts seemed to be unaffected by the same paralysis.

Melina struggled to fight against the pressing weight. She yelled in defiant rage. At least she tried to. The yell could be heard only in her own head as her mouth only slightly parted. As the creature moved closer, she focused all her efforts on pulling back the trigger again. She slowly wrenched it back, allowing the hammer to crash against the next three rounds. Fire erupted from the barrel as each bullet propelled forward. She could see each bullet spinning in flight as they left the rifle and carried on to their designated target. They sailed toward the creature's face.

To her horror, the creature simply ducked its head to the side. The bullets trudged forward as if traveling through compressed gelatin. They completely missed their mark as the beast raised its head again. This time its gnashing teeth seemed to form a devilish smirk. Now she knew these were nothing less than demons.

The creature reached behind its neck and pulled a rod from a sheath affixed to its back. It held out the object and watched as it began to shimmer and twist. It grew in length, roughly the size of a samurai sword. Smooth coils wrapped around itself forming a menacing spiral from the handle to the tip. The weapon glowed black, the spiral slowly turning in a counterclockwise motion. The beast now held the weapon out to the side as it approached its stationary target.

Despite flexing every muscle she possibly could, Melina couldn't dodge or defend against the blow as the demon raised the mysterious weapon and smashed it into her chest. The impact was devastating. It lifted her off the ground, sending her hurtling backward. She ricocheted off the door frame and flopped to the floor.

Melina gasped and coughed as blood spurted from her lips. Her head was swimming, and her ribcage felt as if it'd been hit by a truck going 70 mph. Melina knew things inside her were smashed and broken, but there wasn't time to linger. She willed her adrenaline-fueled muscles to move.

She pushed up to her knees and shook her head against the brewing dizziness. Her hands pressed against her chest. The pain was tremendous, and she couldn't muster more than rapid, shallow breaths. She then realized that, although her body hurt like hell, she could now at least move!

Her rifle's light was still illuminated, revealing the weapon's location nearby. She moved to pick it up and noticed in the angled light the demon ducking through the doorway.

*Time to go*, she thought as she gripped the rifle and backed up through the atrium. She fired several more times as the beast pursued her. Fast or slow, the rifle seemed to have little effect against their scaled flesh. Nevertheless, a wave of relief struck her as she realized all three creatures had come out of the chamber on the attack. They must not have seen Conor.

Shooting and moving, Melina had a twofold mission: keep them away from her son and try not to get killed. The atrium and its exercise equipment were in disarray. Dumbbells had been tossed about and weight benches were uprooted and toppled. Over by the treadmills, she spotted two lifeless bodies. She recognized Rhonda draped over Charlie like a rag doll. Her gaze didn't linger on the tragic sight; she had to focus on the danger—and make sure the monsters continued to follow her.

Another burst of rounds prompted her to perform a tactical reload before retreating from the room. The beasts remained close in steady pursuit.

### Control Room

For a brief moment, satisfaction washed over Norman as he stood at the blinking console. The dim secondary lights flickered and powered on. He had restored the ship's power. Well, not all of it. Just several of the emergency power nodes, but this seemed a good start. The critical systems would now be functional, and this meant that CARIE should be back online.

"CARIE. Report!" Norman exclaimed. No response. He called out again as he toggled the communications switches. "Come on, CARIE. Where are you?"

Suddenly a familiar voice sounded from the ceiling above him. "Massive hull damage. Cause: incendiary. Assessing . . . Power system failure. Cause: unknown. Possible collateral damage from the explosion. Assessing . . . Foredeck immobile. Thrusters inoperable. Rear deck still operable. Power core intact. Emergency power initiated. Emergency power system failure."

Norman abruptly stood. CARIE was running a diagnostic scan of the ship and the recent events. It was good to have her back. Her rapid scan and report continued. "Gravitational field accelerated. Pressure increasing. Pressure stabilized. Hull damage isolated. Weapon systems engaged. Weapon systems disabled. Interference detected. Cause: unknown. Additional lifeforms detected. Assessing . . . Crew multiplied. System override initiated. Cause: unknown. Foreign energy source detected. Crew diminished. Full system shutdown. Reboot . . ."

Norman interrupted CARIE's assessment in order to make some sense of her report. "CARIE, desist. You said there was a lifeform multiplier and then reduction. Please explain."

"Yes, Captain. Prior to being disabled, I detected the emergence of additional lifeforms."

"How many?"

"Six."

"How is that possible?" *You are not alone.* Norman remembered that it was the last thing she'd reported before the system shutdown. "Describe the nature of the lifeforms."

"The source is unknown."

"Are you still able to detect them?"

"Affirmative."

"What is their location?"

"Three are moving toward the power core room."

"And what about the crew?" Norman asked.

"There has been a massive reduction in the crew. I detect seven members remaining."

*What was going on? Had our ship somehow been hijacked? That would be impossible.* Norman suddenly heard footsteps bounding toward him. Then he heard the sound of two loud thumps as if someone had hurled giant sandbags against the wall. Muffled screams echoed in the corridor outside the starboard door.

CARIE then spoke again. "Captain, secure the door immediately."

Norman didn't hesitate. He raced forward and adjusted the locking mechanism just as the latch pulled back to release the door. The lock held the door closed. He slowly backed away, holding his breath.

"Crew diminished. Four remaining members. Two lifeforms closing in on your position."

"I could use more information, CARIE. What am I up against?"

"Unknown, sir. Based on the recent show of force, may I make a recommendation?"

Something smashed against the door, and it buckled. Another subsequent strike caused it to bend inward some more. "Yes! What do you recommend?"

"Run."

CARIE could often be relied upon for very good advice. Norman took her up on the suggestion and hurried to the opposite door. He opened it and stepped through just as the other door was torn out of its threshold and sailed into his captain's chair.

The overhead emergency lights provided enough cursory light that Norman could now see the layout of the corridor in front of him. He felt relieved he didn't have to feel his way along the walls, like he had done earlier. He moved forward, toward the power-core room and the other lifeforms congregating around that area as reported by CARIE. However, it wasn't long before the door behind him opened and a tall, looming figure stepped through. It looked as black as the void of space, with mysteriously shimmering armor covering its thick legs and forearms. Gray-black scales coated its head and torso, but its eyes glowed crimson, like melted candle wax embedded in weathered stone.

He knew the creature didn't have friendly intentions, so he moved as fast as he could. Up ahead, he could hear sporadic gunfire. His instincts told him it probably wasn't the best idea to move toward a firefight, especially since he was unarmed; however, the alternative meant going face to face with the gruesome enemies in immediate pursuit. He came upon the door leading to the power core. He peeked inside the open door and noticed it was both undisturbed and unoccupied. The creature behind him closed in and now looked to be accompanied by at least two others. Just before he moved inside to shut and secure the door, he looked to his right and saw the source of the gunfire.

Melina was standing in the corridor about ten yards away. She crouched down and fired a volley of shots in the opposite direction. She then raised up and retreated toward him. Norman called out to her. "Melina!" She turned her head and spotted him. "Quickly! In here!" he shouted.

She simply nodded, turned, and lumbered over to him the best she could. As she reached the door, Norman spotted the reason for her tactical retreat. Three additional creatures were charging down the hallway. Melina reached the threshold and saw the other monsters closing in on her position from the opposite direction as well. They had been flanked and surrounded.

Norman grabbed her shoulder and pulled her into the room. As he moved to shut the door, one of the creatures reached forward and thrust its arm out, effectively stopping the door from closing. Melina screamed as she took a giant step backward. Norman stayed on the door, struggling to close it and keep the enemy away.

The creature was holding some type of bizarre club in its hand: a glowing black coil spiraled around a solid shaft of metal alloy. Norman reached out for it in an attempt to disarm the monster. Melina, who was familiar with the weapon's power, yelled out to warn him, but it came too late. He touched the spiral and felt the recoil effect; it practically dislocated his left shoulder. He steadied himself once again and pressed his weight against the door. He felt added pressure as one of the other creatures now pulled on the door. "I can't hold it any longer!"

Melina didn't have a clear shot at the enemy's head. Instead, she opted to blast the weapon. She fired two bursts at the club and the hand holding it. The weapon dropped from its clawed grip and landed solidly on the floor without a single bounce. Knowing he couldn't hold the door much longer, Norman released his grip and lunged for the weapon. Based on its size and that of the creature wielding it, Norman had mistakenly assumed that it would be far heavier than it actually was. He gripped it in both hands and took a step back alongside his wife.

Norman raised the weapon and took an aggressive stance like a pinch hitter waiting for the perfect pitch. The creature shoved the door back inside the threshold and stepped inside. Two of its companions moved in as well, like predators looming over their fearful prey. Norman took another step back and bumped into the shoulder-high canister containing one of the energized power cores. He glanced down at it and then at his wife.

Melina fired another burst at the nearest creature and watched it flinch. The bullets couldn't penetrate their skin. Her rifle clicked as the slide locked back. The last of her magazines was now empty. She let the rifle hang and grabbed the sidearm wedged in her back. She pulled the trigger in rapid succession, unleashing all seven rounds into the first beast tracking upward from its chest to head. The last three bullets pounded directly into its face and forehead but ricocheted away with little effect. Then without an ounce of hesitation, she dropped the pistol and turned the rifle upside down, holding it by the heatguard like a makeshift club of her own.

She was out of options, out of breath, as her lungs fought against collapse, but ready to fight to her death. She glanced over at Norman, his hand resting steady on the power core. She looked into his eyes and read his next intentions. She nodded. "Conor and Titan are safe in the rear sleep chamber. I led these bastards away from them."

Just then, the creature to the left halted its advance and canted its head. It then turned and uttered some harsh sounds to two of the other beasts still positioned in the corridor. Melina heard them leave at a hurried pace—their immense footsteps crashing against the floor with curious speed. Had they understood what she just said? Were they going after her son?

"Norman! They're going for Conor! Do it now!"

The captain looked away from his wife and raised the mysterious weapon high overhead. "Your friends will never make it," he said. "My son gave me this idea."

Melina reached out and touched his shoulder as Norman brought the club down hard against the power core.

In a white flash, the power core room exploded in hot fire, incinerating everything. The ship tore apart as the forward deck disintegrated into a ball of fire. The connection to the rear deck splintered and ruptured just as it sealed off, sending it careening into the void of space.

# CHAPTER 3

**Vesputi Galaxy**
**Sector 7—Gobi Region**
**Gregor Monolith**

"Sir, we've located two survivors." The familiar voice of the Commander's Primo Officer sounded in his ear.

"Excellent," he responded. "Prepare for extraction."

"Copy."

This was surprising, yet extremely fortunate, news. In an instant and with a single transmission, his peculiar expedition to the outreaches of the Gobi Region suddenly went from unremarkable to extremely fortuitous. Perhaps this journey into hostile territory would now justify to the Tribunal Elders his insistence on exploring the emergence of the foreign object.

Three days ago, Supreme Commander Makon Welcos had received information about a foreign object spontaneously emerging in the Gobi region. Its path was tracked, and its trajectory calculated, but its movement appeared stagnant. Although it appeared foreign to the Vesputi Galaxy, it seemed unremarkable in size and purpose. However, something about it had drawn him. The Tribunal suggested that it be left to scavenging crafts; after all, strange debris, even of much larger size, frequently passed into the reaches of their galaxy.

What was it about this particular object that had piqued his interest? He stroked his closely trimmed black beard and viewed the image of the damaged craft on the wisp glass in front of him.

It was the picture.

The original telescopic image of the object had been faint due to the distance, but it seemed familiar to him. He brushed his right hand across the pixilated mist in front of him. The image of the small craft spun in an arc. It stopped its spin, and he then reached out to grab a handful of the mist, bringing it closer. When he opened his hand, the microscopic lights formulated a new picture in his palm. It showed the rear port side of the ship. A painted diagram could now be seen clearly. He held it up and stared at it. The symbol brought feelings of unease and discouragement. Maybe, just maybe, it might bring new hope this time around.

He flung the image at the larger mist, and it consumed the screen in front of him. Now he better understood why he'd risked this mission into hostile territory. This discovery would be considered a very significant find—even to the hard-headed Elders more interested in the innermost sectors than what the outer rim could possibly offer. But survivors? No, the Elders mustn't learn about any survivors.

The woman seated at the console to the Commander's left abruptly sat upright. "Commander, we have incoming. Conflict appears imminent." Makon moved over to her area and stood at her shoulder. Valitat Bithos, his trusted Vice Commander, had been in his service for more than six solar years. She was younger than he, but she hadn't let her youth and beauty impede her progress within the Jopali Elite Fleet. Her combat strategy and tactical application in crisis were remarkable.

They both looked at the smaller screen mist in front of her. Three exotic ships appeared, each one large and formidable, yet even their largest was about a quarter the size of their Gregor Monolith—a combat flagship without any known rival. The aggressive ships moved into a flanking position. The sleek razor lines of the ships' exterior indicated the likelihood they belonged to a scavenging clan.

The Gobi region was well known for its roving pirates, marauders, and warring factions. The nearby planets harbored criminals and bloodthirsty creatures of all kinds. Many explorers, brave adventurers, and even smaller Jopali defense fleets had ventured into this region only to never be heard from again.

Makon knew this mission would be risky, which is why the Elders had discouraged it. Perhaps it was for fear of losing the Commander and his crew of 552 veteran graduates; more likely, it was the loss of the fleet's most formidable ship. The absence of the Gregor Monolith would be a tremendous blow to the planet's interstellar defense system, and a hostile takeover of its weapon systems could prove catastrophic. Fortunately, by military decree, once a ship had designated a Supreme Commander, only that individual could relinquish the ship to another or dictate its deployment. No one was going to deter Makon from deploying his ship and crew on this particular mission.

The biggest of the three ships had now moved within firing range. "Should we engage?" Valitat asked. "If we take down the primary ship, the others may flee." The Commander didn't respond. Concentration marked his face as he stared at the screen. These scavengers had a strategy. He just needed to figure it out. It would be absurd and disastrous for ships to try to take on the Monolith in battle. Even three potentially powerful ships such as these would be far outmatched.

As he continued to monitor their movements, he noticed the ships didn't attempt to flank the Monolith—they maneuvered around the foreign vessel. No, the broken ship called *Odyssey* moved toward the primary ship.

Makon stretched out his arm and tapped a blue square on the console. This cycled the optics display of the mist generator screen. The gravitational fields flashed into view. The foreign ship manifested a simulated gravity field. However, around its exterior, another force field surrounded it. This field extended from the largest ship.

"It's being pulled. The broken ship is hostage."

"Should we fire in order to disrupt the takeover?" a man asked. The question came from the Combat Advisor, now standing behind his superiors. "It would free the ship and permit us to open up a full assault."

"No. We played into their hands here when we sent the exploration party onboard the target. If we strike, then a simple adjustment in the field's gravitational pressure would crush the object and everyone on it. We'd lose our whole team in an instant. We must be patient."

"And the other two ships? I can activate our secondary weapons systems and destroy them with optimal efficiency." The advisor made some quick calculations at his terminal. "Based on positioning and current power levels, our shields should mitigate 98% of the potential damage from their counterattack."

"Your assessment is appreciated; however, an attack would prompt a flight response. They would destroy our target, and all our people on it, in the process."

"Perhaps. Yet if the target is absorbed into the ship, then we will lose it. We will not be able to pursue and apprehend these ships. They are faster than us, and we would lose them once they generate a warp hole."

"You are correct," Makon said. "This is why we must be patient and rely on our Primo Officer and his team's abilities."

Just then another transmission echoed out. "The sleep chamber has been opened, and the subjects are awakening. Stand by . . ." The Primo Officer's voice seemed distraught as his words came across in a pitch higher than usual. Valitat shot Makon a look of concern and stood up. With a simple hand gesture, he calmed her and instructed her to sit back down.

"One of the subjects is aggressive. It's attacking!"

Makon spoke aloud. "Stand down. Do not engage."

Primo Officer Iopo Lex knew better than to question the Commander. "Copy. Suggestions for containment?"

"What is the nature of the beings?" Makon waited a long moment for a response. "Officer Lex?"

The Communications Technician addressed the commander. "It appears that the enemy has interfered with our transmissions. We are no longer in direct communication with the insertion team."

Makon remained still and calm. His crew couldn't tell his mind was processing hundreds of bits of data and rapidly running scenarios based on all the known elements of the current dilemma. But they did know their Commander would make the best decision based on the circumstances.

Three enterprising pirate ships poised to attack while stealing the target ship right in front of their eyes as they helplessly watched. One foreign spacecraft with precious cargo and an insertion team of six specialists. Only Makon knew the potential value of this ship's cargo, and how its falling into nefarious hands could produce devastating consequences. However, those two lifeforms apparently had now assaulted his team. Makon closed his eyes for a moment. When they reopened, he not only knew the proper response, but he had already determined the outcome. It wouldn't be without consequences.

"I will respond," Makon said as he reached to the right and activated a button on the control panel. The panel hissed as it rose from the depths of the console and revealed a golden belt. The belt glowed a dim amber hue until he pulled it forth and affixed it around his waist. Then the belt's glow subsided.

Makon then addressed the eight persons in the control room. "Maintain vigilance in my absence for an encroaching assault party. I will advise shortly on the situation with the foreign craft." Makon then turned to Valitat. She stood firm—poised for action—her hands tucked formally behind her back. She was wearing the black uniform of the Monolith, but with the black sash indicative of the rank of Vice Commander wrapping her waist and matching her long dark hair. Others around her were similarly dressed, yet without ranking sashes. Makon knew the battleship and its vast crew would be in very capable hands in his absence.

"Commander, we will have to disable the shields to enable your transport," Valitat stated.

"I am aware," Makon replied.

"This will make us susceptible to attack or invasion. Is this our most favorable option?" Makon respected Valitat and highly valued her tactical insight. Without uttering a word, he simply nodded to her and then spun around to face the exit. She accepted the gesture and felt the reassurance it provided.

As he approached the room's exit, the solid Ionium door wavered like ripples in a pond before dropping into a crevice in the floor like a velvet curtain. It opened into a larger, dim room. The room glowed purple from long light tubes stretching from floor to ceiling. Numerous circular pads lined the floor. They were deep black and seemed to be rolling in dark mist as if they were cauldrons brewing the pure night sky. Sharp blue light encircled each pad like halos encasing pure emptiness.

Before exiting the control room, Makon turned back, glancing once more at the screen situated at the front of his ship. The painted image on the side of the *Odyssey* lingered. He hoped this symbol would bring good fortune to his people.

He punched out his arm and extended his fingers at the screen. Just as he closed his fingers into a clenched fist, the image and the mist disappeared. Makon then reached behind and flung out the tail of his floor-length crimson robe before stepping into the transport chamber.

## Odyssey Sleep Chamber

Makon Welcos arrived onboard what was left of the *Odyssey* deep space explorer just as he had expected. The transporter had functioned well, landing him in some type of common area just outside the room where his team had inserted.

This area of the spacecraft looked like a small battlefield. The walls were broken down in places and peppered with small holes. He recognized what he determined was some sort of exercise equipment—altogether primitive—but it appeared to be broken and damaged. Two fallen bodies—a male and female—were discarded beside one of the benches. Before he could inspect the deceased further, he heard a scream from the sleep chamber. Makon moved to the doorway just in time to observe one of his officers fly through the air and ricochet off one of the sleep pods. The officer skidded across the floor and came to rest just near the Commander's feet.

Officer Haviro quickly gathered himself and pushed up to his feet. He instinctively pulled his sidearm to mount a counterattack until he felt a heavy hand on his shoulder. The officer turned, looking up at the towering Commander dressed in his hooded robes. He immediately lowered his weapon and trusted in Makon's undisputed wisdom. The others in the room turned their attention away from the relentless creature and awaited direction.

Makon stepped into the room. His presence alone exuded authority and strength. The remaining soldiers had taken up defensive positions in an effort to avoid personal danger while still containing the threat. The insertion team were wearing their battle armor, complete with visored helmets. It surely kept Officer Haviro from sustaining injury during his brief flight across the chamber, but once he spotted the threat to the team, Makon understood that the armor had contributed to the problem.

A large, four-legged creature stood near the far pods. It was colored black like the shores of Aquinox and gnashed long, white fangs. It was about the size of a feritu cub—but it moved more like a ravitx. Either way, it was poised and ready for combat. As he watched the beast for a moment, he soon understood. It was protecting something.

That something popped its head out of the pod and began to climb out. Makon's expression changed as he spotted the frazzled brown hair of the boy. Fear and confusion marked the boy's pale face. This was understandable and rather justified given the circumstances.

Makon peeled the hood away from his face and stepped forward. "Commander! Beware of the alien creature," Primo Officer Lex said.

Without stopping his progress, the Supreme Commander addressed the team. "Everyone must immediately exit the room and set up defensive positions in the next room. Prepare for a heavily armed assault squad. We will most certainly be boarded in less than a minute."

Iopo Lex acknowledged the command and repeated the order as they funneled into the atrium and took cover positions—their pulse rifles charged and at the ready. Makon's attention never diverted from the boy and the beast, even as the nine intruders appeared in the next room and became engaged in a fierce gun battle. The Commander wasn't concerned about the result. It was his job to accurately predict the outcome. The result would be common—what typically happened when the brave and foolish dared to engage his Elites.

Makon stepped closer to the beast and put out his hand. This gesture was first met with a vicious growl. Then the boy said something and placed his palm on top of its head. The beast quieted and sat down. The nature of this command and obedience impressed him.

The boy said something to him, but he didn't respond. Instead, Makon released the enclosure on one of the pouches on his belt. He then dug both thumbs into it and pulled them out. Nothing visible was in his hands, so this didn't cause alarm. He then tilted his head and looked directly into the boy's blue eyes for a long moment. He then whispered, "*Vir fortis.*" The boy gave him a bewildered look but didn't have a chance to respond. Makon moved too fast.

In one swift moment he pressed his left thumb against the boy's neck and the other upon the beast's temple. Each thumb depressed a virtually invisible lens onto the skin. The translucent pad activated with a twinkle of blue lights, and in less than a second, both subjects were rendered unconscious. Calm had been restored.

The battle outside the sleep chamber lasted a mere 47 seconds. The scavenger crew had transported into the middle of an ambush with the Elites prepared and waiting, thanks to the Commander's forethought. They greeted the unwelcome arrival with a merciless display of superior battle tactics and firepower.

Makon applied a bracelet to both the boy and the beast. The small tokens stretched around the wearer and then constricted upon contact. They then began pulsating a deep violet glow. Makon stood and pulled his hood back over his head. "Prepare for immediate transport."

"Exact," Primo Officer Lex responded.

In an instant, Supreme Commander Welcos arrived back on the Monolith. He moved away from the pad, leaving the rest of the party in the transport chamber. He stepped over a dead scavenger and greeted Valitat with a simple nod before moving to the main visual mist. He brought up a panoramic view of the Odyssey and the three scavenger ships. It was without surprise that the *Odyssey* suddenly collapsed on itself. Meanwhile the other ships engaged their primary thrusters and began to flee.

"How many intruders boarded?" Makon asked.

"Fifteen," the Combat Advisor replied.

"Survivors?"

"They fought valiantly . . . and poorly. None survived their ill-fated assault. Your prediction had us fully prepared to receive them. We met their aggression with a commendable Gregor Monolith response."

Makon nodded in approval. "Any casualties?"

"Only minor injuries have been reported."

The scavenging crafts now began to pull away from them in a hasty retreat. "Commander, the ships have yet to leave the range of our primary weapon systems. Shall I send a volley?"

"No. They have suffered enough death by our hands this day. Our actions were defensive and reactionary, and they surely regret their interference with our mission. We must refrain from delivering retaliatory punishment."

The Commander then sensed the arrival of Officer Lex. He turned to him and stepped away from the others in the control room. He then spoke softly. "Prepare the foreign cargo for the voyage to Jopal. Speak to your team. There will never be an utterance of what was recovered. Secret them onboard, and maintain the slumber lenses until instructed otherwise."

Iopo Lex indicated his understanding. Discretion was often expected of his insertion team, and the Supreme Commander's purpose or commands were never questioned. Unless someone wore the tunic of his Vice Commander.

Valitat moved to her Commander once his conversation with Officer Lex had ended and he had departed. "Has our mission achieved the desired result?"

"Yes."

"Did you find anything of merit?" she asked.

Makon now turned and looked at his most trusted companion. "I found . . . possibility. A very curious possibility."

# CHAPTER 4

**Vesputi Galaxy**
**Sector 3**
**Jopal**

Conor woke from his troubled dream to find himself in another dream. His body was engulfed in luxurious softness. The fluffy blanket covering his body not only felt warm and comforting, but it smelled sweet, like a medley of fresh fruit.

He had slept under the stars. A majestic starscape unfolded above him. As he lay back and absorbed the spiraling cosmos, something felt out of place. He wasn't outside, and he wasn't on the *Odyssey*. This was much too comfortable to be the sleep pod.

He pushed the cover away from his torso and sat up. As he did so, the cosmos faded away to reveal a domed ceiling. The entire ceiling gave off a light illuminating the strange room. The room itself seemed pretty bare. To his right, long drapes covered what must be a window. To the left was an open doorway, and a lighted panel marked the wall on the far side of the room.

Conor swept his legs over the side of the bed and dropped to the floor. Balance left him, and he was forced to crouch down and extend a hand to stop from falling. The gray floor appeared cold and hard, but it was surprisingly soft on his bare feet, like a freshly trimmed patch of grass. He stood but had to steady himself against the bed. It was then that he realized the bed wasn't actually touching the ground. It was levitating.

He crawled underneath it to try to figure out how it was just floating in the air. He made it to the other side with ease because it was floating about two feet off the floor. He then tried pushing it to the side, but it held remarkably firm. There was only one thing left to do.

Conor climbed up on the bed again and jumped. The bed was remarkably bouncy, and he managed to gain some incredible air. The mattress felt like a spring-loaded trampoline that almost caused him to bash his head on the domed ceiling on his third jump. This startled him, and he plopped back down on the cushioned blanket. Looking up at the domed ceiling again, Conor began to wonder. The ceiling's apex must have been about at least thirty feet high. How could he have almost put his head through it way up there? It probably was a good idea to stop. Besides, he began to feel dizzy.

Now would be a good time to figure out where he was. Conor stepped to the floor, more cautiously this time, and moved to an open doorway off to the side. This room was much smaller. It looked like some sort of bathroom—except that he couldn't find a toilet, shower, sink, or anything else that would make it a bathroom. A small panel on the wall glowed blue. It looked like a clear invitation to reach out and touch it. He pressed his finger to the light and stepped back, not sure of what might happen.

Water flowed outward from a small hole above the shelf he hadn't noticed before. Rather than spilling onto the shelf, it collected into a floating mass, like a giant droplet. The water drop was about the size of a watermelon. It just hovered over the shelf as if devoid of gravity. Conor touched his finger to it and felt the wetness. He then smelled his finger, but it was odorless. Definitely water. He bent forward and pressed his lips to the suspended water. It was cool and had a refreshing flavor. He leaned in and drank more fully, not realizing until now how thirsty he actually was.

At that moment, he noticed that he was being watched. He looked to his immediate right and spotted a boy his same size standing right next to him. He was shirtless, barefoot, and wearing loose-fitting gray pants that bunched at his feet. Conor stepped back from the water shelf and noticed the boy moved the same as he did. "Hello," Conor uttered.

"Hello," the boy said back. Conor tilted his head to the side and watched the boy imitate him. He then recognized he was staring at his twin—only older than he remembered. Conor brought a hand up to his face, and his twin did the same. He squinted, and the boy repeated it. Conor stuck out his tongue, and so did his lifeform reflection. It was both unnerving and exhilarating at the same time.

He stepped forward and waved his hand through the image. It was some form of lifelike hologram. This was so much better than a mirror! After making a few more silly faces, Conor stepped back and took a fighting stance. "Daoooyaaah!" He launched a right punch followed by a straight kick and watched the image replicate every movement.

After another minute of shadowboxing his image, he turned away and stepped out of the bathroom. He spun around quickly to see if he was following himself, but the image remained in the room. "Cool," he muttered with a smile. He then took in the rest of the peculiar room and spotted the large curtains on the opposite side. It had to be a window. A glance outside might give him a better idea of where he was and what was going on.

As he approached the curtain to pull it aside, it swished to the right before he even touched it. This weirdness caused him to stop and hesitate. He moved his right hand out from his side as he stood directly in front of the window. The large white curtain moved and then fell back into place. He swept his left hand outward, and the curtains parted again, causing the left side to move. Of course, now it was time to use both hands at once. He spread his arms like an eagle, and the curtains instantly opened wide. They shut once he brought his hands back down. Each time he moved his arms, however slightly, the curtains corresponded.

Conor brought his hands wide and then swung them in coordinated movements like a conductor before a symphony orchestra. The curtains danced in front of him, slaves to their puppet master. Time for the big finale . . .

"Ahem." A soft noise from behind him startled Conor out of his window-dressing masterpiece. He turned and spotted a girl standing nearby. She was young, maybe his same age or a little older. Her hair was dark and pinned close to her head except for two long tendrils that framed her light-brown face like a painting. Conor was just as startled by her presence as he was by her beauty.

Her lithe frame was covered by a pale-blue robe, parted in the middle and fastened by a thick black belt around her waist. The robe was sleeveless and carried down to her bare feet. She looked elegant, like a princess—like no one he'd seen before. It was then that he became conscious of his bare chest and grew timid.

As if perceiving his awkwardness, she spoke. "Your tunic is in the wardrobe." Conor looked bewildered. What wardrobe? The girl sighed and moved to the wall. She pressed her hand against a cluster of small bumps, and a section of the wall wavered as if it were made of cloth. An open chest emerged, exposing a light, cream-colored tunic. She studied him for a moment and canted her head to the side. "You can also stop playing with the window. The shutters are purposely closed, and you won't be able to see out." She then turned to leave out a doorway that Conor hadn't noticed before. "Don't scratch it. The sensation will pass in a cycle or two."

"Don't scratch what?" Conor asked, but before she could answer, he knew exactly what she meant. He brought his fingers up to his left ear and felt a small horizontal scab just behind his ear. He hadn't noticed it before, but now he felt an uncontrollable urge to scratch it.

The girl shook her head and then turned to leave. "Please hurry. He is waiting for you."

"Who?" Conor scratched behind his ear like a dog with a terrible tickle.

Her eyes met his. "Your father."

### Jopal
### West Mertio Observatory

Lead Stellar Observer Novac Riv finished sending the critical message to his respected colleague, Wilda Ti, stationed at the Academy. She would absorb the value of this discovery more than any other, and hopefully provide some insight into its cause.

Novac understood the drastic consequences for Jopal and the rest of the star system if his data was correct. And it had to be correct; after all, precision was his forte. Nevertheless, he'd checked the data flows nine times. Clearly something was happening. Something horrifying. And he needed to alert others to this anomaly.

Sweat trickled down his forehead as he frantically gathered his materials. A hasty trip to the Academy was not in his current schedule, but other things would have to wait. He grabbed the star map image replicator and disconnected its power supply, stuffing it into his light travel sack.

Calculations still swirled in his head, distracting him from the here and now. Novac glanced at the roasted gillip and glazed wasa root still sitting on a cold plate at the edge of his desk.

It had easily been more than eight hours since he'd eaten, but hunger always conceded to urgent science. He stopped and surveyed the tabletop. He should have all he needed.

A soft touch on his shoulder made him jump. "Are you certain you need to make the trip?" Novac's assistant asked. He turned to face her as he slung the sack over his shoulder.

"I need to go," he replied.

"But it's a long flight. Why not try the transporter instead?"

"Kim, you know how much I trust those things. It would have to be the end of the world before I step into a black hole for the sake of convenience." She gave him a worried look. "All right. You got me. It would have to be the *immediate* end of the world before I disembodied myself."

"You also hate flight," she offered with a scowl.

"Lesser of two evils, I guess. I have no choice. A simple message and freeze images of the far sun, Tiptokon III, would do little to convince others of the importance of this discovery. I have to go there in person. I have to be able to face the doubters and meet their hesitation and skepticism head on."

His assistant stepped closer to him. She placed her hands on his shoulders and looked him in the eyes with a sad longing. Her unrequited love for this brilliant man stirred up anxiety and heartache at the thought of his departure. "You travel safe and comm me when you arrive. I'll wait to hear from you."

Novac's mind was too distracted to appropriately acknowledge her worry as a genuine concern and unrelenting desire for him to be with her. He was already preparing the delivery of his message to Wilda Ti and the rest of the esteemed Academy staff. Perhaps this discovery and his early warning would earn him a position on the Overwatch Council. He would take his place beside Wilda, and she might finally then recognize him and his many merits.

"Agreed? You promise?" Kim asked.

Novac snapped back to the present and realized that he'd been asked a question. "Of course," was his response, although he had no idea what he had promised to do. No matter. Kim was good at reminding him of scheduled events and other obligations. She'd make contact after he arrived and let him know what she needed from him.

"The flight departure is in two hours. You have enough time to eat before you board. Having something in your stomach will make the ascension more tolerable for you."

"Thank you. It has been a long while since I've eaten."

"Are you sure you don't want me there with you?" she asked, hoping he'd change his mind.

"You don't have anything you would require for the trip," Novac said.

"I could pick up what I need in transit. I could even borrow one of your shirts for sleepwear. The important thing is that I would be there if you needed me."

Novac patted her on the shoulder. "What am I going to do without you? I really do need you." The words washed over Kim like a cool breeze on an intolerably hot afternoon. Maybe he did see her as more than just an assistant. Maybe he had contemplated a more intimate relationship between them. Maybe . . . Then the next words slapped her in the face like a frozen snowball. "Without you here, who would watch the lab? I really need you to keep me updated on Tipper 3. It's of vital importance. Can you do that for me?"

Kim nodded. She couldn't muster any other comment because she felt like she'd been kicked in the gut, punched in the face, and tossed out a high window to land in a field of stabbing thorns. Novac thanked her and then turned to leave. As he hurried through the door, he disappeared without glancing at her. She'd been wholeheartedly rejected.

But wait. Had she really been rejected? What if Novac just didn't know how she felt? What if he just wanted to be respectful and professional because he didn't know how she truly felt about him? After more than three years together, they had become a great team and complemented each other really well. Her spirits began to lift, and a smile emerged. He would miss her on his trip and be happy to see her again. Upon his return, she would finally tell him how she felt.

**Jopal**
**Premier District**

As unsettling as it was, Conor could have spent a full day going up and down on the floating staircase. He stood on a shoulder-width pad that glided down from the top floor to the bottom of the massive home. At least it seemed like a home. After all, it did have at least one bed and windows with some rather haunted curtains. Although the place was bare of photos or artwork, the walls were vibrant and seemingly alive. Miniature lights embedded in the walls moved to create shapes and images like clouds moving across a rural landscape or ocean waves crashing on a deserted beach. It was amazing—like nothing he'd seen before.

Conor had also realized that if he turned around, the floating staircase pads would shift direction and then take him back to the top. This was now the third time he'd made it to the bottom. It was then that he spotted the strange girl waiting. She didn't seem very happy with him. Conor smiled to hide his embarrassment. "Uh . . . I don't know how to turn it off."

"Reach out your arm."

"What? Why?"

"Do it." Conor reached out his arm as he neared the bottom, and the pad carried him down to the floor. It hovered briefly before lowering to the ground. The boy nodded and stepped off the pad toward the girl. Without another word, she turned and walked down a wide hallway before stopping to place her hand to a panel beside a door. The door shimmered and fell away, exposing a well-lit room. The girl didn't enter. She waited for him to move forward before following behind him.

A lengthy table to his immediate left first caught his attention. It was decorated with numerous types of exotic foods and bizarre flowers. He stared for a moment realizing he was actually quite hungry, but the food looked too pretty to eat. The long buffet table was positioned in front of a chain of large, shuttered windows. No curtains, though.

Across from the food display rested another table. It was round and had three chairs; the one facing him was occupied by an impressive man with rich brown skin and wearing a crimson tunic similar to the cream one he had been given. His hair was cropped close to his scalp, and his dark beard was also neatly trimmed. He stood as Conor entered the room. This made his presence only more imposing. A giant smile creased his mouth, putting Conor a little more at ease.

"Greetings," he started. His voice was deep and powerful enough to feel in one's bones. "Please have a seat and join me for the pre-night meal. You must be hungry." He noticed the hesitation in his guest. "Don't let this day's strangeness affect your appetite. There is much to show you, and you will undoubtedly need strength."

Conor started to walk but checked behind him to see what the girl wanted him to do. She pushed her head to the side to indicate for him to move forward. Conor turned back to the man and moved closer. He heard a soft *swoosh* behind him. Without looking, he'd seen enough sci-fi movies to know the door had just closed.

"Come, sit. But first, please gather some food and bring it to the table. You can eat while we speak."

Conor walked to the table and surveyed the food. Brightly colored melons and round fruits interspersed with plates of stacked meats and bowls of thick creams. Although everything looked like nothing he'd seen before, their juicy, colorful appearance made them appetizing.

"You can trust that everything is not only edible, but delicious. I highly recommend the halit fruit." Makon noticed the boy's hesitation as he held his empty plate. "It's the red one with the white spikes." Conor reached out and placed one on his plate, unsure if it were a fruit or some creature that might wobble and bounce right off his plate. He then plopped several slices of darkened meat next to the curious fruit. He grabbed another food-like item that looked like a miniature yellow watermelon before shuffling over to the table.

He checked the stability of the chair before sitting. He was actually relieved to find it wasn't floating. A series of interesting utensils were placed in front of him. He picked up the one that resembled a spoon on one end and a two-tined fork on the other. It seemed like an efficient marriage between both common utensils. He felt the man's eyes fixed on him as he dug the spoon end into the recommended halit fruit. It tasted like a sugared mango. Its deliciousness disappeared into his belly before he knew it.

"I thought you would appreciate it. That's one of my favorites." Conor then tried the meat. It was tasty as well. "My name is Makon Welcos. What are you called?"

The boy stopped chewing but didn't look at the man when he answered. "My name is Conor. Conor Hawk."

"A pleasure to meet you, Master Hawk. I hope you are feeling well. You've had quite a journey."

Hunger and shyness gave way to his curiosity. He needed some answers. "Where am I?" Without awaiting an answer,

Conor shot-gunned a series of questions in rapid succession. "What happened to the ship? Where is my dog? How do those curtains move upstairs in that room? The girl said I was meeting my father, but I don't think I know you."

"Many questions, Master Hawk. I can understand. Allow me to answer them as best I can. You are in my home and you are welcome for as long as you wish. The girl is my niece, Tiera. I estimate she is roughly your same age. How old are you?"

"Twelve."

Makon processed his answer for a moment. "Hmmmm. Yes. You were, perhaps before you went to sleep in the pod. Your body hasn't aged much due to your sleep state, but you're now older than you think you are. How much though? I don't know. Don't know how long you were floating asleep in the stars." The Commander noticed the boy's expression change as that information appeared to disturb him. "Ha. Ha. No worries. No use dwelling on the things outside our control." Makon then folded his hands in his lap and his face grew serious. "As for the hard questions, I will not withhold the truth. The ship you were found in has been destroyed. Not by me, of course."

"And my father?"

"I don't know. Was he with you on the ship?"

"Uh," Conor uttered while trying to press his memory for an answer. "I . . . I can't remember. Why can't I remember?" Conor's anxiety grew as he set down the utensil and started to push away from the table. His frustration became visually evident as it began to turn to anger.

"Please relax, Master Hawk. You appear to have suffered a post-traumatic memory loss, possibly triggered by the cryogenic sleep."

"What does that mean? I can remember my name. I know who I am. I just don't know how I got here in this weird place. Is this a dream?"

"No, Conor. You're not in a dream."

"Feels like it."

"I bet it does. I completely understand. You'll get used to it, though. Quicker than you think."

"I was on a ship. With my dog. I don't remember much else. Why can't I remember?"

"It's just fine. Relax. The memories will come back, perhaps when you've had more rest. What's the last thing you recall?"

Conor stirred in his seat. He shut his eyes. "I remember only a feeling of heaviness, like a deep weight in my stomach. Darkness. Everything was so dark. But I can't remember who I was with. I see flashes of faces. I think my parents."

"I'm sorry. I don't know who you see. Hopefully, you will remember in time. You were likely floating abandoned in space for some time. I suggest a post-traumatic event because your vessel was not recovered completely intact." Makon recalled the disarray and carnage he'd observed when he boarded the *Odyssey.* He wasn't about to share those details with the distraught boy. "Do you remember what might have happened onboard?"

Makon observed the boy's breathing increase and felt his mounting tension as he watched him search his fragile memory. Conor's face contorted as he sifted through images, both intense and likely terrifying. "Enough!" Makon's voice boomed. It startled Conor, yanking him back to the present. He looked at the formidable man but noted only peace in his countenance. "I do not want your thoughts there anymore today. We will discuss it at a later time when you are ready. I want your thoughts and strength here this day. This is a new beginning for you."

He waited for Conor to settle into a calmer state before speaking again. "I don't have all the answers you seek. I do not know the fate of your parents. I trust you will have to embrace that on your own. As for your dog, if you mean the remarkable black creature found with you, then I have good news."

"Where is she?" Conor was relieved, yet anxious.

"I imagine it is a pet of yours."

"Her name is Titan. She is friendly. A good dog."

Makon smiled as he remembered the extreme difficulty his Elite insertion team had in dealing with the dog. "Yes, I have met her. She's safe on the lower level. I have my staff caring for your little Titan. Very appropriate name choice, I must say."

"When can I see her?"

"Soon. Like you, she is trying to adjust to her peculiar surroundings. But don't worry, she is being looked after. I've made sure of that." Makon pushed himself away from the table and moved to the far end of the room. "Come. There's something I want to show you."

Conor stuffed a piece of meat in his mouth and followed the man. They stopped at the large, shuttered window. Makon extended his right hand from his side and then traced a half circle in the air. He then swept the hand to the side. The window sighed as it began to slide to the right, exposing a vast balcony. The platform exposed an oasis of manicured exotic plants and trees. The trees towered high above, twisting their way toward the sky. An elegant fragrance permeated the air as the man and boy walked a smooth path.

It was then that Conor looked down and saw rows of clouds under his feet. He was walking on what appeared to be glass, giving the impression that they were sliding across the sky itself. He hesitated a second but realized he hadn't fallen yet, so it must be safe. As they continued forward, he studied the brightly colored, occasionally fluorescent, vegetation.

The leaves and flowers glistened in sharp hues of green, red, and various shades of blue and yellow. However, it wasn't the mesmerizing beauty that stoked his curiosity; it was the fact that everything seemed to be stretching toward the path. No, not toward the *path*. The plants were reaching out to the man leading the way. Every now and then, Makon would trace his fingertips along an outstretched petal. The flower would then respond by coiling in a random pattern as if it had just touched royalty.

After a few minutes of traversing the dense labyrinth, they came to the path's end. The vegetation subsided, and they were now surrounded by white skies. Makon stopped and looked out at the world. Conor took a spot next to him. He couldn't help but feel uneasy with the sensation that he was walking on the sky. "Don't be concerned. The floor beneath your feet is heavily fortified, and you won't be able to move forward any further than we already have." Conor wasn't sure if he could trust that. All of his senses told him that if he took one false step, he would plummet to the ground a mile below. Makon smiled at his unsteady companion. "The wall in front of you is invisible."

"Oh."

"Well, Master Hawk, it has to be invisible. Otherwise, we wouldn't be able to fully enjoy our experience."

A nervous chuckle escaped the boy. "Of course."

"Ha! My son, you may not believe me now, but you will one day grow very accustomed to this feeling."

"Okay," Conor replied. There was no way he would ever be comfortable surrounded by clouds—no matter how thrilling this was.

"Come and see," Makon said with a gesture. "Look down." Conor leaned further forward and peered down at the strange landscape under the shifting clouds. "Welcome to Jopal. Your new home."

Under the seemingly floating balcony Conor could see a vibrant landscape far below interspersed with lush, exotic jungles. The twisting trees stretched high into the white and lavender sky, their elongated branches extending upward like massive stalagmites.

Makon's home was nothing less than a majestic palace cut into a high mountain, making him an overseer to the world below. Cascading waterfalls blasted from the cliffs beneath them, emptying into a wide river. A double-masted ship pushed through the dark waters—its crimson sails unfurled to the cool wind. Conor turned around, looked upward, and noted that the massive building carried upward with several levels above and towering spires pushing through higher clouds. Conor suddenly felt overwhelmed by the grand scope of the palace and the strange world below.

The large man placed his hand on the boy's shoulder and extended his other arm. He pointed up and toward the clouds above. "Look there." Conor noticed three round globes in the far sky. "Those are the suns of Jopal and the rest of the Nivror system. The large one is Tiptokon Major. The red one next to it is called Mitaj. And the smaller one, farthest away . . . the dim one." Makon paused and squinted as if in thought. "That one is called Tiptokon III, 'Tipper 3' for short. All three provide the light and life to this star system.

"I understand that this must be quite overwhelming right now, but you have somehow entered a new galaxy from your own. We call it the Vesputi. It is home to millions of stars and planets, though we have intimate knowledge of merely 368 worlds—27 of which are relatively inhabitable. The Jopali fleet and other Federation members have not been able to venture out into the deep reaches as much as we would like to. Our exploration efforts have been moderately sidetracked for quite some time. In fact, contacting your ship on the outer rim of Gobi in Sector 7 was even discouraged due to our current state of affairs."

Makon removed his hand from Conor's shoulder and tucked it into the wide sleeve of his robe. He searched the boy's face to anticipate his emotional response. First, he saw disbelief, but this soon morphed into anxious curiosity. "I perceive you have questions. Please ask."

Conor shifted his feet and nervously scratched his forehead. "First, am I dreaming?"

"Ha. Ha," the large Commander reared back with a bellowing laugh. "In a way, it might seem so. But actually no." He reached out and pinched Conor's arm.

The pinch didn't hurt, but he got the message. "So . . . I am really in a new galaxy?"

"Yes. The Vesputi."

"On a planet called Joopaa."

"Jopal," Makon corrected.

"And this is your castle?" Makon nodded. "Are you a king?"

Makon stifled a chuckle. "No. This is just my primary house. I have four others. Two on Jopal and one on the utopian planet of Cio. It's a paradise. We will have to travel there one day. You above all others would really appreciate it there. My last home is found on Bravand-Hiy. That one is a little further out, and it's not as accommodating. Perhaps one day you will prepare to endure a voyage there.

"This particular home, where you are now, is my base of operations in a way. It lies closest to that," he said as he pointed toward the metropolis. A massive white building could be seen floating over the rest of the city. Even from this far distance, it still seemed imposing. It was shaped like a crescent moon resting on three towers. A larger object encircled the top of the crescent's tip like a suspended halo. The building was as beautiful as it was bizarre.

"That is called the Towers of Prudence. It is where the Elders reside, as well as the strategic operations for the Jopali defense. I am Supreme Commander Welcos, commander of the Gregor Monolith, and a Premier Advisor to the Collective Federation Council." He sensed that Conor didn't quite grasp that part. "In other words, I am a leader in our defense of Jopal and the other Federation planets. I am a soldier and a thinker to the governing Elders and my people. Oh, and I have a really big ship."

This drew a smile from the boy. "Actually, you've already been on the ship. You just happened to sleep through the journey. I'll take you on board and introduce you to the crew. Would you like that? The ship is twice as big as this house."

"I'd like to see it."

"Good." Makon paused for a moment and lowered his head. "Now I will provide your directives. These must be adhered to at all times. Do you understand?"

"Uh. Not really. What do you mean?"

"Conor, you are no longer from your home planet."

"You know where I'm from?" Conor interrupted.

"Yes. It is known by several titles. Solo Blu was once its name. It goes by another name of late. Now, please let me finish. You were found in Jopal's Ged district alone and with severe head trauma. This is how I discovered you. It will conveniently explain your oddness and lack of familiarity with your current surroundings.

"My oddness?" Conor interrupted again.

"Yes. You will be quite odd to the rest of us. Don't you feel odd?"

"I guess so."

"Don't take offense, young man. You'll eventually get the hang of things, though I fear the oddness will never wear off."

"Oh. That sucks," Conor said.

Makon chuckled. "Don't you worry. In time you will have to embrace your oddness, and others will marvel. You'll understand more later, but for now, your story goes that I had pity and adopted you because your family had perished during the plague altercation. You will now be introduced as my son. It's rather fitting since we resemble one another."

Conor furrowed his eyebrows at the last remark. There was virtually no resemblance between them.

"Ha. Ha. Ha," Makon laughed as he perceived Conor's confusion. "You don't agree?"

"No. Not really. Your skin is black, and mine is white. Plus, you're really big."

"Master Hawk, do not remain fixated on something as insignificant as skin tone. You will soon come to realize that we have much more in common than you now realize."

Conor decided to drop his argument. Besides, he detected he didn't have much say in the matter.

Makon continued, "As my son, you will enroll in the Academy. I have already made the arrangements. Six cycles from now, I will transport you and Tiera for orientation. In the meantime, my niece will take you to the city tomorrow. She will work to get you adjusted to your new environment and expose you to some of our world's many wonders."

"What's a cycle?"

"My apologies. I should not assume that everything translates perfectly to you. A 'cycle' refers to Jopal's rotation on its axis. It is similar in length to a 'day' on your home planet. Likewise, a 'circuit' describes the length of time to orbit between our suns, Tiptokon Major and Mitaj. It equates to a little more than one of your 'years.' Don't worry. Your translator will handle it all from here on out. Do you have any more questions or concerns?"

After a few moments of silence, Makon determined it would be best to avoid overwhelming the boy. "I think you have had enough for now. You should finish your meal and return to your room. You need more rest. There has been much information and sensory stimulation." He turned away from Conor and began to walk the path back to the food hall. He then stopped and spoke again. "Yet, I will unlock your window shutters so you may study the landscape more if you wish."

Makon's head then lowered. "Master Hawk, you mustn't let anyone know where you come from. Only a very select few know the truth. Others have been sworn to silence. It is for your own safety. Do you understand?"

"Yes. Kind of," Conor responded.

"Good enough." Makon then canted his head to the side as he peered over his shoulder back at the boy. "One other requirement. Do not show your anger. It will betray you."

"I'm not angry," Conor said, confused.

"Good," the commander uttered as he led them back through the botanical garden.

# CHAPTER 5

**Jopal**
**Mertio, Capital City**
**Kipri District**

The city was clean. Aside from the massive floating buildings and the intermixing of aircraft with ground vehicles, Conor couldn't help but be impressed with the cleanliness and organization of the city center. From the puttering hover vehicles to the shimmering skyscrapers, the entire city seemed animated and alive. His wide eyes scanned from side to side in an attempt to absorb his immaculate surroundings. Some of the buildings were grounded, but their walls still pulsated with swirling, ever-changing designs.

Although it was heavily populated, the city didn't appear overcrowded. Dense hanging gardens gave an organic appearance and sensation to the city, as if it grew out of the planet's wild jungle. Native Jopali people mixed with other strange species as they participated in daily commerce. Conor's first glimpse of a creature caused him to pause and stare. It was dressed similarly to him, in a hooded tunic and a wide belt around its waist. Its visible face and hands held a bluish hue with scaly skin. It appeared reptilian and moved with quiet grace as it surveyed the hanging lights for sale in a nearby shop. Two smaller creatures swarmed around its legs like children in a game of tag. The tall one bent down to address them before turning back to a particular fixture.

Conor followed Tiera as they passed behind the shop. His gaze still studied the creature and its younglings. One of them ran directly in front, causing him to stop to avoid knocking it over. It spun out of the way, undeterred, and returned to its mother. She turned and faced Conor. Its blue eyes met his, and it smiled shyly. "Excuse us. They are jittery because it's time for a snack," her voice whispered through a translucent device fashioned over her mouth. She then noticed the girl standing near Conor. "Blessings," she said with a reverent nod.

Conor managed to crack a smile, but it did little to disguise his bewilderment. He kept staring as he walked until colliding with Tiera, who had stopped in front of him. She turned to him with disdain painted on her face. "Stop staring and pay attention."

"What is it?" Conor whispered as the female creature turned back to the shop attendant.

"She is Cresvich. A mother and children. She's as much right to be here as you or I. There are many visiting residents on Jopal from nearby worlds."

"But it . . . she spoke, and I understood her," Conor said.

"Of course, you did."

"Does everything speak my same language?"

"No. No one in this galaxy speaks your tongue," Tiera replied with a scoff.

"Then how?" Conor asked.

"How do you understand us, them, and we understand you?"

"Yeah." Tiera moved closer to Conor and touched the tiny scab behind his right ear. "Remember this? It's a translation-modifier implant. Everyone has one. It automatically detects and instantly translates any particular language to your own setting."

"How is that possible?"

"Speaking is just a grouping of sounds. The modifier alters them to sounds you can decipher in your own tongue. I don't really know how it works, but I know it will translate more than 40,000 guttural imitations. Though it doesn't work on beasts like the one you came with. They communicate differently so you won't receive feedback on their sounds, but we can communicate with some beasts intuitively. If you want to learn how it actually works, though, you'd have to speak with a Riostovi and get them to explain it to you."

"A what?"

"Riostovi. V-Techs. That's what we commonly call them. They are a peaceful species from the distant moon of Rios. They're innovative beyond comprehension and superior in the laws of science to any known species in existence. Almost all advancement in technology comes from them, from weapons and gravitational manipulation to space travel."

"So, the V-Techs designed all this?"

"Pretty much."

"Wow. What's the coolest thing they've invented?"

Tiera thought for a moment. "That's hard to say, but you haven't lived until you've tried a Cloud Dart or stepped on a Dark Disc."

"What are those?"

"I'll show you later. Let's keep moving." They continued walking, or more like gliding. The path carried them like a moving walkway. Tiera stopped at a vast, borderless pool of water. She watched and waited. Water suddenly sprang forth in a spiral design. But rather than falling back to the pool, it stayed suspended as other water spurts danced around it. Tiera and Conor stood side by side for a few moments.

"I love this fountain. You know, it never makes the same pattern. Every time it's different," she said. Conor didn't reply, but he did think it was pretty cool. Even better than the water drop in the strange bathroom back in Makon's palace.

"Blessings," two passersby uttered when they noticed the boy and girl at the fountain. Another group of four Jopali approached them and greeted Tiera. One took her hand and bowed his forehead against the back of it. "Blessings upon you, my countess. It is an honor to see you this day."

"The honor is mine," Tiera offered as she placed the pads of her first two fingers against his forehead. The old man bowed again before ushering the group away from her. She then noticed Conor staring at her.

"Are you like a princess or something?"

Tiera chuckled. "No. Nothing like that. They only recognize me and approach to pay respects to my uncle."

"He's like a king, right? He told me he wasn't, that he was some kind of commander or something."

"Supreme Commander of the Gregor Monolith and the Elites."

"Yeah." Conor nodded. "Something like that."

"Well, that's it. That's why he has such status."

"So, he's a celebrity because he's a commander?" Conor asked.

"Exactly. On Jopal our military leaders are revered as heroes. They command respect and admiration. Very few of us have the ability to wage war."

"Anyone can be a soldier," Conor contested.

"Perhaps where you come from, but not on Jopal. Only a very small percentage can manage what it takes to deliver death and destruction across worlds and space."

"Oh, that's strange. But I guess he is a pretty high rank. I don't think my people worshiped our soldiers. It didn't mean much."

"It's not worship. More like reverent admiration."

"Still. It seems bizarre to me."

"That is sad, Conor Hawk. Perhaps your people don't see things right."

"It's too late now. Doesn't matter."

Tiera noted a hint of anger in his eyes. "Why? What happened to your planet?"

"I don't really know," Conor said as he turned away. He closed his eyes and allowed himself to fly to a distant memory. "I can't really remember. I just know it got dark, like no light whatsoever. After the darkness fell, I don't know. But people started dying." Conor winced as he stared off. "I don't even think I was there."

"Were you attacked?" Tiera asked with interest.

"Um, no. You mean like by aliens? I don't think so. Who would attack us? We didn't see anything like that . . . at least . . . I don't think so. You know, I can't even remember my family. My home. Nothing, except feeling darkness and then some images of my ship once in a while."

Conor's face went stony as his mind drifted. Tiera tried to bring him back. "We are at war."

It worked. She instantly got Conor's attention. "War? With who?"

Tiera bit her lip for a moment before continuing. Her uncle had instructed her not to discuss the war or overload the newcomer with too much information. He didn't want to discourage him or instill any fear. "Never mind. Let's move on. I need to show you the observatory."

Conor suspected there was much she wasn't telling him. She was a lot like her uncle. Makon refused to speak to him about the fate of his parents and had taken his dog to some unknown rehabilitation farm or something. These people didn't like to share too much with him. Now he finds out there's some kind of big extraterrestrial war going on, and she'd refused to elaborate.

He couldn't help but feel excitement at the idea of an interstellar war. What did they look like? Were they like the alien woman and her children in the market? They seemed pretty passive, though. Oh, well. He'd have to wait to figure that out. Perhaps his new "father" would speak with him more about it at some point.

Conor felt he could trust the formidable Supreme Commander, but he also knew he wasn't very forthcoming with information. He glanced down at the remarkably comfortable boots on his feet. At least they were pretty hospitable people.

**Jopal**
**Kipri District**
**Towers of Prudence**

"It had been vacated. The vessel itself was only a section of the primary spacecraft," Makon Welcos stated.

"Commander, were you able to determine its point of origin?"

"Not specifically, no."

"Did it originate in this, our Vesputi galaxy?"

"I don't believe so," Makon answered. This inquisition with the High Elders was about to get difficult, more so than the original one, where he'd requested permission to investigate the *Odyssey* ship on the Gobi's outer rim. He found himself calmly standing with his hands clutched behind his back, addressing all 10 Elders as they peered down at him from their high thrones in the Arena of Veritas.

"What would you estimate to be its point of origin, Commander?"

"Its construction left much to interpretation. It was rudimentary and rather crude." Makon had to be careful of his word choice. If he misrepresented any facts in his account, the Elders would be alerted. The arena had been designed to solicit truth from the testifier. Deception would be detected by the change in the aura surrounding the speaker. Each of the Elders sat in front of a micromist permitting them to monitor his vitals and the energy surrounding him. Heartbeat, respiration, perspiration, and one's energy aura all remained under constant scrutiny.

Makon knew he could regulate his body mechanics through subtle manipulation of his words. At least he would try. A display of deception would result in severe consequences; however, the Supreme Commander had to keep the discovery of Conor a secret. He was worth the risk of punishment. But would the Elders be so easy to convince?

"Commander Welcos, did you uncover anything of value from this mysterious spacecraft?" one of the inquisitors plainly asked.

"Please understand the Gregor Monolith was attacked by raiders shortly after coming in contact with the vessel. The Elite insertion team managed to escape the ship's interior just prior to it being destroyed via a gravitational collapse initiated by the enemy."

"Was this enemy apprehended?"

"Negative. They perished in the fierce combat. Their ships then fled the area. We were unable and unwilling to make pursuit."

"What could have been of such extreme interest to these 'raiders'? It appears quite daring for them to engage a ship as formidable as yours."

"I did not manage to determine their intention or motivations. They must have—"

"Understood," the High Elder interrupted his colleague's inquiry. "Yet you have neglected the original question. Did you recover anything of value or of Jopali interest?"

Makon understood that the Elders were not easily fooled or persuaded. Not only could they read him inside and out, but they surely had access to all relevant information and manifests.

He would have to answer honestly. "We did uncover something. Though I'm not sure of its value or interest to the tribunal."

"Go on," the High Elder urged.

"A four-legged beast. It is equal in size to a feritu, but I imagine it's in early stages of growth. It is incapable of communication but is currently under observation and study."

"Very well, Commander. We have received confirmation of this creature prior to this inquiry. Please report promptly on its relevant analysis."

Makon nodded, relieved that the inquiry seemed to be coming to an end. The High Elder glanced to the two other Elders seated on either side of him. They all nodded in agreement of some unspoken issue. Perhaps it wasn't coming to an end.

"Commander Welcos, was there anything else discovered and transported to Jopal?"

Makon sighed deeply. There was no way he could answer without either exposing deception or giving away the discovery of Conor. He hesitated before answering. "Esteemed Elders—"

"Interjection." One of the Elders suddenly stood and addressed the room. "I request a brief recess so that the noble Supreme Commander can enjoy a reprieve and collect himself."

The High Elders turned to one another. After a moment, they nodded in unison. "Very well. The tribunal shall vacate the Arena of Veritas for the precise duration of 25 minutes."

Relief washed over Makon. Although it would be short-lived, he was still pleased to have a few moments to formulate a response that could still possibly minimize Conor's clandestine transport and mitigate the reason why this had gone unreported. This reprieve was a gift not often afforded to testifiers and was clearly granted out of their respect and admiration for him and his past endeavors on behalf of Jopal. It seemed that heroism did bring reward—at least 25 minutes worth.

The panels under his feet dimmed, signaling they no longer monitored his body mechanics. Makon stepped down and turned from the room under the watchful eye of one Elder in particular.

### Kipri District

The market ended just before a grouping of large cylindrical objects floating 100 feet from the ground. They were similar to one another, resembling giant silos. "What are those things?" Conor asked his guide.

Without looking, Tiera answered, "Those are communication relays. They are AI driven, gathering information on flight patterns and directing incoming and outgoing flights to and from the planetary surface."

"So, they just hold really big computers," Conor stated as he stopped and craned his neck. His eyes climbed all the way to the top of the cylinders, noticing they culminated in sharp spires. This time, Tiera glanced over at the flight communication hub and turned away. She then did a double take, turning back to the cylinder towers. Something was odd. They usually rotated, shooting streams of light high into the atmosphere.

"What is it?" Conor asked, noticing the girl seemed perturbed by the towers.

"No. Nothing. We'll ask someone about it once we get to the observatory." She then led them away.

"What's that?" the curious boy asked as he meandered in wonderment, despite Tiera's attempts to move quickly and with purpose. She knew what he was referring to. The atmospheric purification construct would likely distract any newcomer to her planet.

"That is the APES," she said.

"The what? That's called 'apes'?" Conor replied with a snicker. Tiera didn't find it humorous. Probably because she was an alien, or because *he* was now the weird alien. Either way, she didn't laugh.

"Yes, A.P.E.S. The Atmospheric Purification Energy System. It ensures Jopal always has pure air for its residents. Every city has at least one. Mertio has three."

"Neat. I thought it would be something cooler than that. I mean, it looks cool and has a cool name, but it's not too exciting."

"Without it you would be choking on your own tongue right now," Tiera offered. "Now that actually would be cool. Please come on. I'd like to get there before Uncle's meeting is finished."

As they walked the distance to the observatory, Conor continued his visual exploration. He did his best not to wander off or stop too often. He was perceptive enough to know the strange girl got irritated with every pause, sidetrack, or question. However, it didn't fully deter him from pausing, getting sidetracked, or even asking a ton of questions.

Up ahead, Tiera finally spotted the entrance to the magnificent observatory. It had been a long and tedious journey, thanks to the curious tag-along, but her morning perked up just by seeing the building in the near distance. Her uncle sparked her love of the stars at a young age by first taking her here. He encouraged her preparation for the Academy, but as the only child relative of Supreme Commander Welcos, her attendance was a foregone conclusion.

For many years, she would visit the observatory almost every day, but thinking on it now, she hadn't been here in a long while. The last time she visited was with Makon, who instructed the director to take them on a private tour of the facility. It was in preparation for her first year of the Academy, and it exposed her to more stellar knowledge than she'd ever experienced in all the other many visits combined.

The observatory was large and round like a column of huge donuts stacked on top of each other. It stretched high into the air and rounded at the top with an invisible dome, giving it the appearance of being roofless. Three relatively smaller columns flanked the main building. They held most of the investigative and administrative sections. Although the main building rested on the ground, its upper levels could detach from the primary base and hover above. The observatory had a telescopic capability that would enable it to extend into the lower atmosphere for better range and cleaner imagery. Tiera had experienced this only once, during the tour sanctioned by her uncle. She was pretty certain her presence at the time went against protocols, but uncle had a way of getting others to bend to his will. Tiera didn't complain. This usually went to her benefit.

"What is that?" Conor asked. Tiera had heard the same question at least a dozen times before this, but she wasn't bothered this time because she'd anticipated it.

"That's the observatory. It's lowered right now, but the upper part can separate into the sky and even extend practically out of the atmosphere. I've been inside it one time when it did that. You'll really like it because you'll be able to explore more of our galaxy. Uncle wanted me to bring you here today." She then muffled her voice. "Besides, there are other people inside who can deal with all your questions."

"No. Not the building. What is *that*?"

Tiera stopped walking and turned around to see Conor facing away from her, staring upward. She moved her eyes away from him and spotted what he was pointing toward. High in the sky, just beyond the thin layers of sheet clouds, she could make out small black dots. They moved, growing in size as they drew closer, and there were at least forty of them.

The black dots shifted from a disorganized mass of pinheads into a stacked formation as they accelerated toward the ground. Within moments, Tiera's curiosity switched to fear as the black dots took shape into aircraft resembling winged rockets. Their flight moved so fast three ships flashed overhead before Tiera could even react. She reached out and grabbed Conor's shoulder. "It's an incursion!"

"A what?" Conor shouted as another ship shot down toward them. The ground around them tore apart as a series of pulses erupted from the ship's cannons. Conor remained still as the craft flashed overhead, continuing toward the city center.

"An attack!" Tiera shouted. She then dashed toward the observatory. Two more ships flashed over Conor, but as they flew closer, they appeared to slow in midflight. One ship turned over to its right, and Conor caught a glimpse of the pilot—a fearsome, hairless creature with a dark face and hatred in its eyes. The pause in time lasted but a moment, and the ships screeched onward. It was then Conor realized that the ships were headed toward the same destination as Tiera and he were.

"Tiera! No!" Conor shouted, but she was too far ahead with chaotic destruction swirling all around for her to hear him. He had to stop her. Conor sprinted forward as fast as he could. After a short distance, he caught up to her and grabbed her shoulder, pulling her backward and completely lifting her off her feet. He noticed the look of shock on her face as he lifted her and spun her to the ground. Before she could utter a word, Conor hunched over her as eight torpedoes pummeled into the massive observatory.

Fire and ferocious debris exploded outward in a long, deafening moment. Conor felt the pressure shockwave bang into him. He tightened and strained his back muscles against the wave of force, feeling it try to uproot and toss him and the girl like a Wiffle ball in a hurricane.

Conor resisted the explosive force and opened his eyes to look down at her. It was the first time he saw something different in the strange girl. Her eyes were soft now, and it made her even more pretty. But that didn't last very long. Tiera snapped her fright away and pushed him back off of her as she climbed to her feet. He held her hand to steady her. "Thanks. I'm okay," she said. Conor knew that was the signal to let go of her hand.

They both stood in awe as the building continued to shed its shape in a smoldering cascade of destruction. The observatory had been utterly destroyed. Conor forgot about the other spacecraft still circling overhead as he wondered if anyone had survived the explosion. He was about to urge them to go toward the wreckage to see if they could help, but Tiera took off running in the opposite direction. This didn't seem like her.

Conor ran after her and called out, "Where are you going?"

Tiera pointed to the squadron of enemy ships overhead. She ran under their flight path. "I know where they're going next! The temple!"

*Oh, crap!* Conor thought. He'd just remembered: *Commander Welcos was in the temple.*

# CHAPTER 6

**Jopal**
**Kipri District**
**Towers of Prudence**

The door to the solitude chamber slid open with a *swoosh*, and an Elder stepped into the hall. He spotted the Commander precisely where he expected him to be. Makon calmly sat in the small space reserved for quiet reflection. He knew that someone was slowly approaching but didn't look up. The Elder tucked his arms into the deep folds of his robe and stepped closer. "Commander, speak with me a moment."

Makon uncrossed his legs and slowly stood. He looked upon Elder Waan with a sad smile and reached out his hand to give his arm a squeeze. They then turned together and walked the length of the empty corridor toward the ascension chamber. As the Elder approached, the door scattered into tiny particles, exposing a yellow light. The light moved in slow waves from the bottom of the chamber to the top. The Elder hesitated a moment. Then with a slight cant of his head, the yellow waves shifted and started in the opposite direction.

Without a word, he stepped forward, and the light carried him down. Makon followed behind him. The yellow waves washed over him, carrying him downward. He wasn't sure where his friend was now leading him, but he assumed it wasn't going to mean good news.

After leaving the ascension chamber and walking another long corridor, they came to a large, dark room. Elder Waan moved to a specific spot on the floor, and the room suddenly began to illuminate like the rising of the sun. He stepped off the floor panel once sufficient light had been restored.

Makon briefly glanced around. He hadn't been in this area of the Towers before, but that went without saying. No one was permitted to tour, roam, or explore any part of the Towers without explicit invitation and observation by one of the Elders or a designated proxy. To be honest, Makon had never felt comfortable inside the entire place; the surroundings were too sterile for him to appreciate. However, this particular room did quite pique his interest.

It looked like a warehouse—more like two or three warehouses joined together, branching out into three wings. From where they stood, he could see the room's center some distance away with two other halls splitting off into other directions. Not only was the room massive, but it seemed to be . . .

"Yes, we are moving," the Elder said as if reading Makon's thoughts. "Ever so slightly. Most who are escorted here do not perceive the rotation. The room moves with Jopal's axis. This has been known to encourage balance, bringing mind and body into harmony. It helps with study." Makon nodded. "I am not surprised you were able to discern this movement," the Elder continued as he moved away to a long, slender column. "You have gifts."

"I assume you did not bring me here to discuss my attributes, Elder Waan."

The Elder reached out his hand and waved it in a downward motion. The column rapidly began to collapse. His hand moved again, and the column halted. Another slight motion and the column moved gently upward as if he were scrolling on a computer screen. "No, Commander Welcos. I don't wish to discuss gifts and attributes. I'd prefer to address foolishness." He then flicked his hand to the right, and a tremendous display shot out from the column. Words, pictures, and graphs illuminated the space in front of them from floor to vaulted ceiling.

Although he utilized the same particle technology on his ship, the vast amount of information presently laid out impressed him. He directed his attention to the giant sphere rotating in the center and immediately recognized it by the peculiar land masses and deep blue waters. His heart dropped into his stomach.

"Welcome to the Archive, Commander. We know much more than you think we do."

**Kipri District**
**Exterior**

The ships screamed overhead as Conor and Tiera ran toward the Towers. Luckily, they hadn't been singled out as specific targets yet as they dodged falling debris and cannon blasts. The enemy targeted shops, high-rise homes, landmarks, vehicles, and even fleeing people as they unleashed destruction upon the city.

Conor trailed slightly behind the girl, unsure of the way, but he was certain she knew the primary target would be the temple and the Elders inside. She moved with speed and purpose, but with enough caution not to lead them in the path of an incoming cannon blast. She ducked and pulled Conor down beside her as two ships approached, circled once, and then targeted a group of Jopali citizens huddled at the entrance to a nearby building. Conor rose to yell for them to move, but Tiera restrained him. "Too late," she uttered, shaking her head.

She was right. The front of the building exploded as multiple cannon blasts found their mark.

Then a deep rumbling noise sounded overhead. Conor looked up to see a larger ship hovering above them and two others sliding in to flank it. The aircraft's edges were sharp and angular, but it moved much slower than the first ships.

They seemed to be built for something other than speed and quick aerial assaults. Suddenly, the bottoms of the ships simultaneously disappeared and began to glow with a bright red light which carried all the way to the ground. Conor and Tiera found themselves washed in the same red light. "I'm assuming this can't be good, either," Conor said.

"It's definitely not! Run!" They took off in a sprint as numerous small pods spilled from the ships. They accelerated toward the ground but appeared as if they'd been dropped rather than shot downward. Conor then realized aircraft often dropped bombs rather than firing them. His pace quickened in an effort to outrun the blast zone. He didn't even notice that he'd run right past Tiera. He also didn't notice the gnewtrussel running beside him, the rolling canister of koli juice, or the giant crate of fresh but ash-covered sweet fruit. That is, until the koli juice rolled underfoot, launching him awkwardly into the air and face first into the sweet fruit all while under the curious scrutiny of the timid gnewtrussel. The quick, slender creature hesitated a moment to look over the strange boy who'd just flown into a pile of food, but then fled once Tiera made her way over to him.

"What are you doing?"

"I tripped," Conor said as he wiped pink mush from his face. He picked a pile of the squishy melons off his lap and began to stand, but Tiera slammed her palm into his chest to keep him still. She then dove on top of him and spun so she was now actually sitting on his lap. She flung the fruit, attempting to cover them up as best she could before leaning back against his chest.

As if it wasn't bad enough to have tripped and fallen in a giant pile of weird fruit, now he had a grouchy alien girl sitting on top of him and telling him to be quiet. Even though her hair smelled like caramel apples, it still tickled his nose every time she moved. Yep, definitely caramel apples—no nuts. And he swore he had some squishy fruit jammed in his ear, but every time he moved to pick at it, she yelled at him in that hushed whisper kind of yell where you know it's a whisper, but you're really actually being yelled at.

Conor felt awkward. Awkward enough to forget there were ships flying around trying to kill him. Awkward enough to forget he was the alien on an alien planet. Awkward enough to forget there were tons of bombs dropping down and about to explode at any moment. Wait—bombs! He craned his head around Tiera to see what happened when the bombs hit. Maybe this was a special fruit that would shield him from the blast. Maybe Tiera would protect him in some way. Maybe the bombs would forget to explode.

He watched as several bombs made contact with the ground. He winced, anticipating giant, fiery explosions, but that's not what happened. The bombs weren't bombs at all. They were pods filled with large crouching bad guys. Conor breathed a sigh of momentary relief. Then he noticed what came exploding out of the pods and didn't feel relief at all.

These aliens were tall, bald, and ugly. Of course, one might think twice before saying that up close, since each one carried some sort of long lance crackling with electricity and wore black armor that twisted around their limbs and torso as if it were organically connected to their skin. The pitch-black armor rose in sharp edges all the way to the forehead as if its design had been inspired by underground caves, leaving only small portions of the hands and face uncovered.

The pods kept falling like tremendous, nightmarish raindrops. One fell, and the alien immediately began running. Others followed suit, and soon an army of fierce warriors now rushed toward them. Some would stop and fire their weapons with a loud crack, but most of them seemed to be running in the only direction that luck would have—straight toward them and their pathetic fruit-filled hiding place.

"Keep quiet, or I'll kill you myself," Tiera whispered. At least it wasn't another of those whisper screams. Still, it didn't do much for building friendliness into their relationship. The aliens were getting closer, and the closer they got, the less confident Conor was in their ability to win this game of hide-and-seek. For a moment, he found comfort that they would at least get the girl before they got to him. But then he banished that awfully rude thought as quickly as it came. Besides, he actually liked her. No, that's not right. He didn't actually like her. She was cute, but he didn't like her. He liked that she was cute. That's it. That's the one.

Oh, well, cute or not, they were about to be blasted by alien bad guys any second, so no one was going to be cute for much longer. As the aliens approached, several of them slowed to a walk. One in particular stopped and began looking around. Could it smell him? Could it smell Tiera's caramel-apple hair? Perhaps it could smell the squishy fruit. What if they just happened to be surrounded by this guy's favorite snack?

"Why did it stop?" Conor whispered to Tiera.

She turned her head slightly to answer. "I don't know. Stay quiet."

As if he had to be told that. He held his breath and tried to turn himself into squishy fruit. It wasn't working, because the alien kept coming closer. Conor glanced down and noticed Tiera's hand moving to the inside of her cloak. Knowing what he knew about her, it was probably a weapon. This could either be very good or very bad for them. She was now holding a small, cylindrical object in her left hand. The creature now stood right in front of them, looking down, right at them.

Its slender, black eyes narrowed as the armor slithered around its elongated head. Though the jet-black armor covered most of its body, Conor could spot the creature's deep-blue skin under exposed sections at its elbows, knees, and other rotational pivot points. Thick black veins coursed along its toned muscles as if the alien's body were in a constant state of flex. It snarled, drawing Conor's attention back to its face. Wide, oval nostrils poked out from the armor's guard just above a gaping mouth filled with broken and jagged teeth. They looked long, sharp, and menacing, making Conor wonder if they'd cracked from crunching on too many bones.

Tiera steadied herself, prepared to strike if the alien came three steps closer. That's all she planned to allow. Three steps, and she would attack. If she waited until being discovered, then she would lose the element of surprise. And she would need every possible advantage to take down this warrior.

It stepped forward again, hunching low, digging its nose at the strong odor below. It got too close. If she didn't strike out now, then the enemy would make her regret her hesitation. She clutched her weapon in her hand and lashed out, but her arm caught on something. No, it was the boy's hand holding back her arm. She tried to shake his grip, but he held her pretty tight. That's when she noticed the warrior had diverted its attention elsewhere. It stepped forward just beyond them and continued past.

Once certain no more enemies lingered nearby or were headed toward them, she pushed herself from Conor's lap. He also stood and cleaned some of the slime off his tunic. "Close one. That thing almost—"

"Don't ever grab me like that again," Tiera snapped back without even looking at him.

"What is wrong with you? That monster could have killed you."

"It's a Kravii warrior. The ones we are at war with. You know nothing. Just accept it."

"I know that you suck."

"I don't follow the translation of that," Tiera muttered.

"Of course not. Why would you know what it means to suck? You'd probably want to take it as a compliment anyway."

"Stop talking. We need to go." She chose a route away from the Kravii fighters and began to follow at a quick pace but safe distance. Conor took a deep breath and followed.

### Towers of Prudence
### Interior

Elder Waan studied Commander Welcos' face. The battle-proven warrior/celebrated leader stood unfazed by the particle display. He sifted through some of the listed statistics and archived images before folding his arms behind his back and turning to the Elder.

"What do you see, Commander?"

"Elder Waan, I have always respected your wisdom and esteemed our friendship," Makon answered. The short, weathered old man nodded in acknowledgment. "Why do you ask questions you already see answers to?"

"It is not always the answers that provide fulfillment. Much more perspective and intellect become evident as one formulates an appropriate response."

"You have shown me the archived collection on the blue planet," Makon offered.

"That is correct, though it now goes by another name. That will be a discussion for another occasion. Why have I shown this to you?"

"You want me to know you have discerned what I located in Sector 7."

"True, but too simple for both of us. I have brought you here per your own request." Makon canted his head and, after a long pause, broke into a smile. Waan's expression didn't change. "You need my help. That was painfully clear in the Chamber of Veritas."

"Yes. I need your help. I don't want the council converting this child."

"Why not? It is a great privilege to be selected, and his specimen is ideal for the process."

"Let him learn and grow, make mistakes and experience defeat. I wish to adopt him as my own and enroll him at the Academy."

"The Council will not agree. There is much need for a capable deliverer. Many years have passed since our last, and there will be much anticipation to initiate the analysis. It will be of great benefit for Jopal and the many systems we serve. As it has proven before."

"Analysis? Don't you mean experimentation?" Makon asked, displaying disgust.

"They are one and the same. A young specimen would be fortuitous, as his growth and progress could be studied and mapped, perhaps extracted and duplicated in others. The benefit could be astronomical to the defense program."

"It won't be a benefit for him. You know what happens during conversion. We have no idea what toll it would take on a child from that galaxy."

"Great potential is lost if the process is delayed and age sets in," Waan urged.

"He should choose it for himself if it has to be done at all. Let him grow. I'll train him. He won't disappoint."

Elder Waan turned away and bowed his head. "I'm afraid there is—" Suddenly the tower shook like a rung bell. He stumbled but caught himself against the column. Before they could fully gain their bearings, a multitude of other crashes caused the building to bob like a buoy on a stormy sea. The library buckled and began to tear apart around them.

The middle of the room caved, falling away into the cavernous space below. A loud crack sounded high above them, and Makon saw the archive column break apart. The large sections of liquid crystal flipped upside-down, plummeting toward the hunched Elder.

Makon sprung forward.

**Towers of Prudence**
**Exterior**

Conor and Tiera came to an unexpected halt. The smaller spacecrafts circled the Towers like a swarm of killer bees strapped with missiles. Defense shields were clearly inoperable as explosions rocked the floating building. A group of six ships screeched across the sky overhead, banked toward the top levels, and then unleashed a focused strike. The barrage of violent energy smashed against the glowing pinnacle, causing it to erupt in a shower of sparks and fire.

Tiera's mouth dropped full open. The Elders often convened in the light pinnacle portion of the Towers—precisely where her uncle would be. She screamed but lacked the breath to give it any volume. They could only stand and watch in horror as the gravitational lift released, dropping the tower base from the sky.

The final crash cratered the ground like a meteor impact. It uprooted Conor, sending him hurling backward. He opened his eyes and pulled himself upright to find Tiera already on her knees, pounding the soil in frightened rage. The dust cloud from the wreckage billowed out, swallowing them like a menacing fog.

It became hard for Conor to see much around him. His ears still rang, and he felt more alone than he had since he first woke from the sleep chamber. The dust lingered, but in the silence, he started to see large shapes moving quickly in and out of his narrow field of view.

Tiera still slumped over with her head in her hands, tears streaming down her face. Conor didn't recognize it at first, and the girl had no idea what loomed directly above her. He squinted and saw one of the warriors slide out of the smoke and dust. It stepped around some debris and leveled its eyes on him. Conor held his breath, freezing all his muscles to that spot right there. His eyes flashed to the girl. Although she was sitting directly underneath its long, muscled legs, the creature hadn't noticed her. It snarled and brought up its staff, spear, or whatever it was. The weapon began to spark with dancing electric current. That soft voice in Conor's head told him to move. If it were louder, he might have listened, but his body wasn't going anywhere.

The ground began to rumble and shake again. Conor wondered what this creature was doing. Was this staff weapon powerful enough to create an earthquake?

Then—in a flash—the huddled girl lurched upward, striking the staff with her right hand. The weapon rebounded up toward the creature's head, the arced electricity grazing the side of its head armor. It screeched in pain and surprise and then lashed out toward the small girl with the long weapon. Tiera bent her torso backward like a graceful circus performer, causing the warrior to miss her. Then she sprang to the side to evade its secondary strike.

Tiera attempted a counterattack, but its armor easily repelled her effort. The Kravii moved quicker than she'd anticipated, catching her arm in its taloned hand. It lifted her up to face level and flashed its jagged fangs before flinging her through the air like a banana peel. She slammed hard against a torn afro plant and rolled for a short distance.

Conor watched as Tiera ended up face down. She groaned as she grasped her side and rose to her knees. He felt relief to see her move because the crash landing into the frilly plant looked quite painful.

His attention then diverted back to the creature, but he spotted a handful of similar warriors. Great. Now there was more than one. Conor squeezed his eyes shut and reopened them. His luck couldn't possibly be this bad. But it was. Of course, it was.

The monster now stood flanked by four other warriors. The ground rumbled again, and they staggered during the quake. Conor used the diversion to stand and dash toward Tiera. By the time he reached her, multiple charged-energy weapons targeted them.

Three loud cracks thumped in Conor's ears. He winced, anticipating the devastating impact, but nothing came. One warrior crashed face first into the ground, followed by two others. The remaining two turned to face the new threat, but they never had the chance to engage before being cut down. The smoke parted enough for Conor to spot what looked like an angry group of Jopali troopers moving through the smoke like a hungry shark through cloudy waters.

One of the troopers nodded in his direction before shouting an order and pressing on to the next target. As he helped Tiera to her feet, Conor figured out what had caused all the earth to tremble. No fewer than 20 large guns emerged from the ground and now fired upon the enemy space fighters. More Jopali troopers surged from the tunnels below the city to engage the foreign attackers with fierce combat.

Tiera stumbled forward toward the wreckage of the fallen pinnacle. Her steps were heavy and her gait wobbly, like a blood-drunk zombie. They came across dead and wounded troops from both sides as they crossed the battlefield. Kravii warriors now made up the majority of the carnage near the city's center, but the fighting continued as Jopali artillery guns targeted and decimated the remaining airships. Most of the aircraft fled in retreat to the upper atmosphere as the Towers collapsed.

Jopal's defense systems appeared to have been slow to respond, but the momentum of the battle drastically shifted once they became functional. The enemy fled the battlefield, scrambling back toward their drop ships, but the Jopali cut them down as they tried.

Conor turned back to the rubble at his feet. As the smoke swirled about, dust stinging his eyes, he reconsidered. Perhaps this was "mission accomplished" for the Kravii. He now struggled to absorb the complexity and tragic wonder of his surroundings. He was standing on an alien planet that had just been attacked by other aliens. Despite feeling accustomed to death and combat somehow, he still felt genuine sorrow for this planet's victims.

Troopers began to bustle around the main entrance of the lower main towers building. It had suffered heavy damage but had survived the onslaught. Most of the occupants escaped during the first wave of air strikes, but Conor detected movement from the inside. A toppled column slowly rolled away, and a silhouette eclipsed the entryway.

Conor watched the gathered troopers level their weapons at the imposing figure, but a quick movement flashed in the corner of his eye. Tiera left his side, sprinting full speed toward the figure.

Conor hesitated to follow her. He decided to give Tiera some space, but he still wanted to get a better look at what was going on. He moved to a mound of broken materials that seemed flimsy, like light plastics, but oddly felt slick and wet, though it was neither. As he neared the top, he could see the figure moving toward the girl. Conor flailed his arms to adjust his balance.

Just as Conor scrambled up and reached the peak, something sharp suddenly stung him in the back of his thigh. He lost his footing and tumbled down the heap with a loud yelp. By the time he'd spun all the way to the bottom, he was half-buried and feeling as foolish as he did in the crate of slimy fruit. This was turning out to be a truly terrible, awkward day.

He dug out his legs and stood up. Depending on what they used on this planet to clean their tunics, Conor figured his outfit may just need to be scrapped altogether. He reached his right hand to the back of his leg and craned his neck to check it. A ragged hole in his pants marked the area of the sting. It throbbed, but he didn't feel any blood, just a bruise. What kind of bizarre bug had bitten him? His mind formulated wild images of the kind of insects he might face on this planet, and his imagination didn't hold back.

Conor took a step forward, wincing at the tight pain, but it subsided as he moved. He still felt more foolish than hurt for toppling over like a clumsy bowling pin. At least no one saw him fall. Everyone looked preoccupied with watching Tiera's uncle emerge.

Feeling more excitement now than humiliation, Conor scurried overtop and around the debris to get closer to the entrance. That's when he noticed a tall man with long, dark hair pacing him a short distance away. He was wearing a black, floor-length tunic whose ruffled, dirty appearance embodied the day's combat experience. A stern expression creased his face as his piercing ice-blue eyes scrutinized Conor, making him feel uneasy. Clearly, the man had seen him fall and must think he's a clumsy idiot.

Conor looked down to avoid the stare and took several steps farther away. He glanced up again to see if his observer was still tracking him and was glad to see the stranger turn. The man moved with purpose away from the crowd as if he had somewhere better to be. He looked like a Jopali, but he seemed different from the other soldiers. Was he even a soldier? The tunic didn't look like the other uniforms, yet it was imposing in its simplicity—simple black with only a single purple line of embroidery on the back of the left shoulder. Conor found him odd. Maybe he'd ask the Commander about him, and maybe he'd get a straight answer.

Makon draped his arm around Tiera as several troopers debriefed him on the situation. Conor moved closer to the only two people he knew in the entire galaxy, but a large crowd had begun to form. Apparently, Makon's position as Supreme Commander made him their present deliverer.

Conor got close enough to see Makon and Tiera just beyond the crowd as they stood on the raised entry platform. He wanted to go to them but wouldn't risk wading into the mass of bodies. Everyone seemed to be fixated on the survivors of the building's collapse, except for one. That eerie man stood watching him again, and sure enough, he spotted the cold stare.

Conor looked away back to the platform. Makon had disappeared, and another quick glance afforded him the chance to spot the creepy, purple-stripe guy moving toward him. Conor's muscles tensed, and his heart rate increased. He had to get away from this guy.

He wanted to move forward but now found himself swamped within the crowd. Many more people had gathered, trapping him. He could barely move. The voices around him grew louder, almost deafening. Too many people and nowhere to go. Every time he shuffled past someone, three more blocked his way. Conor's vision went in and out of focus from sharpened details to blurriness. His mouth began to dry, and his head swirled with dizziness. Panic surged, and he felt his limbs weaken. He struggled to breathe but couldn't resist the helpless feeling of drowning. His vision narrowed and began to darken as he sank down.

Suddenly, a heavy hand landed on his shoulder and lifted him. A deep whisper against his ear then chased the anxiety away. "Relax. I am here."

Conor's vision returned, focusing on the man pulling him from his internal abyss. Makon's calm face hovered above him like a beacon. He had never been so relieved to reunite with a relative stranger before.

# CHAPTER 7

**Sector 9**
**Hadak-5**
**Riptide Coves**

Darkness hung over the jagged landscape like a magician's cape, perpetually shrouding the planet's character in mystery. It was vaguely lit by the stars above, but the thin atmosphere did little to discourage the continuous bombardment of stellar debris. While the dark made a visit to the lesser planets undesirable, the raging winds tearing across the terrain made mere existence in the environment quite treacherous.

Hadak-5 was the smallest of the nine lesser planets found in the Nopa belt in Sector 9's distant reaches. Its aptly named *Riptide Coves* remained the most precarious destination. With the average wind speed of 140 mph, shredded granite, pulverized nettlebone, and shadowdust swirled around at vicious velocities.

The inherent danger associated with this twisted deathtrap made inhabitation impossible—and visitors to this desolate planet were either fleeing from conflict, had crash-landed, or were just plain crazy. Yet, on this occasion, none of those reasons explained why the Kravii stealth cruiser had just touched down among a group of towering stalagmites. The sharp formations stretched from the ground like a contorted demon claw, creating an overhang, thus shielding the ship from the debris field.

Utirot, the ship's commander, exited first. He was fearless in life, unstoppable in battle, and would never be led in any situation without the promise of glorious conquest and all its spoils. He wore the traditional organic armor but carried a shoulder-high, U-shaped staff—the marking of a fearless Battleborn Chief. Nine other Kravii Knights exited both lateral sides of the ship and fanned out around the Chief. Their armor reacted defensively to the harsh environment, instinctively expanding and wrapping limbs and areas of exposed flesh to provide maximum protection.

The Knights scanned the area for other signs of life presence or movement—anything that could be deemed a physical threat. The darkness felt heavy and formidable. Even the blinding spotlights from the ship's exterior seemed to shrink back, as if fearful to glimpse the horrors lurking in the dark. Other than the blistering wind, they appeared to be alone.

The Battleborn stepped forward. He peered into black, but his senses stretched beyond the limitations of eyesight. Despite the appearance of dark solitude, he felt the presence of another. One of his Knights stepped forward to speak. "The dark is too thick, and no other light is seen. Our thermal scans detected nothing when we flew over the area." His words carried forth, raspy and labored.

Utirot wasn't quite listening. He watched the darkness. "Here we stand!" he bellowed. "It is done. The citadel of Jopal has fallen . . . as you requested." His other Knights strained to see what their leader was talking to, but it didn't work. Apparently, Utirot must've been able to see what they couldn't, or sense its presence somehow. They didn't question him, though. That would be a deadly mistake. "Show yourself. I know you're there. I can smell it. Smells like smoldering ash."

Several minutes passed, and Utirot now paced back and forth. He began to feel frustration and started to doubt whether this meeting would take place. But it had better happen, or heads would roll. Utirot hadn't gained notoriety from being known as the most patient. As a warrior, he was stubborn and impatient. As a Chief, he was the same. The only difference was that, now, he could get away with it.

The darkness moved. One of the Knights near the leader perceived it first. "Chief, there," she uttered. She felt sure she saw something, but it looked like a pitch-black object moving against a black canvas. The other Knights readied their weapons, scanning the black for movement, or whatever it was their companion had spotted. None dared utter a word. They waited with building anxiety. No one had met this new creature. They had only received a message demanding the attack on Jopal in exchange for the gift of the mysterious cloaking technology and the healthy return of their revered Lord Raider, Gilgorst.

The Knights also knew better than to act out of turn. This was Utirot's stage, and punishment would be severe for anyone forgetting this.

Utirot peered into the area the High Knight had indicated. He brought his black staff forward and pointed, the U-tip arcing intense lightning. "Ahh. There you are. Show forth, and let's end this gathering."

The blackness swirled just at the edges of Utirot's dark vision. It gathered into a mass that quickly developed limbs and the form of an *upright* (a term commonly referring to those creatures who moved on two legs, pods, pistons, or fyrds). It stood tall and firm, roughly the same stature as a Jopali, but not as muscular as the typical Kravii.

Once the figure formed, it remained stationary, faceless and wearing an unclassified robe. Utirot didn't know where this being had come from, but he sensed it wasn't something to underestimate. Nevertheless, this didn't mean he wasn't prepared for a fight—an opportunity to demonstrate his own true brutality. He gripped the staff tight, feeling the material flux in his palm. No one moved as time passed slowly and silently as if adrift in space. The wind howled and swirled with violence, but everyone remained too fixated on the hooded figure to pay it undue attention.

Utirot dragged his slim tongue across the bottom of his jagged teeth. This encounter quickly became irritating. "The citadel of Jopal has fallen." He waited for a response from the stranger, but no reaction or response followed. "Our attack destroyed much of their principal city. Mertio is wasted. We did our part. Now it falls to you."

Silence lingered like a chilled morning dew. Utirot snarled, opening his jaws to speak again, but the robed figure spoke. "Observation." The word carried forward like a sharp whisper before fading in the howls of the wind.

Utirot canted his head, causing his organic armor to shift slightly. He processed the one-word response for a moment before finally understanding. He turned to the female warrior on his left and nodded for her response. She stepped forward. "The cloak you produced allowed our ships to pass the planet's atmospheric defenses long enough to enter the atmosphere undetected. Our strike would have been detected and repulsed without it."

"Observation," the figure hissed again.

She looked at Utirot in confusion and then offered an answer. "Yes, observation. The Observatory."

"Destroyed?" the dark image asked.

Utirot stepped forward and spoke. "The city burned. Citadel and Observatory. Our fleet presented a successful attack, and now it is on you to deliver. Where is our Lord Raider? Show us Gilgorst, or I'll tear you apart."

The figure neither spoke nor moved. Utirot raised his staff. It began to shift and twist on itself. Its U-shaped end stretched into elongated sharp points. "Deliver him, or I will show you now the painful death you have earned." Just as Utirot and his soldiers stepped forward, the figure brought forward both his hands. A dark, shimmering mist streamed outward until filling the area, clouding the lights from the ship. The particle-heavy mist encircled the light until snuffing out each one. They now stood swamped in a heavy darkness.

Utirot depressed a recessed area on his gauntlet. His armor began to glow an ultraviolet light, outlining his figure and producing a dull purple glow around him. The other guards did the same. As one of the Knights moved to activate his armor light, he suddenly felt a pain shooting up from his belly to his throat. He gargled death in his throat and collapsed dead. The Knight next to him heard the garbled scream and turned to see what happened. The darkness remained too thick even for the glow of his armor to pierce it. He motioned for the three other Knights beside him to advance. They crept forward, their lifetime of rigorous training and savage combat guiding them with calm in the face of fear.

The air grew heavier with every passing moment. The particle mist now swirled around their heads. It disoriented them and seemed to be a lifeform of its own. It then attacked, pushing into any open orifice—eyes, ears, throat. The Kravii organic armor could do little to thwart the assault. Intense pressure in their heads and chests caused paralysis and agonizing organ failure. Dark blood seeped from their eyes and ears as the mist consumed their insides. They fell dead where they stood, their bodies mere hollowed-out carcasses.

The remaining five Knights took defensive positions along with Utirot and discharged their weapons into the dark. Electric bolts shot out haphazardly in multiple directions. However, their attacker remained either too fast or cloaked to be seen. Their bolts couldn't catch a target.

Then flashes of red like glowing snakes of light cut through the black. Within moments, Utirot stood alone among his intrepid Knights, their torsos gutted, crusted, and cauterized. He glanced around him to see they had fallen, their armor flayed open and still glowing hot.

Utirot spun to his left, spotting the shape of the assailant. He lashed out with the staff-spear, attempting to carve into his enemy. His blow met only empty air as the target moved away. The soft glow from his armor only illuminated enough around the immediate vicinity, so he could see the swift assailant only when he moved in close. "Stand and fight me," he snarled as frustration built to anger.

The enemy moved too fast, his presence hidden by the darkness. The red glow danced now in the dark. It moved slowly, slithering as it cut through the night. Utirot followed its mesmerizing movement, knowing the enemy had to be near. The weapon was strange, eerie. In all his days of ruthless combat, he'd never seen one like it.

The red light suddenly flashed out toward him like a serpent's strike. Utirot darted to the right, but it caught his left arm, leaving a deep gash, cutting through the armor as if it were fine linen.

The Battleborn recaptured his balance and swung blindly to fend off any other incoming attack. He felt his arm tingle and start to go numb from the wound down to his taloned hand. Acting quickly, he grabbed the middle of the staff with both hands and tugged outward, so that it rotated and split in half, creating two equal-length spears, both razor-sharp and deadly.

As the numbness started to more fully embrace his left hand, his fingers weakened, and the spear fell to the ground. He glanced down and found it wasn't his spear that dropped. His severed arm still held it tight as it lay at his feet.

Utirot felt the creeping numbness inching up his shoulder to his neck as well. It was disturbing, if not distracting, to say the least. However, he maintained his firm grip on the remaining blade and searched around for his adversary. Without warning, the crimson glow flashed again, this time from behind, lashing out at both of his legs. It dropped him to the ground, sinking him hard to both knees. Pain shot through him, climbing up his back. He started to stand but his legs had already started to weaken. He let out an agonizing cry of rage.

On his knees, he waited not for death, but for a chance. One chance to deliver an equalizing blow to his enemy. He had one good hand left and had killed more than a few foes from a grounded position. His mind remained quick to process the fight before him, but he had yet to understand what sort of weapon or foe this was. All was unlike any he'd ever seen in his 30 years of combat and warfare.

He heard a sharp scratching, and his eyes drew forward to the hooded figure. It stood silent, simply watching him. Utirot canted his head to the right and looked up at him. "Come closer," he uttered, "so we can share this death together." The hooded enemy didn't move. It remained faintly visible, still cloaked in black against the dark background. "Why? Why attack?" Utirot uttered through labored breath. "We had an agreement. Where is our Lord Raider?"

"Here," the enemy whispered. The figure then brought forth his hand and tossed a capsule to the ground. The object landed with a thud and then began to agitate rapidly. It cracked open in a silent explosion of dust. The dust began to swirl and circle much like a tiny whirlwind.

Utirot knew what came next. Nevertheless, he grinned, his upper lip curling in a final look of both hatred and satisfaction. "Vengeance will seek you. That is my promise."

“Svatich nol chispa,” the demon replied. The particle swarm pushed forward towards the Battleborn like a wave of tormented souls stretching out to claim another victim. Utirot held firm, disappointed yet steady for his moment of death.

# CHAPTER 8

**Jopal**
**High Grasslands**

Conor and Tiera stood together, well, at least close by one another, near the top of Mount Calibos, looking out over the cliff into the great ravine. They were at the edge, and, more than anything else, Conor wished for a handrail or bungee cord. To say he felt uncomfortable would be an understatement, but Conor accepted the challenge. He had to.

It was obvious to him Tiera was showing off for her friends in hopes to scare him. But he refused to take the bait. He walked to the cliff's edge, simply hoping nothing else happened.

"Hey, Tiera—let's go! We probably need to get back! I'm sure your uncle's waiting for us by now," one of the other girls said. Tiera turned to face her friends a short distance away. She just shrugged and turned back to face the chasm.

"You see, sometimes strong gusts of wind will pick up from the bottom of the pit and carry all the way up. We can ride it, you know," Tiera said to Conor.

Conor didn't want to turn away from the edge. He also didn't so much care to ride any winds that might pick up from the bottom or from the side—or any other which way, for that matter. He risked a step back or two. Maybe she wouldn't notice, but, of course, she did. He picked up her smile out of the corner of his eye. He wasn't surprised by it. After all, this moment was why she brought him here—to issue some sort of challenge, demonstrating she was tougher than he.

"Hey! Come on, you two! Let's go!" the girl named Yaoli shouted again from her perfectly sensible position far away from the edge. It seemed to Conor the other girls were ready to go, and he could have been easily convinced to leave as well. It seemed like everyone was waiting on Tiera. Most likely a common occurrence.

Tiera brought her arms out and up and breathed in deep, taking in as much of the free, thin air as she could. Keeping her eyes closed, with her head tilted back, she said, "Breathe it in while you can. You're gonna miss breathing like this."

Of course, Conor had no idea what she was talking about, but he risked taking his eyes off the edge to watch the strangely attractive, super-cruel girl doing her breathing exercises. After savoring a moment when she wasn't making a snide comment at him, he clapped his hands together, nodded, and turned away from the edge. Tiera sensed this and quickly spun around, racing back to her Rumbler. Conor felt a little bit winded, as he still was trying to adjust to the new atmosphere, so he decided to let her win this race. Besides, he knew his chances of beating this warrior-athlete were slim.

Conor felt a sudden blast of wind pushing up from behind. He turned around, sensing that it must be the whirlwind Tiera had mentioned. He took a few steps back and waited to see what this cyclone looked like. "Hey! I think that whirlwind is coming!"

Tiera had already made it back to the Rumbler and gathered with Yaoli and Iora. They all heard Conor cry out, saying something about the whirlwind. Tiera turned back to the ravine. She paused for a moment, waiting to see what would happen when the cyclone up-drafted and pushed Conor back off his feet. Then she caught the scent—a piercing, pungent, and nasty smell. She recognized it, knowing what came after.

"Tiera, wait!" Yaoli, the petite girl with short, spiky purple hair and rigid pants cried out. But it was too late. Tiera had already engaged the switch on her Rumbler, spun around, and was starting across the field back toward the unsuspecting boy.

Conor stood befuddled as he watched Tiera shouting something and waving her arms in the air as she guided the two-wheeled craft with only her knees. It was impressive. She moved it pretty fast, just not quite fast enough.

Conor's nose caught a strange odor, like sulfur coming up from the depths. Then came the sound—the drum-pounding, loud, whooping noise like fan blades on a giant aircraft.

Tiera continued to shout, but it was muffled, especially now with the numbing sound rising up from below. Conor turned his head, but before he could see the source of the noise and the odor, a blast of air caught him from behind, launching him forward. He toppled over, spinning into a somersault, missing the chance to see what was rising behind him before being tossed.

The wingspan on the Crestadon beast was equivalent to a midsize Jopali merchant-class ship. Its wings flapped hard and loud as it crested the ridge and caught the first sight of the boy. Its fangs dripped heavily with saliva, thirsting for an afternoon snack. Tiera knew this and maneuvered her Rumbler between the beast and the boy. She leapt off her hovercraft and let out a cry Conor hadn't expected could come from something her size.

The monster now hovered above them both, its full form in view. Its legs and arms were like tree trunks; its tail lashed about, giving it balance as the wings kept it aloft. Its head loomed large above its muscled chest and back. The fangs hung long and sharp as its taloned claws stretched and curled, poised for a merciless attack.

"Don't move!" Tiera shouted. "Don't run," she said softly, almost to herself, as she felt terror mixing with her courage. The Crestadon locked its cold eyes on its target and prepared for the first dive attack.

Tiera reached behind, placing both hands at the small of her back. She flung aside her tunic revealing a light double holster holding two upright batons, bright silver-chrome in color. The *Paraeo.* When one would wear the accompanying bracelet, as she did now, it became a formidable weapon. She pulled one of the twin batons with her right hand, holding it out to her side.

The Crestadon paused, observing her afternoon snack now potentially posed a threat. Tiera began to move to the right and thrust her left hand out to the side. This caused the other *Paraeo* to fly out of the holster and into the air. The baton spun in a circle, lifting above their heads. Tiera manipulated its movement with her spread fingers, distracting the beast away from taking a massive bite out of the boy. The weapon halted in midair, an arm's length from the beast's nose. As the monster stared at the twirling baton, Tiera caused it to spin faster and faster, now giving the blunt instrument the ability to cut.

Sweat began to bead up on Tiera's brow. She knew she could hold the creature at bay for only a moment and hoped this might deter it. Or frighten it off. She continued spinning the *Paraeo* with twirling fingers, inching it closer to the creature.

She watched the Crestadon switch its gaze from the twirling baton to the boy and then back again, as if weighing its options for primary attack. Conor didn't risk even the slightest movement. "Conor!" Tiera suddenly shouted. "Run!"

The Crestadon sized up the threat in front of it. He swiped at it with its right paw but missed as it moved away too quickly. Tiera still kept it spinning.

Conor seized on the distraction and dashed toward Tiera. The creature roared, attempting to swipe at the threat again. This time it caught the *Paraeo*, knocking it to the side. Tiera regained focus and redirected the weapon back toward the creature. She then bent low to the right and thrust her hand forward to send the other baton screeching toward the creature's chest with extreme violence, like a warrior's javelin. It struck the monster in the armpit. Not the devastating blow she'd hoped for, but it proved enough to stun it.

After being struck, the creature moved to the right, wincing from the pain with a high-pitched screech. Tiera now repositioned both of the *Paraeo* batons. She saw Conor standing next to her and the Crestadon refocusing for its next attack.

It bellowed a deep, ferocious roar. Tiera began spinning the batons again. The creature moved forward, and Tiera launched both of the batons at it, one hitting its shoulder, the other striking it in the jaw. This time, the blows did not deter its momentum.

"Move!" Tiera shouted as the beast swooped toward them. She managed to dive out of its grasp as it swept a massive claw at her and Conor.

When she hit the ground, the batons also fell away. She rolled and regained her stabilization. Conor also ducked the first blow. The second one caught him.

Its massive arm smacked him in the chest with a backhanded swipe. It struck Conor with tremendous force, sending him flying backward. He toppled airborne into a backflip until crashing down to one knee. He hadn't intended the aerial acrobatics, but the momentum had done most of the work. He was surprised when he didn't feel injured—just winded. The attack felt as if he'd been hit by a giant balloon. He checked his body for damage, but everything seemed fine.

He then looked up and saw how far he'd been launched. He found himself a healthy distance away from the monster, but now it surged toward Tiera. Her batons lay scattered on the ground between them. Conor looked further off and saw the other girls a safe distance away still shouting. His thoughts rattled between running toward them and safety or toward Tiera and danger. He made a quick decision and found his legs pumping fast, taking him to a third option.

Tiera rolled to her right and then burst up into a quick sprint as the beast tried to strike again. She evaded and circled quickly around to its back. Unfortunately, the creature knew too well how to ensnare a feisty prey. It crouched down and sprung up, gaining lift as its wings beat hard twice. The blast of air caused Tiera to stumble backward.

As quickly as it had left the ground, the beast dropped. Its sheer heft and size caused the ground to shake, knocking her down again. Tiera scrambled, desperately trying to get away. Her hands clawed at the dirt to regain her balance and footing. She got to her feet but then smacked face first into a heavy wall of tendon cartilage as the Crestadon extended its wings. As she toppled back, it reached down and grabbed her leg, lifting her high, dangling her upside down like a slab of drying meat.

Tiera was now staring directly into its gaping maw. Its eyes were shining like fire as they gazed upon the afternoon treat. She bit back fear the best she could, and with all her energy, Tiera bent forward grasping at the claws pinching her leg like a vice, holding her captive.

She scratched and picked at the claws wrapped around her ankle. "Come on," she breathed. "Give me back my foot," she said, as she yanked hard trying to pry apart the talons. She knew she didn't have time.

At any moment she expected to be freefalling down into the creature's throat. Her fingers caught the fastener on her boot. She unlatched it and managed to finally slide her foot out.

The Crestadon flapped its wings to take off. Tiera dangled, holding on to the claw with both hands as they moved farther up from the ground. Tiera knew she had to jump before it managed to gain too much height. The longer she waited, the more devastating the fall would be. Just then her Rumbler zoomed into view below her, with Conor at the helm of the controls.

"Hurry!" Conor shouted. "Jump!"

She didn't need to be told twice.

She released her grip and landed with a thud and a slip as her feet gave way on the loose gravel. She clambered back to her feet and tried to sprint to the Rumbler, but her bootless foot handicapped her. She bent down and unfastened her other boot, taking it off and flinging it aside. The harsh gravel dug into the soles of her feet, but at least now she could run. She reached the Rumbler, grabbed the rear handle with both hands, and vaulted into the seat behind Conor. Her arms wrapped around Conor's waist.

"Go! Go! Go!" she shouted, fearing the Crestadon would smash them at any moment. "Move fast," she said as she reached around with her right hand and pushed the throttle switch all the way forward.

The Rumbler accelerated with a boost, racing toward Yaoli and Iora, who were already tearing across the landscape, one on a Rumbler and the other a Spotter Pod. The Crestadon didn't appear discouraged from engaging in a pursuit; she didn't intend to lose her lunch buffet so easily.

The three land speeders raced away, wind blasting their faces as they pushed the machines to their limits. Tiera's tight squeeze around his waist offered Conor comfort as he tried to manipulate the strange controls. He felt her suddenly release her grip as she thrust out both arms behind her. The *Paraeos* spun on the ground before shooting toward her. She caught them in both hands and rotated backward on the seat to face the beast flying above. She flung both batons straight up at the pursuing monster, desperately hoping for good hits.

The creature failed to notice the two massive bullets before they smashed into her skull. The brute force from the baton strikes didn't disable her, but it disoriented the creature enough to knock it off kilter from its flight. She'd been flying too low in an effort to pluck the girl off the back of the machine, and her right wing dug into the dirt. The Crestadon rolled violently over a snapped wing bone in a turbulent cloud of scattered debris. Once it stopped tumbling, it lay slumped over, defeated, and destined to seek out a different midday meal.

The batons returned to Tiera once again, and she swung her legs around to face forward. She replaced them into the scabbard and wrapped her hands around Conor's waist again as they sped away behind the other girls.

"What was that thing?" Conor asked over the hum of the motor.

"That was a Crestadon—depending on its hunger level or our proximity to her nest, it can be friendly or extremely aggressive. She didn't look too friendly today."

"No. Not that thing. I mean the weapon that you used against it. It's pretty cool. Can I get one of those?"

Tiera looked at the back of his head with perplexing scrutiny. "No," she said, shaking her head. "You're strange."

Conor shrugged his shoulders and accelerated. "I'll just ask your uncle, then. He'll probably give me a set," Conor mumbled just loud enough for her to hear. He couldn't see her expression, but he hoped it had made her cringe.

**Jopal**
**Welcos Palace**

The Rumbler spun its massive tires on the loose dirt, churning up dust as it carved its way through the cavernous overhang built into the mountain. They skidded to an abrupt stop before Tiera slammed the vehicle in reverse, choosing an open spot next to a glider. She'd taken over the Rumbler's operation since leaving the Grasslands, both thrilling and terrifying him the whole way back with her borderline reckless driving.

The girl bounced off the vehicle and started running to the ascension lift. Conor moved slower, fascinated by his new surroundings. They were in some type of garage or hangar. He counted no less than three aircraft, what looked like two hover machines (because they were hovering), and another Rumbler, this one in black, unlike Tiera's red one. The waterfall cascading down the open wall both hid the bay and drowned out the echoes generated by the expanse. The tumbling roar of the water would surely muffle any calls out for her to wait for him, so he didn't try. Besides, it wasn't like she would wait up anyway.

Conor hurried to reach her just as she mounted the lift. He turned around inside the open chamber to gain one last view of the majesty of the Commander's hidden collection. "Your uncle has a lot of vehicles."

"Yeah," Tiera replied while adjusting stray hairs gone awry from their furious ride through the canyon. "This is just the Toy Hangar."

"Toy Hangar?" Conor asked, now getting a bird's eye view of the ships docked inside.

"These are the ones for play and excursions. Uncle has another bay for the leisure and luxury stuff. He calls that one the Ego because everything in there—"

"Boosts the ego?" Conor asked.

"Yeah, I guess. He doesn't think of it as a good thing, though. Usually takes out those ships and rovers when he's meeting important people like ambassadors, council members, and stuff." The lift carried past the palace's ground floor and up to the midsection. They slowed to a stop and stepped out of the undulating yellow waves. "Come on. Uncle said he'd be waiting for us in the study when we got back."

She couldn't wait for the study's oversized portal to give way. The particle mist split down the center, and Tiera squeezed through as soon as she saw a large enough gap. Conor didn't share the same urgency, so he waited for the portal to finish opening before entering the room. Based on the general majesty and vastness of the overall palace, Conor found himself surprised by the layout of the study. He expected volumes of books, dim lighting, walls coated in dark wood, and the smell of rich mahogany. Instead, the room was anything but a room.

Crystal clear waters carried from the false horizon to crash as soft waves on the white sands around his boots. It didn't feel like he was walking on sand; it was still flooring, but the illusion captured all the other senses. Colorful birds cawed overhead, and the sweet smell of tropical fruit blended with the salt of the ocean to transport one's mind straight to the islands. The water reached for Conor's feet, and he didn't know whether to move away or see if it would soak his shoes.

"It won't get you wet," Tiera said, noticing the boy's hesitation. "It's just an illusion."

"Oh, okay. Still. Seems very real."

"Yes. Those V-Techs really know how to put on a show," Tiera replied. Conor remembered the alien race of innovative designers who seemed to have their hands in everything around here. He kind of wanted to meet one.

Tiera pointed to a thatched hut nearby. "Uncle will be in there, probably." Conor followed behind her as they approached a large hut in the middle of the beach study. Its doorway opened to face the water and was covered by a single, thin cloth that swayed lightly in the breeze. There was a breeze in the study? Conor felt it on his face. Yep, there was a breeze in the study.

Tiera moved the linen curtain to the side and stepped through. Just as they entered the room, they spotted Makon, seated opposite a strange, hooded figure.

The man was well-built and athletic. He moved with grace and precision as he stood up almost immediately upon them entering. He faced them for only a moment as he moved swiftly across the floor and ducked past them to exit the hut. He paused at the doorway, looking slightly over his shoulder. "We will see soon enough," the stranger uttered. With that, he was gone.

"I believe we will," Makon responded under his breath. Clearly, their conversation had been interrupted by the two young adventurers.

Conor watched him depart, but in the grand scope of his exposure to recent events in the High Grasslands of Mount Calibos, he didn't see anything of significance about the figure. That is, until he noticed the subtle embroidery across the upper back of his black tunic. A thin purple line stretched from the shoulder seam to the mid-back. It was the same guy from the day of the battle in Mertio. The one who watched Conor trip and fall down the mound of rubble when he got stung, and then hung around like a creepy monk.

Tiera, however, didn't pay much attention to the other figure and directed herself straight to her uncle. "Would you believe that I took down a Crestadon today?"

Makon turned away from his parting guest and looked at the two children who had spontaneously emerged in his tranquil hut. "I see there is much excitement. You must have something quite astounding to tell me."

Tiera took a deep breath and straightened herself. "Yes," she said as she tried to calm her breath. "I took down a Crestadon today. It was amazing! I used the *Paraeo* batons you gave me last year for my birthday. I had practiced with them quite a bit."

Conor had never seen her so animated before. Turns out she actually knew how to smile. "Yeah, you could tell she'd practiced with them," he offered. "It was pretty impressive."

"I am pleased to hear it," Makon said as he adjusted in his plush lounger, crossed his feet, and picked up a slice of halit fruit. "And you, Conor? What were you doing during this endeavor?"

Conor thought back on the event and didn't have anything really cool to say. He did remember getting launched into the air like a sack of marshmallows, but he didn't want to share that part. It didn't sound remarkable. More embarrassing than anything else. It sounded weak, and he felt the need to impress this Commander rather than disappoint him.

"You have to let me tell you!" Tiera interrupted. "This thing was huge with fur and fangs just as long as I heard they would be. In all the times we had been out there, I had never seen one, even though I'd heard that there may be a nest somewhere nearby."

"Where, exactly, did you go?"

"We went to the south. Agali Fissure."

"That's pretty far out. I didn't anticipate you taking Conor out that far, especially with the events from three days ago." Tiera shuffled her feet a bit and sat down at a table tucked off in the corner. She started to look dejected, as if she were about to get reprimanded. Instead, she sprung up again. Excitement had taken too much of a hold on her, and she needed to finish her story. Makon listened as she told him more about the monster and her heroics. He waited for her to finish and then folded his hands. A stiff pause chased the joyful levity from the room. "And what about the young man here? How did he perform?"

Conor thought it was an odd question. Why did he care so much about his performance? Tiera didn't seem too keen on talking about him, though he did help in saving their lives. At least she wasn't too proud to briefly explain how Conor ran to the Rumbler and did a halfway decent job at operating it before she soon made them switch positions.

"Is that all?" Makon asked. Tiera nodded. "I'm proud to see you were able to take care." Makon turned to Conor. "Thank you for watching out for our common interest," he said as he nodded in the direction of Tiera. The girl furrowed her brow. She didn't like the sound of that. Clearly, she'd been the one watching out for this boy. She also didn't like being referred to as their *common interest*.

Confusion swept over Conor. Makon must've been joking about him taking care of his warrior-niece. Surely it was the other way around—her watching out for him. Tiera appeared angry now, and Conor felt awkward. It was time to change the subject. "Who was that?" He asked.

"Who are you talking about?" Makon asked.

"The man in the black," Conor said.

"That was a Paladin. You need not worry about him," Makon offered.

Conor tapped on the side of his jaw just below his ear, making sure his translator device was working correctly, because he had absolutely no idea what the Commander was talking about. "I've seen him before," Conor added in an effort to elicit more explanation.

Makon turned to him. "That does not surprise me as much as you think it should. You will very likely see him again." The Commander's ambivalence toward the man and what it meant for Conor to recognize him did not ease the boy's suspicions.

Yet, he'd learned by now the Commander liked to remain cryptic in his statements for some reason.

Makon pushed himself from the low-rise lounge sofa, rising to his feet. His long robes cascaded down to the floor. "I'm pleased to see your adventures today brought good fortune, good storytelling, and good training. I would normally chastise you for lack of caution, but I have recently discovered that, due to the events of the attack and the decimation of our cathedral—The Towers of Prudence—the Academy will begin the next session in two days' time."

"That doesn't give me more than a day to spend with my companions," Tiera said, displaying clear agitation. "And you had me spending most of my time dealing with this boy here." Conor could've been offended by the remark, but he'd half-expected it. After today's incident, he figured she'd soon start to soften up to him. But obviously not too soon.

"For your safety and the needs of the Federation, you must be in attendance. As you must know, I have been tasked with much to do about our defense and countermeasures with regard to the attack." This time, Makon turned to Conor. "The Elders have fallen. On the upside, this keeps our secret safe. That is, until you choose to expose it. And you will."

Conor shook his head with a furrowed brow. "No. I won't."

"Oh, but you already have," Makon said with a hand gesture toward the doorway, signaling out the departed Paladin, but he still deliberately remained ambiguous. Conor wasn't sure what he meant or how much it mattered if people found out where he came from. After all, what was the big deal? There were already so many different kinds of aliens wandering around just on this one planet alone.

"Come now," Makon continued. "We need to prepare for our ascent to the Academy."

Tiera was still brimming with frustration, but nevertheless, she turned to leave the hut. She wasn't quite ready to leave, but she knew better than to question her uncle. Arguing with him never worked. Besides, on a good note, the Academy was pure awesomeness, and she couldn't hold back the excitement that thought held for her, especially with it being her second term.

"One more thing, Tiera." The girl stopped just outside the doorway. "Next time you go exploring, you may want to rethink your footwear. I hear latch-boots are a sensible fashion." Tiera turned away with a huff and marched down the false beach toward the exit.

Makon waited for Tiera to leave before speaking to Conor again, catching him at the thin, white curtain. "She's incredible, isn't she? Intense but pretty impressive nonetheless."

"Yeah, I suppose. For the record, she did have boots. She had to take them off when—"

The Commander quieted him with a hand gesture and quick nod. "I know. But what's more imperative, Conor Hawk, is that you aren't ready for the Academy." A smile crept across his face. "But, in truth, the Academy isn't ready for you."

"But, what's the Academy? What am I expected to do?"

"All in time. You will find out everything. All in time." Makon moved forward and placed his large hand on Conor's shoulder. "There will be a surprise waiting for you when we arrive."

Knowing he wouldn't get any more of an explanation from Commander Welcos, Conor just smiled and stepped back onto the virtual beach. Tiera had already exited the study, and from the look of it, she didn't have any intention of hanging around him. No matter. He could use a break from Miss Sassy Pants anyway.

Makon's large arm draped across his shoulders, heavy but comforting. "Don't worry about her. She'll warm up to you. I want you to come with me."

"Where?" Conor asked.

"I want to show you something." Makon walked out onto the virtual beach and into the empty ocean, strolling toward the horizon. Conor followed into the waters, knowing he wouldn't sink or even get wet, but still half expecting it. He continued following Makon as the water illusion grew deeper, climbing up to his waist, his chest, and over his head. He felt anxiety creep in, though he was still breathing. They were now walking underwater, still descending. Conor stopped and looked around. The waters were crystal clear, so he could see underwater wreckage of a crashed vessel and undersea wildlife swimming all about.

Makon sensed the boy had stopped and turned to face him. "Pretty fantastic, huh? Don't worry—we aren't actually underwater, but you wouldn't believe what this illusion cost me. Ha!" He then turned and continued down the ramp through the undersea spectacle. "We're almost there."

Conor started forward again, reassuring himself that if a giant shark or anything similar swam up to him, it would be nothing more than an illusion. The ramp ended at a giant slate wall of black onyx. Makon swiped his wrist against the wall, and it began to peel away into moveable slats from the center outward.

Makon glanced backward a moment, flashed a smile, and uttered, "Shortcut."

The vertical slats gave way to a massive hangar bay cut into the mountain. Granite enclosed the massive expanse on three sides, with the only visible opening at the far end, but its entry was marked with a roaring waterfall. At first glance, Conor spotted at least four ships, but as they walked further into the sequestered bay, he noted twice that many. Some were sleek, with sharp lines and narrow cockpits, while two others looked like frigate ships that would need a small crew to operate.

Conor moved slowly in between the docked ships, wondering what the Commander needed with so many. This must be the Ego Bay Tiera had referred to.

Makon tapped the side to a long, open-topped cruiser and waited for the steps to descend. He gripped the side and climbed into the cabin. "Over here. We'll take this one," Makon said. Conor moved away from the bright-red speed craft, looking back at it once more before reaching Makon's choice. "Those fast ones are fun, but I actually want you to see things, not zoom by them. You'll get your speed fix another time."

"Where are we going?" Conor asked as he plopped down in a large comfy chair whose material resembled soft leather.

"That depends on you. Where should we go?"

"I don't know. I don't know this place much. Let's just stay away from the Grasslands if that's okay."

Makon laughed. "I think you've had your fill of that place for a while. I want to share a little more of Jopal with you before you head to the Academy. Tell me about your home."

"I don't remember much. I remember I was on a ship, I think."

"Before that. Do you remember your planet?" Makon asked.

"Kinda. I have images of cities and buildings." Conor thought harder, closing his eyes and pushing his mind to remember. "I remember people were afraid. The days got darker, and the nights got longer."

"No. No. Don't tell me about the end. Tell me about your home. What did it look like before the dark? Did you live near a beach or a mountain?"

"It was green. We had lots of trees around us. And grass. We had a large lawn."

Makon smiled. "Good enough. I know just the place." The Commander tapped the wisp panel, and the twin engines engaged with a soft hum. The ship moved silently backward, suspended in the air as they backed out of the dock. Makon redirected the ship and pushed them slowly toward the waterfall. As they drew near, he tapped the screen again, and the water stopped flowing. They passed under it, and the water trickling on top of Conor's head confirmed this one wasn't an illusion. Makon brushed the water off his forehead. "Open top. Figured we'd better turn off the water first."

Conor spun around in his seat to look back on the fortress as they moved away. The waterfall sprang forth again from unseen ducts cut into the mountain. The ridiculously ornate palace the Commander called home began to shrink in the distance as Makon flew them down through the valley.

Jagged rocks reached up to touch the hull, but the expert pilot kept the vessel just out of reach. They pushed through the valley as it opened to a bustling river, and Conor watched as they cruised over the water with its wide fishing boats and luxury ships. They turned to the north, away from the stretches of Mertio.

Makon pulled the throttle to gain altitude and decrease the duration of the excursion. He turned to Conor. "We have a beautiful planet here . . . when it's not being pummeled with torpedoes. You'll find many things that may just remind you of home."

Conor nodded and held to the side as they climbed a bit higher. The ship moved through the sky toward the wilderness. The shores of the capital blended into the horizon as multicolored vegetation fields now covered the landscape canvas. A mountain chain grew in size as they moved closer without climbing. He risked a peek over the side. A sprawling forest appeared below, and they began to skim the treetops as Makon brought the craft lower without reducing the velocity. They were so low Conor could reach out and touch the canopies stretching up toward them. He heard the scratching on the ship's underbelly like fingernails clawing, trying to break it open. Then came a loud thump, and the ship rattled and rocked.

Makon startled. "Where'd that one come from? Tree must've been a bit taller than I anticipated. We're okay, though. Don't worry. Almost there."

The Commander dipped the ship down and to the right at a narrow opening in the forest. They zipped past the thick columns of trees lining their path like soldiers poised on an ancient battlefield. The ship carried up a steep hill leading to a mountain. Makon powered down the ship and brought it to a stop at the top.

"Here we are," Makon said as he stepped back from the control panel. The stairway extended to the ground, and he began to descend. He waited for the boy to reach the ground before guiding them along the hilltop away from the ship. He paused and inhaled a deep breath. Conor imitated him, taking in crisp air.

"Feels good, doesn't it?" Makon asked.

Conor nodded. "It smells good."

"What do you smell?"

"It's like pine but sweeter, as if cotton candy and pine needles had blended together."

"Good call. I hadn't thought of that," Makon said with a smile. "It's the trees. Maybe we'll change the name to the Candy Pines. I thought you might like it here."

"I do."

"Does it remind you of home just a little bit?"

"Well, I suppose. It is green. I love the trees and feeling the grass under my feet."

"I thought so. So much around the palace and the Academy, as you'll soon discover, is a simulated illusion. It looks great, but you lose the smell and the feel of just being absorbed in the reality of a place."

Conor spun around slowly, taking in the majesty of the towering mountains at their back and the Candy Pine forest below them. He then looked over to the Commander. "Have you always lived here?"

Makon smiled. "It's my home now, but no. Like you, I came from very far away. Feels like a lifetime ago now. I've seen much of what the Vesputi Galaxy has to offer, but Jopal is still my favorite. It's not just the scenery and the environment, but the people. You'll soon find that you have more in common with them than not. They feel and think the same as you. The same things motivate and scare them. And in spite of our ongoing war with the Kravii, they remain resilient and hopeful for a peaceful future. Perhaps it's just how they are or because of the war, but they don't concern themselves with pettiness. They focus on what's important."

"What's that?"

"Well, survival, I figure." Makon squinted and looked across the valley. "No, I think it's more than that. The Jopali value life and growth. They strive for peace, but who knows? I've seen peace tear civilizations apart more than war ever could."

"How long have they been at war?"

"Ever since I can remember. They founded the Federation to combat the Kravii. That was rather recent because Jopal wasn't the only planet under constant threat. And let's face it, Jopal needs all the help it can get."

"Why? It seems they have great weapons and the best ships," Conor asked.

"We do now, thanks to a random excursion to a tiny, forgotten moon. There we discovered the little Riostovi V-Techs. Who could've known a crash landing on an insignificant moon could lead to so much advancement?" Makon drifted back into memory, and a smile formed as he recounted to the inquisitive boy. "They were such a curiously strange species—peaceful and fiercely intelligent. There wasn't much to their little moon, and not many of them existed altogether."

"If they are so good with technology then why were they so hidden?"

"Good question, Conor. You see, they didn't have the raw materials to do much. I mean, they did the best they could with what they had on their moon, but once we introduced them to our resources, they were able to build wonders."

"Like weapons?"

"Yeah, sure. They wouldn't have ever needed to construct weapons for their own purposes. It's like they are the one species not motivated to kill each other. It was a strange concept for them at first, but they came around when they learned about the Kravii threat. I'm sure you'll come across one at some point."

"Who, the Kravii?"

"No. Yes. I mean the V-Tech, but you'll definitely see more Kravii. You already have, and that's the whole point of the Academy."

"To fight the Kravii?"

"Them and other threats, but mostly the Kravii."

"Why are you at war with them?" Conor asked.

"It's not by our choice. They are so many, and they want Jopal. Their planet is overpopulated, so they kind of need to branch out into other worlds."

"Why can't they just move here peacefully?"

"That's a nice thought, Conor, but the Kravii thrive in darkness. They would fully alter the beauty of this world. They have about 10 offspring to every mother, each one born and bred for combat. It's like they spring out of the womb with bloodlust and knife in hand. We wouldn't want them living among us. It'd be like inviting the town bully to move into your house as a roommate."

"Can't they just find a different planet where people aren't living?"

"Don't I wish," Makon said with a tap on Conor's shoulder. "You've got the right idea, but they don't think that way. The Kravii are accustomed to just taking what they want, and they've been pretty successful at it. After all, for a warrior race, where would be the enjoyment in not invading and conquering? I believe that's half the goal of their conquest—the satisfaction in taking it."

"Oh," Conor said as he looked away back to the trees.

"Enough about all that. They'll teach you all you need to know in the Academy courses. Come, I want to show you something," Makon said as he turned and moved across the hilltop. They continued at a leisurely pace until the Commander finally paused and turned to the right to face down into the valley below. Conor did the same and noted something peculiar. The trees spread out from this vantage point in the form of a wedge as if this very spot pushed them outward, or they were guiding the traveler to where they stood.

"You see that there?" Makon asked with a signal of his raised hand. "Look far away, to the horizon." Conor looked as far as his eyesight would carry him, but he didn't see anything of significance.

"What am I looking at?" Conor asked.

"Nothing now," Makon offered with sorrow in his voice. "Until recently, from this hill one could look out across the forest and the plains and just barely catch the levitating Towers of Prudence. When the light from Tiptokon, Mitaj, and Tiptokon III would converge on the pinnacle, it would cast a blanket of rainbows over all you could see. It was truly remarkable."

"What's so special about this place?"

A smile came back to Makon's face. "See for yourself," Makon said as he stepped back revealing a large grouping of black crystal stone a short distance away. Conor looked at it and then back at the Commander. Makon just stood in silence, still staring at the horizon as if inviting him to go take a closer look.

Conor moved away, taking cautious steps toward the stone. For some reason he didn't comprehend, he felt a reverence, as if there were something sacred about this moment. As he moved closer, he felt a vibration in the air. It wasn't uncomfortable or distressing, but instead felt rather invigorating. He felt energized and lighter as though he could move swifter and with greater clarity.

He reached out and touched the stone, feeling the smoothness of the material. It pulsed energy through his fingertips. He pulled away due to the alarming sensation.

"Don't be afraid," Makon said, suddenly appearing at his side. "It won't hurt you."

Conor reached out again, this time placing his full palm against the rock and sliding it around. The energy trailed up his arm until it engulfed his entire body. "What is this stone?

"The stone is called Dark Bloodsalt, mined from the cold lava mountain of Fi. It's virtually indestructible. The name comes from those tiny rivulets of red you see running through it. However, the energy you feel isn't coming from the stone. It's coming from that," Makon said as he pointed to a glowing object jutting out of the stone cluster.

Conor spotted a slender black column rising upward, a handle to something embedded in the Bloodsalt. It glowed white, emitting energy that carried throughout its captive stone. Conor climbed the rock cluster to get closer to it and view it fully. The column was indeed a handle to something. Decorative panels marked with odd white runes ran along its surface, from its gold-capped tip to the other end partially buried in the rock.

It wasn't fully buried though. Something else was exposed. At first glance, he thought it was part of the rock, but now he could see the shape of a black, glossy arc. He traced his fingers along it, being sure to avoid what appeared to be a lethally sharpened edge. As he touched the glossy shape, he noticed the glowing energy transferred to his hand.

"The Harbinger's Bane," Makon whispered. Conor stood, taking a step back from the weapon, though unwilling to take his eyes and attention away from it.

"What is it?" Conor risked asking, enthralled with its magical wonder.

"It is an axe smithed from the same Dark Bloodsalt holding it captive. There are several legends attached to its creation, but I'll offer my favorite. Many years ago, two of the ancient Elders journeyed far in search of a particular Mystic. They commissioned him or her to fashion this weapon, and it proved to be more than they expected. Both Elders lost their lives bringing it home."

"How?" Conor asked.

Makon traced his hands over the weapon's handle without grabbing it. He pulled the white energy along his fingers like smoke. "The Mystic imbued the axe with this strange energy that ultimately drained the Elders of their vitality. The legend urges that only the true Harbinger can wield its power, just as only they can pull it from its home in this rock."

"Why would anyone want a weapon that drains your energy?" Conor asked, now stepping away as if the magical axe were infused with poison.

"Relax. It won't hurt you. The energy only harms in large doses. It is said, the true Harbinger will feed off the weapon's energy rather than the other way around, granting them unfathomable power in combat. So, as you can imagine, many tried to wield it only to fall ill from its effects. Besides, it's too heavy for most to lift. In their wisdom, they entrenched it here, never to be pulled again."

"Did you ever try to pull it out?"

Makon laughed. "Of course, I did, but the thing wouldn't budge. Go on. You try. Give it a tug."

"You sure it's safe?"

"It won't hurt you. See if you're the chosen one," Makon said with playful sarcasm in his voice.

"Like the story of the Sword in the Stone?" Conor asked, recalling the fairy tale from back home.

"Something like that," Makon replied with a smile. He then grew quiet and somber as he watched Conor move close to the axe again. He watched intently as the boy wrapped his hands around the handle and bent his knees to give it his best effort of strength. The energy wrapped around Conor's hands and forearms. He felt stronger as he gripped the handle. This weapon could be his as the chosen Harbinger! He flexed the muscles in his arms, back, and legs, and pulled upward.

The axe didn't move.

Conor adjusted his grip and tried again, straining hard against the cold grip of the rock. No luck. On the third try, Conor thought he felt it budge, but it stayed sunk deep within the stone. Before he could try for the fourth time, he felt Makon's hand rest on his shoulder. "I couldn't lift it, either. Perhaps the legend of the Harbinger's Bane is nothing more than that—just a legend."

Conor's head sunk as he dropped his hands. For a moment he thought he might be special. "But I hoped . . ."

"The story of the chosen one, the deliverer bestowed with power and ability to save people and planets, is just as you said, a story. A fairy tale. Look here," Makon said as he turned the boy to face him. "I believe we become who *we* choose to be. It's not chosen for us. You can be great, with or without a stupid axe, but that ultimately will depend on you and the hard choices you make. Just know this: the hero's journey is a rough and lonely path born of selflessness and bathed in sacrifice."

"I don't want to be a hero," Conor replied.

"Ha, ha," Makon chuckled, cutting through the dramatic tension of the moment. "We shall see. No one chooses to be a hero. They just make heroic choices, and *bam*!" he yelled with a clap of his hands. "A hero is born!"

Conor forced a weak smile and began to climb down the rock. He reached the smooth grass and paused, again absorbing the majesty of the view. Makon moved behind him back toward the ship. Conor hesitated, basking in the axe's white energy, almost saddened to leave its invigorating sensation. He looked back on the Bane one last time before turning away.

Conor moved out of the weapon's mystical energy field, feeling a sudden loss within his muscles and bones, as if fatigue had set in.

And the Harbinger's Bane sank ever so slightly back into the Bloodsalt.

# CHAPTER 9

**Jopal**
**Northern Starbase**

The ship called the Gregor Monolith was ginormous. It was like a slow-moving city, which made sense, because much of the crew apparently lived on it practically full-time. When Makon had brought Tiera and him to the ship in the luxurious transport, Conor first thought they'd arrived at some strange floating building that was attached to other buildings. It turned out to be the Commander's ship. Conor had just barely gotten around to exploring a small fraction of the palace, and now he was faced with another giant platform of exploration.

However, the thrill of the ship's presence was nearly eclipsed by the people. Crowds would gather wherever the Commander went. Apparently, his palace had to be far removed from the masses because people would swarm wherever he went just to get a glimpse of him.

A large gathering congregated around the ship's fence perimeter, surrounding the entryway into the pavilion housing it. Cheers erupted as their dark-tinted hovercraft approached. Clearly the Commander was a celebrity. No—more than a *celebrity*. This was *adoration*. And in a time of war, they appreciated their hero more than ever.

Supreme Commander Welcos said some parting words after leaving the hovercraft and escorting Conor and Tiera onto his mothership. Other crew members bustled around as they prepped the vessel for liftoff.

The Gregor Monolith was so massive Conor barely sensed their movement as they lifted, but they moved fast. Already out of the atmosphere, the ship set course for the Academy. He'd been told it was like a planet unto itself. From the surface of Jopal, the Academy looked like a tiny version of the planet's four moons, so it must be big.

Conor had been left to himself, so he naturally began to wander somewhat aimlessly. It wasn't that he was looking for something to do. He just needed to explore—to find the most curiously interesting parts of this floating city built for war.

Another kitchen? Well, at least it could be. He located a strange, vast room with multiple open levels. It looked like a kitchen because people seemed to be eating while others prepared different foods in front of them. He didn't find this interesting at all. He wasn't hungry, and though it looked exotic and unusual, there had to be more spectacular things to see on this monstrous ship.

He then spotted a corridor to the right and decided to take that venture. This one appeared to be less frequented by others. As he walked down the corridor, the floor panels lit up for him, adding a gentle white light in addition to the overhead blue lighting.

He got nervous for a moment, becoming unsure about getting lost. But then he realized the Commander could likely find him with ease. He was that type of man—to know everything going on within his ship. Conor stopped and glanced all around. Besides, he already was quite lost, so what was the point of worrying?

Then he saw something that sparked his interest. Three Jopali soldiers rounded the corner of the hallway to the left. He recognized them from the battle several days before. Days or whatever they called it—*cycles*. The soldiers looked to be excited or agitated, and he overheard something about weapons. Weapons. This definitely could be interesting.

He tried to trace their movements to figure out where they had come from. This ended up being easier than he thought. The hallway opened up into a massive arena with distinctive, leveled structures.

The mysterious room had numerous alcoves and wall partitions set aside for what appeared to be different forms of combat. A long hall at the far end held stationary and moving targets and was marked for ranged weapons. Conor had stumbled upon a type of training area.

It seemed all but empty as he ventured deeper into the massive room. Assuming he wouldn't be welcome here if found, he promised himself not to touch anything.

On the wall nearby hung several forms of long spears but with rounded ends. What would be the point in a dull spear? Must be something different. He moved on, absorbing the environment like a spy on a scouting mission. He came across some smaller tools or weapons. He reached out to pull one off the wall but hesitated. Better not. He didn't know how to operate any of them, and recent experience proved the technology remained outside of his understanding.

Conor had been exposed to plenty of weapons before. His mind flashed to a ferocious woman handling a long blade. She sheathed the sword and pulled a pistol from her thigh holster tactically engaging encircling artificial targets. Fast, precise, and merciless. Who was she? He knew her. Was it a memory, or something he'd watched on the simulator?

Suddenly, a loud boom sounded up to the left. The level above him. He heard it again and decided that's where he really needed to go. He looked for stairs, but, of course, there weren't any. Maybe they had one of those floating stairways again. This was becoming a complicated undertaking.

Conor moved to the far-left wall. A particular pad on the floor seemed out of place. He stood on it and waited. Nothing happened. He did the next best thing he could think of. He jumped up and down. Still, nothing happened. There had to be a switch somewhere.

He started to move away but then had another thought. It seemed too simple but might be worth a shot. He sneaked back over to the floor disc and uttered the word, "Up."

Without warning, he began to ascend in midair. He could feel the disc beneath him, but it was invisible. It became clearly evident what he should do next. "Down." The disc halted for only a moment and Conor began to descend. Way too easy. "Up." He reversed direction again. Before he could really test the elevator pad's limits, a loud boom echoed above him.

Time to investigate. But first, he just had to know something. "Down." Conor got all the way back down to the floor, took a deep breath, bent his knees, and said, "Up . . . Fast."

The pad accelerated as if shot from a cannon. His knees buckled as if he were now spring-loaded. "Stop!" Conor yelled, and the disc abruptly halted, sending Conor airborne. "Ahhhhhh!" He couldn't help the involuntary outburst. Terror quickly turned to giddy joy as he continued to soar high with tremendous velocity like a torpedo through weightless waters. His smile spread wide as he propelled upward, until he saw the fast-approaching problem. The ceiling was closing in—or vice versa—and he didn't seem to be slowing much at all.

"Woooah!" he yelled as it became clear he was going to crash into the hard shell. He instinctively put out his right hand to buffer the impact. He grimaced, shut his eyes, and braced for the forceful collision. This was going to hurt. But it didn't. His hand touched the ceiling and he stopped in midair. He hovered there, his hand lightly pressed against the hard textile ceiling.

How strange.

Conor risked opening his eyes. He first looked up at his hand pressed against the ceiling. He looked down and found himself at least 60 feet off the floor. *What is going on? And why am I not fall—?* As if triggered by the very thought, Conor began to fall. The second rush of the day wasn't as fast as the ascent, but it was still awesome. Of course, the landing was going to be a problem. "Ahhhhhh! He yelled as he flailed his arms. The floor moved closer and closer. He shut his eyes again as he landed face first with a thud.

He lay on the floor with arms spread wide, hugging it. He rolled over and stared up at the ceiling again. *Did that just happen? Why am I not dead, or at least hurt?*

He stood up and took a deep breath. Then he checked his body for injuries. Nothing broken. What a strange ship! Somehow, he survived, so his next decision was whether to cut his losses and return to the cafeteria for a now much-needed drink or hop on the disc and do it again!

He decided on neither—to simply continue his exploration. The elevator disc had returned to its original position, and Conor stepped back on. "Up . . . Slow!" Pretending to be a missile needed to happen only once today.

The disc stopped at the upper floor. He stepped off to the left and into another room. It appeared empty. The three other soldiers must've left.

Just then the booming echo sounded again three times on the floor right below him—second level. Conor still had to investigate this. Besides, everything else on this floor seemed to be shut off and vacant. It looked like a bunch of white space and clear partitions. *Level two it is.* With that, Conor stepped on the disc and descended at a slow, normal pace to the floor below.

He found himself facing a large wall with a break to the right. He knew the noise had come from the other side. He stepped away from the disc and then moved around the wall to his right. He tried to stay low, quiet, not knowing what to expect.

Dang! He couldn't see anything so low to the ground. He hugged the half-wall and craned his head around the corner to catch a glimpse of the soldiers in training. He didn't see any soldiers. What he did see made him feel pure terror. A Kravii warrior stood just several feet away, its back slightly hunched. Its organic armor slithered and pulsed. How did it even get on the ship? Had the ship been attacked and boarded, and no one noticed? No alarms sounded. No bustling chaos that should accompany an invasion.

The Kravii spotted him or smelled him. Conor didn't know which and didn't think about it. The creature jerked its head immediately in his direction and flashed its jagged teeth.

Conor dashed back behind the wall, but the creature was already pursuing him. He fell back and opened his mouth to yell but couldn't find the sound. It crept closer and displayed a wicked black dagger. It appeared to pulse with swirls and trails of blue. Conor crawled backward and finally managed a yell. "Heeeelp!" This certainly didn't deter the Kravii. It seemed to relish the boy's fear. The dagger raised and then *"Crack!"* The arm holding the dagger flung to the side. Another rifle crack split the creature's head. The Kravii slumped to the floor. The warrior dissipated into a yellow mist before blood could ooze from its cleaved skull.

"A simulation. Couldn't have really hurt you, but you have to appreciate the realism." The boy looked up and spotted five Jopali soldiers looking down at him.

Conor simply nodded.

"You shouldn't be here," the shortest soldier offered.

"I bet he knows that," another said.

"We should report him to the Commander. Academy students, especially first-terms, aren't permitted in the training forum."

"You don't recognize him, do you? This is the kid from the outer-rim ship." The black-haired man stepped around the other soldiers and extended his hand to Conor, yanking him up to his feet. "I'm Primo Officer Iopo Lex. What's your name again?"

"Uh, Conor. Conor Hawk."

"You're damn right, it is! Man, now I remember that day on your ship. That was crazy!" Conor didn't react. "Oh, yeah. You don't remember. You were out. Comatose." Iopo Lex shook his head back and forth with a smile. "These guys remember it, too, I bet. They probably still have the bruises." He bent forward as if to whisper so the others couldn't hear it, but he clearly wanted them to hear. "Bruised egos mostly," he said with a laugh.

A large, bald-headed, bearded beast of a man slapped Iopo Lex on the shoulder. "Are we done here? I'm hungry."

Without looking back, Iopo continued speaking to the boy. "Bradok is still upset. He's not used to being tossed around like a child's toy."

"Bye," Bradok muttered as he pulled on the arm of the soldier next to him.

"All right, I'll catch up with you. I'm going to help Conor out and make sure he gets back to where he should be." The other soldiers turned to leave. "Hey, how about that shot? I took that slither down."

"Sure," Bradok replied. "It's a shame that the real ones don't go down that easy. These simulations don't even carry Lanzas."

"Whatever," Iopo uttered before turning back to the boy. "It was a good shot, right?"

"Sure. Looked good to me," Conor said. "What's a Lanza? Is it that long spear-thing with the electricity?"

"Have you seen one? It's a *Kralanza*, but we call them Lanzas for short. A single shot from one will put a hole right through you. Well, maybe not *you* though."

Once he saw the others were out of earshot, Iopo Lex spoke again. "It's all right, little friend. I know your secret. Well, those guys do, too, but they don't really understand. You know what I mean?"

"Uh, no," Conor replied.

Iopo reached up and scratched his thick black hair set on top of a mostly shaved head. "Well, I mean. You're not from here. You're different."

"I know. I'm from a different galaxy. Why does that matter so much? There are people and things and creatures from a bunch of different worlds walking around everywhere."

"Yeah, but you're different."

"How?"

Iopo Lex scrunched his face and scratched his head again. "Um . . . well. I don't know. You look and talk just like us Jopali, but you aren't. You follow?"

"Kinda."

Iopo thought for a second. "Commander Welcos knows. I don't know what he knows, but he knows he wants no one else to know, you know."

"You're confusing."

"And so are you, my friend." He wrapped his arm around Conor and led him through the training labyrinth. "By the way, I saw what you did with the Bounder. It was freaky, but spectacular."

Conor looked at him sideways. "You mean the elevator-disc thing?"

"Yeah. It's called a Bounder, but I've never seen it do that before. You're savage crazy! I love it. Don't worry. We're gonna take a different way down."

**The Academy**
**Entry Dock**

When the Gregor Monolith docked in the main entry port, it was as if time had slowed. The bustling port came to a standstill. Cargo draggers and transports halted. People ceased their conversations to turn and watch it descend. Even the oxygen ventilators seemed to churn quieter. After all, it wasn't just the majestic ship and how it eclipsed all else in its vicinity that was awe-inspiring. It was its *cargo*—the Supreme Commander himself. He'd arrived and would be mingling among them at least for a short while.

The bay door at the ship's mid-belly hummed. A deep hush hung heavy over the spectators below. They impatiently awaited the first glimpse of the Supreme Commander—poised to erupt in glorious cheers and reverent applause. A true hero's welcome.

Two girls risked breaking the silence. "Do you think Valitat Bithos is here?" the Jopali child whispered to her older sister.

"Yeah. Definitely," she whispered back. "I can't wait to see Iopo Lex. He's just all-parts amazing."

"And Tiera? Is she gonna be here?"

"Yes. Shhhhh. Of course, she's a second-term," the girl answered.

The girls quieted as the gold mist swirled from the open bay and generated a gangplank that sparkled in the violet glow of the Monolith's underbelly. Per the custom, the Supreme Commander would be first to descend to accept the preliminary cheers. The little girl caught a glimpse of him and almost screamed. The unmistakable crimson flap of his robe billowed just below the overhang.

He stepped into full view. A giant among leaders. Supreme Commander Makon Welcos. No introduction was needed. He looked regal, dressed in a black tunic under his customary dark-red robe. Tribute music now blasted from unseen speakers all around the dock. This was the moment.

He descended in glory, flanked by his most cherished—Vice Commander Valitat Bithos and his niece, Tiera Welcos. Cheers erupted from the hundreds gathered, effectively cordoned off by beams of blue light shooting up from the floor. The screams of delight practically drowned out the overhead music.

Something was different, though. "Who is that?" a Jopali man asked his female companion as he continued to clap.

"I don't know," she replied while shaking her head and still clapping. Quiet confusion slipped through the crowd as they watched the Commander with his entourage. He hadn't been seen in public as much recently due to the attacks, so his presence at this Grand Circuit Academy Initiation proved even more significant.

Two columns of ornately uniformed warriors trailed directly behind the Supreme Commander. His Elite Squad. Elite in ability, training, experience, and appearance. They were easily recognizable by their beige uniforms with blue trim. They wore tactical vests adorned with defensive mechanics and offensive weaponry. A gauntlet covered each soldier's left forearm, their Vulcan Bo held in their right hand in its extended form. The Vulcan Bo was the traditional weapon and marker of the Elite, golden with red circlets decorating its length as if dividing it into segments. Only those familiar with the design and introduced to its use knew its full potential.

However, what sparked the general curiosity was not the pageantry of the Supreme Commander and his Elite, but the stranger walking beside him. Tiera stood on Makon's right, with Valitat Bithos at his left. Rather than walking directly beside the Supreme Commander, she remained at the left of another. A boy no one had seen before. Given his position in the formation, this boy held significance, though what that could be remained a mystery.

Conor felt the searing gazes from the crowd. He didn't belong there. He knew it, and they knew it. But so did Makon. He waved at the crowd and thanked them with a gleaming smile. He approached the blue light towers and moved within arm's reach. People stretched forward to touch his robes and accept his handshake. This physical contact with a living legend was priceless and would be worth free tavern drinks back home just for sharing the experience.

After he made contact with dozens of appreciative spectators, he stepped back and looked over his squad, Vice Commander, Tiera, and, finally, Conor. He winked at Conor. Makon turned back to the crowd and held up both hands. The applause and shouting faded to a hushed calm.

He waited for the tribute music to stop. It became the only sound in the bay. A few moments passed and the beat continued. Makon looked over his shoulder to Valitat Bithos. She shrugged. He glanced at Tiera, and she smirked. Clearly, the music wasn't stopping.

Patience slowly turned to awkwardness as the multitude waited for the thundering anthem to subside. Makon began to move. At first, they weren't quite sure what to make of his antics as he lifted his left leg and put it down and his arms swayed in and out. The smile never left his face as he now peered down at the floor. He brought his hands in front and then above his head, then behind his back. His feet shuffled back and forth. People began to smile as anxiety turned back to glee once again.

Makon was dancing. He looked around to his entourage again as if encouraging them to move along to the melody. Valitat felt uneasy but took her leader's cue and shuffled her feet back and forth. "It's a great tune, right?" Makon hollered. "I've always loved it." He turned to Conor and shouted, "They play it whenever I show up to these things! It's my theme song!"

First, Conor thought it was strange, but then he started bobbing his head, and thought it'd be pretty cool to have one's own theme song. "Wait!" Makon yelled. "Here it comes! My favorite part!" The music crescendoed and then fell into more hypnotic beats.

The multitude enjoyed watching the Supreme Commander spin, sway, and bounce to the beat. Then, suddenly, as if out of nowhere, Makon took a step back and then sprung forward into an impressive front flip. He landed steady, before dipping into a side split just as the music stopped.

The crowd cheered their beloved hero—this time for his charming entertainment. Makon stood and adjusted his tunic and massive robe. He bent down to Tiera and whispered, "It's always about the timing."

"Nice split," she offered.

"Thanks." His hands went up again in appreciation for the applause, but then he brought them slightly down, holding them out with palms facing outward. This was the next cue to settle down.

The people from Jopal and all around its neighboring planets held their cheers once again in anticipation of hearing what the beloved champion had to say. "Friends, neighbors, colleagues, and nobles. I wanted to take this moment here and now to address what you have all been wondering." He pointed to his left at the boy by his side. "This here is Conor Hawk. He once was lost but now is found. He is mine—my son. Therefore, he is yours—your son. Make him welcome. And forever be grateful for the gift he is to all of you." The people clapped and let out a few hoots here and there, but it was in no way close to the reception which accompanied the Supreme Commander.

Makon bent down and whispered to Conor, "Don't worry. They'll warm up to you sooner than you think." He smiled and then pointed to Tiera on his right. "You already know my niece. She's pretty cool, too." The applause grew louder for the beautiful, astute, and capable niece of the Legend. Tiera smirked at her uncle's diminutive comment and raised her hand to wave at her fans.

Makon turned and began to move away from the Gregor Monolith. A Jopali woman with short, white hair and dressed in the formal uniform attributed to the Academy quickly marched toward him. She wore a form-fitting suit that stretched from wrist to ankle. It was a single, pitch-black piece wrapping her arms down to her wrists, a short collar at the mid-neck, and carried down to her knee-high black boots. A crimson tassel draped her like a ring of Saturn. It slung from its attachment on her right shoulder, across her chest, and looped at her belt before carrying up to reattach at the back. Despite the organized formality of her dress, the look on her pale pink face displayed anxiety.

"I must apologize, Commander Welcos," she said as she reached her right hand out and placed it on Makon's left shoulder. He responded with a smile and imitated the gesture. She continued, "We had no idea you were going to stop and address the people. You've never done that before, and we hadn't prepared to stop the tribute music. I felt shock and disappointment, and take full responsibility. Please allow me—"

"Oh, Wilda. Stop," Makon interrupted. Sometimes her obsessive propriety unnerved him. "I didn't tell you because I didn't know I was going to do it. I made the decision after assessing the situation and the confused state of our spectators. You need to learn this. Sometimes we need to change things up at the last moment."

"I'm confused by this. What do you mean?" Wilda asked.

"There are times in our leadership when we may need to deviate from the plan and stand by that new decision in a situation that is unprovoked, and unprecedented. You should work on this."

"Fortunately, Commander, the volumes of standard operating procedure I have mastered and memorized over the years have prepared me to respond in any situation known or predicted in the galaxy. As you know, the Elders have provided this knowledge with specific instruction never to deviate because their wisdom and foresight have dictated the proper response in any given situation."

"Clearly. Unless, of course, there's music involved," Makon said with a smirk. Wilda Ti let her hand fall away from the Commander's shoulder. She felt the sting from that remark. Makon sensed it and knew that the Academy's Chief Administrative Leader (referred to as the CAL for short) was too rigid and fixed in procedural rules and established protocol to deviate from the manual. He couldn't really blame her. Her vigorous study and exceptional ability to retain information had served her well to climb through the ranks and land the highly coveted command of the Academy.

"Wilda Ti, that was a joke. Please take ease. Besides, I'm sure the people enjoyed my dance skills."

"Perhaps. I, for one, thought you were having a stroke."

"Aha! That was a joke!" Makon laughed and looked at her expressionless face. "Hmmm. Perhaps not. You're a tough crowd."

They walked together through the bay as the bustle restarted in full force. Makon's team dispersed to their prearranged security checks and duties associated with the securing of the ship and its carbon refueling for redeployment. "It's going to be a good year. We need this training to move fast and hard, Wilda. The Kravii are becoming more brazen and relentless. The attack on Jopal was unprecedented in its devastation." He thought of the fallen Elders and the destruction of the Towers toppling around him. "And the cost. Tremendous. The enemy has something new. We don't know yet what it truly is or might mean in the war ahead."

"We still don't know how they got past our defenses. That's never happened before. Was it their cloaking?" Wilda asked.

Makon shook his head. "No. It's not of their own design. We've beaten that technology, thanks to Niganio and his team of Riostovi masterminds. We truly don't know what happened. They're steadily working on it, but it worries me. What are the prospects for an attack here, at the Academy?"

"Commander, that would be unprecedented," Wilda responded with extreme confidence.

"Humor me, Wilda."

"Improbable. The enemy has tried in the past, and our defenses have dusted them at the very onset of a skirmish. A frontal assault would be suicide, as we have previously demonstrated. They wouldn't dare attack."

"Okay. But what if?" Makon urged.

"What if? What? I don't follow."

"Let's assume the Kravii got stupid all of a sudden and did attack."

"Our long-range, portal interceptor missiles will pulverize them immediately upon arrival."

"What if it's a massive fleet?"

Wilda Ti felt a tinge of frustration but knew better than to show it. "Commander, you already know that it's a continuous massive barrage of firepower, like a wall of impenetrable fire."

"Yes. Yes. I know it very well, but there's always a chance."

"No chance, sir," Wilda insisted.

"Fine. Nevertheless, I want your security forces vigilant at all times. And I'm reinforcing your cadre with additional troops as well as two of my Elite to assist as advisors and proactive support."

"That won't be necessary," Wilda Ti responded. Makon turned his head to look at her with steely eyes while they continued to walk. She kept her head straight but saw him out of the corner of her eye. She didn't risk looking over at him.

Makon faced forward again. "It is already arranged. But because I consider you a close friend and I so very much value the cargo you now have, namely my two cadets, I will let you choose who remains from my squad."

"But, sir—"

"Choose. It's a limited-time offer."

"Iopo Lex and Bradok," Wilda blurted out.

"Wow! That didn't take you long. You want my number-one guy!" Makon craned his head to the side and made a *tsk* sound with his mouth. After giving it a thought, he remembered his children—their safety being paramount. "Deal. But I have to ask, do you want Bradok because of his massive size, skill, and ability, or because you think he's sexy?"

"I would never make a decision based—" Wilda Ti caught herself in Makon's jest and stopped when she spotted his smirk in her peripheral vision. He was toying with her, like always.

Instead of playing into his hand, she decided to change the subject. "I would like to go over your agenda before we reach the Overwatch Conference Room. You recall that, at 1300 hours, you will be delivering the welcome speech to the whole of the Academy. Afterwards, you are arranged to portrait with staff and stand-in with me for the endowment of new instructors. Then finally, before departure at 1900 hours, you will—"

"How many?" Makon asked.

"We have seven new instructors," Wilda replied, anticipating this question.

"As I was saying. Prior to departure . . ." Wilda Ti continued speaking, but Makon's thoughts turned elsewhere. He stopped a short distance away from the conference chamber. Wilda Ti was now a step ahead. She turned back and faced him. "Commander?"

"I almost forgot. Have all the arrangements been made for our little companion?"

"Yes, but," Wilda Ti hesitated. "First off, it is hardly little in size. And second, I need to formally caution against it. The training has been well received, but she's so volatile. We just don't know what will happen with so many recruits around. It's dangerous, and this is my Academy. I really hesitate to take such a risk."

Makon placed both his hands on her shoulders and smiled. "Wilda. Wiiiildaaa. Please relax. Do you trust me?"

"It's not a question of trust."

"Do . . . you . . . trust . . . me?"

"Yes," she said with a frustrated sigh.

"Good. You should. Everything will be just fine. Make it happen. We will continue with the training and accommodations, so you and others feel safe. But you will soon see how progress will exponentially increase." With that, Makon dropped his hands and moved toward the conference room. She stopped him at the doorway. "What else? Get out with it," Makon urged.

"In addition to the Kravii issue, there is another concern with Novac Riv."

Makon nodded. "Tragedy. The loss of him and that of his staff at the Observatory is immeasurable, and they will be deeply missed."

"No, you don't understand. Novac is here."

"What?" Makon asked with squinting eyes. "Why would he be here? First of all, the man can't tolerate travel. Odd for someone who studies the stars for a living. The man would rather have others explore them, but . . . Hold on. That means he's alive." Makon smiled. "Finally, a sliver of good news."

"Yes and no."

"Hmmmm." Makon waited for her to elaborate.

"I mean, it is fortunate he survived the attack. Yes, for sure. However, he spoke with me briefly about a concern and would like an opportunity to promptly address the Overwatch Council. He appears quite troubled."

"Novac is well respected, and I'm sure it will be of some importance. However, it will have to wait. The matters concerning our immediate defense and countermeasures clearly take precedence." Makon tapped the thin gold band on his wrist, and the chamber door began to dematerialize.

# CHAPTER 10

**The Academy**
**Entry Bay**

Conor stayed close to Tiera with the hope she might give him some direction, but this didn't happen. She ran into a group of her friends and forgot he was there. Conor recognized Yaoli with her unmistakable lavender, spiked hair, as well as Iora, the thick-waisted girl who seemed to laugh when she talked. Tiera hugged a third girl who didn't look at all like the others. She had a grayish skin tone that looked wet to the touch. She didn't have hair on her head or body, but rather thick, black coils stretched from her head to her lower back. They resembled corded rope, like dreadlocks. She was attractive, despite the physical differences, and she seemed to be someone Tiera had truly missed over their time away from each other.

The girls continued to talk about their activities over the break, their adventures together during their first Academy session, and other cadets Conor didn't know. When Tiera began to recount her experience during the Jopali invasion, Conor noticed he was a detail conveniently excluded. He took it as a cue to move away and go off for a bit on his own since he now felt as appreciated as a lingering guest at bedtime.

There were so many people—mostly Jopali, but interspersed with others who looked like the dreadlocked, wet girl. A family of three giants walked past him, and he almost got knocked backward. Conor craned his neck to look up at them. The tallest one looked down at him with fierce, intimidating eyes, but then he smiled and continued on. Fortunately, it didn't look like there were many of the giants—because getting stepped on wouldn't be very pleasant.

Other curious species crossed his path—some with large, tucked wings, others with water tanks on their backs distributing moisture across their scaled flesh. Many kids, some smaller than him and others much larger, meandered along with their parents trying to get registered for courses, mingling, or touring the loading dock to check out the Monolith and some of the other ships. Everyone appeared to belong, no matter how bizarre they looked. Conor seemed to be the only one out of place. No family. No friends. And no clue of where to go or what he was supposed to do.

Conor straightened his black, waist-length tunic, looked down at his slip-on boots, and decided that now was as good a time as any to explore this massive, fabricated world called simply, *The Academy*. Before he took another step, he felt a *whoosh* of wind that caught his face and hair. A bluish blur moved to his right and wove through the crowd. He watched it for a moment until it disappeared out of sight.

Conor took another moment to take in the spectacle of the crowd and all the strange people and creatures. He started to feel a little overwhelmed. He didn't like crowds very much unless he could view them from a distance. Besides, he remembered what Iopo Lex told him about the Academy. Its overall size was that of a moon, equal to the Yevi moon orbiting the planet Mokoli. Whatever that meant. All he knew was that he was on a space station the size of a moon and that there had to be some pretty cool things to see. He didn't anticipate being missed.

Conor finally left the entry dock and found himself in a corridor after feeling like he'd walked long enough to have disappeared into another time zone. The corridor led to a massive round room. There were five large cargo doors, each one without any markings or description. The walls carried upward, far, and out of sight, as if he were standing at the bottom of a topless tower. What could be up there? How could he possibly get to the top? He needed one of those Bounder elevator discs. That'd solve this little exploratory problem for sure.

Having been left with only five options on where to wander next, Conor applied excellent precision decision-making tactics. He closed his eyes, raised a pointed finger, and spun around in three circles. When his eyes opened, his finger was pointing dead in the middle of two doors. Go figure. Decision-making tactical Plan B. Left or right? He was right-handed, so naturally the best choice would have to be the door to the right.

Conor moved to the chosen door and studied it. It was made of a solid metallic material. It felt strong and solid against his palm. Now, how to open this thing? If only Makon would've stopped talking to him in riddles and just handed him a simple manual to figure this place out. It could tell him all the more important things—like which things were actually food, or how to open freaking doors. He studied the surface, looking for some lever or handle, but couldn't find anything other than a smooth surface barrier. Dead end.

He stepped back and sighed. He wasn't in the mood to go back to the entry dock and deal with that crowded mess again. In his frustration, Conor lifted and swung his fist down against the door. It unexpectedly buckled against his blow. That shouldn't have happened. His first thought was shame because he'd just dented a pretty fancy, expensive door. But then, a curious confusion crept in. How had he just dented this thing? He hadn't even hit it that hard.

Now the dilemma. Should he hit it again and try to tear it open, or should he walk away and pretend he was never here? Well, he'd come this far, and it just seemed too late to turn back now. But the thought of destroying a door didn't really sit well with him, either. He stepped back to think. Weird place after weird place. This whole Academy might even be stranger than the alien planet they'd just left. Then he remembered Makon Welcos' palace with its bizarre disintegrating doors, floating staircases, invisible walls, and freaky water faucets. There had to be an easy way to open this door.

"Open," Conor uttered. Nothing happened. "Ajar." Nope. "Move yourself to let me pass," he boomed in the deepest voice he could muster with arms spread. Still nothing. No buttons. No levers. Not even a raised or glowing panel in the wall or floor. How did this stupid thing open? Wait. What if it opened only to those who belonged? Those who were authorized to pass through. It was worth a shot. Kinda like a password or authorization.

He took a deep breath because, after this, he was fresh out of ideas. "Conor Hawk."

The panel beneath his feet suddenly glowed purple. He knew there'd be a glowing panel somewhere! The light washed over him as if in some verification sequence. Then it went out, and the door turned to the customary golden mist. Conor scratched the back of his neck in relief. He'd been granted entry, which meant two things: somehow, he had already been authorized to enter, and somehow the Academy already knew who he was and what he looked like. Creepy, but cool. As he began to step through the doorway into another hall, he only hoped it would be more exciting than the endless tower room. *This exploratory mission had better be worth it.*

**The Academy**
**Overwatch Conference Room**

"Yes, as I said earlier, all of the Elders have been killed. I should know. I was there in the Towers when they fell. The only reason why I still stand before you is because I got blown into the ascension shaft with the first blast. I almost fell to my death, but I am quite resourceful in a crisis," Makon said.

"And we are grateful for your resourcefulness, Commander Welcos, but without the foresight and knowledge of the Elder Council, we are operating in the dark," one of the three noble dignitaries said.

"That is not true. We are a capable force with our ample knowledge, significant firepower, and resources that surpass the Kravii in all ways."

"Not anymore," the councilmember quipped.

Makon frowned at the defeatist attitude permeating the room. "Look, I am grateful you have all made it here for this impromptu gathering of the Overwatch," Makon offered, "but we need to arrange an offensive counterstrike sooner than later. If we're just going to sit here and pull our hair out trying to figure out how the enemy managed to surpass our detection systems and mount such a devastating attack, then we'll all just end up bald. And no closer to a resolution. We've studied the available data. We've looked at available replays. All we can see is that they entered our atmosphere undetected and that the attack came swiftly. We will come back from this and promptly avenge our beloved people. However, there is something else extremely concerning."

"What is it?" Wilda Ti asked with worry in her voice. Makon's tone seemed ominous.

"Why such an attack? Sure, it was precise and therefore highly effective. But whatever cloaking technology they may have surely could have been used to infiltrate with a battleship or three. Or an entire fleet. Why didn't they? They could have invaded and set us at total war on our home planet."

"Perhaps their technology hasn't reached that capacity," boomed a voice from the back of the room. It came from

Councilmember Haz, the giant seated in the back corner merely because there wasn't sufficient room for him at the table. He'd joined them from the endangered planet of Wildora, and he didn't often speak, so his words carried weight.

"That is possible, even quite likely," Makon responded. "But I'm not comfortable waiting for them to master that ability to cloak a fleet, or to see what they plan next."

"Hopefully, you bring us a solution, Commander Welcos, and not just words of caution and concern," a gray-haired dignitary uttered as he adjusted his black robe.

"You know me better than that, Councilmember. I do have an objective, but I don't have the plans or means to carry it out just yet," Makon replied.

"Let's hear it. As the last one in contact with the Elders, I'm certain you were provided with some helpful insight into this predicament."

Makon thought back to the afternoon of the attack and his meeting with the Elders. Nope, there wasn't much discussion on the Kravii; it was more of a disciplinary session that was about to turn pretty bad for him. The Elders hadn't been aware of an impending attack, and Makon didn't want to sour the Council's perceptions of their beloved Elders. Besides, this left him a very persuasive tool right now which couldn't be challenged due to their unfortunate demise.

"Although they hadn't foreseen the attack on our capital, they did speak of a lurking danger. One that could not be repelled by our current defenses. A danger we would have to face head-on. They didn't speak of it directly, most likely because it still remained in shadow to their abilities. But they did offer to tell me that I was to be chosen to lead our fleet to the enemy and mount an overwhelming offensive to drive them to their ruin."

Makon looked around at all the pensive faces. Adding the backing of the Elders to his initiative would definitely secure their approval for his attack. They were playing right into his hands because, whether or not the Elders would've sanctioned his initiative, Makon wanted nothing more than to punish those savages.

"Very well, Commander Welcos. Speak to us more of this massive counterattack," Haz offered. "Though you must grasp that a direct assault on Kravos would be nothing short of suicide. We haven't the collective military force or firepower. They outnumber us five to one."

Makon took a deep breath and began, "Actually, it's more like 10 to one. And I agree, we can't afford a frontal assault. However, if we do nothing, untold death and sorrow will prevail over our entire Federation unless we drive the enemy back. Without action, we will be stuck as we are, pressed back on our heels, reeling from devastating loss. The enemy will come again—of this I have no doubt. And unless we answer with the full force of our military, we will be defeated. We will shortly be faced with our destruction and undoubtedly thrust into darkness until we simply cease to exist."

Although the Elders hadn't actually offered Makon this wisdom, the councilmembers were about to be persuaded to sanction whatever he proposed. Unknown to everyone in the chamber, the Commander's words couldn't have been truer.

**Gobi Region**
**Unnamed Moon**

The intercepted message displayed on the wisp screen. The dark figure sat without movement as the feed began in the cockpit of the stolen marauder ship. Behind him lay the hollowed-out remains of the spacecraft's former owners—six pirates who'd been spotted and trailed by an unknown enemy to the black moon. It served as their base of operations, but on this occasion, their lives had been cut short within moments of landing their vessel.

A female's face materialized in the screen's mist, and the audio started. "Novac, it's me, Kim. I'm sure you know of the attack on Mertio by now and that all of our work has been destroyed, along with the Observatory. I barely escaped out the trash chute once the Kravii fighters began their assault. Unfortunately, I am one of only a few survivors. Oh, I hope you're okay."

The ash-skinned assassin waited still and patient. This last intercepted message could be innocuous, or it could be significant.

The woman on the screen showed clear anxiety and fear. "Did Wilda Ti and the Overwatch Council listen to you? Hopefully, they did. Losing Tiptokon III will have a devastating effect on our entire galaxy. Darkness will rise, or fall, whatever." She was emotionally agitated. "But you already know this. We need them to listen. Of course, you know this, too."

The figure slowly rose to his feet like a phantom. No sound. No extraneous movement. He moved slowly but swiftly through the cabin as the woman's voice on the wisp screen spoke to an intrusive audience. "I'm so happy you're safe. We can rebuild our research together using the telescopic projector available at the Academy."

The assassin spun his head to look at the message screen again. He scowled in disgust. Another observatory needed destructive attention. Along with these two individuals who've discovered too much too soon.

"I'm coming to see you," Kim's message continued. "I just need to get some things together . . ."

The assassin walked away from the pirate craft and flicked his wrist behind him. A round metallic ball laced with glowing blue markings fell to the ground and rolled away. It came to rest under the belly of the ship and began to tremble. It broke apart along its glowing seams and caused a catastrophic implosion, crumpling the ship in on itself until disappearing into a self-contained black hole.

He paused in the darkness beside a jagged rock formation, glancing around at his barren surroundings before beginning to climb the air, step aft r step as if ascending without wings. The air then hissed, and he continued forward into a deep-violet glow. The inside of a cockpit hung in midair. The air hissed again, and he disappeared inside the cloaked ship.

The assassin took his place in the center of a glowing ring—the source of the violet light. His hand stretched out from his swirling robe that churned slowly around him like thick smoke. He rested a black hand on a suspended orb about the size of a hormone-enhanced grapefruit. Thin smoke began to ooze from the orb and filled the cabin all around him. Within moments the aura of a cavernous chamber materialized, and he found himself still kneeling inside the purple ring but as if transported elsewhere. Somewhere much darker and cold.

He waited. It wouldn't be long. His message was expected.

Out of the darkness, two red dots appeared in the distance. The assassin spoke one word, "Sedit-Kal." The name given to him like the other Kals before him. One of very few chosen.

The red dots moved silently closer until they blazed crimson in the dark. Eyes of blood and fire.

Sedit-Kal spoke. "Observatory destroyed. Kravii contacts eliminated. Federation Elders eliminated. Second observatory must also meet ruin. Two more deaths imminent," he spoke, considering the female called Kim and her companion at a place called the Academy. The eyes gleaming within the pale, ashen face extinguished as the shadowed figure turned away. Nothing more needed to be said. The assassin removed his palm from the orb, and the smoke retracted back, leaving him once again inside the cockpit.

The cloaked ship's engines fired without sound or burst, and the invisible ship ascended quickly before accelerating toward the moon's atmosphere. Unseen. Unheard. Like a spirit of death.

**The Academy**
**Exterior Kravos Pod**

Conor was standing before another massive door. At least this one had markings—one word etched into the frame above with large, glowing letters—Kravos. Cool name. This was it. Finally, something worth exploring around here.

If Tiera had been truthful with him, this doorway should transport him to a replica of another world. A world called Kravos. He was apprehensive, but not afraid. After all, this was some type of training facility for children. He assumed danger would be present, but not life-threatening. After all, they wouldn't want to go off killing their cadets. At least, he hoped they wouldn't.

Like the other doors, this one didn't have a panel or lever. No doorknob or secret writing illuminated by special moonlight. Must be his name again. He took a deep breath and muttered to himself. *Kravos, here I come.* He then declared, "Conor Hawk."

Nothing happened. No movement. No particle clouds. Nothing.

He tried again and again, louder each time. Still nothing. Frustration began to brew. The name thing clearly wasn't working. He must not be authorized for the fancy Kravos world. They didn't want him to get in here, which made him want to do so even more.

There might still be a way in. He shouldn't. Nah, he definitely should. After all, his "father," Supreme Commander Makon Welcos, would surely cover for him.

Conor placed his right palm against the hard, metallic surface and stepped back with his right foot. He cocked back his right fist for a moment and then punched the door with all his might. His fist landed with a loud smack, but the door didn't crumple like the other one. It didn't hurt his hand, but it didn't have the effect he had hoped for. Before he could wind up for a follow-up door smash, he noticed movement from both sides of the doorway. Three blocks emerged from both sides and began to energize. They levitated in the air and shot out black electricity across the span of the doorway. He could smell and feel the pulsing energy as he stood close. The energy appeared odd. He hadn't seen electricity like this before.

As often happens, Conor's curiosity won out over fear and rational thinking. He brought his hand close to one of the arcing electric lines and hovered it just above. He reached down and touched it with his open palm. His skin began to tingle as it swam around his hand and fingers. He pinched it, pulling it toward him. It bowed out from the door, forming an arch.

Suddenly a voice echoed overhead. Or was it in his head? All he knew was that it was loud. "What are you doing?" The voice sounded calm yet stern.

Conor stood cemented in place. "Who? Me?"

"This is a restricted passage, and your admittance is unauthorized. Return to the Entry Dock at once."

Conor yanked back his hand and watched as the black current still swirled around his fist. He shook it off, flinging it down to the ground with a splash, and then did what any self-respecting twelve-year-old would do. He ran.

The corridor stretched far into the distance. He had no idea if he could outrun the voice of authoritative doom in his head, but he was determined to give it a try. He came to a fork—well, a two-pronged fork. Left or right. Both looked the same. A glance over his shoulder granted him a little hope. No one was following him. Time to go left.

The bright walls whisked by, giving him the illusion that he could run pretty fast. He didn't feel like he was moving that fast, and he wasn't even tired. Must be the oxygen supply or the odd, but super-comfy slip-on boots the crewmembers of the Monolith had laid out for him. After all, he'd seen crazier things than magical boots since waking up in this strange galaxy.

"You can stop running," the booming voice echoed around him. It sounded like a robot. He knew better than to listen to a robot when in trouble.

"No way," Conor muttered. After all, maybe they didn't know who he was, and he could make a clean getaway back to the Entry Bay without anyone noticing. That was the plan anyway. Yeah, they definitely didn't know who he was. Everything would be fine.

"Conor Hawk! Stop running," the voice commanded. Okay. They definitely knew who he was. Time for Plan B. He didn't have a Plan B. Just keep running appeared to be the only Plan B he had so far.

The voice distracted him enough for him not to notice the corridor no longer continued straight, but instead spiraled like the belly of a coiled snake. The pathway curved upward to the left, and Conor didn't break stride. He noticed the lighting began to dim, but as he got closer to the top, or what he figured might be the top, the space opened up.

He rounded the last corner and stopped dead. The slick blue floor disappeared beneath him. It was still there. He could feel it. He just couldn't see it anymore. Empty space engulfed him as he crossed into a massive chamber.

It looked like he'd stepped out from the confines of the Academy and wandered into the expanse of the Vesputi galaxy itself. Was it real? The majestic cosmos of the Nivror Solar System swirled around him. Three suns pinned against the blackness off in the distance, while a greenish-brown planet hung much closer, surrounded by three moons. A crimson and blood-orange wave of stardust churned behind it as if a deity had dipped his brush in cosmic paint and in one broad stroke painted a swath of beauty across the black canvas.

No walls. No ceiling. No floor. He walked forward as if tiptoeing on specks of light across the void. If Makon hadn't introduced him to this illusionary marvel back at the Jopali palace, he might've freaked out. But this reality thrived on what could be felt rather than seen. They liked to remove visual barriers to the observer. It would take some time to get used to.

Conor walked the width of the space until he came to what he sensed to be the floor's edge. His hand stretched forward. He couldn't feel anything, but he knew the wall existed.

He continued to gaze into space, and a vague memory began to form in the hazy distance of his mind. He saw a port window in a spacecraft. His vision peeled back from the window to see the whole of the ship. It was primitive compared to the Monolith and everything else he'd experienced in this galaxy, but it felt familiar. Had he lived on the ship? Who had he lived with?

A woman's voice echoed in his ears without words. It was hard to think. He could see people moving about, but they had muted faces as if some electronic smudge had redacted them from his memory. Were they his family? Maybe. Hovering portraits moved in and out of view as if riding the rails of a cobweb through forest fog.

Conor's frustration began to surface, but he was jerked back to the present by a loud *whooshing* sound as if a door had been opened and shut by some unseen force. But what door? He stood alone, surrounded by nothing but the solar system.

Something had to be nearby because he definitely heard a door open, or close. The other side of the expanse must have some other way in or out. Though, if he were being honest with himself, the thought of running down the spiral instead of up seemed pretty exciting. Just a quick inspection of the invisible doorway, and then he'd go back.

He'd made it to the other side and didn't see any sign of a doorway or window or anything like it. After taking some time spinning around the area looking for something that might not even be there, he turned back toward the downhill spiral. He started back across the cosmic floor but hesitated a moment and looked back. Then he saw it.

There was a corridor made of blazing stars against the dark. He could see it from where he stood, but if he shifted one way or another, it disappeared. Surprised that he couldn't see it before, now it appeared plainly obvious. The doorway contained an arch and jutted out from the wall like a cylinder. As he moved closer and to the front, it began to fade again from view. An optical illusion. Conor changed his angle of approach and found it again. This thing was tricky.

He felt for the side of the cylinder and made his way to the front. There wasn't actually a door, just a pathway through an archway of stars and space. He moved forward, first thrilled with the sensation of an astral tunnel, but then he began to feel dizzy. Conor decided to shut his eyes and just walk forward with his arms outstretched. Small steps led to bigger, more hurried ones. He just wanted to get to the other side of this tunnel. He didn't even care where it ended up—he just wanted to get there already.

His hand passed through something soft like a curtain. The temperature changed. He'd definitely entered another room.

This was good. Finally. He opened his eyes now, but it didn't matter that he did. No more stars. No more light. He stood immersed in pitch-darkness.

He waited for his eyes to adjust, but they couldn't find any light, as if he'd traveled into the depths of an underground cavern. His hands blended into the black in front of his face, and he could only hear his heartbeat throbbing in his ears.

It was the only sound at first; then he heard something else. A faint sound. The sound of something slithering across the ground, or someone slapping a wet towel down and dragging it behind them.

Conor's senses homed in on it. Vision gave way to sharp hearing, and he managed to determine the relative location of the eerie, slimy sound. Whatever waited in the dark could likely see or smell or sense him in some way. What it was, Conor had no clue. But he didn't want to find out. He closed his eyes to better focus his hearing; after all, his eyes didn't do much good for him right now.

It moved closer. He could not only hear it, but he now caught an odor of retched bile. It circled to Conor's right, sizing up its prey. Conor took a few steps to his left to prevent being flanked. He didn't know how he knew this. He just did. "Step like a ninja," he thought. His hands came out in front of him to deflect and defend.

Suddenly the thing lashed out a barbed tentacle but missed. Conor ducked his head to the left and felt drops of goo splash against his cheek and neck. Another attack came low for his ankle, but Conor managed to step aside just in time to avoid it. He then rolled and sprung back to his feet. Maybe he could actually get behind the unseen monster. His breathing grew heavier as he sensed a more concerted attack.

A tentacle darted out and lashed against his thigh. He winced from the impact but didn't lose his footing. Another struck him low again, cutting at his left calf. The creature could either be blind, too, or just playing with its food. Before Conor could change direction again, four immense tentacles lunged for him. They wrapped around his right arm and leg, while another struck him in the gut. The fourth missed him completely, just above his forehead.

Conor absorbed the blow to his stomach with a quick exhalation of breath and dug in his heels, fighting back against the creature's effort to reel him in. He clawed at the tentacle wrapping his right forearm and tore it away. The one on his leg tugged against Conor's resistance as he stepped back. "Aaaagh! Get off me!" Conor yelled. Once again, the boy's tenacity proved too much, and he broke free from the monster's grasp.

Conor now moved back to his right, sensing the creature's movement. He could hear it climbing—moving upward. It was clearly undeterred, seeking a position of advantage above him! Not good. Conor rolled backward to create some distance. It had to be somewhere above him. He could feel it. But how high above and how close, he had no clue.

Conor continued to move backward. He envisioned it creeping and slithering along the ceiling toward him. But that's not what it did. Unseen by Conor, the creature spread against the top of the roof, its tentacles gripping against the surface like a leech on exposed flesh. Two of its tentacles gripped a large piece of scrap metal wedged just above it. With a quick yank the metal dislodged, exposing a powerful vacuum. The scrap metal had served as a closed window to the void of space, a window now becoming a sucking hole of doom.

Conor resisted against the vacuum's pull but was lifted off his feet. He flew toward the opening and the creature just below the aperture at an uncomfortable rate. He yelled and brought both hands in front of him in hopes of thwarting the creature and maybe stopping himself from being pulled into space.

A beam of white light then penetrated the dark, illuminating the creature and its intended meal. That's when Conor saw it. The monster's gaping mouth drenched in jagged teeth waiting to receive him. The pocket of stars above illustrated a second form of death. *Choose one,* Conor thought. Either a lunch snack or a frozen corpse.

The light glinted off the monster's six orange eyes, each one fixated on Conor—his trajectory making him a tasty missile aimed for the back of its throat. Before he could consider what it might feel like entering the creature's belly, Conor felt an impact on his lower leg. At first it started at mid-calf, but then began to climb and swirl around his leg until it reached his upper thigh.

He stopped flying. He still remained suspended in midair, but at least he wasn't moving forward toward an unsavory death. Conor now felt himself being pulled in the opposite direction. He looked down at his leg and picked at the galvanized metallic claw squeezing his leg like a python. "Leave it!" a voice yelled from behind.

Conor rolled over in the air and looked back. He knew someone was there, but all he could see was the piercing light. The creature brought two tentacles up to shield its eyes from the uncomfortable light and started to move back down toward the floor. It found the scrap metal and lifted it with relative ease to close the vacuum.

Once the hole was again obstructed, Conor dropped to the ground and slightly bounced on impact like a plastic water bottle. The monster now moved toward him, undiscouraged by the other occupant with the light projector. "Get up! Let's go!" the man said as he retracted the grapple. It released the boy's leg and shot backward like a roll of measuring tape. Conor scrambled to his feet and chased the light as it entered the star tube. Conor found it much easier this time to navigate the tunnel with the light beam ahead.

Once they emptied out into the large observatory, the man turned back to the arched doorway and swiped his wrist across it from left to right. The familiar gold mist emerged from the edges of the arch and crafted a solid door. "Will that hold it in?" Conor asked as he tried to catch his breath.

"Let's hope. Are you winded?" the man asked.

"Yes . . . yeah. Did you see that thing?! We just ran from a monster the size of a boat. A big boat. It planned on eating me!"

"You're not tired. Stop breathing hard."

"What are you talking—?" Conor furrowed his brow at the man's concern over his breathing rather than the creature that had just tried to kill him. But then he realized he was right. He wasn't tired. "Okay. So what? I'm not tired. Just scared out of my mind!"

"That's fine. Understandable," the man replied as he affixed the grapple to his belt.

Conor studied his rescuer for a moment. The man stood slightly taller than he. His shoulder-length hair came together in a messy ponytail. He was wearing a high-collared tunic which stretched down to his low-cut boots. A uniform not entirely unusual. He'd seen it before. He'd seen this man before. "Follow me. I'm taking you back to the Commencement," the man said as he turned toward the downward spiral.

Then Conor spotted the thin embroidery across his shoulder blade. A single purple line. First the destruction of Mertio. Then Makon's study beach hut. Now here. This guy was definitely a stalker. He decided against bringing it up, to not risk antagonizing him. After all, he did just save his life. "Are we just going to leave that thing in there so it can try to eat other kids?"

"We can't defeat it now."

"Why not?" Conor asked.

Without turning around, the man held up both of his empty hands. "Obviously, no weapons."

"Makes sense. Later then . . . with weapons." Conor smiled. He wanted to be present when they blasted that beast back to the hellhole it had crawled out of. "Why is that thing living in there?"

"It must be comfortable. Better than out there," he said as he pointed up to the left toward outer space. "It's not supposed to be here."

"What is that place?"

"It's the Tranquility Chamber."

"It didn't seem too relaxing to me."

"No, I suppose not," the man said with a smile. "This is the Star Deck. Supposed to elicit tranquility and oneness with the Vesputi all around you."

"I didn't feel peace. It's too weird for me. And you need to kill that thing."

"Sure thing, Conor. On your command."

"You know who I am?" Conor asked. The man nodded as he began to descend the spiral. "I know who *you* are," the disheveled boy added. The man stopped and looked down at the frazzled boy, waiting for more. Conor swallowed before continuing, hoping he hadn't angered his stalker. "You've been following me around, haven't you?" The man just looked away and began walking again. "I've seen you. I thought you might want to hurt me, or not like me or something."

"I don't like you," the man declared, offering honesty over decorum.

"Oh. That sucks. Thanks for saving me, anyway."

"You're welcome."

"Who are you? Why have you been following me?"

The man closed his eyes and took a deep breath. "If I tell you, will you stop talking?"

"Okay," Conor replied.

"I'm called Anibal. And to clarify, I haven't been following you. I've been watching you."

"Same difference," Conor muttered. "Well, why?"

"No," Anibal shook his head. "It's none of your concern. Now, stop talking."

"Whatever. Fine." Conor walked beside the mysterious man for a bit and then remembered they were descending the spiral. "If we're not talking, then I'm going to run."

Conor then took off sprinting down the corridor, hugging the turns and feeling light as his footsteps glided with ease. Anibal watched him run as the distance between them quickly grew. He heard the boy holler as he moved out of sight. He then shook his head and asked himself with as much patience as he could muster, "Why me?"

# CHAPTER 11

**The Academy**
**Entry Bay**

Conor reached the bay a significant distance ahead of Anibal. His rescuer now seemed more cool than creepy, but enough mystery lingered around him to put Conor on edge. The massive flight deck still held the magnificent ships both big and small. Some appeared lean and built for swift travel or precision airstrikes, while others had more rounded, robust shapes as people-movers or artillery bombardment. He spotted a number of fancy dignitary ships with minimal defenses but an abundance of luxury and comfort. Of course, the Monolith still managed to dwarf them in all categories. Conor had looked for the ship—a shred of familiarity, or at least as close as he could get to anything relatively familiar at this point.

The area still teemed with people of various alien species, with the majority hailing from Jopal. He moved closer to the nexus of the gathering and then stopped short. Anibal soon caught up, and Conor sensed him standing by his side. "Okay. Now what?" Conor asked. "I don't know where I'm supposed to go, what I'm supposed to do, or if anyone even cares."

Without looking at him, Anibal answered, "We'll get you there. This part doesn't matter. Parents are leveraging the courses they want their children to attend. Political and social contacts are made here. Inquiries into who are the new instructors for which courses. All that nonsense. None of it matters."

"How come?"

"They think their opinions make a difference here. They don't. The Academy Council lends its decision-making authority to the Board."

"What's the Board?" Conor asked.

"They decide the direction your training will take. There are two paths, and it's decided for you in the Second-Circuit. You're in First-Circuit, so for you, it doesn't matter yet."

"What are the training paths?"

"They will explain it to you, but I already know—" Anibal cut his sentence off as he noticed some uncommon commotion up ahead. People began yelling and darting to either side as something parted the crowd like a rogue ship through open water. It moved fast, and its path aimed directly toward them!

Within moments, they spotted the reason for the fuss, as a family dove to the left to avoid being trampled. A large storm-gray four-legged beast rushed toward them. Its jaws hung open, exposing rows of sharp teeth and a destructive capacity for violence. Four Academy staff members raced behind it in a vain attempt to intercept, but the beast easily left them behind in its wake of turmoil.

Anibal flipped his tunic to the side and assumed a fighting stance, with his right leg in a brace position. He reached over to Conor and gripped his shoulder to move him behind and out of the way, but Conor's legs remained fixed, and moving him proved much harder than anticipated. Instead, Anibal stepped in front to shield the boy from the inevitable attack.

As he quickly formulated a plan of counterattack, Anibal couldn't have anticipated what happened next. Suddenly, Conor rushed forward—straight toward the charging beast. Anibal's first thought was that the child was fearless. Then he just considered his move to be reckless and stupid, no matter how fearless. He lunged to intercept Conor, but the boy moved too fast. Conor and the beast were on a collision course, and he wouldn't be able to prevent the first strike.

The beast lunged and Conor wrapped his arms around its belly. They both toppled to the ground to everyone's horror. Conor lay on his back with salivating jaws hovering over his face.

Anibal moved on instinct to close in on the creature and prevent a lethal strike. A curved weapon emerged in his hand, his fingers lightly gripping the soft-coated hilt. The blade itself glowed with traces of gold light infused in the foreign metal. Just before plunging the dagger into the beast's neck, he hesitated. Screams of terror didn't spill from the boy. He heard laughter.

Makon Welcos stepped forward from the crowd and yelled, "Hold!" in an effort to stay Anibal's attack. Fortunately, the Shadow Paladin had already accurately assessed the situation. Makon lowered his hand.

A man was standing at Makon's side. He was bald, his skin a tinge of orange with black designs tattooed throughout his body up to his jawline. "Why does he hesitate? Save the boy."

Without looking down at the Fian technician, Makon answered, "There's no danger here."

"Isn't the boy being mauled?" the Fian asked with concern.

Makon smiled. "This isn't an attack, my friend. This is a reunion."

Conor continued to hold the beast as it drenched his face with wet kisses. "Okay. Okay. I missed you too, girl." He finally managed to push the overjoyed dog off of his chest and stand up. He petted and nuzzled her neck as Anibal tucked his weapon away.

"I take it you are familiar with this beast," the Paladin stated as his battle-tension subsided.

"It's my dog. Her name's Titan. But she's a lot bigger now than I remembered!"

The word for "dog" translated loosely to an animal similar in appearance to this one, but far less formidable. Anibal lowered his apprehensions when realizing it resembled an intensely loyal and often domesticated animal. "She came with you, did she?"

"Yes," Conor replied while still holding her neck.

"She's dangerous when provoked?"

Conor stood up fully and rested his palm on Titan's forehead. He looked over at the Paladin and nodded. "Don't provoke her, then."

"Fair enough," Anibal replied.

They hadn't noticed the approach of the Supreme Commander. He reached out and petted the dog. Titan spun around and leaped up to greet him. Makon scratched her behind the ears for a moment before saying, "Platz." Titan suddenly relented and ceased to climb him. "Sitz." She then sat beside Conor, her tongue dangling off her mouth's edge. Makon turned his attention to the boy. "We've been working on her training, though her strength and stubbornness have been a lesson in patience to the training staff. She will stay with you during your year here at the Academy. Do you approve?"

"Of course, I do. She stays with me?"

"Not exactly. She will have her own accommodations, but you will be able to visit with her as often as you wish until we feel she's well adapted and won't present a danger to other trainees and staff." He leaned down and cupped his hand to Conor's ear. "She tends to knock people over . . . a lot." Makon smiled and stood straight. "Either way, we've introduced some commands that will help you with her obedience, but otherwise I'm going to leave her in your capable hands."

Makon turned his attention back to the onlookers and started back in the direction of the Monolith. "Come. It's almost time for the Commencement, and you'll want a good seat. Have you seen Tiera around?" Conor shook his head. "Let's go find her."

### Main Auditorium

A soft bell chimed overhead. Most of the attendees had already entered the auditorium and gathered in their seats. Conor happened to be one of the last to enter. So much for a good seat.

Recruits filled the room, although it could've easily held double the number in attendance. The ceiling opened to the stars, giving the appearance they weren't inside the orbiting sphere anymore. Conor would've been more impressed if he hadn't already been exposed to a similar observation chamber earlier—an experience that ended in a rather terrifying moment with an actual space monster.

He patted Titan on the head. "You stay here, girl. You can't come in, but I'll be back soon." He then looked for a nearby seat and began to move to a row and seat close to the exit with his dog now standing as a sentinel in the doorway. As he started to enter the row, someone grabbed his arm and pulled him back. Conor glanced over his shoulder and found a familiar face.

"Come on. Don't sit there," Tiera whispered. "Follow me. You'll definitely like it better in the back." She then moved up the ramp to the right. Conor looked at Titan with a worried expression, hoping she'd stay put. He then followed Tiera up the ramp all the way to the back of the amphitheater. Three soft tones sounded around them, and the lighting began to dim. "Hurry, Conor. If we don't get to our seats, we'll be stuck."

Though this didn't make much sense to him, he couldn't doubt the urgency in her voice. Tiera shimmied between the seatbacks and five other students who'd been savvy enough to find their seats much earlier than them. The peculiar girl in the dreadlocks raised her hand to signal Tiera and her guest to the two seats she'd saved for them. As Conor scraped the back of his legs against knees to find his seat, a woman stepped out on the platform.

Wilda Ti stood out in front of the crowd of students. "Welcome to another year of training at the Academy!" Her voice boomed all around them. "Are we ready to stand as one and vanquish darkness and tyranny?!" The students erupted in screams and cheers. "Then let us begin." Her platform began to raise and slowly spin. It carried her high and low, left and right. Conor recognized it to be a sort of elevator disc. It made him smile. He loved those things.

Just then he found himself sinking into his chair as the bottom caved in a bit as if he were now sitting in a hollowed-out eggshell. He looked over at the girl on his right and noticed a wide smile. Clearly, she loved every moment of this. The other students also sank in their seats as well, so it wasn't that Conor's seat was broken. But what happened next made him wish the seat came with armrests or at least a seatbelt.

His seat lifted, carrying him high above. The other chairs raised as well as if they rested on floating bleachers that cascaded downward toward the front platform. He soon found himself high above the others, looking down at the tops of heads and a floor that seemed no longer to be present—or at least visible. The kids around him let out yelps of excitement as they also lifted.

Conor gripped the sides of the seat and leaned over trying to gather some idea of how high they actually were. He couldn't fully tell, but fearful uncertainty mixed with exhilaration. He sat back, fixing his gaze on the presenter at the front. Now wouldn't be the time to expose his slight fear of heights. Laughter chirped in his ear, and now he understood why Tiera had been so passionate about sitting in the back. Best seats in the house. If you wanted to watch everything like a perched bird.

Wilda Ti spoke again once the seating had been rearranged in classic Academy fashion. "Some of you are returning for your last session before being assigned to your career positions. Others of you are here for the first time. Whether it is your first session or last, make no mistake, you are critical to the preservation of the Federation. You have been chosen to perhaps hold the esteemed distinction of Academy graduate.

"You will be praised and celebrated in your homeland; looked to for guidance, leadership, and inspiration. You will be beacons of hope, trust, and a symbol of the might of our collective union." This seemed pretty cool. Wilda Ti glided about the auditorium sometimes above all of them and sometimes right at individual eye level.

"Your lives are henceforth forever changed. They don't belong to you anymore." That part didn't sound so good. "You represent something much more profound and enduring than you could ever obtain on your own. As such, there will be extreme conditions, peril, and challenges placed before each one of you." Again, this part didn't sound good. "But conquer your fears. Lay aside your weakness. Grow in strength and honor, and upon graduation you will reap the rewards of being one of us—one of the elected bearing the mark of Academy alumni." She then lowered her collar to expose the coveted mark of the Academy on her neck—a black, triple-star divided by three golden halos. The golden halos glinted as they continuously traced their path around the outer star. There was an animated tattoo of the same symbol on her uniform and displayed all throughout the orbiting training sphere. Conor wondered if he could get a motion tattoo like that with a wolf's head or dragon. Probably not, but maybe a question for a later time.

"After our presentation, the First-Circuits will learn their respective factions. When you return for your second term, you will be assigned a squad within your faction. Some of you will be pilots, others infantry, fleet engineers, ground artillery, or naval officers. Your training will then be dedicated to the maximization of your potential within that squad. If one falters in their duty and responsibility toward mastery, the whole of the squad will suffer. The faction itself will be deficient.

"When the war games begin, you will experience either this deficiency or a mighty synergy as you achieve glorious victory or devastating defeat. The dangers here are vast, complex, and real—as are the same dangers you will face out there. Savaging pirates, renegade scoundrels, menacing beasts, and, of course, the true enemy—none other than the savage Kravii."

Just the simple utterance of the alien force elicited a disquieting feeling of unease and dread to sweep over the recruits. Conor leaned over to Tiera. "Is she serious?" The girl shot him a look of disdain and rolled her eyes. She peeled back her sleeve and displayed a long, curved scar on the underside of her forearm running from wrist to just below her elbow. She looked Conor in the eye and raised her brows before sliding her sleeve back into place. She told him plenty without uttering a word.

Conor had already encountered the fearsome Kravii on two occasions. Tiera didn't know this. Since he could've been injured during the simulation on the Monolith, he was still counting that one, too. His thoughts drifted from Wilda Ti's welcome speech, first because it didn't seem too welcoming, and second because he couldn't get the Kravii warriors out of his head.

His chair suddenly spun to the right and dipped. The movement jarred his thoughts back to the presentation. "So now I give you our beloved champion, Supreme Commander Makon Welcos!" Wilda Ti exclaimed as she stepped off the platform to give space to Makon.

The Commander raised his arms in greeting to the cheers and then slowly lowered them to entice the trainees to silence.

Conor joined in by clapping, and then he felt his chair center itself and begin to lower. The same thing happened throughout the auditorium as if in sync with the Commander's arm movements.

"Aw, come on," Tiera blurted. "Leave it to him to spoil the fun and the best seats in the place."

"You know how the Commander is, Tiera," the girl to her right said.

"I know," Tiera replied as she sat back and folded her arms.

The Commander waited for the chairs to return to their original, stationary positions before addressing the audience. "My apologies, but now is not the time for theatrics. I don't plan to take much of your time. I only wish to extend my gratitude for your ability and willingness to serve your home planets and the Federation. We are under a continuous threat, and, with the recent attacks, the enemy has grown exceedingly bold. Study hard. Train harder. The Academy will give you the tools to succeed, but you will become the weapons. You are a defensive imperative to protect and defend our families against subjugation and annihilation.

"You are our hope. Our future. I believe in you. Believe in yourselves. Believe in each other. That is all I have for you. Be well, and good luck."

Makon then took a step forward. This was a signal for everyone to stand. Conor guessed as much because that's what everyone did. The next thing he knew, the tall, dreadlocked girl grabbed his hand as he reluctantly stood. Tiera grabbed his left hand.

"Rise!" Makon shouted.

"As one!" the crowd replied in unison as the girls thrust their combined hands into the air. Conor looked all around and noticed everyone holding hands in a sea of unity. Makon nodded, signaling for the recruits to lower. Tiera released his hand as suddenly as she'd grabbed it. The other girl released his hand a little slower.

The Commander exited the platform, and the trainees began to chat among themselves.

"That was short but sweet," the dreadlocked girl said to Tiera and Conor.

"All the better," Tiera replied.

"Either way, your uncle can definitely ignite a crowd. I preferred the dance earlier, but this was good, too," the girl offered.

"If you say so," Tiera replied with a smug expression.

"You still hoping for the pilot class?"

"You know me. Hasn't changed. What about you?" Tiera asked.

The girl shrugged. "I still don't know. I mean, it doesn't matter anyway. They'll just assign us where they want us. Not much choice in the matter. Maybe not for you, but the rest of us, you know."

"What are you talking about?"

"You're Tiera Welcos. You'll get wherever you want."

"Why? Because of my uncle?" She shifted Tiera a sideways glance. "Shut it. No special treatment for me. I put in the same work as everyone else. More so. If anything, you know my uncle. He'll influence them to put me somewhere on his ship so he can watch over me."

"A spot on the Monolith would be fantastically awesome! Every recruit in here would push their mother down an ascensor shaft for a chance at that. Ooooh, maybe he'll make you one of his Elites. You'd totally look hot in that tight little uniform twirling the Vulcan Bo around and slaying anything in your way."

Tiera rolled her eyes. "Like that would ever happen. Not that I would want it anyway." She then looked at Conor, who'd been listening to their conversation, and gave his shoulder a push. "If anything, uncle would make this freshie an Elite."

"You think?" the girl asked as she eyed Conor.

"I wouldn't understand if he did. He can't even walk right half the time. Could you please move faster?" Tiera nudged Conor again.

Guess it was time to go. He had no idea where he was going or what to do next, but that seemed to be the norm, and getting out of Tiera's way seemed the best idea right now.

Conor moved down the ramp and then remembered Titan just as he spotted her still perched at the exit where he'd left her. It was funny to watch the other cadets approach the exit, notice her sitting there like a slobbering gargoyle, and then opt for one of the other exits.

Her tail wagged as soon as she spotted him. He patted her head, and they exited together. Tiera and the other girl exited behind them. Once the beast of a dog moved away, the other trainees felt more confident in taking the same exit. Though they did give a wide berth to the boy and his odd creature.

"This is Ari," Tiera said. "Ari. Conor."

The strangely attractive girl with the granite dreadlocks and wet skin smiled at him. She then leaned toward Tiera and whispered, "He's short, but not as odd as you said he was." Conor wished he hadn't been close enough to overhear.

"Just wait and see," Tiera replied with her customary eye roll.

"He's cute. though." Conor was happy to hear that part. Although the awkwardness now rose like cold bath water.

"Whatever, Ari. Let's go."

Conor needed to say something to not seem odd. "Uh, so what's next?"

Tiera tilted her head toward him. "You heard the CAL. Now you're going to be assigned to your faction. We already have ours because we are Second-Circuit. Ari and I are going to the Rehab Center."

"Okay. I'll just—"

Tiera cut him off. "You can't come with us. You need to get assigned first."

Ari noticed the perturbed look on the boy's face and smirked. She then stepped forward and grabbed his elbow, pulling him away. "Come on, Conor. I'll help you out."

Tiera watched her friend drag the nuisance away. "Ari, what are you doing?"

She turned her head to the side as she playfully dragged on Conor and said, "Don't worry. I'll meet you there."

"Fine," Tiera muttered as she watched them disappear into the crowd. She then looked down at Titan. "I'm not hanging out with you." As if the feeling were mutual, the dog simply looked away and trailed after Conor.

**The Academy**
**Vesputi Passage**

Ari had led Conor and Titan through the entry dock, bypassing several curious passages she referred to as the Pilot Module, Time Sphere, Teleportation Channel, The Forge, Wormhole Deck, and Recreation Grounds. Every time they passed one of the passage portals Conor couldn't help but bite his lip to hold back the urge to access each one. Despite the vastness of the Academy Sphere and all the magnificent exploratory wonders it held, they traveled with relative ease and efficiency. Ari explained it as a corridor built like a tree trunk with numerous branches—each one leading to a distinctive world or training area.

She hesitated at one doorway marked as "Tretch." At first, Conor thought they'd reached their destination, but then he realized she wasn't trying to access it. She placed her palm against the cold metal door and bowed her head. Conor thought to speak but stifled back his words once he sensed the girl's sorrow. "This is my home world."

Conor stood silent. Now wasn't a good time for questions or odd comments. Clearly, the girl missed her home. It must've been some time since she'd been there. After a few prolonged moments of silence, Ari finally pushed back from the door and moved away. He risked a question. "Would you like to go in?"

She shook her head. "No. We can't," she said as she held up her wrist to show the black bracelet infused with gold swirls. Conor was now wearing a similar one. "Our entry is restricted. Only level-four recruits can access it. Too dangerous for us lowers, I guess."

"Even for you? Since it is your home planet."

"Yeah. Still can't see it. You wouldn't want to go there, anyway. You wouldn't last three minutes."

"Oh. What's it like?" Conor asked.

"Fire. Lava rivers. Heat winds." Sounded like a crappy place to grow up. She was right. It didn't seem much like a vacation spot. She continued, "Dragors everywhere."

"Dragons?" Had he heard her right? Now his interest piqued. After all, who wouldn't want to see a dragon? He'd have to wait three years to see a dragon? That wasn't fair.

"Dragors," she corrected him. "You don't want to meet one. Trust me."

"Do they fly?"

Ari squinted. "Not quite. They bound, though. Pretty high. Otherwise, they're fire-spitting nasties who consume everything they see." Although he didn't feel like being eaten or burned like a crispy steak, Tretch World jumped high on his list of places to explore. At least just to poke his head in and see what they looked like. It was more appealing than the underwater place they'd passed earlier. "Come on, we're almost there."

Conor followed her away from Tretch until they reached another gateway nexus. The area was vast, with merchant shops and carts selling various items from weapons and curious trinkets to clothing and snacks. The aroma of exotic treats wafted throughout the bright atrium, and Conor didn't know whose hunger was more enticed, his or that of the massive dog at his side, wagging her tail like a submarine propeller.

Ari was unfazed by their surroundings and navigated the labyrinth of storefronts as if she'd been born in one of the alleyways. Conor struggled to keep up while also taking in all the distractions. As his gaze averted to the flying banners above the shop to his left, he suddenly felt like he'd been kicked in the hip. He took a step back and glanced down to his right. A small pointy-eared creature with grayish skin had landed hard on his butt, dazed from the impact. Before he could gather himself, a portly Jopali man reached out and snatched him up by his shirt collar. It yelped and squirmed in a futile attempt to escape.

"I caught you this time, little thief," the man said with a wrinkled sneer. He then pried a small round sphere with hexagon shapes etched along its surface from the creature's tiny hands.

"Nooo!" it yelled, sounding only like a whisper. "I need that."

"You do? Then purchase it with V-Coin like everyone else."

"I can't afford it," he whispered back.

"Of course not," the shopkeeper said as he waved an orb strapped to his palm across the creature's wristband. "Yep. Says here you can't afford much more than a pioti sandwich," he added as he stared at the bright orb in his hand.

"You charge too much," the creature blurted.

"Sure, I do. I'm the only one who carries these in the entire Academy market. Now, we all know what happens to thieves. Immediate expulsion and banishment. It's time you go, and good riddance."

"Please, no. I can't leave. I have nowhere to go."

"Looks like the Topar slums, or maybe they'll be nice and send you to vacation on Tretch." Conor didn't know anything about Topar, or what a pioti sandwich might taste like, but he knew Tretch wouldn't be pleasant. He looked over at Ari and spotted her glaring at the shopkeeper. She clearly had taken offense to the last remark but opted for a death stare over calling him on it. The creature had his head bowed now, and Conor spotted tears brimming his eyes.

"How much does the shiny ball thing cost?" Conor asked.

The shopkeeper finally noticed him. "It's rare. That makes it expensive."

"You don't even know what to do with it," the creature whispered. This angered the Jopali man, and he shook him.

Conor reached out and steadied the small captive to stop the jostling. "I don't have any money, I don't think." He looked to Ari, and she simply shrugged. "Maybe we could figure something out. I mean, you got the ball back."

"It's a Nova Bulb," the little creature and shopkeeper said, simultaneously.

"Fine. You have the bulb," Conor replied. "Let's just all agree that he's . . . What's your name?"

"V-23." Conor leaned forward closer to the creature. He must not have heard him well because of the whispering.

"Sorry, I didn't hear you because you're still whispering," Conor said.

"He said, 'V-23,'" Ari remarked. "You heard right. All of the Riostovi, or V-Techs, as we call them, have numbers in their names. Oh, yeah, and he's not whispering. That's his voice at full volume. They're all like that."

Conor stuck his bottom lip out and nodded. Then it dawned on him. This little creature was one of the alien genius-level engineers Makon had told him about. Things had just got super interesting. "Okay. V-23. Cool name, I guess." He turned back to the man. "V-23 won't be back at your store ever again. Right?" he asked while passing glances back and forth between the two.

"No," the Jopali said with a shake of his head. "Not good enough. I'm tired of his stealing, and unless either of you care to pay for it—because look, it's scuffed now—he's going to the Disciplinary Board for recommended expulsion."

"Do you have any money?" Conor asked Ari.

She covered her wrist. "You mean, V-Coin?"

"Uh, yeah. What's V-Coin?"

"Vesputi Coin. You don't know what V-Coin is?"

Conor felt stupid. "Yeah, of course I do," he said, shaking his head. "I just heard it wrong, I guess."

Ari shrugged. "I don't have nearly enough. I'm not paying for his crime, or for that stupid bulb."

"I'll pay for it then, once I get the coin," Conor offered. Without warning, the shopkeeper swiped the orb across Conor's bracelet. He then glanced at the peculiar device and looked away. He immediately turned back at it and gazed for a moment. His eyes grew wide as a bewildered expression befell his countenance. Without looking back at Conor, he thrust the bulb into his chest and released the V-Tech creature.

"Here. It's yours. Paid in full," the shopkeeper said as his demeanor softened.

"What?" Conor asked. He stood as confused as everyone else.

"I've never seen this before," the man muttered under his breath. He shot Conor a sideways glance with one eye closed. "What's your name?"

"Conor Hawk."

"Never heard of you, Cadet Hawk, but anytime you want to shop for anything you need, come find me. I'll get you the best prices for the best merchandise." He then turned and left.

"Uh, yeah. Sure." He shared a shoulder shrug with Ari before V-23 snatched the bulb away from him.

"Thank you. Thank you. I am in your debt, Master Hawk."

"Conor."

"Master Conor." Before he could tell him to drop the "Master" part altogether, the Riostovi boy sprinted away.

"Congratulations," Ari said as she placed a hand on Conor's shoulder. "You have now inherited your own personal V-Tech shadow. I wouldn't want one tagging along after me, but he's all yours."

"Is that a bad thing?"

"Don't know. Might be a good thing. Who knows? But I do know they are fiercely loyal, so good luck shaking him away any time soon."

"Well, he left  in a hurry," Conor said.

"It's not you." Ari leaned in and touched her lips to his ear. It felt mildly sensual, though he knew it wasn't intentional. "I think he was scared of your beast. Everyone is." Conor realized that she was referring to Titan and chuckled.

"Are you?" Conor asked.

"Nah." She bent over and scratched Titan behind her ears. The dog relished the attention and began to hop around. She rose up and climbed Ari for extra attention. She giggled and continued tickling Titan down her flanks. "I've met much more fearsome things than this big beauty." She pushed Titan back down, and the dog instantly calmed. Conor had never seen her so obedient to a single touch before. "Come on, let's get to the Recruit Towers before Tiera punches me for taking too long hanging out with you."

They cruised through the market at a quicker pace. "I do know one thing, though," Ari said as they passed a cart adorned with luxury bags and shoulder packs. "Somehow you're worth a lot of coin. Should be easy to make friends."

"I don't want those kinds of friends, Ari. Don't tell anyone."

"Consider your secret safe, so long as you don't forget about me when you go shopping," she said with a smirk.

"In that case, hold up." Conor moved to a cart with an elderly woman surrounded by multi-colored sweets. He smiled at the woman and pointed to a blue and yellow round ball on a stick that closely resembled a lollipop. Something familiar. "I'll take the red-and-purple one, too."

"Oooh. Good choice," Ari said.

"Thank you," Conor said as he allowed the woman to swipe his wristband. He handed the red-purple candy to Ari.

"I love Smoke Pops. You certainly know how to spoil a girl."

"Yeah. Who doesn't love the Smoke Pops?" He did his best to not be odd by letting on he had no clue what he'd just bought.

Ari wasn't daft. She laughed. "You'll see. Give it a try." Conor put the candy pop in his mouth and immediately felt the tingling sensation of sugary coldness. Smoke began billowing from his mouth like a damp log tossed on an open fire. He pulled the pop from his mouth and chuckled. "You look good as a Dragor," she said through a smile. She then tasted hers and blew out a cloud of sweet-smelling vapor. She reached out, gathering some of the vapor. It crystallized in her hand. She smiled and tossed it above her, letting it sprinkle down like drizzling rain. Her face, locks, and shoulders now sparkled. "Who doesn't love a little glitter now and then?"

**The Academy**
**Residential District**

Conor's expectations shattered. Based on the mundane sterility of the corridors and entry port, he falsely assumed they'd step into a boring dormitory. Instead, he found himself in more of a tropical paradise. The metallic floor gave way to white sands leading to a crystal sea in the near distance. It reminded him of Makon's palace study, only more elaborate and immense.

Manicured gardens brimmed with wide palms and vibrant flowers fluttering in the soft breeze. Conor absorbed the beauty with an open jaw. Lush, puffy pink-and-white clouds circulated in the blue sky above. They moved as if painted by an unseen artist, forming shapes and masterful designs.

"Welcome home, Conor," Ari said. "You impressed?"

"Yeah."

"I was, too, the first time."

"What are those?"

Ari followed Conor's gaze upward. "Oh, the clouds. They're pretty spectacular, right?"

"What are they doing?" Conor asked as they swirled around until finally forming the shape of an astral star.

"Communicating."

"How so?"

"Everything here at the Academy serves some purpose. Look around. This place is unlike any other on the sphere. It was designed to promote relaxation and serenity, to be a place for us to recuperate so we're rested and ready for the next set of trials, territorial exploration, or disaster of a training course."

"And the clouds?"

"The clouds. They are simply depicting the Nivror solar system. All its planets, moons, space stations, and celestial wonders—even the Academy shows up from time to time. Just don't sit and stare at them too long."

"Why? What will happen?"

"You'll be the oddball staring up at the clouds all day and miss all the fun," she said with a slap on his arm. "Come on." She then slipped out of her shoes and scrunched her toes in the sand. "I think this is the only place I missed on break. Everywhere else can kill you."

Conor followed suit and removed his shoes and socks. To his surprise the sand didn't feel like sand at all. Rather than gritty, it felt like stepping on tiny bubbles that lightly massaged his feet with every step. They marched forward as the exotic jungle carried with them on their left.

As they walked, the majestic wonder of the tropical paradise began to wear off. No matter how beautiful the environment appeared, it still felt contrived. Just like the world simulations, everything in this place was a fabricated replica of something or somewhere else.

"Here we are," Ari said as she stepped off the sand onto a blue surface that looked like an inflatable quilt. She dropped her shoes and slipped her first foot back in.

"Where is here?" Conor looked around and didn't see anything resembling a destination.

"There," Ari replied while balancing on one foot to get on her other shoe. Conor craned his neck upward. He could see the underbelly of a suspended building high above them. Parts peeked out from the clouds as if it rested on their pillowtop. Up again. Everything had to be up in the air.

As if reading his mind, she said, "We sleep above the land because our time as Federation officers will mostly be spent above it anyway. As cadets, we're expected to do the same. They often deactivate the gravity drive, so we get accustomed to weightlessness, too. It just happens, and we have to adjust. Frustrating when you're bathing. Trust me."

"Okay. Why not? How do we get up there?"

"Simple. We jump."

Conor looked at her funny. "We just jump?"

"Yes and no. Tap your bracelet twice. That activates the jump pads."

"What jump pads?" Conor asked while putting on his second shoe.

"You're standing on them," Ari said with a smile. She then tapped her bracelet twice, and the blue padded square under her lit up. It now glowed green. She braced as the pad whistled. An instant later she shot upward with a scream. "Don't forget to bend your kneeeeees!" she exclaimed as she launched upward like a missile.

As nerve-wracking as it seemed, it still looked pretty fun. He looked around and found himself all alone, except, of course, for Titan. She stood still, as bewildered as he. Conor looked around for someone to provide some clarifying pointers. No one. He didn't even know where he was going, much less how to land when he got there.

He took in a deep breath and squared his feet on the pad. One more breath and remembering to bend his knees, Conor double-tapped his bracelet. He watched the pad turn green beneath his feet. No turning back now.

One moment the whistle sounded, the next, he was airborne. He flew through the air with tremendous velocity, moving faster than he had even on the Bounder—terrifying and exhilarating at the same time. He determined he'd soon have to get used to flying.

The air whipped his eyes, and they began to water. Conor stopped holding his breath and tucked his arms at his sides. If this ended up being a one-way flight, he might as well make it count.

He hadn't realized how fast he was moving until he shot past Ari as if she were paused in mid-ascent. He looked down at her and spotted a face full of disappointed puzzlement. Moving at intense speed, the structure swiftly came within arm's reach. His head breached a soft bubble at the base, but it did little to slow him. Was that supposed to be the brakes?

Conor flew up the side of the building closest to him. Something was wrong. He looked down as he continued upward and noticed a group of kids staring up at him as if he were a misguided rocket on a crash course. Ari popped up inside a bubble and landed on solid ground with ease. But not him. Apparently, he was destined for the top unless he did something to stop.

He began flailing his arms, hoping to latch onto a window ledge, waving banner, maybe even a spire or dangling mane of long blond hair. But there wasn't anything to grab. The whole place was shaped like a giant cone with slick sides. He just kept bouncing off every time he got close enough to touch it.

Just as Conor had resolved himself to a never-ending flight of doom, a massive hand reached out from inside the cone and snatched his arm. The hand plucked him out of the air like a baseball just about to make it over the left-field fence, pulling him right through an open portal in the curved wall. Half-dizzy from the rapid flight and abrupt halt, Conor fell straight to his butt. He steadied his head and looked up at his rescuer. Way up. He hadn't fallen on his butt—he'd been dropped.

A giant, easily three times his frame, bent down to look closer at him. "Hello. I thought you might want to stop flying and come back down."

"Ha. Yeah. Pretty much. Thanks," Conor rattled off.

The giant smiled and straightened up. Nope. He was easily *five* times his size. Despite having clear intentions of avoiding the rare Wildorians at the Academy, Conor had just been saved by one. Guess they might not be so bad after all.

"I am Jip," the giant bellowed.

"Conor."

"You don't know what you're doing, do you, Conor?"

"Not a clue. All I know is this is where I'm supposed to live. A weird, glowing cushion shot me up here straight through a bubble that was probably supposed to stop me. And now I'm talking to a giant inside a big, floating cone building. That's just been in the past ten seconds. You should hear about the rest of my day."

The giant Wildorian simply dropped his hands and walked away. He obviously didn't want to hear about the rest of his day. Conor pushed up to his feet. "Thanks again!" he shouted.

Jip turned and waved a bear of a hand for him to follow. Why not? What could possibly go wrong next?

# CHAPTER 12

**Vesputi Galaxy**
**Edge of Sector 6**
**Gregor Monolith**

The massive expanse of a battleship coasted through the stars, Valitat Bithos poised at the helm. She sipped from a cold beverage in her hand and closely monitored their approach. "There. That moon," she said as she pointed to the visual display. "We'll tuck in behind it and deploy from there."

"Yes, Vice Commander. Changing trajectory to target the moon of . . . What's it called again?"

"I'm not concerned with its name. It's not our destination. We're just using it as cover for the insertion."

"Very well, Vice Commander. Moving to the moon of Whatever," the engineer said as he motioned on the mist board with his hands to guide the flight path.

"If I'm not mistaken, it's the Moon of Kol," Makon interjected as he moved to the helm display.

"Acknowledged. Moving to the Moon of Kol."

Valitat looked at the Commander with a furrowed brow. Makon just shrugged. "We're just outside Kol's orbit. One must assume that the Moon of Kol is an acceptable name. Am I right?" He spotted an eye roll from her as she turned away and sipped from her cup again. He didn't even try to mask his smile.

They stood in silence for a few moments before Valitat broke it. "Under good conscience, I have to question if this is the right action." She hesitated and placed a hand on her hip.

"Go on," Makon urged.

"We are inserting into Kravii-influenced territory, without Federation knowledge or approval, on one of the most faction-riddled spheres in the Vesputi galaxy."

"Correction. Known. One of the most unfriendly, violent spheres that we know of."

"I don't follow," Valitat replied.

"There could always be worse ones we just don't know about yet."

"Fine. I'll agree with that, but its meaning is superfluous."

"I like when you agree with me, Vice Commander," Makon said with a smirk. He then reached out toward her. Without looking at him, she handed him her cup. He took a sip and then handed it back. "You do always make the best cocktails."

"Must be why you keep me around," she replied, both of them knowing how untrue that statement was. She then noticed the Commander had dressed down in rugged pants and a matching gray overcoat with a sidearm affixed to his right thigh in a drop-down holster. "Wait. Are you seriously going in yourself?"

"Why not?"

"Because it's dangerous. No, not dangerous. It's just stupidly suicidal, and you and I both know you're not getting out of there without some kind of violent altercation."

"Do you doubt me and my negotiation skills? Okay, who here also doubts my abilities to peacefully accomplish this mission?" he asked the rest of the flight deck. No one moved to answer. "Let's place a bet. I wager a two-day stay at my villa that we can get in and out without any trouble. Who's up for it?" Every member of the flight deck enthusiastically raised their hand. "Come on. No one here has faith in their Commander?"

"See?" Valitat chimed. "Everyone wants to take that bet because we know enough about Kol and its inhabitants."

"Moon," Makon uttered.

"What?"

"The Moon of Kol. We're going to the third moon. There's nothing on Kol."

"I know that. You know I know that. Stop trying to irritate me."

"Fine. Consider the irritation ceased."

"I highly doubt that. As I was saying . . ." Valitat paused when the engineer stepped in close.

"Excuse the interruption, Commanders," he interjected. "But we're docking behind the Moon of Kol and then deploying Commander Welcos to the Moon of Kol. Same name but different sphere. It can be rather confusing."

Makon thrust out his arm and pointed directly at the engineer. "Yes. He's onto something. Let's call this one the Second Moon of Kol. We shall deploy to the third moon of Kol, which is called the Moon of Kol because some of us lack creativity, but we will avoid Kol altogether."

The engineer shrugged. "Fine. Move us into position behind the Second Moon."

Makon spun back toward Valitat with a grin. "Now, you were going on about my brilliance and how I have the best ideas ever. Please continue."

Valitat scoffed. "Not quite. What I was going to say is we also know enough about you and how you tend to handle things. We don't doubt you. I, for one, just doubt your sensibilities."

"Confidence booster for sure, Val. Much appreciated. But, aside from marching into the Kravii Command Center and demanding intel, this is the fastest way to get some answers to how they managed the cloaked attack on our home."

"I'm not so sure this is a safer option than busting through the Kravos atmosphere, guns blazing and taking on the whole Kravii homeland."

"Oh, but it is. Besides, I'm taking Haviro and Shila along with me. They'll have my back." Both Elite officers were standing behind the raised helm, dressed similarly to their Commander.

"Shila's been an Elite for less than half a year, and you think this mission is suitable for her?" The Vice Commander didn't give a thought to the fact the newly appointed Elite Squad member was standing within ear-shot. "Too bad you just gifted Iopo Lex to Wilda Ti and the Academy to serve as a security guard." Makon's countenance changed from jovial and good-natured to one of scorn. Valitat had overstepped, and she knew it. She took a deep breath. "At least take more than two members with you."

"Nah. It'll be fine," Makon said, his scorn softening. "You forget, I left Bradok at the Academy, too." Makon remained relentless in his jovial stabs, fully realizing Valitat wasn't truly bothered by it. "Besides, we can't go in with a crew, or we'll definitely draw attention and possible trouble. I want to be low-key and quick."

"You are the exact opposite of 'low-key.' If you're recognized, the whole lot will be fighting over who gets to take you hostage and collect the ransom. Or even just kill you and collect the reward for the head of the Federation's most esteemed Commander. You make lots of enemies."

"Yes, I do," Makon replied as he placed a brimmed hat on his head. "But I have stronger friends. We'll be in contact with the trackers activated the whole time. You'll see us, and we'll hear you. But I'm not leaving without finding someone with answers."

**Ipit Solar System**
**Moon of Kol**
**Scavenger Skiff**

Makon and his two Elites docked their small scavenger skiff alongside several others matching in size and appearance. The Federation maintained a number of crafts like this one for clandestine missions where Federation presence and identification wouldn't be practical for infiltration. They disembarked from the vessel and absorbed the atmosphere. Random gunfire pierced the perpetually dark sky made possible by Kol's virtually permanent eclipse of the Ipit Solar System's lone sun.

The three moved steadily, each of the officers flanking their Commander. This wouldn't work. Makon paused and let his officers walk past; then he moved to the right, behind Officer Shila. She hesitated a moment before realizing her leader's intentions. She was now in charge of their little party to throw off any suspicion or recognition of one of the rare Supreme Commanders in the galaxy's mightiest fleet.

Shila moved to a storefront and hesitated. It looked crowded inside with a merchant openly selling arms, blades, and various other gadgets suitable for aggressive piracy. Perhaps they should question the store owner. Over her right shoulder, she saw the Commander continue forward. Perhaps not. She took a few rapid steps to take the lead again as they crossed deeper into the marauder village.

"Disorder" would be the first word to come to mind describing the scene. People and creatures wandered about without much purpose or design. No force existed to police the inhabitants, as everything and everyone held self-governance. The buildings stretched high but stayed shabby, thrown together with wood, metal, or whatever material they had on hand. Patrons poised on patios overlooking the street or clung to corners, lingering in the shadows, planning whatever devious behavior might come to mind.

Suddenly, a large six-legged beast came barreling out of an alley right toward them. Its thick fur mane stood on end and its ravenous jowls hung open. The large beast towered over the tallest man, and its tail acted like a clearing broom as it whipped and lashed against anything in its way. Four men chased after it; two of them met the broad side of its tail and were tossed into a table of drinking buddies like wads of paper.

Screams rang out as the beast rushed forward, but they didn't come from the Elites. As it got closer, the three experts merely stepped aside and let the parade go by. Shila moved her hand off her pistol and let her coat flap cover it again.

They soon moved to what looked like a saloon. A large crowd filled its space, spilling patrons out to the walkway. It carried up high, roughly six or seven stories by her count, each floor marked with a crowded patio. Gunfire came from no less than two of the floors. A body came toppling down from the fourth floor and landed face down in the dirt next to Makon. No one flinched. This was common here, and an overzealous reaction would signal them as strangers.

Makon looked down at the man and back up at the building. He looked down again as he sensed movement. The man pushed himself up to his knees and coughed. He glanced up at Makon and brushed dirt off his chest. "Ugh. That hurt," he uttered with slurred speech. Makon turned away, certainly unimpressed. "Well, it worked last time. I need another drink," the man muttered as he stumbled off.

Only a slim possibility existed they'd manage to find someone intelligent enough here to answer some questions. Makon knew that one misstep or unappreciated gaze, and the whole tavern would erupt into a war zone. Risk far outweighed reward at this venue.

The Commander shook his head, and they moved on.

They now moved through a multitude gathered around a ring dedicated to the battle joust. They pushed through the boisterous mass of galaxy pirates and mercenaries to the edge of the pit. From his vantage point at the rim's edge, Makon observed numerous rows descending into the pit.

Cheering spectators shouted down at the competitors—a weaponless bout between two bloody gladiators. The one had silver skin and swung fists of scaled armor. The other looked much smaller, a long braid of red hair swinging past his shoulder blades. Blood coated his right shoulder and cascaded down his arm from a deep cut to one of his pointed ears. He moved fast and graceful but must've been caught by one of the large Harev grunt's blows at some point.

The Harev now swung wild and hard, unable to connect with the twisting and spinning Magart war slave. He moved swiftly with the calculated precision and lethality of a jungle panther. Strength and power versus speed and smooth technique.

Makon turned away from the fight. He already knew the victor. The Commander and his Elites clawed back through the crowd to the street. Shila took the slight lead in their travel wedge as they moved again, deeper into the twisting bowels of the town's labyrinth.

One spectator turned, taking greater interest in the departure of the three rogues than the brawl below. A pair of gold eyes glowed dim through a form-fitted helmet as the integrated HUD flashed identification credentials on each of them. The last image displayed the coveted prize of all prizes—Federation Supreme Commander Makon Welcos.

A gloved hand palmed the underside of the opposite forearm and two dull beeps sounded in the helmet. The suit shifted with a shimmer, and the figure disappeared, now invisible to the eye and any other optical enhancement. Targets marked; it was time to follow.

**The Academy**
**Residential District**

Conor followed the giant around the spiraling corridor wide enough to fit a family of Jips side by side. The place had been built with giants in mind, or maybe even something bigger. The corridor wrapped itself like a python around a massive tube-shaped center stretching from the bottom all the way to the top. Doorways lined the interior tube. *Must be the living quarters.*

They eventually reached the bottom, and Jip simply pointed to a woman seated nearby in a high, plush chair. Conor looked up and thanked him as his steps thumped away.

Conor moved closer to the Academy official. She wore the typical black uniform accompanied by a wide smile. "Cadet Hawk," she greeted him. "I wasn't sure you were coming back to join us. In all my years here, *that* I have never seen. You shot right through the barrier constraint as if it wasn't even there."

"Sorry."

"I will get the technicians to work on it immediately. But if it happens again, you know what to do next time."

"No, not really. The giant over there pulled me down."

"Well, Cadet Hawk, we can't always rely on giants, now, can we?"

"I guess not."

"Good. So next time, if there is one, you resolve the problem yourself."

"I'll try. But I don't know how to. I can't fly."

"No, Cadet Hawk. No. You certainly cannot," the woman said with a grin and chuckle. "Now, how about we get you to your residence?" She waved her hand over a small sphere with purple clouds swirling around its surface. A mist screen materialized in front of her, and she moved images with her hand as she searched for the recruit.

Conor watched the ball and its clouds rapidly changing from blue to red and back and forth. "Okay. There you are." She tapped a finger in the air, presumably on his name. "Hmmm. That's odd."

"What?" Conor asked as he watched the clouds in the sphere change to black.

The woman simply shot him a glance and turned back to the screen. "No problem, Cadet Hawk. You just haven't been assigned a faction at this time. But we do have your residence. You are going to be in number 10-484. You are with . . . Ha! That's strange."

"What? What's strange?"

"All of it, Recruit Hawk. I wonder if this was intentional or an oversight. I'll look into it, but, for now, just head on up." She pointed to the lift pod behind her. It marked the middle of the massive tube at the cone-shaped tower's center. "Be aware—there may be a change forthcoming, but for now, move along." She swiped the mist screen away and slumped back into her comfy throne.

Conor stared dumbfounded for a moment and then moved behind her. Then he paused and turned back. "What about my dog?"

"Dog?" The word struck her as bizarre and didn't quite register. "Oh, the beast of yours," she said without moving from her chair of luxury. "The beast doesn't reside here. It has its own quarters. You can retrieve it in the common areas. Some are restricted, like the residence."

"She is waiting for me."

"Where is she waiting, Cadet Hawk?"

"Way down there on the beach," Conor said as he pointed down through the puffy clouds.

"Nonsense, Cadet Hawk," the official corrected.

"No, really. I left her there when I went flying all the way up here."

"No, she's not there. Upon activation of your bracelet the collar around her neck directed her back to her quarters. The beast will be available for your companionship at a later time."

"When is that?"

"Move along now, Cadet Hawk."

Conor stifled the frustrated anger brewing in his cheeks and turned away. He moved to the lift pod and stepped forward. He couldn't find any buttons or levers, and nothing spontaneous happened. He was about to yell for some assistance when a cluster of five recruits came dashing toward the pod. They pushed inside, barely noticing him as they continued laughing and chatting as if they'd been friends for ages. They all looked similar in appearance—similar in that they came from the same planet.

The tallest of the recruits, with a fair complexion, and brown hair like Conor's, turned to him. "Thanks for waiting, mate."

"Yeah. No problem," Conor replied as he watched intently to see if he knew how to move the lift. The same boy waved his bracelet at the portal. The others continued talking as the gold mist formed a door panel and they began to move. He began to feel uneasy because he felt the other boy watching him. The others barely even noticed he was there, but this one moved closer. He now looked down at Conor and tilted his head to the side.

"You're definitely new here, mate."

Conor looked at him and took a deep breath. "Yeah, so?"

"What level are you on?"

"10-484."

"Level ten," the older boy said.

"Yep," Conor said as he began to brace for some bullying. The boy nodded and then suddenly grabbed Conor's left wrist and thrust it toward the door. Conor tensed, balling his right hand into a fist. Five against one in a lift didn't give him the best odds, but if a fight was what the older boy wanted . . .

Before Conor had decided to lash out at his aggressor, the boy released his arm, and a soft chime sounded. He then smiled. "Level 10 is coming up. Didn't want you to miss it."

Conor now felt mixed emotions of relief and embarrassment. He wondered if the other boy knew how close he'd come to getting punched. The pod slowed, and the mist-formed door dropped. Conor paused and then moved forward.

"Hey, mate!" the older boy called to him. Conor looked back over his shoulder. "The name's Adin. I'm Fourth-Circuit and can remember what Circuit One was like for me. We all go through the same stuff the first year. It gets easier. You'll get it."

Conor nodded as the mist formed again, closing in the pod and sending it back on its path upward. He doubted anyone could compare their first day to his. And it was still just the afternoon.

# CHAPTER 13

**Moon of Kol**
**Black Tar District**

The night seemed to darken in this particular corner of town. Shila continued to lead the group under the subtle direction of their leader, but as they ventured deeper into the darker corners, she became less secure of their ability to get out. They kept to the shadows, stealing the small spaces from those who might be lurking, watching, scheming to do them harm or offense. She lowered her head to mask the rising uneasiness, but her eyes stayed on a swivel, seeking potential threats.

"Here," the Commander's voice whispered into her earpiece. She stopped and looked around. Tall, bleak buildings made entirely of mirrored glass lined both sides of the alley. They juxtaposed with the rest of the dilapidated marketplace, shedding off the appearance of impoverished dilapidation for one of opulence. "The one to your left."

Shila turned to the sheet of glass that looked like a smooth, black, starless sky. The three stood side by side gazing at their own reflections.

"I feel like we're being watched," Haviro whispered.

"Believe it. We are," Makon replied.

"There's no entryway. Where do we go in?" Shila asked.

Makon stepped forward. "Only those who know, know."

"You been here before?" Haviro asked.

"Long ago. Before the Federation," Makon said as he stepped forward and placed the toe of his left boot against the glass, where it submerged into the dry soil. "I remember. Though I'd like to forget." He then placed his right palm against the glass. An unseen rectangle of black began to shimmer like a calm sea suddenly catching a gust of wind. "Hopefully, this visit goes better than my last one," he muttered as he stepped through the shimmer.

Shila was now the last one in. The shimmer eased to solid glass once again. She turned to look back, and, just as she'd assumed, she had a clear view of the dark alleyway behind. They'd entered a vast circular room with no ceiling, walls that stretched to the sky, and a balcony overlooking the depths below. A group of huddled renegades paused their conversation as they entered the unmarked building. Blue smoke billowed from the golden eyes of a tall man dressed in red armor as he brought the curved pipe away from his lips. Two others, also in similar armor, flanked him while holding their flame lances at the ready.

Makon glanced to his left, not looking up from under his hat's brim. He offered a subtle nod and then headed over to the wide winding staircase. Haviro and Shila followed behind him, but, before descending below with their Commander, they couldn't help but glance over the thick, wooden balcony. The staircase coiled far below into a pool of purple light. Thunderous booms from powerful speakers carried the rhythmic melody all the way up to them at the top. They couldn't determine the layout of the space below, but they knew they'd have to quickly scan the environment once they'd reached the ground level. The Commander would expect nothing less.

The Elites descended together, with Makon now leading the way. Their leader's cover became unnecessary. "The Monolith can no longer track us. We fell off their screens the moment we stepped inside," Makon said as he moved slow and sure down the stairway. "The volume of the music will drown out our comms once we reach the bottom."

"What is this place?" Shila asked as her hand glided down the polished banister.

"It's called The Cavern. But some refer to it as paradise. You won't."

As they moved around the last bend in the staircase, the atmosphere changed. Literally. The temperature dropped, and the air became heavier, thicker. Purple light glowed through the smoke, providing limited visibility. Other than random sets of glowing eyes and the bright hues from fashionable beverages, violet decadence ruled the sight picture. Dancing shapes moved to the melody, while others sat calm, watching.

"Remember, I'm looking for someone with particular information. Everything else is just lethal distraction. Increase your ear volume so that we can hear one another somewhat." Shila and Haviro each moved in opposite directions; she took the left flank while he blended to the right. "And one more thing," Makon said in normal pitch to potentially carry over the bass. "We have no friendlies here."

Shila methodically pushed through the purple haze attempting to study the layout and patronage. She moved under the stairway, staying close to the wall but made sure not to touch it. The black rock walls seeped with translucent slime, giving off the appearance of it moving, breathing as if alive itself. She couldn't decipher the origin of the music; no musicians or stage presented as she continued on her path.

Numerous dark shapes crowded The Cavern, but she couldn't make out much through the purple smoke. She needed to enhance her vision. "Optic. Dark." The lens cushioned over her right eyeball activated. It cast the room in a shade of hunter green and black. This helped her locate the larger shapes like the robust circular bar. Multiple forms moved inside the bar distributing drinks and curious food. A large floating sphere with 68 numbered hexagons hung toward the room's center. A round table with a crowd of players cheered and sneered as the sphere spun and the number 14 illuminated. Shila had heard of the game before—Biru—though she'd never risked her coin on it. A simple game with built-in complexity. Now might be the best time to try it out and get close to someone with the information they needed.

Two more similar spheres spun at opposite sides of the room. Each of the tables entertained plenty of players. She moved to the center Biru, the one with the most occupants. As she pushed through the haze, she noticed something peculiar about the players, though she wasn't positive until she uttered, "Optic. Heat."

Her lens changed to infrared heat signatures. Most of the patrons now manifested half-moon red-yellow shapes on top of bodies of deep blue. This stabbed her gut with sharp anxiety. Only one species displayed that type of image due to their organic armor. The Kravii.

Shila stopped short of the Biru table and hesitated. This wasn't a club, tavern, or pleasure kitchen the Commander had led them to. It was a Kravii haven. She and her meager team of Elites wandered as wolves into a den of dragons.

One of the Kravii spotted her and scanned her like an uncooked meal. She had to exude confidence in this moment or be challenged as an outsider, and probably risk being torn apart. Shila squinted and lowered her head. She dug three hexagonal coins from her vest pocket and finished her trek to the table under a cloak of confidence and poise. She'd trained close-quarter combat against hordes of these fiends and fared better than most. But there was a glaring difference between simulation and live interaction. The real thing never liked to go down easy.

Shila walked straight toward the curious Kravii warrior and pushed between him and a robust woman wearing a silver-horned mask. She didn't look up at the Kravii. Instead, she flicked one of the horns to let the woman know she'd better move over, and then stuffed her coins into the chute on the tabletop. Blue mist spewed from a spout next to the chute and materialized into a screen with numbers 0–68 along with color cubes, arrows pointing up and down, and odd and even.

She understood the ease of the game relied on a player being able to select whether or not the next number would be even, odd, greater or less than the number before it. They could also select the color from the spectrum of six. The payout for that type of play was minimal. The real strategy came in determining the pattern of the numbers based on the set displayed. She'd have to guess the next number if she learned the pattern. The large payouts came from learning the pattern early and making subsequent markers accordingly. Much higher payouts flowed the more numbers a player could guess. However, the advantage to the host lay in the simple fact that the patterns would only carry forward based on the preset number, and the pattern changed as new numbers emerged. The large payouts were only afforded to those who bet on each number.

This was of little concern to Shila. The current pattern showed 7, 8, 5, 10, 3 with the total pre-set at eight. She studied it for a moment and knew the next number. She bet a small amount. It was a safe bet so as not to draw newcomer envy from her swarm of enemies. The number 12 hit, and her credits doubled. That felt good.

She noticed the Kravii savage seething to her right. It lost and didn't like her winning. He really wasn't going to like her next bet, then. This time she chose the next number from one of two possibilities—1 or 13. She went with 1; when it hit, the

Kravii smashed his claw on the table. It didn't do damage to the table's frame, but it got everyone's attention. Meanwhile, Shila's coin doubled again, and she couldn't resist smirking.

She thought about cashing out for a fleeting moment but resisted that type of stupidity. She had one more number to win on at a 4–1 payout!

Suddenly a soft whisper tickled her ear. "Don't play that number." She didn't have to look up to know Haviro's voice. "It can be addicting, and apparently you're a natural at this game."

"One more," Shila urged.

"Fine. One more. But get it wrong."

"No way."

"Lose, Shila. It's too dangerous to win here."

"I hate you," Shila muttered as she punched in a bad number. The sphere spun and cycled through the number bank until landing on the winner. But she lost. So did the Kravii, but it savored the small victory in the female mercenary's defeat.

Shila pushed back from the table and jabbed Haviro in the hip. "You're no fun."

"Fun? Of course, I'm fun. I'm also smart," he said while walking away. "Have you been able to locate the Commander?"

"Uh. No, I don't see him."

"I lost him during my perimeter survey. That concerns me," Haviro said.

"No wonder. You happen to notice where he brought us?"

"You mean this underground gambling cave-den overflowing with Kravii?"

"Indeed," Shila said.

"Nope. I hadn't noticed."

"You think the Commander knew this was an enemy hangout?" she asked.

"First of all," Haviro started, "Everyone here is an enemy for the right pay. And second, you don't know the Commander that well."

"Guess not. Either way, we need to find him quickly and get out before we have a serious problem, you know, getting out."

– ✳ –

Makon pushed through the door leading into a long, narrow room. It was designed for storage, but it'd been converted to hold various distinctive arms from shock rifles and pistols to fire lances and blades—curved, jagged, long and slim, light and heavy.

"What are you doing here, strange one? Get out!" one of the three men at the opposite end of the room shouted. He was one of two red-shelled soldiers flanking the proprietor, a large, muscled man with blue-black skin sitting at a wide desk with stacks of V-Coin on one side and a young female nimerith perched on the other. Jewels decorated his pointed ears and five horns jutted out from thick black curls. More twisted horns pierced through his forearms, biceps, and bare chest like stalagmites sprouting from a cave of flesh.

Makon ignored the guard's command and instead turned to one of the weapon displays. He pulled down a small dagger and inspected it. It was heavier than one would expect a dagger to be. Its long hilt made it great for driving penetration, but this diminished its practical concealment. However, concealment didn't factor into its overall purpose.

"Did you hear me? If you have business, then you can speak with me outside. This office is off limits to the uninvited," the guard bellowed. He moved around from behind his boss to the side of the desk.

Makon pinched his fingers and ran them up the width of the blade. "You have quite a selection here, but this weapon in particular has always fascinated me." As his fingers moved up the surface, the blade's length began to stretch. "It's both primitive and majestic all at once. Truly fascinating."

"Did you not hear me? Put the weapon down and step outside."

"Sorry. Can't do that," Makon said, his face still shadowed under his hat.

"You'd better, or it's the last bad decision you'll ever make," the bodyguard said with a snarl. He lowered the fire lance in Makon's direction.

"I need to speak with him. Not you." Makon slid his fingers back down the blade, causing it to retract. He lowered it even farther until it disappeared completely into the hilt. He then held it in his outstretched palm and moved steadily toward the desk.

The blue demon behind the desk leaned forward and smacked the nimerith on her thigh. Her butterfly wings fluttered, lifting her from the desk. She glided away down the corridor past Makon without looking at him. When she got to the doorway, she lowered to the floor and glanced back once at her owner. He nodded to her and waved her away. She eyed the mysterious rogue in the long, gray trench coat. He seemed quite sure of himself. But not for long. She knew what came next.

The door closed behind her, and Makon grabbed the top of a chair somewhat in his path. He dragged it across the floor behind him, the scraping of metal on unpolished rock irritating the beast with sensitive hearing. "So, you want to speak with me. Only me? You don't have an invitation or anything of my interest, so I'm afraid this'll be a painfully short meeting."

Makon reached the front of the desk and spun the chair around. He set the dagger on the desktop in front of him and sat himself calmly in the chair. "Now there's the problem right there. You've already made a mistake. I'm not here for your interests. I'm here for mine." Both guards aimed their lances at the brazen threat.

"Ha! Now I don't even care to hear anything you have to say," the horned boss said with a chuckle.

Makon smiled and shook his head. "You know what truly disappoints me? When pathetic gangsters work really hard to show they're tough and dangerous by displaying all these exotic weapons. Take that dagger there in front of you. I bet you have it because it's pretty with all its squiggly designs on the hilt. It's so neat how it expands and contracts, almost like a toy."

"I know my weapons. You're boring me."

"Wait. I'm getting to the best part," Makon said as he rolled it back and forth. The three men watched intently, poised to blast him if he attempted to activate the blade. "I bet you think it's still just a dagger."

"What is it then?" the guard asked. Makon looked down, and then, in a flash, drew his sidearm and fired three shots. The first penetrated the guard's mouth to his immediate left. The second burned through his nose before exiting the back of his scorched skull. The third shot struck the other guard in the throat, tearing away cartilage and soft tissue. He fell back, gurgling as his neck melted like charred marshmallow, just not as sweet-smelling.

"It's a distraction," Makon uttered.

The Commander then side-stepped just as a tremendous blast ruptured the underside of the desk right in front of him. Before the beast could bring the hand cannon up from underneath the barrier, Makon lurched forward and tore away a long horn from the fiend's bicep. He drove it hard into his opposite forearm and twisted. The beast grimaced, flashing jagged teeth and fangs.

"Release it," Makon urged as he pressed the barrel of his firearm into the beast's temple so hard it caused an indentation.

"Bring your hand up to the desk, or there will be three of you wishing you'd conducted business differently today."

"I know you, don't I?" the beast asked as he brought the other hand up to the desk's edge.

"Yes, Siv Ro. You do," Makon said as he released the horn and pulled off his hat letting it plop on the desk. He kept the firearm aimed at his head for good measure and compliance. "Optic. Clear." The lens in Makon's right eye switched from X-ray to normal vision. Both eyes now took in the golden hue enveloping the corridor.

"Ha. Ha. Ha. Captain Windevil. Been a long time."

"No, not Captain. Commander. Supreme. I've upgraded. I'm Federation now."

"Hardly an upgrade. From free man to servant of the Masters," Siv Ro said with a sneer.

"The Elders are dead."

"I know. I've heard. Who do you serve now, Commander?" he asked with mocked disdain.

"Retribution," Makon said.

"Oh." Siv Ro nodded. "Years long gone but never forgotten, I see."

"I do owe you, personally. But that's not why I'm here."

"You'll never leave here alive. I guarantee it," Siv Ro threatened. Makon tilted his head and looked directly into Siv Ro's blazing blue eyes. "Right. The great Captain Windevil. Terror of the skies."

"That name's been retired," Makon replied.

"Maybe, but the stories live on."

"Good. Only my enemies need fear."

"Am I your enemy, Windevil?"

"You serve the Kravii, so I would say you are."

"I serve no one but myself. They pay better. They want war. I deal in bloodshed. We have a mutual understanding. Besides, I prefer their company and business to the irritation of the whining Jopali. Just the mere sound of their voice pricks my ears and aches my head."

Makon dug the barrel into Siv Ro's face just below his right eye. "I can take away your headache right now. Take the whole damn head away with it."

"What do you want?"

"Information," Makon said. "Tell me what you know about the attack."

Siv Ro smiled again and licked the front of his teeth. "I know you guys weren't ready. I know they tore your chief city apart and blew away your tower like a pile of flowers in a windstorm. Tell me, Windevil, did your Masters see it coming?"

"Tell me what you know!" Makon bellowed.

Siv Ro rejoiced in his assailant's frustration and continued his agitation. "Because if they didn't see it coming, then what use were they? A blind foreseer is no more than a beggar. How's your faith now, Windevil?"

"How's your arm?" Makon grabbed the horn jutting from Siv Ro's arm, jamming and twisting it deeper. Siv Ro grunted and snarled at the surge of pain. Black blood trickled down to the floor. Makon half-sat on the desk to face his opponent for the interrogation.

"I don't know anything. Ugh. Heard patrons celebrating the victory. How easy it was." The pain radiated up his shoulder.

"Cloaking. Tell me about the cloaking. It's new, and the Kravii don't have that level of advanced technology," Makon pressed.

"Neither do you."

"Where did it come from?"

Siv Ro looked up at Makon. "That there is the mystery."

"Give me a clue then, before I decide Windevil should emerge from his retirement." Makon brought his finger down to the trigger and pulled. The firearm recoiled as a blast sliced through the top of Siv Ro's ear.

"Aaaaagh!" The beast bucked and shouted as he clutched his bleeding ear.

"No more games, or the next one goes through your head."

"No, I'm serious. It's a mystery. The Kravii Battleborn Chief, Utirot, has gone missing. His entire squad disappeared. He's the only one who knew about the tech. And he's gone."

"Where was this Battleborn last seen?"

Siv Ro gripped the top of the desk and shut his eyes. His breathing steadied but grew deeper. "Windevil," he whispered, "You are a bold and savvy man, but you're also reckless." Before Makon could respond, Siv Ro flexed his arms and grunted, driving all his might upward from the desk's edge. His power flipped the massive desk over, sending Makon toppling with it. The firearm went off, launching a shot into the ceiling.

Before Makon could scramble to his feet, Siv Ro loomed over him. His clawed hand gripped the overcoat, hoisting the Commander all the way up to eye level. Makon brought the firearm up, but a blue hand swiftly swatted it away. Siv Ro slammed Makon down on the top of his shoulder before flinging him far against the wall. Makon soared backward but reached his arms out behind him and braced against the impact. He hit the surface without injury and calmly dropped down to the ground on two feet.

"I guess we're gonna get that payback after all," Makon said as he stretched his arms up and brought them around to his waist in a circle. He stepped forward, turned to face the wall, and ran up it until both feet were planted. He pushed off with tremendous force launching himself at his adversary like a furious missile of muscle. Makon collided with Siv Ro's thick-muscled legs with enough force to bring him down. The beast fell backward with Makon landing on top.

Makon moved fast. Super-fast. Close-quarter combat wasn't just his specialty—it was his playground. His movements were swift, graceful, and thunderously lethal. He first landed a fist strike on the beast's jaw as he moved around him to the left. He brought his right knee across Siv Ro's belly and punched him again in the face with a right cross. Siv Ro reeled from the blows and brought his arms up for defense. Makon neatly wrapped the beast's extended right arm, still slick with blood from the horn-stabbing, and tucked it under his left shoulder. Pinning him down, Makon delivered three more punches before overextending the right elbow across his shin. Siv Ro winced from the strain but then screamed when Makon snapped the bone.

He released the now-flimsy arm and stood. Siv Ro rolled back and forth in pain. Makon stepped over him and collected his sidearm, placing it back in the holster. He then moved to the busted desk, brushing aside a few pieces of debris. He fished his hat out from under the toppled chair, pinched the top, and placed it back on his head.

"Good thing Windevil is retired. Otherwise, you'd have more than a broken arm and a bruised ego. Here you go," he said as he yanked an embedded horn out of his own collar. Blood trickled down Makon's shoulder. "You can have this back." He tossed it down at Siv Ro and watched it bounce off his chest and clatter to the floor. He adjusted his fedora, pulling it snugly in place, before moving over to the felled beast. "Now, you got distracted from my last question. Where was the Battleborn Utirot last seen?"

# CHAPTER 14

**The Academy**
**Residential Tower**

10-484. Conor found the portal to his room. He took a deep breath and exhaled. He then raised the wristband toward the doorway and watched the door fall away to the floor. He stepped forward, and the cold blue light shifted to a warm natural glow like overcast sunlight through a bay window. He took a few more steps into the vacant room, and the door closed itself behind him.

The room wasn't huge, but it wasn't small, either. The farthest end of the room held two rectangular beds, large and long enough to fit a single person comfortably. A desk with a low-backed chair neatly tucked against it separated the beds. One of them had a bluish gold sphere roughly the size of a basketball plopped in the middle of it. The other bed, and the two similar beds marking the left and right sides of the room were still unclaimed. Each had a single folded blanket placed at the bottom. Conor moved to the center and looked up at a long, levitating cylinder hanging in the air above a low, round table of dark glass. Two large half-moon couches encircled the table. He patted the cushioned back of the couch and traced his hand around its curved back while studying the cylinder. He didn't have a clue what it did other than essentially being the room's light source. The top end glowed yellow, spreading light across the high ceiling and back down to the room below.

He plopped down on the bed to his immediate right. The padding was comfortable and familiar enough. He relaxed, finding a sense of relief in having the moment to himself. His eyes swept the room and found nothing else curious to explore other than three other spheres lined up by the doorway. One showed red, and two others were plain black. Those two looked deactivated. The red one and the blue one on the far bed swirled with activity.

One of the spheres must be his, but he didn't know which one. He thought about inspecting them since they were the only curious items left in the room other than the floating light cylinder overhead, but he found himself lying back and sliding his arm beneath his head.

This is what he needed—the comfort of collapse after a busy day. He closed his eyes as thoughts traced back to the luxury of Commander Welcos' palace bedroom. Then an unfamiliar thought crawled into his mind—one of a similar room, though much smaller. The bed held the same size and feel, but it wasn't in a cone-shaped tower in the sky. Not in the sky, but in space. A ship with a room he slept in many nights with Titan on the floor beside him.

His mind lingered on this distant memory as if it were passing through a sea of fog. It flitted in and out of sight and feeling, his mind going back and forth to the ship and his present surroundings.

Conor found the small room again in his mind. He could picture the bed under his body, hanging his hand off the side and petting the soft fur of the dog below. If he turned his head to the side, he could picture the gray, metal dresser bolted to the wall. A picture frame with three people centered on its top. A stoic man with a trimmed beard and crow's feet wrinkles framing his eyes, an athletic woman seated beside him. A boy's smiling face perched on her shoulder. Above it hung a poster of his favorite superhero—his red cape waving in the wind. He remembered all this.

Conor held onto the memory, and sleep overtook him.

Finding himself in a familiar dream, Conor's mother moved to him and smiled. She held out a piece of toast with raspberry jam, offering it to him. Conor sat up in bed and reached for his breakfast, but she suddenly pulled it away and took a bite. She laughed and turned away. "Your breakfast is waiting in the kitchen. Come on."

Conor looked around and found himself in a different space—a bedroom from a time before space rockets, space stations, and his galactic space travel. He recognized the sky-blue paint that carried down from the walls to the carpet as if the color couldn't be contained to only four sides of the boxed room. Absorbed in happy blue, as if drowning in island waters, Conor sat up in bed. The double window invited in the morning sun, providing a portal outward of the summer green surrounding the house tucked into the wooded suburbs.

The buzz of locusts caught his attention, the drone feeling both uncommon and familiar. A redbird pounced along the branches of the massive maple tree eclipsing a third of the window, her chirps drowned out by the returning insects.

Conor turned from the window's showcase of nature's serenity to the one of violence neatly organized among the blades of carpet. A battle scene ready to be played among his action figures took up much of the floor space as the mighty soldiers in green armor stood ready to defend Earth against the invading army of aliens armed with mystic rifles and double-bladed energy swords. This would be the afternoon's activity, before his mom told him to clean his room for the hundredth time.

After all, he didn't have school today. News of the asteroid prompted his parents to keep him home. Thank God for space debris. Any excuse to stay home from the life-sucking tedium of school sat just fine with him.

The smell of hash browns and scrambled eggs caught his attention now as the aroma wafted in his nostrils. He was definitely home. And it felt good.

"Mom," Conor called out.

"Yes, sweetheart?"

"I miss you."

His mother turned around full and faced him with a smile. The piece of toast fell from her hand, oddly fluttering to the ground like a leaf from a distant branch. "I miss you, too." Her expression suddenly changed to etched worry. Her sundress morphed into a black uniform and a military-grade assault rifle materialized in her hands. The blue walls turned to cold gunmetal gray, and the window morphed into a porthole with a view of emptiness. The pleasant lure of bacon shifted to the sting of fuel and disinfectant, and nature's music converted to the roar of churning engines. A wave of black crested behind her and crashed through the doorway, swallowing everything in heavy darkness.

Conor woke with a jolt and bashed his forehead against something hard. He reached forward to rub his head and felt a strange sensation like he was moving. He opened his eyes and stared at the ceiling—only it was really close—about an inch from his nose.

"Look," a voice called out. "He's awake." Conor rolled to his side and looked down at two people sitting on the couches below. "If you're done napping, you should come down."

"Wha—okay," Conor replied. He felt them watching him as he tried figuring out his current situation. Zero gravity. Weightlessness. It was unexpected, but not something he hadn't experienced before.

Conor rolled backward in the air and placed both feet against the ceiling. He then pushed off sending him back down to the floor. He realized in midflight that he'd probably pushed too hard, because he shot downward with intense velocity. This was new. Exhilarating, but again, unexpected.

"Woah! Slow down," the Jopali boy with blond hair exclaimed. The floor came fast, and Conor braced with his extended arms, unable to roll over to his feet in time. Rather than crashing against the hard floor, he was surprised to find himself stopped and in a handstand. It was purely unintentional, but it must've looked pretty cool. He then pushed slightly with his fingertips and found himself upright. He gripped the top of the couch to hold stationary, so he didn't float upward again.

Two boys were staring at him from the opposite couch. Next to the kid from Jopal sat another. He looked different. He was wearing a crimson tunic under a black, hooded robe. His hands were tucked deep into the sleeves, and the long hood shrouded most of his face.

Conor turned away from the boys and looked around the room. One of the black spheres was now lying at the foot of his bed, and the other was resting on the bed in the far corner. The bed across from his and behind the boys had been overturned on its side. One end of the blanket was tucked into the bed frame and the other end stretched to the wall forming a makeshift fort like the ones he'd constructed as a young boy.

"He likes it darker than the rest of us," the boy said. Conor nodded. "They turn off the gravity deck whenever they feel like it. Next time you may want to strap down before you sleep. Otherwise, well, you already know what might happen. But you gotta tell me how you did that."

"What?" Conor asked.

"The way you flew down here. And then that sweet handstand."

"I can't fly," Conor corrected him.

"Well, you definitely know how to fall. You did it with . . ."

"Grace," the boy in the hood hissed.

"Indeed. Lots of grace," the Jopali said in agreement.

"Thanks," Conor said. "When I figure it out myself, I'll teach you."

"Like I said, they turn off the gravity sometimes without warning, and we have to adapt. Luckily, they warn us when it's coming back on, so we don't fall on our face. Doesn't look like it'll be a problem for you, though."

Conor shrugged and lifted himself up and over the couch. He took a seat but started to lift. Then he noticed the fair-skinned boy had his one leg tucked under a soft strap keeping him seated. Conor found one under his right leg and tucked himself behind it to stay in place. He then studied the two strangers, who had to be his assigned roommates.

The Jopali boy noticed Conor staring at the cloaked figure seated by his side. "Yeah, he's different. He doesn't have the same issues with gravity as we do. Kinda just decides not to have it affect him."

"What does that mean?" Conor asked.

"He can, I don't know, control things he wants."

The mysterious boy looked up at Conor with blazing green eyes. "I choose to sit."

"All right. Got it." Conor couldn't help but feel awkward in the boy's presence. He was a mix of odd and scary, especially with the glowing green eyes and the striations on his face. "Well, I like the fort you built."

The boy didn't reply. Feeling the unease of the silence, the Jopali boy spoke. "Okay. I'm Byrovi Jilok."

"By—?" Conor tried to clarify the mess of syllables just thrown at him.

"Just call me Byro. This is Keil."

"Uh. Kill?" *Did I hear that right?*

"Yeah, Keil. He's got an easy name to remember," Byro said.

Conor brought his hand up to his face as if scratching an invisible beard while avoiding eye contact with the super-strange, intimidating kid. "But his name is Kill. That's pretty messed up, don't you think, a bit?"

"You say it wrong," Keil whispered. "Listen closer. Keeeeeiiiil."

Conor nodded, but drawing out the sound just made it even creepier. "Okay. Keeeel. I got it. My name is Conor."

"Conor Welcos, right? You're the Commander's son," Byro remarked.

"No. Yeah. Not exactly. My name is Conor Hawk. The Commander sort of adopted me, I guess."

"I'm from the Hati District," Byro offered. Conor nodded, but Byro soon realized it wasn't registering with him. "It's in the south region. One midsize city and lots of jungle fields. You haven't heard of it?"

"Yeah, of course," Conor lied. How soon would it be before these people figured out he didn't know anything about Jopal?

"What about you?" Byro asked.

Conor bit his lip, struggling to remember the name of the area Makon had told him. He couldn't recall, so he tried to be as vague as possible and hoped it would stick. "The central area."

"Well, obviously. That's where the Commander lives. How did you meet him?"

"He just found me. I was alone. Well, I had my dog, too."

"Oh, yeah! That beast is yours. Is it terrifying?"

"Terrifying? No. She's just a puppy."

"That is one gigantic puppy! I want to meet it. Will she try and take my arm off?"

Conor scoffed and shook his head with a chuckle. Keil slowly tucked his legs and began to float up from the couch. The other boys watched him levitate like some enlightened, eerie sage. "What about him?" Conor asked. "Where's he from?"

"I don't know. Let's ask him," Byro said. "Oi, Keil. Where are you from?"

"Everywhere. Nowhere," the little floating monk responded.

Byro slapped his thigh. "See? Exactly. That's exactly why I stopped asking." Keil continued floating until landing softly behind his bed. The blanket then slowly slid over his shelter. "And there he goes. Not much for conversation, that one."

Just then the door fell open, and a little gray creature pounced into the room. He briefly looked around and leaped up high in the anti-gravity atmosphere. He directed his attention solely on the floating tower module as if no one else were around. His arms and legs wrapped around it like a monkey on a suspended tree log, and he scampered up to the top. Conor and Byro exchanged a look of bewilderment and then continued watching as the creature released a latch just below the light dome.

He fiddled with some buttons and coils before yanking out the panel and leaving it dangling. He then pressed his face against the cylinder as he dug his arm deep inside. A face of stern concentration quickly turned to jubilation once he found what he'd been looking for. He pulled his arm out of the device, replaced the panel, punched some buttons, and closed the latch. "All done," he said. "Prepare."

*Prepare for what?* Conor wondered. Then he felt it. He sank down into the confines of the cushioned couch. Gravity had been restored even though the cylinder tower remained high above them. The creature shimmied down to the bottom and then let go, dropping down to the table on his hands and feet like a nimble cat. He then spun around and sat right there in the middle of the glass table.

"Hello," Byro said.

"Hello to you. And hello to you again," he said to his onlookers.

"You know each other?" Byro asked.

"Of course. This is Master Conor. I am—"

"V-Tech, obviously," Byro said, cutting him off. "You made that quite clear."

"V-23," Conor blurted and shrugged. "It's one name I find easy to remember. We met earlier in the market."

"I guess you're our fourth mate," Byro said.

"Truly," V-23 said in his whispery voice. "I requested Master Conor's room." This reminded Conor of Ari's cautionary remark about having a V-Tech shadow. She was spot on.

"What were you doing up there?" Conor asked.

"A secret. The atmospheric towers all have a remote device hidden inside," V-23 said as he turned over his palm displaying a small rectangular piece. "Now we control the lights, gravity, and weather effects."

"Weather effects?"

"Don't ask," Byro inserted. "You'll be grateful not to wake up in a torrential downpour, hurricane winds, or with your bed covered in snow when you get back from evening meal."

"Wow," Conor blurted while looking back up at the tower. He had a newfound respect for the machine's awesomeness.

"V-23, that's your spot over there by me. My name's Byro. Over behind the other bed hiding under the covers is Keil."

The Riostovi hopped off the table and moved toward his side of the room, which consisted merely of a bed and a black sphere on top of it. He plucked the globe off the bed and rolled it between his hands as if inspecting it for imperfections. He then tossed it over his shoulder into the center of the room. It didn't bounce when it landed, but it didn't thud either. "Not mine."

Conor watched the ball plop like a soggy plum, only without the juicy mess. "How do you know?"

"You know," both V-23 and Byro said in unison.

"Go and see," Byro urged. Conor moved from the sofa and bent over to pick up the black sphere. He expected it to weigh a bit more than it did, but it felt like more of a sandbag than a ball. As he handled the sphere, his reflection came to the surface. No, not really his reflection, but rather a motion image of him. He recognized different parts of the day, from the arrival on the Gregor Monolith and his reunion with Titan, to even a view of him flying high past the tower check-in. His flight journey didn't look as impressive as he had hoped it would.

The sphere started to vibrate, and its black color glowed bright white. "What's it doing?"

"Don't worry. It's not dangerous," Byro said. "Just go and set it over there by your bed."

Conor moved to the bedside and cautiously set it down as if it might explode at any moment. He then took several steps back just in case it actually did. The ball stopped vibrating and began to grow and morph. It collapsed in a pool of ooze on the floor, still glowing white.

"Here's the best part," V-23 said as he walked closer to it.

Conor thought to hold him back to keep everyone at a safe distance, but then he realized the little gray alien most likely understood the object much more than he did. All three boys watched in wonder as the ooze climbed up itself taking on a different shape. It was now square with rounded corners. It then folded over on itself like a cresting wave, finishing its metamorphosis into a smooth, reflective trunk complete with a lid.

"Wow," Conor whispered.

"Yes. I always enjoy watching the transformation," V-23 said.

"Cool. From ball to box," Conor said, half amazed at the mystical technology and half unimpressed by it simply becoming just a box.

"No, Master Conor. Not just a box. Go and open it."

Conor shrugged and moved to it, now hoping it was a treasure chest. He reached down to lift the lid but found it locked.

"Use the pulsero," V-23 instructed.

"Pulsero?" Conor asked. V-23 tapped the bracelet on his own wrist. "Oh, right." Conor waved the pulsero across the front of the trunk, and the lid split in half and lifted. Gray mist formed and swirled around both separated tops of the lid. He looked inside the trunk but just saw more fog. It looked empty. "Now what?"

"Now you tell it what you're looking for," V-23 said.

"What I'm looking for?"

"Yeah. What do you want?"

"Okay. I want a snack." The left mist then suddenly displayed a collage of pictures of distinct edible items. Conor didn't recognize most of them, but he assumed they were what the trunk had to offer in terms of snacking. He swiped his finger across the images, and they scrolled up, down, left, and right. He finally recognized something, and his mouth spontaneously watered. He pressed a finger on the image of the halit fruit he remembered tasted like a juicy mango. All the images then disappeared. "Uh. Nothing happened."

"Yes, it did," V-23 said with a smile. "Reach for it."

Conor listened and slowly dug his hand into the fog. He felt around until his palm rested on a round object with rubbery spikes. He grabbed it and pulled it out of the trunk. It was red and white, bizarre looking by any measure, but its sugary goodness was not easily forgotten.

"Ha. ha. Guess you're hungry," Byro said. "You did sleep through last meal."

"Wow," Conor uttered before bending forward to look past the fog. He couldn't see through it, so he knelt down and dug his hand around for what else might be inside. Nothing.

"You won't find anything until you select something else," the tiny V-Tech said as he perched on the top of the couch, watching his every move with gleeful fascination.

"What else is in this thing?"

"Whatever they put into the inventory," Byro answered. "They pre-load it with items we're allowed to have. Weapons and stuff like that are off limits outside of training grounds, so there's nothing like that in there. But clothing and equipment items you'll need for session are all inside. Obviously, some fruit, too."

"Yes, but you can add things," V-23 said. He bounced to the other side of the room and activated his own personal sphere. Once it assumed its trunk form, he waved the pulsero across the front and watched the lid open itself. V-23 then dug a round object from a pouch strapped to the middle of his back. Conor recognized the coveted Nova Bulb he'd purchased earlier in the market to prevent the V-Tech's expulsion to some wasteland or prison.

V-23 dropped the bulb into the mist, and it hovered, suspended in air. The mist encircled it and rotated the object on its center axis as if it were analyzing its schematics. The bulb then fell away and disappeared. V-23 waved his hand at the lid again, causing it to drop, both its slats joining again in the middle.

Conor turned back to his own trunk. "So, anything I buy at the market I can bring back here and this thing will just keep it for me?"

"Yep. It holds a lot of stuff," Byro replied. "In fact, it's heavy now. You won't be able to move it. Good thing you picked a good spot before you activated it. There was one girl here who I heard left it on her bed when she transformed it. It broke the bed and dropped right to the floor. She had to spend the entire session sleeping on the floor like this guy," Byro said as he pointed his thumb over his shoulder toward Keil.

"No lifeforms," Keil offered as if summoned to speak by Byro's mockery.

"Yeah. Don't climb inside it," Byro said with a chuckle.

"Why not?" Conor asked as his curiosity awakened.

"I don't know. I just know you'll never be found again. Ask the V-Tech. It's his people that come up with all this stuff."

On cue, V-23 interjected, "It's simple black hole synthesis application. In its mildest form, of course."

"Of course," Byro said with a shake of his head. "That clears it up. Black hole synthesis. So, we have four black hole boxes in our little room. Nope. Not dangerous at all."

"Infinity Chest. That's what they're called," V-23 offered as he spun around and plopped down on his trunk.

"I like the name," Conor added. "Not so sure I'm comfortable digging around inside it anymore, though."

"Perfectly safe. Um . . . I think," V-23 said as he began to contemplate it more. "No. Yes. It's fine. There's a particle inhibitor allowing for the passage and absorption of one item at a time. It's archaic technology. Perfectly safe."

"How about that one time that boy—" Byro began to ask.

"Nope," V-23 cut off the question. "That was his fault. Stupid boy."

"All right then," Conor said as he closed the lid with a wave of his hand. "Perfectly safe."

Byro craned his neck to the side to eye the gray Riostovi boy. "Whatever you say. I guess they wouldn't want to have anything hazardous around that could potentially harm Federation cadets," he offered with an exaggerated eye roll.

"You'd be surprised," Conor said.

"No. Not really. This is my second session here. I wasn't being serious."

"This is my first session."

"Mine, too," V-23 said. "Actually, am I in session?"

"Why not?" Byro adjusted himself to spread out on the couch. "Keil and I have trained with V-Tech once in a while. You guys aren't very good at combat. Or piloting. Or strategy. Or water traversal."

"I can swim," V-23 blurted, offended by the criticism.

"Great. You can swim. And climb, too. Saw that a few moments ago with the atmospheric tower. The V-Tech are mostly engineers," Byro said, now turning to Conor. "In all fairness, just about all our advanced weaponry and gear comes from them."

"Yes, and it's old. Your people still can't figure out light jumping," V-23 said, still bothered by Byro's assessment of his warfare capabilities.

"Yeah, we have," Byro argued with a furrowed brow.

"No. Jopali just uses the technology we create. You don't understand it."

"What's light jumping?" Conor asked. Bad question. Both boys just looked at him like his head had fallen off. Before V-23 could offer an explanation or Byro could spout a critical jab, the door behind them opened. Byro immediately sat up, and V-23 stood frozen at the sight of the four tall Jopali cadets standing in their doorway.

The first stepped into the room wearing an aura of entitlement. "There you are," he said, pointing directly at Conor with a smirk. "We've been wanting to meet you."

The other one stepped forward, standing next to the first. The two looked like identical clones. "I can already tell we don't like you."

# CHAPTER 15

**Moon of Kol**
**The Cavern**

"Were you able to locate another exit point?" Haviro asked Shila, hoping she could hear him over the bluster of the gambling den. "I couldn't find anything except these nasty walls and ugly faces. I'd hoped you spotted something on your end. Otherwise, it's a race up the staircase of doom and a long trek back to the skiff." He turned around to try to spot her through the haze. "Shila, do you copy? Are you back at the Biru table? Come oooon."

Haviro pushed through the smoke back toward Shila's last position. The heat optic displayed a mass of blue bodies with red-yellow heat signature heads huddled around an object on the floor. As he moved closer, one of the Kravii warriors stepped aside to reveal his partner doubled over on her hands and knees.

He drew his weapon and raised it to fire on Shila's assailants, poised to turn this place into a war zone. Suddenly, he was kicked from behind between the shoulder blades, sending him stumbling into the enemy cluster. His head struck the ribcage of one of the large, armored beasts, causing him to stagger from the blow at his back and the collision in front. Haviro turned and raised his weapon to fire on the aggressor behind him and was surprised to see her flitter down to the ground. Assaulted by a nightmare fairy. Shouldn't be too out of the ordinary in a place like this, but a nimerith sighting was pretty rare. And never a pleasure.

The Kravii warrior seized upon the Elite's hesitation and wrapped a massive arm around his chest, dragging him off balance and swallowing him close to his body. He plucked the firearm from Haviro's right hand and flung it away. He stretched out the Elite's arm, effectively immobilizing his prey. The nimerith strolled closer and grabbed Haviro's jaw with her soft, charcoal-colored hand. "You shouldn't have come here."

Haviro shook his face out of her grasp. "I agree with that. We'll leave."

"No," she said with a smile. "My man is already dealing with your companion down below. You and the girl are mine."

"You obviously don't know who's down there," Haviro said.

"He's already dead."

"You're probably right, someone is definitely dead, but not the one you think."

"You're cute. I want to play with you," the nimerith said with a smirk.

"I don't play very nice, harpy."

"Neither do I," she said as she flashed sharp fangs. She drew closer to his face, her hand pulling it to the side, exposing the side of his neck.

"That's not a good idea," Haviro said as he winced.

"Perhaps not for you," she hissed in his ear. "But I want a taste."

"No, really. I haven't bathed today, and even when I do, I hardly ever wash my neck."

"It's been long since I've tasted Jopali blood."

Haviro cringed and struggled to free himself from the Kravii's grasp. As he fought against the warrior, the pressure on his chest grew, feeling like being pinned under a cargo ship hauling water rock. He felt the nimerith's breath on his neck and sensed the fangs drawing closer.

A camouflaged figure stalked the scene, moving among the crowd unobserved like a haunting ghost, poised to stir up mischief or terror. He snaked between the Kravii warriors with ease and calculated grace, moving into an optimal combative strike position. Trailing the three incognito Jopali Elites from the battle pit and into the bowels of the Cavern had proved simple for the Shadow Walker. It also proved fortuitous. Capturing the Federation's Supreme Commander would bring in some serious V-Coin. Adding two Elites to the bag made things really interesting.

The Walker raised the pulse cannon, directing it toward the incapacitated Elite about to have some blood extracted from his neck. One troubling thing about premium bounties though—dead ones didn't reward so much, and that would be a waste. The Walker sighed, and then pulled the trigger.

A sudden blast cracked through the thumping bass music, and the pressure on Haviro's chest lessened. He immediately seized upon the loosened grip and ducked underneath the massive arm. In one swooping move, he pulled the Vulcan Bo from his waistband, twisted the handle and ducked to the right. The weapon activated upon the simple twist of the handle, and it expanded as it spun rapidly. The coiled end heated with the intensity of oozing lava.

He struck low for the beast's knee, effectively defeating the organic armor and tearing through flesh and bone. The Kravii fell away easier than he'd experienced in past encounters. As the warrior crashed hard to the floor, he noticed the back part of its skull was missing. The wound was cauterized and still smoldering. Only a truly powerful projectile could have defeated the organic armor and caused such a lethal wound. He didn't have much more time for consideration because about eight other Kravii moved in to tear his limbs off. And one demon fairly intent on eating him. Well, biting him at the very least.

Haviro's weapon was now several feet in length, its tip spinning with hot devastation. He twirled it above his head and then around his waist and back up again with practiced expertise. His maneuvers kept the enemy at bay long enough for him to reach down and grab Shila's shoulder. He yanked hard. "Get up! Could really use your help!"

Shila pushed herself to her feet and struggled to regain her bearings. The unseen blow to the back of her head produced dull, throbbing pain, leaving her still uncomfortably dizzy. She stumbled and steadied herself against her partner. She fought to steady the room still spinning around in her head. She managed to pull her Bo and expand it, but rather than set it spinning, she leaned against it like a cane.

"Hey," Haviro shouted as he swung his weapon at a warrior. The Kravii dodged, but the one next to him took a hit in the chest, sending him backward. Though the warriors hadn't brought their *Kralanzas*, they were still armed with wicked cutlery—large, jagged blades appearing as menacing as they were effective. "I can't handle this on my own. Need you to snap to it. Now!" he exclaimed as his Bo deflected a thrust from one of the blades.

Shila shook away the ache and gripped her weapon with both hands. She set her feet and brought it around, up, and down with force on top of another blade aimed for her partner. Haviro felt a tinge of relief as he noticed his defenses were now doubled. But this feeling quickly subsided when he noticed a pack of red-armored guards swarming from openings in the slime walls. His back pressed against Shila's as they watched the Kravii encircle them.

"Whirlwind. I got high!"

"Go!" she said in a trained response.

Their Bos were now expanded to full length, roughly as tall as each stood. Haviro lashed high. Shila went low, her heated coils now spinning. They struck from opposite directions and at different levels. This caused disruption to the enemy's attack and caught several unprepared for the dual attack. Four of them either took blows to their lower extremities or their upper bodies. Others dodged and deflected but took crippling damage to their blades as the coils shredded at the honed metal.

A Kravii broke through their whipping defenses and kicked Haviro in the hip, sending him forward and off balance. This enabled another warrior to land a crushing punch to his face. Haviro dropped to a knee, reeling from the heft of the blow. Shila stepped in front to shield him and intercepted the lethal strikes from the two blades slashing through the smoke toward his head. The fight grew more difficult as the Kravii adapted to their defense tactics.

The young Elite fighter lashed at a warrior encroaching from behind. The Bo struck him squarely in the arm, but with his free hand, the warrior gripped the weapon below the coils and held on. Shila pulled back on her weapon, but the foe's inherent strength proved too much and yanked her off balance. She still managed to dodge a sweeping strike from a second warrior, but her counterstrike kick to the groin had little effect, like a cotton ball thrown against a wall.

"Aiiiiiiwaaaaaa!" A deep-throated yell suddenly carried all across the room. Along with it, red streaks of devastation slashed through the haze like a laser light show. Makon stood atop the floating rotund bar and repeatedly cracked off his firearm into the red guards and Kravii warriors surrounding his soldiers. The flurry of firepower scattered the warriors enough for Shila and Haviro to collect themselves and retreat toward the staircase. The Commander had redirected their attention and now was taking the brunt of their attack.

The Cavern converted into a battlefield. Tables overturned to become ballistic cover from Makon's onslaught and the indiscriminate flame bursts from the guards' fire lances. Uninvolved bystanders plowed for the staircase like a stampede of startled wocoks. The music still thumped, a backdrop to the gunfire, but no one paid it any mind except for one. The gunslinger on the bar-top heard it, using it to fuel his adrenaline. None were close enough to him to notice he moved to the rhythm, or see the smile creased on his lips.

"Woah," Makon blurted with a grin as he spotted three guards hurrying toward his position. Their lances activated in unison, unleashing a massive fireball directly at him. Makon shifted, crouched, and leaped high toward the ceiling just before the flames scorched the entire bar.

The guards watched the rogue launch into the smoke like a rocket. They lost him in the heavy haze that grew thicker as it climbed to higher elevation. They waited with fixed anxiety for him to come back down.

Meanwhile, the other Elites sneaked to the stairway, but stopped short when they noticed a blockade of Kravii intent on thwarting their escape. One of them spotted the escapees, signaling them out with a clawed finger. Haviro grabbed Shila's arm and pulled her to retreat back into the Cavern. They hugged the near wall to eliminate angles of attack. The Kravii pressed forward with malicious intent until cornering them with their backs against the far wall. Haviro and Shila glanced at one another and simultaneously raised their Vulcan Bos. Ten fierce Kravii warriors against two Elites. Neither of them had faced so many in hand-to-hand combat without the rest of the squad. One of them had never even faced a Kravii outside of simulations.

"One more round," Haviro shouted. "Let's make sure they remember it." He twisted the center causing a second coil at the opposite end to ignite and spin. Things were about to get real messy.

"Rise!" Shila shouted with fury on her face, her hands twisting the raised Bo with a fierce grip.

"As one!" they exclaimed, shouting down fear and debilitating anxiety.

The Kravii snarled, baring sharp teeth along with their lethal swords and density axes. They charged forward with ravenous intent. The gap between them and their trapped prey closed fast, but before they could reach them, the smoke above them parted, swirling around the legs of an organic missile. It toppled once in midair before crashing into their path. Coat flaps fell to the sides of the wearer as he crouched and slowly rose.

"Hello," Makon said as he stretched his arms out wide. "Let's have some fun." The initial shock from the Commander's bizarre arrival faded, and the Kravii moved to punish the newest enemy. Only one of the Kravii warriors realized what was about to happen. He recognized what, or more specifically, who they were dealing with now. Before he could warn his troops, the onslaught had already begun.

Makon dodged the first two arching strikes, one from an axe and the other a blade. He countered with punches and kicks to both warriors, their organic armor cracking under the ferocity of his blows. He spun and twisted like a cyclone as he pushed through them with swift precision—his blows causing damage and disorientation.

His technique embodied art, the movement so swift it appeared that the others were moving in water, and his power sounded with each crunch of armor and bone. Five warriors were already incapacitated or had been flung a healthy distance away before the two other Elites could join in the fray. Makon set upon his targets, leaving Haviro's and Shila's Bos for efficient cleanup.

One of the Kravii thought for sure he marked his victim for death as he brought his powerful axe down on the unsuspecting enemy's head. Makon was turned away, busily delivering multiple strikes to a warrior's throat and upper torso. But the warrior was wrong.

Makon suspected the impending strike. He made this clear when he reached up and caught the axe blade in his hand. Shock rippled through his body as by its design. The density weapon should have pulverized the entirety of his opponent's arm; instead, his victim savagely yanked it out of his hands and tossed it away like a child's toy.

Makon turned to him with fire in his eyes. The best option would have been to flee at that moment, but the Kravii didn't have that instinctual option. Instead, he lunged at the Commander with both claws. What happened next, the warrior didn't know. He found himself on his back, his right arm immobile, and teeth crumbling out of his mouth.

The skirmish had lasted only a few moments—17 seconds to be exact. But a congratulatory celebration would have to wait. Additional red guards and a mass of Kravii swarmed down the staircase to join the fight. "I think it's time to go if you guys are ready," Makon said.

"Definitely," Shila replied, winded from the exertion.

"But the stairway is the only exit," Haviro offered. "The only way out is up, and that looks like one hell of a challenge coming down it right now." Haviro couldn't count how many warriors stormed forth. It looked like an avalanche of black terror spilling down the steps and onto the Cavern floor.

"Yes, up is out. But not that way." Makon grabbed Haviro's Bo and stretched it out to the wall. He dragged the hot coils against the oozing black entanglement of vines. The walls screeched and tore away, peeling back to reveal the rock underneath. Makon stopped the sweep when he found the vertical cracks of a hidden door. "There it is. These walls are nasty, but they don't appreciate heat."

Makon handed Haviro back his weapon and then kicked forward into the carved rock. It crumpled in on itself, revealing an opening with a very tall ladder. "Go!"

Haviro ducked inside first. He reached the ladder and collapsed the Bo. He started to climb and then paused to look back at Shila and the Commander. "Let's go!"

"Go on," Makon said to the new Elite.

"What about you?" Shila asked.

"I'll lead them away and join you at the top."

"How?"

Makon smiled.

"Here, take my Bo," she said, offering up her weapon.

"Where's the fun in that? Keep it." Makon watched Shila step through the wall and drew his firearm. He began firing into the sea of Kravii as he moved away from their exit, deeper into the room. Blue Lanza blasts now answered his own firepower. "Easy, now," Makon blurted before diving behind the Biru benches. This batch of warriors had brought out the big guns and had come ready for a firefight.

**The Academy**
**Residential District**

Two sets of identical Jopali twins, a male pair and a female pair, now faced off with Conor, Byro, and V-23. Conor noticed the look of worry etched on his roommates' faces. They stood taller and visibly stronger than he and his new mates. Judging by V-23's retreat to his bed, this wasn't about to be a pleasant interaction.

"How'd you get in here?" Byro asked. One of the twins stretched out his finger, pointed to him, and then brought it slowly to his lips.

"We're not here to talk to *you*," the other twin said.

The female twins stepped around and stood behind the curved sofas, each one resting their left hand on top as if their entry had been rehearsed. They had long black hair pulled back from square-jawed faces, and their tunics stretched over an athletic build. "We've come to talk to the Commander's new son," they said in unison. At that point, Conor didn't know if they were twins, clones, or robots.

The first one in the room crossed over closer to Conor, sizing him up. He was wearing the black tunic laced with blue and gold like the other three. He and his clone had buzz-cuts and dark eyes, their forms large and imposing. "The Commander does not know how to pick 'em," he said with a shake of his head.

"The girl is okay," the other twin said.

"Tiera's not bad. Makes sense at least. But this one is a runt." He leaned closer into Conor. "You don't belong here." Conor stared up at him with as much courage as he could muster. He knew better than to look away. That's what this guy wanted. Of course, Conor couldn't help but agree with him—that he didn't belong there. The guy had no idea how right he was about that.

"You should go home," the female twins interjected.

"Yes, little boy, you should really consider it. I mean—look at you. So out of place here. You're going to get hurt in training."

"He won't survive," the female twins chimed.

"No, definitely not. Won't your father be sad to hear of your death?" The mention of Conor's father caused anger to stir. It showed on his face. "Ooooh. You're mad now. Nice." The twin turned away and looked down at the black trunk. "No faction yet, I see. Oh, well. Whichever you're assigned, we'll make sure you enjoy yourself."

He walked around in a wide circle, studying the rest of the room, mostly concentrating on the Infinity Chests. "You are with us," he said, pointing to Byro. "I don't care who you are—don't bother telling me. Just remember your allegiance. As for the two runts without an alliance, well, let's just hope you're assigned the victorious blue."

His twin stepped forward. "It's better to serve . . ."

"Than be destroyed," all four declared.

"You've made your introductions," a raspy voice sounded from the corner as Keil ascended from under his makeshift fort. "It's now time for you to leave."

"We have no quarrel with you, Mystian," one of the twins blurted.

"Your interruption has stirred a quarrel," Keil hissed as he now hovered cross-legged, suspended in air. The shadow-faced, hooded boy floated. At first, Conor thought the gravity had been deactivated, but he checked and found his legs still planted on the ground. No, the creepy alien was definitely floating. If Conor had known the meaning of "surreal," he would have described it as such. So, he went with "creepy." The best part was that the clones didn't like it, either.

"If you don't wish to leave on your own, I can make you," Keil whispered, now suspended in the air directly above the four intruders. They swallowed the threat with distaste, turned, and calmly left the room without another sound. When the door shut, Conor wasn't sure if the true threat had just left, or if it was tucking itself back down to bed. Either way, he felt a sense of relief that the bully twins had gone.

Byro breathed a deep sigh. "Didn't expect that. I hate those guys."

"What was that all about?" Conor asked.

"The Collective. That's what they call themselves. They dominate, causing the blue faction to win every competition year. They're like bred for combat or something since they were able to walk. During their first two years, they were the best at everything from piloting and combat to scaling, tactics, and freefall."

"At least they're on your side," Conor said.

"I don't think so. They're only on their own side. Who knows? You might be in their faction, too."

"Hope not."

"Are you sure?" Byro asked. "I mean, it's better to serve than . . . "

"Be destroyed," Conor and Byro said together in a mocking tone. They laughed. Even a slight snicker sneaked out from Keil.

"What was that all about anyway?" Conor asked.

"They don't like you," Byro replied.

"Yeah. I got that part. But why?"

"They don't like the Supreme Commander. Since you're his son, that hate transfers, I guess."

"Why don't they like him? Everyone else does."

Byro shrugged. "On that fantastic note, let's close out this day and get some sleep. First training starts in the morning, and first round is always brutal." Byro retired to his bed. "V-Tech, could you put out the light?"

V-23 swiped his remote, and the room darkened. Conor sat on the side of his bed, and, after a few moments, lay back. His thoughts raced. This place was just too plain weird. *Round one tomorrow. Brutal?* What was he doing here? Minutes spun away as he reflected on the day's adventures and curiosities.

He finally sat up on his elbow, deciding to make the most of the situation. "I don't suppose that trunk has a pillow in it, does it?"

### Moon of Kol
### The Cavern

Haviro slid open the hatch and took a quick peek at the surface above. He peered down the same alley they'd walked down earlier. He watched the last of a group of Kravii entering the

Cavern through the main portal. "Hey, it's all clear," he said as he extended a hand to Shila, pulling her up to him. Once they both exited, he kicked the hatch shut.

"What about the Commander?" Shila asked.

"Looks like they didn't spot us. Let's get back to the ship and straight out of here," Haviro said, surveying the area and effectively ignoring her question.

"The Commander," she repeated a little louder, to make sure he heard her.

"What?" Haviro asked, clearly distracted by his scan of their position, looking for incoming threats.

"Commander Welcos. We can't just leave him."

"Oh, yeah. He's fine."

"What are you talking about? There's a whole Kravii army down there by now."

"He'll be fine. Just hope he hurries. Let's go."

"We can't leave!"

"Yes, we can. And we will. Otherwise, he'll be annoyed that we waited." Haviro turned and took a few hurried steps before stopping, realizing Shila hadn't followed. As he turned to look back, the black paneled glass exploded outward from the main entrance. A Kravii warrior took the brunt of the impact with his head and shoulder before coming to rest against the alley's opposite wall. Several other warriors fell into the alley as the Commander stepped through the opening. He glanced left and then right before running toward his Elite companions.

Makon slowed as he approached but didn't stop. "Why are you waiting around?"

Haviro gave Shila a scolding glance. "See?"

"You may want to hurry up," Makon said as he picked up his pace. "There's a lot of bad guys right behind me." The Elites raced away down the alley to the main street. Shila glanced back at the Cavern entrance and saw the enemy spilling out in hot pursuit. She pulled her weapon and fired as she ran, hoping to slow them a bit.

They didn't stay on the main strip very long. Makon led the way, taking them through shops and side streets in an effort to divide the enemy force and make it harder to track their escape. Fortunately, a foot chase through the streets wasn't an uncommon occurrence in this town. Most people just took a step out of the way, not wanting to have any part in the skirmish.

"You know where you're going?" Haviro yelled. He had become sufficiently disoriented in their twisting escape and wasn't sure if they were headed to the landing pad or back to the heart of the Kravii hideout.

"Of course, I do," Makon answered as they turned a corner and ran right up to a walled building. "Unless something changed." He touched the wall with his palm. "Hmmm. Crap. This is new." All three turned around and faced the three Kravii who'd managed to keep up with them.

Haviro moved toward the enemy and extended his Bo. "Claws out! I'll draw their attention."

Makon smiled and slapped his hand on Haviro's shoulder, causing him to stop. "Probably not the best option," he said just as more warriors streamed into the alley behind the first three.

"I agree. We need another option."

"You had it right. Claws out. We go up," Makon said as he reached to the left side of his belt and pulled a black device over the knuckles of his left hand. He extended his arm up and squeezed the pad now in his palm. Four rigid darts shot out from the knuckles, each carrying a thin tail of crystallized thread. Three of the four darts dug into the side of the polished rock at the top. He never seemed to get a perfect four embeddings, but he only needed one to stick, and three out of four wasn't anything to complain about.

Shila and Haviro followed suit, each extending their claws to mirror the Commander. Makon squeezed his palm again and instantly lifted high and fast as the crystal thread retracted. They all reached the summit as crackling Lanza bolts peppered the area of their landing. They didn't wait around for a lucky hit and continued their race through the smuggler town, this time from rooftop to rooftop.

They hurdled obstacles and leaped over small gaps between the buildings, avoiding the raging gunfire from below. A clawed hand grabbed Haviro's foot from below as he traversed from one building to the next. He stumbled and fell forward before self-correcting into a dive roll. Warriors now scaled the walls to pursue them along the rooftops, while others followed along the street.

They managed to fight them off and keep the pace. Makon cut left along one building and then jumped up to the last rooftop. As he crossed over the border, he noticed they'd reached the end of the row. He looked over the edge and then stepped back just as Shila and Haviro joined him. "We have a problem."

"Long way down? We've done worse," Haviro said as he leaned forward to gauge the extent of the drop. "Oh. That is a problem," he muttered as he reassessed the drop. The distance to the ground didn't cause concern, but, rather, the battalion of Kravii warriors amassed below. A nearby troop carrier had deployed to the area and reinforced the local contingent with sufficient warriors to attack a moderately fortified Federation base.

Haviro stepped back from the edge to avoid taking a charge bolt to the underside of his chin. "I think we need to turn back." Makon looked up at him from his crouched position and flicked his thumb over his shoulder. Shila and Haviro looked behind them and saw roughly twenty Kravii savages clambering up the buildings and otherwise racing toward them. "We're trapped."

"I hate this place," Shila said. "Never coming back here." She began firing at the rooftop aggressors.

"Commander, what's your plan?" Haviro yelled.

Makon glanced over his shoulder to judge the distance between them and the enemy. Then he proned out on his stomach. "I think we should all get down."

"What?!" Haviro yelled as he rapidly fired his sidearm.

"Yeah. Hit the ground. I know you looked down, but I think you failed to look up." Haviro glanced upward and immediately dropped to his belly.

"Shila! Incoming! Take cover!" Haviro shouted over her blaster fire and the Kravii exchange.

The Gregor Monolith now breached the clouds, hovering over the town like an omen of cataclysmic destruction. It released a barrage of heavy cannon fire, showering the rooftop from high above. The Kravii armor was no match for the heft of the charges. Warriors catapulted from their positions with tremendous and devastating force. Explosions riddled the rooftops as the warriors were either peeled apart like husks of corn or flung from the buildings. The lucky ones took cover from the firestorm but altogether gave up their pursuit of the Elites. Self-preservation now took precedence.

Makon pushed up to a crouched position, seeing that most of their pursuers had been eliminated. He then pointed to the ground below, signaling for the battalion to be targeted next. Before the Kravii could redirect their artillery on the airborne threat, the Monolith unleashed two capsule bombs. They moved slower than torpedoes, but they produced a greater area of impact. Makon knew their design and had seen their effect enough times to know what was about to happen. He just hoped the bomb radius wouldn't reach their position.

The orbs crackled with blue flames as they sped toward the Kravii military. Warriors scattered, attempting to scurry out of the death zone, but the bombs touched down with a splash of azure fire. The anti-personnel ordnance generated minimal concussion bursts, but the death toll proved significant. The flames carried in waves, a ripple effect, consuming all life within reach. They licked up the side of the building, nearly reaching the three crouching Elite.

Once the blast heat subsided, Makon stood up and leaned over the edge to risk a glance. As he'd hoped and predicted, the Monolith had cleared away the Kravii force. The heavy weapons and troop carrier still remained, but the orbs had left o one to operate any of it.

"That there's a good woman," Makon uttered, picturing Valitat at the helm as he saluted upward to the looming flagship.

"I second that," Haviro replied.

"I think it's time we got off his moon," Shila muttered.

# CHAPTER 16

**The Academy**
**The Forge**

With only a small bowl of exotic fruit in his belly, Conor stepped through the portal with Byro and Keil into the world designed specifically for defensive tactics, combat enhancement, and all-around physical training. A gladiator's paradise.

A ring rested at the near center, large enough to hold horse races, but without visible stands or high walls. A stretched oval stood out from the rest of the space by its distinctive flooring—black checkered panels encircled with a ring of red. Off to the left, he recognized a shooting range. A massive building with transparent walls and rows of targets lined up declared its purpose. As they walked by, Conor spotted two shooters inside engaging multiple targets, both moving and static. It looked like they were holding pistols, but he couldn't hear any sounds of gunfire ringing from outside.

"This place is called the Hero's Forge," Byro offered to his awestruck companion. "We come here twice a day at a minimum, but it's always available and open to us. It's typically for Combatives, range, strength, and agility performance."

Several recruits scurried past them as they traversed the expanse between the arena and the range. They were dressed in the similar athletic blue-and-black uniforms as he and Byro. The fabric was light and stretchy, with a fancy Federation haloed-star logo imprinted on the left shoulder. Most of the cadets wore the pants and long-sleeved version like him, though others chose short-sleeved or sleeveless tops. Conor didn't mind blending in with the other cadets for once. Besides, the uniform felt remarkably comfortable.

Byro then pointed to a globe on the left. "That's what we call the Jump Room. Acrobatics and flexibility. You'll like that one. Except when they mess with the gravity while you're in mid-flip." He instinctively rubbed the back of his neck and then pointed off in the distance to their right. Conor couldn't make out what it was exactly, but it looked like rows of benches and odd-shaped machines. Each of the corners had a sunken ring with a post in the center large enough for several people. "That across the way is strength enhancement and endurance. There is never a time when you don't see at least two of the Collective exerting themselves over there."

"What are these?" Conor asked as they walked through three rows of round huts with flat rooftops.

"Private training sessions. I've never used one, but they're probably good for working on techniques away from the group." They continued on into a wide area the size of a football field. It seemed more than just open space because the ground beneath Conor's feet became flexible, like rubber padding. "Our combined defensive tactics are done here. This is where you learn how to handle bullies."

"Or Kravii hostiles intent on tearing your limbs off," Keil blurted.

Byro furrowed his brow and stared at the short, cloaked figure to his right. "Are you serious? I'm trying not to freak the guy out his first morning here."

"Second," Conor corrected.

"First. Second. Whatever," Byro said.

"It is true," Keil whispered.

"Yeah, okay. Sure. All this is to prevent our gruesome death at the hands of an enemy with an untiring intent on killing us, drinking our blood, making us slaves, and destroying our planets. Does that make you happy?"

"The Kravii don't drink our blood," Keil uttered.

"Good to know. Thanks. How about you? Do your people drink blood?" Byro looked into the green eyes staring up at him from underneath the hood. Keil's smirk set both the boys at unease before he turned away. "I reaaaally don't know about you. Do me a favor and stay under your bed-fort when the lights go out, okay?"

"What is that?" Conor asked, looking off n the distance.

"That is why we're here. It's called the Ascension, but we nicknamed it Freefall, since that's what we all end up doing. It's a test course designed to push you to your limit until it breaks you."

Conor turned his attention to the crowd of recruits gathered at the start of what looked like a winding obstacle course that carried up hundreds of feet into the air. Various platforms hovered above, with ropes to climb, walls to scale, moving objects to dodge, and giant chasms to traverse. It looked like a medieval boobytrapped labyrinth had been upgraded with gravity-defying, space-age technology and thrown up into the sky.

"That thing looks crazy, but I was referring to the volcano way over there. What's that?" A towering, black mountain rested in the distance, completely out of place with its billowing smoke and trickling lava trails.

"It's a volcano," Byro said.

"Really?"

"Yeah. It's to work general traversal, climbing, and dead-fall prevention. You'll see it up close soon enough."

"Is that real lava?"

"No, it's candy drizzle. Of course, it's real."

"Oh."

"Don't worry about it. Let's get over to the Freefall. We don't want to be late."

The boys made it to the obstacle course's entrance just as a female instructor in a blue tunic elevated above the group. "Good morning, recruits. To those of you who are new to the Academy, this is the Forge."

"'Hero's Forge' is better. I added the 'hero' part. That's on me," Byro whispered, leaning into Conor.

"The Ascension is the culmination of all your effort, skill, and resilience," the instructor continued. "To this time, no one has bested the path and claimed its prize," she said, now pointing up. Conor trailed his eyes from her fingertip to the pinnacle of the obstacle course. Hovering above all at the very top, a golden light shimmered. Conor couldn't make out whether it was an object or just a light, but it looked like a slice of the sun had been cut away and set on a platter.

"You will each try today—a pretest. You will then test again on the last of the year. In between, you are encouraged to try and try again. Your progress will be measured based upon your advancement in its stages. Circuits One, Two, and Three, do not be troubled. We will catch you. Circuits Four and Five, as always, catch yourselves."

Conor didn't know for sure what the instructor meant, but in the moment, he felt relieved to not be a Fourth or Fifth-Circuit recruit. How were they expected to catch themselves?

"Everyone must go, so who will be first?" More hands raised high than Conor expected. His arms stayed tucked at his side. "Yes, we have a number of brave souls here," the instructor said as she surveyed the thirty recruits under her. "You," she said as she pointed to the first chosen.

A familiar face pushed through the crowd and pounced up the stairway leading to the course's archway entrance. Seeing

Tiera again caught him by surprise. It felt like forever since he'd seen her, even though it'd been less than a day—a long day, though.

He wasn't shocked she'd volunteered to go first. This type of thing *was* her sort of thing. She wore the same form-fitting jumpsuit as everyone else with her hair tucked back and pinned tight. She meant business. The look of intensity on her face reiterated this as she raised her arm to signal her readiness.

"Tiera Welcos," the instructor said. "We have come to expect great things from you. You may begin."

Tiera stepped through the archway and dashed up the first ramp taking her upwards. She was already twenty feet above the ground when she hit the first obstacle—a series of walls of varied heights. She scaled all five of them with ease and style before coming to the edge.

She then came to a series of twisted ropes that moved with the slow and steady rhythm of a serpent moving along a tree branch. She timed her jump with the pace of the rotation and caught the rope at its crest. She snagged it with extended hands and then traversed it to the end with the finesse of a spider monkey. Tiera waited for the next rope to come within reach and then flipped to it with acrobatic grace. As the end of her new rope began to crest and loop around on itself, she released her legs and swung them vigorously. The momentum from her leap carried her to the next twisting rope as it corkscrewed through the air. She climbed up to the next platform without even breaking a sweat.

She paused for a moment to assess the next challenge. Spinning discs moved back and forth in a haphazard manner. There might have been a pattern, but Conor couldn't decipher it from down below.

Tiera backed up a step and then raced forward as a disc came spinning toward her. She jumped, twisted in a front flip, and landed on its center in a crouch. "Now she's just showing off," one recruit spouted as cheers erupted. She jumped to the next available disc when it came from the left and then carried upwards. Before riding it back down on its continuous loop, Tiera leaped down to the next one.

The instructor turned away from the aerial display and offered, "There is more than one way to cross, and the rotational pathways of the discs are never the same for a recruit. If you make it, consider it an accomplishment in itself, as you may fail the very next time."

Suspense laced the air as they watched Tiera continue across the void. She discarded the theatrics as she began to tire and concentrated her focus to an extreme. The last three discs, roughly the size of standard tires, moved in a circle around a vertical and horizontal axis. She focused on one, watching it closely as it neared the position she needed. She jumped before it arrived, anticipating the timing for it to be exactly where she hoped. She landed with a thud, grabbing the disc at the edges and hugging it with her chest. She didn't pull herself up, but rather gripped tight on the edges because she recalled what happened next. Without warning, the disc turned upside down, leaving its rider hanging as it continued its circular journey. It then moved upwards on its y-axis. Tiera waited and began to swing her legs.

When she reached the apex of the disc's path, she swung forward, releasing her grip before it could carry her down again. The momentum of her swing, aided by the disc's movement, propelled her forward. She doubled backward into another flip and landed on the waiting platform. The crowd erupted in cheers and laughter. Tiera greeted them with a quick wave of her hand.

"Impressive, Tiera," the instructor bellowed into the voice amplifier. "She's already achieved farther than most."

"I've never gotten past that part," Byro leaned in and said to Conor. "I don't feel bad, though—neither do most cadets."

"She's good," Conor said.

"That's an understatement," Byro replied as he watched Tiera grab the rope hanging in front of her. There appeared to be a great chasm between her current platform and the next one. Conor wondered if the rope would be enough to swing across. But rather than use it to swing to the next level, Tiera began to climb.

She reached its suspension point aft r a minute of straight climbing and then stretched her arms down between her legs, now climbing down it while inverted. Conor found this bizarre until he noticed the bottom of the rope begin to curl upwards toward the next platform. It attached itself, leaving a rope bridge for the climber. Clearly, knowing the course dynamics and terrain held its advantages.

Tiera made it to the surface, a tower of separated discs spinning in opposite directions. She took a moment to catch her breath before reaching up to grab the disc above her. Immediately, her feet spun away, leaving her dangling by her fingertips. Possessing the agility and poise of a skilled gymnast, the girl made it look easy. She climbed from one disc to the next. However, exhaustion reared its menacing charms, and she lost her grip on the third disc. The stumble nearly flung her away to her death, or whatever was promised to catch her.

After a number of gasps from the other recruits, Tiera brought her left hand back to the surface and pulled herself up. A group of her friends cheered. Conor looked over and spotted Ari staring up at the Jopali acrobat. He smiled at seeing another familiar face and then also found himself cheering on Tiera as she reached the top of the disc tower.

"Fatigue begins to set in and becomes another obstacle to conquer," the instructor noted.

A spiral of eight columns now lay in front of the nimble girl. The pathway seemed impossible. The course's difficulty increased the higher a cadet traversed. It also became harder to determine the challenges the farther away she climbed.

To the spectators, the columns appeared spaced unevenly apart, with each one higher than the next. But from below, they couldn't see that they also vibrated. Tiera jumped to the first one and landed on her feet, feeling the quake rattle her teeth. The platform left barely enough room for both her feet, and the shaking didn't help things. She then jumped to the next one and caught the rim, pulling herself up. The muscles in her arms and back burned. She tried to rub out the ache and stretch a bit, but she had to work to maintain her balance on the shaking column. It wasn't designed to be a rest spot.

She sized up the next leap and crouched to give her legs the spring they needed. She took a deep breath and sprung forward. The crowd gasped as she caught the lip of the column with her fingertips but couldn't manage to hold it.

Tiera's eyes closed in exhausted defeat as she fell backward.

**Sector 6**
**Gregor Monolith**

"You barely made it out of there in one piece and all you have to complain about is that your claw didn't work as well as you wanted."

"Well, yeah, Vice Commander. That is a concern, of course. I can't seem to get more than three, sometimes two of the stupid grapples to grip," Makon said.

"It seems to have worked well enough," Valitat Bithos replied.

"I just want to be able to rely on the gear in a pinch." Makon sat down on the edge of his bed in the Monolith's

Commander's quarters, turning the lightweight metallic object over in his hands.

Valitat leaned against the doorway and crossed her arms. "I'm curious," she said as she scanned the simple elegance of his room.

"No, you're not. Go on."

"Do you really care about that claw contraption?" She now moved into the room and scanned the picture screen projecting from the wall she'd seen dozens of times before. One of the Supreme Commander standing with the Elders. Another with the crew at the time of the Monolith's first flight. Several depicted his beloved Tiera—all action shots. One with Makon wearing a huge smile alongside a beautiful woman. Valitat then turned away and moved to the weapons case. "I notice you don't have any depictions of your son," she said as her finger lightly traced the edge of the Jopali ceremonial blade resting in its display case, a coveted piece seldom issued but for extreme acts of bravery on the field of battle.

"My son?" Makon asked.

Valitat replied with only a slight cant of her head.

"Oh, yeah. My newly adopted. You're right. I need to get something up there. I should have Wilda send one over. Maybe one of him during Combatives."

"Wilda. Right," Valitat uttered.

"I just haven't had much time due to the attack and all. Came on quite sudden. Don't think I've spent longer than a few conversations with him. Just threw the boy right into the fight, you know."

"Was that wise? The Academy could be bad."

"How so?" Makon asked.

"Cadets have been seriously injured. Even died."

Makon chuckled. "Not him," Makon uttered with a grin.

"Why not?"

"You were there when we picked him up. He isn't from around here."

"What does that matter? We're at war, and that place trains them by subjecting them to the elements and dangers of it."

"Let's just say I know him better than you do. Conor's going to do some amazing things."

"Hope you're right. You've done well with Tiera. But didn't you just say you haven't gotten to spend much time with him? So, how do you know him so well?"

"I just know. Now how about you get back to asking your first question about what makes you curious?" Valitat smiled. Makon set down the claw and lay back on his bed. He closed his eyes. "Go ahead. I'm listening. Just a little tired."

"I'm curious as to why you're so concerned about that claw grapple. I mean, do you even really need it?"

"It helps."

"Yes, but I know you're not afraid of falling."

"Nope. But I don't want any of my men to fall, either. Men and women," Makon corrected himself. He then sat up and turned to her with a newfound energy. "Shila was truly awesome today! I'm really proud of her. Tough girl. Sharp, too."

"I'm happy to hear she held her own."

"She did much better than that," he said as his head found the pillow again. He closed his eyes and muttered, "I bet you're getting sick of me always being right."

"Kinda," Valitat whispered. "I'll leave you to your nap. After all, you're going to need it since I believe you decided to send us deeper into the Vesputi for Hadak-5, of all places."

"I'll explain later. When we get there," Makon said. Valitat moved to the doorway. "Oh, and Vice Commander." She paused without turning. "Thank you for saving our butts today. It wasn't the first time."

"Definitely not the last, either," she muttered as she turned into the corridor.

**The Academy**
**The Forge**

Conor moved over to Tiera and Ari as they stood with several other companions. Most of the other recruits had tried and failed at the Freefall by this time, so Conor hoped he'd find her less angry than after she had dropped. Byro tailed behind him.

"You did pretty good up there," Conor offered. "Got farther than most everyone except for some of the older students . . . er, cadets." She looked at him with sharp, cold eyes. Crap. Still in a bad mood.

"I can do better. Just couldn't get that last column. I'll get it, though."

"You were fantastic up there," Byro spouted. "Very impressive to watch. Don't worry. I'm sure you'll get it next time."

"Did better than you," she replied. "You didn't even make it past the ropes."

Byro looked like he'd been slapped in the face. "Uh, yeah, I know. I was just saying—I'm giving you a compliment. And well, my shoulder's sore so, you know, I was climbing with a handicap."

Just then a recruit screamed as he fell off a rotating disc. Conor looked up as the boy toppled to the ground for a moment. The boy's pulsero sparked, and the air around him solidified into pliable gel. It then stretched to the ground, sending him downward as if he'd been shot down a slick playground slide—a really tall one made of silicone.

"I hate that part," Tiera said.

"Really?" Byro asked. "It's the best part. The rest is crazy hard work."

"I love the slide," Ari chimed. Her input eased the tension a bit. "I'm terrible at this thing. Give me a staff or a pulse rifle and I'm good to go. But ask me to jump around on weird spinning and turny things, and I'm done."

"You didn't even make it as far as Byro and some of the first years," Tiera playfully mocked.

"Fine with me," Ari replied with a wry smile. "No sense in wearing myself out before Combatives."

"Sure. Sure."

"I'll let you have the glory of conquering the Freefall. Unless someone else beats you to it first," Ari said.

"Not likely," Tiera replied.

"I don't know about that. There are some pretty agile Fifth-Circuits. And don't forget the Collective."

"They all fell, too."

"Maybe they just needed a practice round, like you," Ari offered.

"Why are you trying to get me mad?"

"I'm not. I'm just stating facts. And how about this guy?" Ari asked while putting her hand on Conor's shoulder. "He hasn't gone yet."

"That's true," Byro chimed in. "Saved the best for last."

"Me? No, I really don't want to do it. Probably fall off the platform right when I get there."

"Nah. You'll do great. I know it. Get up there," Ari urged, trying to spark the boy's confidence.

"Everyone has to try," Tiera added.

Conor looked up as one of the last Fifth-Circuit recruits smashed face-first into a disc he struggled to land on. He now flopped around like a rag in the wind falling from high above. Conor's eyes darted from the tumbling recruit to the instructor, seeing if he'd spot a hint of concern in her demeanor. Her fingers moved to the panel in front of her, but she hesitated, watching the cadet plummet without batting an eye.

The cadet finally righted himself and dug both hands under his opposite armpits. He then thrust out, and his uniform top changed. As he extended his arms outward both sleeves now held a light material from his armpit to his wrist. They looked like translucent wings that allowed him to glide downward with hardly an ounce of grace. It might've been graceful had he been better trained with the wings and less disoriented from the faceplant moments before.

The instructor's hand moved away from the panel, and she watched along with everyone else as the older boy touched down with his feet in a full run. His legs couldn't keep up with the momentum, and he ended up falling and sliding on his belly. He stood up with an embarrassed smile, perfectly content to still be alive.

"Good enough, Cadet. Welcome back," the instructor said without feeling. She tapped the panel once to view a short list of the remaining recruits. "Looks like we have one more First-Circuit, two Fours, and a Five. Make sure your suits are fixed because you'll regret it if you don't." She tapped the panel, and the air above them shimmered for an instant. "Let's have our last First-Circuit come up. Conor Hawk. Ascend."

Conor looked first at Byro and then Ari. Their smiles provided flimsy encouragement. He hoped for a second they might change their minds and not make him go. There was no way he'd be able to do this thing. He could hear the churning of the daunting ropes and a dull buzz emitting from the spinning discs. It didn't help to calm his agitated nerves.

He rubbed his hands together and took a deep breath before receiving an encouraging push from Tiera. A literal push. "Go on. Get to it," she said as she planted her palm on the back of Conor's shoulder, nudging him forward. He didn't stumble or look back. With everyone staring at him, he had no choice but to continue up the ramp and through the portal to the start.

He glanced over at the instructor, who checked him with a slight nod. Time to go. Conor took a deep breath and pushed his legs forward past the fear. Just a quick jog up the ramp and onto the first platform for the multi-wall climb. He stood at the base of the first wall. It was about chest high and didn't look too tough. After all, the other recruits didn't seem to have much trouble with it. His thoughts then raced forward to the rope churn and the disc spin. Those would be much more difficult. How did he plan to get past those obstacles?

He refocused. One thing at a time. Get over the walls first and then worry about the ropes and the other stuff. He reached up and finally grabbed the top of the first wall. Something odd happened. He felt it move. It moved up. He hurried over the top before it could get any higher and then dropped to the other side. He hadn't noticed before that the walls moved upward. Guess the easy obstacle wasn't as easy as he'd hoped.

He raced to the next wall and jumped to grab it before it went higher and out of reach. Pulling himself to the top was quite easy. He swung his legs over one at a time and then lowered himself to drop again to the other side. Not bad. Three more walls to go.

The next wall moved much faster, and he had to move quickly, or else he wouldn't be able to catch the top. It now stretched taller than him, at more than six feet high. A good jump could still get him to catch the top. Conor sprinted forward and planted both feet square. He bent his legs and jumped as high as he could, hoping to catch the top with his fingertips.

He made a solid jump, but with an unexpected result. The momentum of his leap quickly carried him upward, way higher than anticipated. His waist reached above the wall, and his right knee bashed against the rough surface. The collision caused him to topple over it in a flip. He landed hard on the opposite side, smacking his side against the platform floor before bouncing once over the side.

"Aaaaaagh!" he yelled as he accelerated downward, headfirst, down the life-saving silicone slide. He stopped at the bottom and opened his eyes. A gathering of upside-down people stared at him. Some of them snickered. Others just hung their jaws dumbfounded.

"Okay, Cadet Hawk. Two walls," the instructor said over the intercom. "Looks like there's much room for improvement."

Conor wanted to disappear into his shirt. He did worse than he thought he could. Three familiar faces now hung above him. They looked confused. Tiera's face came into full view as she looked straight down at him. "What was that? You only made it over two walls!"

"I can't lie to you, Conor," Ari chimed in with a smile. "That's probably the worst I've ever seen anyone do, but, if it makes any difference, the fall was pretty impressive."

Two hands reached forward and grabbed his shirt by the shoulders. Conor was dragged out of the chute and helped to his feet. Byro then straightened him out with a huge grin. "Man, did you guys see that?! It was awesome!"

"Yep, we saw him crash and burn," Tiera replied.

"Yeah, he did. Spectacularly, I might add. But he nearly jumped clear over the third wall! What were you thinking?"

Confusion still lingered like a mist in Conor's mind. "Uh . . . I banged my knee."

"Yes. Yes, you did. On the top of the freakin' wall! How'd you do that?"

"I just jumped, I guess."

"Whatever. I've never seen that before," Byro said, his words loud with enthusiasm.

"Totally impressive," Tiera said with a sarcastic tone. That answered that. Sarcasm was alive and well even in a faraway galaxy. "What would've been more impressive is if you would've at least gotten over more than two walls."

"Leave him alone. He'll get it. How far did you get on your first try?" Byro asked in defense of his roommate.

"Disc 3," Tiera responded abruptly.

"She's right," Ari added.

"Okay. Well, good for you. Not everyone can train with the Supreme Commander since they could walk. I'm sure that counts for something."

"Whatever you say. Don't be mad because us girls do better than you boys."

"Hey, speak for yourself," Ari chimed in. "I never said I was any good at that thing. I just said I love the slide."

"It was pretty cool," Conor said with a smile. Ari smiled back. Tiera looked at both of them, scoffed, and then walked away. Ari turned to follow. Conor brushed his semi-elastic shirt flat and looked in the direction everyone headed.

"Come on. We have Combatives starting up in a few minutes. Maybe you should pair up with Tiera. I can see she really likes you," Byro said.

"Really? What are you even talking about? You think she actually likes me?" Conor asked with a furrowed brow.

"No. Not in the slightest." There was that sarcasm again. Conor started to follow Byro as he moved to join the crowd, but a heavy hand on his shoulder stopped him short. He then spotted an unexpected face and long hair. "Remember me?"

"Uh . . . yeah. You're the guy who saved me from that thing."

"The Dalex." He nodded. "I'm called Anibal."

"Yeah. Sorry. I've met so many people; I can't remember everyone's name."

"That's expected. Don't forget it this time." That sounded like some kind of warning, so Conor repeated it silently in his head over and over. Anibal was wearing the same black tunic he'd been wearing when they first met. Hopefully he owned more than one, or at least cleaned it often.

"What do you want to talk to me about? I've been keeping out of trouble if that's why you're here."

"That's good. But we both know that'll never last. Trouble seems to orbit you like a satellite."

"Not my fault. Well, sometimes it is, maybe."

Anibal smiled. "I like your honesty." He paused for a moment and looked up at the Ascension as if tracking the path from obstacle to obstacle all the way to the top. "You know what's up there at the top?"

"No clue," Conor said.

"Me, neither."

"You mean, no one's ever gotten to the top?"

"Not that I know of. I'm sure the reward is worth it. Don't you think?"

"I guess. Doesn't look like I'll be the one who finds out."

"You did well up there," Anibal said.

"You obviously weren't here to see it then. I did terrible."

"Oh, I saw."

"I fell."

"Everyone falls. Maybe not as soon as you, but they fall."

"I did notice that."

Anibal looked at Conor and crossed his arms. He studied the recruit for a long while—long enough for Conor to start to feel uncomfortable. A grin then formed wide on his face. "What if I told you, you could reach the top and claim that elusive prize?"

"No way. Impossible," Conor responded.

"You're right. Glad you agree."

"So, you do or don't think I can make it to the end?"

"Master Hawk, it doesn't matter what I think. If you don't believe you can do it, then you can't. No matter how many others say you can, it needs to start and end with you."

"I think I proved today that something like that is beyond me."

"Is that what you think?" Anibal asked, now smirking. "This is going to be fun."

Conor was confused. "Fun? It's not fun. It's crazy and painful. Everything is in this weird place."

"Crazy and painful play an important part. Only the hard things prove to be worthwhile. If it were easy, then what would you recruits learn?"

"I guess that's true," Conor offered. The chime sounded for the beginning of the Combatives class. The other recruits had already gathered on the large football field area as the instructor on her levitating platform began to lecture. "I need to go. They're starting."

"Of course. I'll see you around." Anibal watched Conor start to scurry away. After a moment, he called out to him. "Master Hawk!" Conor stopped and turned. "The Ascension isn't about the climb."

Conor simply nodded and turned away, again without a clue as to what that even meant.

### Sector 9
### Gregor Monolith

"No one lands on that godforsaken planet. Just look at the atmosphere, from outer all the way down to base. There's no way we're taking the Monolith down there."

"That's an accurate assessment, Vice Commander. It appears too treacherous to enter without the ship taking significant—and likely, disabling—damage," the navigator advised.

"I'm pleased we can agree on that. I don't even see the benefit of taking in a smaller craft."

"That, too, would be perilous. Statistical projections are at 34% for a successful landing. With the cyclonic landscape debris, even a clean landing does not guarantee the absence of damage while docked," an engineer added.

"So, give me the projection on a clean entry, landing, and departure," Valitat urged.

The engineer tapped the data needed, including wind speed, trajectory, orbit entry velocity, and gravitational force into her mist screen. "That would be 22%."

"It's even worse than that," Valitat Bithos said. "Don't forget the docking. If the debris field causes damage to docked crafts, give me the best time window before the landing craft is torn apart, or at least disabled."

"Well, the best option would be not to land at all," the engineer said with a sigh.

"Obviously."

The engineer shifted a barrage of data around on the screen. "But I would say no more than 24 minutes. That's being generous considering the probable hits from entry and several small debris strikes while on the ground."

"Copy that. Launch another probe," Valitat ordered.

"Another probe?" A tall man with closely cropped hair moved to the stairway of the bridge. He looked up at Valitat Bithos with anxious scorn. After all, as the ship's Jetson, and in command behind the Vice Commander, it was well within his place to question poor decision-making. "We've already lost four probes. This is our last one."

"Just do it. I want better confirmation on what we saw on the last probe before it exploded."

"We spotted a ship. That's obvious. It looks Kravii." The Jetson pointed to one of the crew members, signaling him to display the image again. The survey tech summoned the image and pushed it upward. An enlarged picture of the suspected Kravii vessel hung in the air above them.

"Though it's partially blocked by the rock formation to the right, we can see by its lines and color scheme that this is a Kravii military-class ship."

"I'm not arguing that," Valitat Bithos said, peering down at him. "I want to see troop presence. We're not sending anyone down there to walk into an ambush."

"There weren't any heat signatures observed."

"Exactly," she spouted. "Who abandons a ship unless it's beyond repair? And from what our image feed showed, it seems pretty well intact. It couldn't have landed too long ago because according to our esteemed analyst right there," Valitat said with a wave of her hand, "it would be pretty mangled outside of 20."

"Twenty-four, Commander," the young engineer offered.

"Thank you, Sarat. Twenty-four minutes."

"I don't think we need another probe to tell us the enemy is down there, and it's a bad idea to send troops into that kind of environment in the first place," the Jetson argued.

"Very well. Your contest is noted. Now send the damn probe." Valitat rubbed her brow with closed eyes. She felt the same anxiety the rest of them did. Without a better understanding of what they were doing here and what they were actually hoping to find, frustration and hesitation would prevail. That could prove problematic.

The Supreme Commander's ways and methods were beyond unorthodox, uncannily successful, but nonetheless reckless at times. It was time to get Makon to share some pertinent insight into this venture, because right now, this trip to Hadak-5 appeared to be just plain foolish.

Valitat grabbed her cloak from the chair beside her. She flung it around her shoulders as if trying to stifle the brewing frustration inside her. "Advise me once we have live imagery. I'm off to get a little more clarity on our current mission."

She marched straight to the ascensor lift and dropped two levels to the lifestyle complex. A large glass wall greeted her arrival. Behind it lay giant palm plants towering to more than three levels above her. A silly little lizard-like apologo pressed itself against the transparent wall. They spotted each other, and it decided it'd been there long enough to know when to move. It wagged its tail and made a quick turnabout to scamper away as fast as it could.

Valitat waved her hand, and the glass in front of her turned to mist. As she stepped through, she felt the cool water droplets but then got hit with a rise in humidity. She shook her head and pressed forward along the dim, meandering path leading deeper into the jungle enclave. The Commander loved the heavy climate of southern Jopal. The heat and humidity were too dense for her liking, but it put Makon at a comfortable state of relaxation. She also knew no one else liked to linger at this atrium setting, so it provided a much higher likelihood the Commander would have the space all to himself.

A cantoo bird called out overhead, as if announcing Valitat's presence to the Master. "Yeah, I'm here," she mumbled. "Might as well let him know." She pushed aside a series of purple-blue leaves and stepped over a felled log from a shift tree. As she stepped over it, even in its fallen state, the bark switched like cascading dominoes from smooth, deep green to a rough, dull brown. *Odd little tree*, she thought.

The rush from the waterfall caught her ears before it came into view. The waters toppled from high above into a warm pool surrounded by lush, swaying plant-life and a white-sand beach. Somewhere below the surface, the water drained, feeding back into the circulation to produce an endless loop for the softly roaring waters. Not every ship came with a tropical waterfall-jungle-beach enclosed environmental atrium. In fact, none other did. It was a gift from the Federation to the Commander after his heroic victory at the Battle of Dohani. The Council asked if he needed anything, and, of course, this is what he'd asked for.

She found Makon floating in the shallow water just beside the beach sand. His eyes were closed, and he looked incredibly relaxed. Valitat looked around for something to throw at him.

*Plop!* The water splashed next to Makon's hip. He didn't stir or open his eyes. "I'm awake. You can stop throwing rocks at me."

"It wasn't a rock. It was a klax shell."

"Was the klax snail still inside it?"

"Don't know," Valitat said with a shrug.

"Probably was. You're that kind of woman. I knew it."

"You don't know as much as you think you do, old man."

"Well, I know enough to know you're miserable right now, standing there."

She shifted her stance and looked up at the tree canopies. The massive leaves stretched downward, reaching for her. "I hate it in here. It's too hot, and I feel like I'm breathing through a blanket."

"The water's nice. Come join me," Makon said as he planted his feet on the ground.

"No. You come join *me*. It's time to get to work. We're nearing Hadak-5."

Makon pushed through the waist-high water toward the woman in the knee-length cloak. "That's good." He continued toward her, moving slowly but with purpose up onto the beach. It was hard not to notice the water droplets clinging to Makon's athletic frame. His muscles were relaxed, but well-formed and clearly exposed since he was wearing only form-fitting aqua shorts.

Valitat made her best efforts to not encourage his ego by showing any signs of being impressed or attracted. She turned away, moving back to the trail that brought her to the water's edge. "Get dressed. I expect you'll finally brief us on what we're doing way out here."

"I need you to do it."

Valitat stopped and turned back to him. "Do what? You expect me to brief the crew? How do you suppose I do that when I don't know what we're doing on Hadak-5?" She threw down her arms in exasperation. "Why are we here, Makon? This place is far away from Federation protection and on the outskirts of an uncharted galaxy. This space is a Kravii playground, and we marched right in. Besides, it's not like we haven't announced ourselves due to that little dance on the Moon of Kol."

"Okay, I'll tell you, but I need you to handle the briefing. I have something I need to do before I go down."

Valitat crossed her arms. "Of course, you're going down there. Do you have any idea of what that place looks like? If we land a ship, it'll be a miracle. If the ship lasts longer than 10 seconds, that'll be miracle number two. If you don't get attacked by the Kravii force, that's probably already there—miracle three." She noticed the flinch on Makon's face. "Oh, you didn't know that there's a Kravii party already docked? Well, there is. We can't spot any troop presence, but a battle cruiser is sitting in an alcove. We have partial visual."

"That's not completely unexpected," Makon said with a smirk.

"It was for me. Maybe if you shared the mission, I could've been prepared."

"We're following up on a lead into the Jopali attack."

"Yes, I figured. But we're here on just a lead. Give me more, Makon."

"Siv Ro."

Valitat kept her arms crossed and canted her head. "That's it? Is that supposed to mean anything to me? Why are you being so cryptic?"

"You're familiar with him. I told you we used to run together in my days before the Federation."

"I thought he was dead."

"Me, too, but he isn't. Our reunion kind of got off on the wrong foot for a bit there, but he eventually came around."

Valitat couldn't hold back her smile, though she wanted to. "You certainly have a convincing way." She shook her head. "What did he tell you?"

"Not much. Only that a Kravii Battleborn Chief named Utirot had a meeting with someone or something out here."

"I am definitely familiar with Utirot. At least the name."

"We all are. Except he and his entire crew went missing. Hadak-5 is their last known whereabouts. Utirot knew about the cloaking that enabled the attack, so I'm hoping we can find something of value on his ship."

"So, there's no Kravii troop contingent down there?"

"Not likely."

"Well, I feel a little better about this. Yet, we still have the atmospheric problem. It could be devastating."

"Can we insert via Dark Disc?" Makon asked.

"No. I wouldn't risk it. There's too much debris. You might emerge with shrapnel in your belly or end up on one of the orbiting jagged-rock formations."

Makon nodded. "How about time dilution?"

"The gravitational pull on Hadak-5 is just a little stronger, so you're going to lose some time to slippage."

"How much do we calculate?"

"It's not significant but will be slower for you. Your short minutes will be hours to us and Jopal."

"Okay," Makon replied, bringing a hand up to wipe away a few water droplets clinging to his beard. "Not bad. We shouldn't be down there too long. I hate losing time when we don't have much to waste." He reached for the stack of plush towels nearby, unfurled one, and brushed it over his chest and shoulders before draping it across the back of his neck. "I still think you should've joined me for a swim."

Valitat ignored the Commander's playfulness. "I'll brief the deck and ready the insertion team."

"Keep the team small. We won't need many troops to investigate an abandoned ship. We'll be back before you miss us."

**The Academy**
**The Forge**

The punch stretching toward his face came slow. Conor could have easily dodged it, but the intention of the training was to parry and counterstrike. He brought up his left hand to deflect the blow and then stepped in close to his opponent while simulating a direct palm strike to the nose. Both combatants then reset and repeated the motions.

"You can go faster if you want," Conor said to Byro.

"You want me to actually hit you? I'm already going at nearly full speed."

Conor shrugged. The practice was pretty easy since they knew where the punch was coming from. They'd already worked on kicks, elbow strikes, knee thrusts, and a variety of punches. It all came pretty easy, and Conor's body moved—reacted—like he'd learned some version of the techniques before, though he had no recollection of any previous training.

Combatives Instructor Nalinia Haz then voiced from her customary levitating platform they would now be moving to the arena. The mass of recruits halted their exercises and started gathering together into their clusters of friends and roommates. Conor and Byro moved to the replenishment stand and selected a transparent-bottled beverage from the display. Conor grabbed a red one. It felt warm, so he put it back. He grabbed a clear drink but thought twice about it when he noticed the contents mysteriously churning around like a slow-motion cyclone.

"The blue one's the best," Byro said. Conor set the clear drink back down and found a light-blue version.

"It's warm," Conor said, holding it up to his face. "And I think it's bubbling."

"They're all warm. Get used to it."

"Is there something inside?" Conor asked as he watched Byro gulp down half of his own bottle.

"Only pure goodness. Try it. Trust me."

Conor slid the retracting lid to the side and took a hesitant sip. It felt cool going down, even though it was warm to the touch.

"You like it?"

"It feels cold once you drink it. What is it?"

"That's the lopo root. Tastes pretty good and replenishes energy. Just don't take the purple one until after training. Oh, and make sure you don't have a boring class afterwards. That one will relax your muscles, slow your breathing, and you'll definitely need a nap."

"Good to know," Conor said as he took another long drink. "So, what's the arena?"

"Remember that red oval we saw when we first came in?"

"Yeah."

"The arena."

"It doesn't look like much of an arena," Conor said, eyeing the red oval.

"I agree with you there. It's not really a true arena. It's for more training—not for spectators."

They walked over to the arena and stood with the others, encircling the center from outside the crimson ring. Some of the recruits started stretching, jumping, and otherwise limbering up. One Jopali girl moved into a handstand with her legs together, then apart, then wide, then to just one hand. She then pushed herself into a full backflip and landed without a hitch. Quite impressive. A few of the others started some mock sparring. Obviously, they all knew something demanding was in store here. Maybe he should start stretching, too. At least that might distract him from the rising anxiety he began to feel in his stomach.

"What are you doing?" Byro asked as he looked down. Conor stretched both arms down to his toes, brushing at the top of his flat-soled shoes with his fingertips. He stood back up and faced his companion.

"Just stretching like everyone else."

"You don't need that. You're already loose enough for this. We've been at it for over an hour now."

"Well, why are they then?"

"Because they're idiots. Don't worry. You'll be fine. This is just a quick spar. We don't go hard at each other until later in the program."

"What are we going to do?" Conor asked, feeling apprehension rise from his gut.

Instructor Nalinia finally announced the next phase of training as if directly answering Conor's question. "Cadets! Now let us see how you can put everything together in a combat scenario. You will engage one on one until I declare a winner, or otherwise stop the match. Don't worry, this is simply a single engagement. We won't introduce multiple combatants or weapons until a little later. I'll even let you select your opponents this time."

"See? It's not that tough today," Byro said with a hesitant smile. Conor simply nodded, not feeling very reassured.

"All right! First two volunteers, enter the arena." Pounding drums suddenly sounded from all around them. The drums were unseen, but Conor felt their rumbling bass in his chest. A tall girl stepped forward. Her long black hair was tied back and up, her blue-black training outfit stretched tight over her slender frame. She walked the ring with all the bravado and confidence of someone who'd won a hundred matches. No one else seemed to step forward to challenge her, but that didn't matter to her.

She strolled the interior, scanning the faces of potential opponents. She came to a boy, matching her in height, but with more visible muscle. He started to step forward toward her, but she placed her hand against his chest and shook her head with a smile. She then moved along. Of course, the boy could've demanded the match with her, but he didn't want that kind of trouble.

Conor remembered her, and the other one that looked just like her. That one stood opposite him on the other side of the ring. She raised her hand and pointed to him—a signal to her evil twin. He felt his stomach sink. The Collective.

Within moments, the challenger now stood in front of him, looking down. She wasn't much taller than him, but it was enough to make her feel advantaged and superior. It worked. Conor felt small and defeated even before she stepped back and beckoned him to join her inside the ring.

Conor hesitated. "Go on. You can take her," Byro said in an effort to encourage him. Conor felt all eyes on him. He picked at his left sleeve and shuffled forward. He then took a deep breath and crossed the line. She waited for him at the center, awash in applause and cheers from the spectating cadets. Conor assumed the others were cheering because they weren't the ones picked for the impending beating he would soon endure.

The Collective twin stood opposite him, dropping into a fighting stance. She looked ready to punish him for something, her smirk sliding into a snarl. Conor took another deep breath and stepped his right leg back, bringing his hands up in front of him. The whole experience felt weird. For the life of him, he couldn't remember if he'd ever been in a fight before. Hopefully, he could remember the techniques they'd just worked on. And hopefully, she wasn't nearly as good as she seemed.

A sudden pop sounded overhead, catching him off guard. He kept his hands up, but the girl had already left the ground, twisting in the air. She spun full around, lashing out her lead leg, and striking him on the right side of his head. The blow knocked Conor off-center, dropping him to the left. As he tried to regain his wits, she moved on top of him. The kick didn't particularly hurt, but the surprise and power generated from the theatricality caught him unaware.

Now she mounted on top of him, sitting on him like one would a saddle, delivering rapid punches to his face. Conor squirmed and blocked them as best he could, but each time he tried to move out from under her, she inched her thighs closer, deeper into his armpits. From his vulnerable position underneath, he couldn't strike back so he did the only thing he could think of. He shifted his weight under her and rolled to his stomach. She seemed to let him. This was good, or so he thought.

That idea changed when she wrapped her arm around his throat. This sparring session had gotten serious, and Conor's mood started to change. It went from fear and shock to frustration. He tried to stand up, but her legs entwined with his, forcing him back down. The intensity of her chokehold began to cut off his oxygen. In that moment, frustration turned to anger.

Conor grabbed the arm encircling his neck and started pulling it away. Although she fiercely applied her technique with expert skill, she couldn't resist the might pulling her arm away from the boy's neck. Conor now stood, the girl's forearm in his right hand. He reached back with his left hand and grabbed the back of her neck. He contracted his muscles, the fibers in his back and arms activating as if infused by liquid steel. Conor lurched forward. The sudden violence of his movement tore the girl off his back and sent her hurling through the air like a wet towel.

She crashed into the line of recruits, toppling three of them over before striking her head hard against the flooring. The recruits stood in silence even as the firecracker sound burst overhead, signaling the end of the match. Conor watched for a long moment as the fallen recruits clambered to their feet and attended to the unconscious Collective member.

A familiar voice finally broke the still silence. "Conor! Woah! That was amazing." He looked over and saw Byro cheering him on. "Come on. Over here," Byro beckoned with a wave of his hand. "You won. Match is over—" He spotted the Collective girl charging at Conor from behind. "Hey! Look out!"

Byro's warnings came too late as the girl leaped up in the air and delivered a flying kick to Conor's back, striking him right between the shoulder blades. But it wasn't the same girl. The one Conor had tossed overhead still lay dazed on the floor. Her twin menace now wanted revenge for her sister.

The blow to his back knocked Conor face down to the cushioned floor. The shock of the strike reverberated up and down his spine, radiating throughout his lean muscles. He rolled over to face the threat and saw the gnarled grimace on her face. She matched her sister in athletically defined beauty and tactical cunning. Her brown hair pulled back in a ponytail revealed a smooth complexion and tapered jawline. The girl might've even been attractive if she didn't act like such a jerk or harbor an immediate intent to injure him.

She wound up to strike him again, aiming for his ribcage with a powerful roundhouse kick. Conor tucked his left arm into his hip to protect his torso and absorb the blow. Just before the kick was able to make contact, the girl's neck jerked back with a violent tug on her ponytail. She slammed backward to the floor with a breath-sucking thump.

Conor sat up to notice another familiar girl with her arms wrapped around the Collective's head like a boa constrictor. As the Collective clawed at the arms and punched at her attacker's face, she began to receive brutal punches to her chest and kidneys.

A series of three explosions sounded all around the arena. The Instructor Nalinia then boomed, "Stop! Clear off!"

The girl climbed off of the Collective's face and stood back. Conor got to his feet and looked at the pretty Jopali native still standing above the downed Collective, her chest heaving as she inhaled deep breaths. He never would've expected Tiera to come to his defense, especially with such brutality.

The other girl stood up and loomed at least a head taller than Tiera. "What's your problem?!" she shouted. "This isn't your fight."

"My reason's the same as yours," Tiera replied, still on her guard but not relenting a step.

"Your strange little boyfriend hurt my sister."

"He's not my boyfriend," Tierra spurted back. She then looked briefly at Conor. "He's . . . he's family, I suppose."

"Then your pathetic family has a problem with mine." As the girl continued, she sensed the presence of the male twins now standing behind her. "The whole entire Collective will—"

"Oh, shut up," Tiera interrupted. "Your name's Rayna. Your sister is Danika. And those two fools behind you are Cyril and Gavril. Why don't you stop with the 'we are the Collective' garbage?"

"I think we should remind you why we run this place," Rayna said.

Tiera took a step toward her. "You don't control anything around here."

One of the male twins, named Cyril, moved closer, stepping around Tiera's tough stand. He walked right up to Conor and smiled. But just as he began to utter his newest threat the instructor set her platform right beside them. She was wearing a look of a warrior's intensity when she spoke to them. "This is over. And unless you would like me to remind you of the difference between the Academy and a basic scholastic school, I would separate. Do it now!"

The Collective heeded the warning and created some space. However, the tension hung like campfire smoke on a humid evening. It was felt. Etched in their faces.

One thing was clear. Conor had some powerful enemies.

# CHAPTER 17

**Hadak-5**
**Inner atmosphere**

Makon's face was a mask of stern intensity as both his hands gripped the steering column tight. A sharp movement to the left caused the fighter craft to veer right, narrowly dodging a jagged rock spinning toward them. He then moved the Tidal fighter up and right again, activating the thrusters to shoot through the center of a cyclone of daggered pilons. "Fire on that piece there."

"Which one?" Shila asked, anxiously poised over the assault panel.

"The big one. On the right."

"Copy." She unleashed a barrage of heat torpedoes at the passively moving formation. The burst shattered the mass into smaller shards, and Makon maneuvered through the cloud of splintered debris.

"How we doing?" Makon asked.

Haviro studied the wisp panel in front of him. The target glowed purple with a trajectory sweeping in a concentric circle toward it. "Good. But we need to get left soon and then come in behind it to catch the landing rock."

"No problem," Makon said as he brought the craft in a swift movement to the left, inverting their ship twice as he did so to avoid more incoming environmental missiles. "Still think you should've come with us," he uttered as he focused on the flight path. At first, both Shila and Haviro were confused because they thought the Commander was speaking to them. Then the familiar voice of the Vice Commander sounded overhead, and they politely ignored the comment.

"You know me. I prefer to stay with this big beast," Valitat replied.

"Look at all the fun you're missing," Makon said. "There's nothing dangerous down here." Just then three large fragments loomed in front of them. They presented too large to go over or under, so Makon expertly brought the ship to its lateral and split the two on the left. His eyes then grew wide as an unseen flat piece moved into view. It looked like they were about to dive straight into a cliff face, until a series of five torpedo blasts ruptured its center, leaving a crack narrow enough to scoot through.

"This one's going to be tight," Makon uttered through tense lips. The scraping of the craft's underbelly on the bottom half of the crack accentuated this fact. Makon accelerated, bursting from underneath the temporary cavern just as the upper half closed on itself. "Thank you for that, Shila," he said without looking at the cannoneer, still busy making holes and gaps where and when needed. "Update."

"Seven GUMs to go," Haviro stated. Geographical Unit of Measurement, or GUM for short, still made Makon think of gnawing on sugary sweetness every time he heard it.

"Almost there," Makon said as he spotted the massive formation off in the distance. It moved slowly in a counterclockwise rotation above a dusty gray plain of granite. As expected, the planet appeared lifeless, but a hiccup more perilous than he originally projected.

Swirling devastation never ceased, as if an endless hurricane was consuming the entire sphere. It would be a perfect spot for a clandestine meeting. If anyone could survive the insertion, it would be free from ambush, reinforcements, or detection from the Federation or Kravii warships.

From her position on the Gregor Monolith, Valitat and other essential crew on the flight deck monitored the Commander's craft on its path toward the target location. They could also survey the crew's movement and vital signs inside the cabin. "Yes, it looks quite fun. Did I notice a spike in your heartbeat pattern a moment ago?" Valitat asked, hinting she knew this insertion was anything but fun.

"Nah. Must've just been an adrenaline surge from the vip juice I had this morning. Just kicked in," Makon said with a slight strain to his tone while he barrel-rolled through an upswell of stalactites. One of the stone rockets impacted the rear right-side fender, causing the engine to sputter.

"That last one got us," Haviro said with a tinge of worry in his voice.

"How bad?"

Haviro moved away from the navigation panel and checked the diagnostic screen. "It looks like . . ." The panel showed a transparent overlay of the craft. The starboard engine went from yellow, which still meant limited functionality, to a bright red. "No. It's out."

"Indeed, it is," Makon said as he felt a diminished power output. In that moment, Makon wished they'd gone with the smaller, faster Whiplash fighter than the midsize Tidal craft. It would've been easier to maneuver it through this churning minefield, but then it couldn't carry all five passengers, and Makon wanted to bring four Elites just in case they encountered undetected Kravii troops.

"You guys still good down there?" Valitat asked.

"Suuuure. Still got one good engine. That's all an expert pilot really needs."

"It's a shame the expert pilot is still up here then," Valitat offered as she sipped her morning fruit splash cocktail.

“Hey, I invited you, but nooooo. I guess this second-rate pilot will just have to manaaaage,” Makon uttered as he manipulated the controls to duck the craft under a wave of shrapnel. “Okay, Shila. Clear a path right there on the left, and I’ll bring us in right under the ledge.”

“That ledge?!” the Elite seated behind the Commander questioned. “We’ll have to thread the space there between that rock face the size of a Jopali Juggernaut castle.”

“Yes, Haviro. That very one. Now, get shooting,” Makon replied. Shila touched the screen to switch to rapid fire and tucked her fingers into six wisp sockets, one for each forward gun. She then worked her fingers up and down like a court reporter on a keyboard. Torpedoes sprayed horizontally from the cannons like a curtain of blue rain, pulverizing the debris into a traversable mist of chunks and shards.

Makon swept the craft from left to right, banking hard to skirt between the ledge and the rock wall. “We need more power! We’ll never make it at this speed!” Haviro shouted.

Makon’s pulse shot up, matching the heart rates of his fellow crew. Haviro was right. This maneuver required more power. “Brace for impact,” he mumbled. His focus intensified.

Valitat watched. Her muscles tightened at the sight. Her screen displayed the Commander’s view through the windbreak of the Tidal fighter. The entire windbreak eclipsed as the mountain rose into view like a rogue wave of rocky death.

**The Academy**
**Planetary Studies Pod**

The adrenaline from the combat training and clash with the Collective, or whatever their names were, dissipated rather quickly as they gathered in the backless chairs for the Planetary

Studies class. About a third of the recruits attended while others were whisked away to more dynamic courses.

Conor looked around at the other students, most seemingly disinterested as they positioned themselves around the instructor's panel in a crescent moon shape. They fidgeted and squirmed in their uncomfortable seats either because they were ready to do something more active, or because they thought they knew enough already.

The instructor first introduced himself as Fivor Yew, a Cresvich from Aquinox. Conor remembered meeting a mother and her children from the same planet while in the Mertio market just before the Kravii attack on Jopal. The Cresvich instructor stood tall and thin, poised and proper, almost mechanical. His voice sounded raspy through the reverse-engineered translucent aqua respirator covering his mouth, but he spoke with enthusiastic eloquence.

He started the lecture with a motion-picture tour of the Academy itself, discussing its history and architecture with more energy than any of the recruits could muster for the topic. Perhaps Conor should have already known this stuff, too, but it all seemed so foreign and unfamiliar to a boy with an amnesiac memory.

Conor learned there were six planet simulations housed within the Academy, worlds where they might eventually have to travel for battle or rescue missions. Worlds that typified the atmospheres and varied terrain of the majority of planets in the Vesputi.

The Academy mimicked these planetary environments with meticulous detail down to plant life, atmospheric conditions, gravitational density, and even imported home species to enhance dramatic accuracy, threat assessment, and tactical engagement. While this element surely enhanced the realistic training initiative, it blew to bits the notion they ever intended to keep their cadets away from harm.

Fivor Yew, with tinted glasses now covering his narrow eyes, confirmed this when he briefly described the first planet—Fi—a cold planet with snow-covered mountain ranges, accompanying avalanches, and limited food supply. Fortunately, not all the creatures would try to eat you for dinner, but the ones that did seemed quite ruthless.

An image of a Likiti tribesman emerged on the screen behind the instructor. It materialized into a life-like model, three times its actual size. The instructor spun around the holographic specimen and began pointing out its anatomical features.

"Razor-sharp claws are filed down to dagger points. The same goes for their teeth. The widened feet," he continued as he pointed at the double-jointed legs, "allow for efficient traversal in unpacked snow. Their hair, or you may recognize as fur, grows in triplicate to absorb and sustain warmth. In fact, if one is seen in a shorn form, it's because the fur was removed as punishment. It is understood if they survive long enough for the fur to regrow, then their punitive sentence has been fulfilled. Most don't survive.

"This one here grows no bigger than the average Jopali villager, but don't be fooled by its size. They are remarkably strong and agile, and will dine on anything with a heartbeat.

"They travel in herds, living a nomadic lifestyle, with the males serving as hunters and the females as the builders and child caretakers. One female will have multiple mates as the male offspring outnumber females three to one. They live and die by their queens, so if you get on her good side, then your chances of surviving the encounter are greatly amplified."

A girl stood in the second row across from Conor. He thought she was getting up to leave or declare something, but she just stood there quietly. The instructor turned away from the Likiti display and pointed to her. "Yes, go ahead."

"If there are species from each planet here on the Academy, then what about Kravos? Are there—?"

"No," the instructor interrupted. "We get this question each time from First-Circuit recruits. We don't house Kravii warriors here. I should've led with this." He cleared his throat and continued. "We tried at first, but they proved too dangerous for the recruits as well as the staff. They refused to adapt to the planetary simulation and tried too often to escape. Ultimately, the few we held were eradicated."

"So, Kravos here doesn't have any Kravii?" another recruit asked.

"I didn't say that much. We do have simulated versions of them. This doesn't eliminate their potential to harm the unwary recruit, but they aren't nearly as lethal as their real-life counterparts."

Conor felt a wash of relief in hearing that part. His last encounter with the Kravii while on Jopal was a nightmare he didn't want to relive for practice, training, or any other reason. "I understand your concern," Fivor Yew continued again, "but we have taken precautions to minimize deadly force engagements. Your pulseros have been programmed to reflect your level of experience and capability when entering a training world scenario. It interacts with a cerebral implant on each inhabitant, and their subsequent response will be subdued, thus reducing the potential for grave injury."

The instructor tapped the hologram, and it reduced itself back onto the screen behind him. "Now let's get back to Fi." A looming mountain range appeared on the screen. Then he swept his arm in a wide circle, and it billowed out, encircling the class. He raised both hands and then slowly brought them down. The temperature in the pod dropped drastically, and digital snowflakes trickled down from above.

"Yes, friends, it just got colder in here. Not nearly as cold as Fi itself, but this will help you understand the planet's environment a little better while we study. Don't worry. We won't stay here long without giving you a chance to get up and move around. And we won't ever visit Tretch in the same day. Going from drastic cold to scorching heat will force a number of you into sick bay. Don't want that."

Fivor Yew swept an arching glance around his audience as if counting their numbers. "It looks like we have a majority of Jopali recruits, as usual. So, in order to understand how the various climates will affect you, we need to embrace an understanding of yourselves and where you come from. Let's start with our individual homes. Each of you activate your immediate desk screens, and pull up where you come from."

Conor looked around at the other recruits as they activated their screens. He copied their movement by swiping his pulsero across the front edge of the tinted glass desk. Tiny yellow particles poured out of a narrow slit in front of him and warped into a rounded screen. "The pulsero is keyed into your ancestral biology and will automatically display your birthplace." Conor swiped across the blank screen, but nothing happened. He looked to his left, and the Jopali girl's screen showed crystal-clear waters and sandy beaches. He watched her face form a smile. No wonder. The girl clearly lived in a bubbly paradise.

Conor couldn't figure out why the boy to his right seemed giddy. A sprawling industrial wasteland scrolled in front of him. It looked dingy, gray, and depressing. *I guess home is always home, no matter how ugly it may be.* He jerked his head back to his own screen when the boy noticed him spying.

"Hmmm. That's odd," Fivor Yew's voice sounded over his shoulder. Conor didn't realize the instructor had made his way around behind him. "Do me a favor and swipe the pulsero again." Conor waved it back and forth across the screen. Nothing. "There must be a glitch with your band. Get it looked at before tomorrow's class. Either way, Cadet Hawk, we are all pretty familiar with your story. I'm told the Supreme Commander found you in the under alleys of Jopal's northeast district while on business. What city was it again?"

Conor hesitated. "What city?"

"Yes. What city did he find you?"

"Uh. I wasn't born there," Conor said in hopes to deflect the question. The Commander had told him once, but that seemed forever ago, and he couldn't remember it right then under pressure.

"Fine. Where were you born?" Now he was in trouble. He couldn't tell him that.

"I . . . uh . . . don't remember." Perfect answer. At least Conor hoped.

Fivor Yew nodded. "Yes, I'm sorry. I forget myself. My apologies." He tapped the pulsero on his wrist and a rolodex of recruits sprang up. He swiped until he got to a picture of Conor. "Traumatic amnesia. Says right here," he said as he read a snapshot of Conor's file. "You were present for the attack on Mertio. He placed a hand on Conor's shoulder. "Must've been terrifying. Don't worry. We definitely need to get your pulsero fixed, then. The biological genetic synapse should connect you to your birthplace. That will do wonders to help with your memory recall. At least we hope."

Just then the portal to Pod 7 opened, and the recruits spun to address the intrusion. Wilda Ti moved with determined purpose right through the mountain hologram to the front of the room. Conor rose with the other recruits to stand at attentive rest in respect for the Chief Administrative Leader.

"To what do we owe the honor?" Fivor Yew asked.

Wilda Ti held up her hand to greet and politely silence the instructor.

**Hadak-5**
**Riptide Coves**

Makon yanked hard on the controls as the Tidal fought against him. His muscles strained as the ship banked right under the maximum available power. They ducked underneath a shard twice the size of their craft, narrowly missing its under-hang of granite icicles. The shard struck the cliff side and burst apart showering them with a cloud of particle dust and falling debris. This didn't distract Makon from his primary goal of not ramming head on into the immovable rock.

He tucked the ship downward in hopes of utilizing some gravity for an extra boost. The gamble changed the angle, but not enough. "I still need more power to finish the turn!" Makon shouted.

"I have an idea," Shila said as she engaged the rear weapons systems. Try this," she said as she activated and fired two rear torpedoes. The thrust from the dual blast boosted them forward, enabling them to make the turn. Well, almost. The left fender took another hit as it smashed against the cliff face, causing it to shear off. The ship now drastically sliced to the right keeping them clear of a disastrous collision. But now they began to spin.

Makon caught a glimpse of the overhang just before it spun out of view. "I see you. We're coming," he said out loud, speaking directly to his preferred landing spot. He cut the power as they moved in a 360; then, just as the overhang came back into view, he ignited the remaining thruster. This briefly redirected the ship and shot them forward out of the spin. He then banked hard to the right, slamming the ship's belly down on the massive rock plain. The fighter craft dug into the unforgiving surface and skidded until slamming broadside into the side of the overhang.

They stopped. Makon released his vise-like grip on the controls and began to breathe again. He visually checked his two co-pilots, who sat just as frazzled. "All right, friends," he said, clapping his hands together. "That went just as intended."

"I don't doubt it, Commander," Haviro said. "But did you also intend on destroying the console and our ability to communicate with the Monolith?"

"Nope. That part was quite unintended."

"How about the part where we won't be able to fly this thing out of here?" Shila asked as she attempted to get a power response from the controls.

"That is also rather inconvenient," Makon said as he rose from the cockpit chair. He then looked to Haviro. "Check on the other two Elites. Get them working on the repairs. Shila and I will get a head start on exploring the Kravii skiff. Then join us over there." He glanced out the windbreak as three large rocks pelted the ground in rapid succession before lifting up again. "Make sure everyone grounds their traversal, or else you'll be swept away in the wind currents."

"Copy that," Haviro responded.

Makon moved past both of them toward the side storage compartment. He bypassed the water gear stacked on top and then grabbed two of the five smaller cases tucked into their assigned slots. He handed one to Shila before turning the dial on his case. "You been trained to use these yet, Shila?"

"I've been using grounders since I was a little girl."

"That's special, but these are intuitive."

"What does that mean?"

"It means we don't guide them with poles. Totally hands free. They work off the wrist bands."

"Oh. In that case . . ."

"Don't worry about it," Makon said, cutting her off. "You'll pick it up quickly. Just watch what I do, do only one leg at a time, and never cross your body," Makon instructed as he fastened one of the two cuffs around his ankles. After securing the second one, he applied the first wrist band. "And make sure the left band is on your left wrist and the left cuff is on your left leg. Self-impalement is uncomfortable and messy."

Shila studied the cuffs and bands inside her box. It was set up to be idiot-proof as diagrams marked all the items as either left or right with each corresponding band and cuff latched together. She plucked the left set out first and attached the band. "I like to do one side first and then the other," Haviro offered as he squeezed by through the narrow corridor. "The Commander prefers to toss them up in the air and see if he gets a match. There's nothing like getting a plasma rod straight through the crotch to readjust your mood."

Makon smiled as he fastened the last bracelet. "Don't you have something you should be doing?" He then bent toward Shila. "I'm not that careless. I always double-check before activating."

"Yes. Yes. I'm going," Haviro uttered. "Have fun out there, and remember to duck."

"Go away," Makon said with a chuckle and a shake of the head. He checked both his bracelets and cuffs and then looked to Shila as she finished attaching the last piece. "Buddy check," he uttered as he compared her right-side wrist and ankle, and then her left.

"These things must be serious," she uttered.

"Your turn. Check mine. You know how it is—trust but verify. A distracted application can be lethal. Besides, who knows who packed these? We just want to make sure you don't have two rights or something in the batch." Makon stood after checking her cuffs and moved to the door. He swiped up on the panel, and the door hissed open. "You all set?" he asked, glancing back at her.

"Yes."

"Good. Let's move." He looked out the open door. The strength of the wind could be visualized by the cyclonic particle batches. A shower of jagged shards swept by just then like a storm of angry javelins. "Hmmmm." He glanced back at Shila. She appeared a bit apprehensive. "Okay, the suit will repel most of the smaller stuff, but I'm not sure about waves like that. There will likely be some punctures."

"Into the suit?"

"Into our bodies. Hold on a moment. Grab us helmets." Makon then moved away from the open door toward the back of the craft. Shila walked to the starboard wall and placed her palm at the center of an octagonal pad. A cabinet opened up with each crewmember's kit secured inside. She took her assigned helmet and slid it over her head. It was sleek and form-fitting, gold in color to match the horizontal stripe stretching across the shoulder blades of her otherwise pitch-black suit.

The visor automatically activated, giving her a clear view as well as a subtle heads-up display in the lower right corner. It integrated with her suit and began to cycle through a readout of her core temperature, heart rate, and $O_2$ level. She wasn't concerned with the oxygen source since they confirmed the planet had a sustainable atmosphere prior to insertion. If not for the cyclonic winds, it might have even supported life.

Makon marched back into the cockpit and slapped two gloves down on the table. "I gather you know how these work." Shila nodded. "Good. If we plan on keeping puncture holes to a minimum, these will certainly come in useful."

**The Academy**
**Planetary Studies Pod**

Wilda Ti stood before the recruit class to make her impromptu announcement. The CAL's interruption of a class was not only infrequent and unexpected but signified a critical announcement. A cause for one's utmost attention. But then, her sheer presence in itself garnered strict attention.

"I must regretfully inform you that, due to the present state of war with the enemy, we must hasten your preparation for conflict. Therefore, Planetary Studies will be postponed as an independent course and its curriculum will be integrated in a more directly kinetic manner."

"How will that be, Chief?" Fivor Yew interrupted. "This material is crucial in their preparation for interplanetary exposure."

"Yes, it is, but these are unprecedented times. Not to worry, you will integrate with the cadets to provide relevant information pertaining to each environment and its corresponding inhabitants." Wilda Ti turned back to the cadets, all poised and sitting on edge. "You will be provided this course's materials for evening study and integration. You are dismissed and charged to report to Piloting immediately."

Conor slowly rose from his seat along with the other recruits as the CAL left the pod, passing through the snow-capped mountains like a phantom. Not having a clue as to where to find the piloting class, he aptly followed the other recruits as they departed the pod and scurried down one corridor and into another. He now understood The Academy layout better since the brief overview in the last class, but it still churned up enough confusion to get him lost.

Like a massive tree branching outward from the core, each simulated world or pod existed on its own branch. One could traverse from one world to the other only by returning to the trunk and then either ascending or descending to another branch.

The ascensor carried upward from the lower branches housing Planetary Studies, Galactic Code/Federation Law, Procedural Application, and Ceremonial Guard—a cluster of required but otherwise uninspiring courses. Conor didn't plan on spending more time than necessary down there. The fun training courses populated the upper levels, and Piloting would no doubt be one of them, even though the last class held his interest more than anyone else. After all, exposure to the intricacies of a foreign galaxy meant more to the newcomer than those who grew up already traversing it.

He entered the pod with his class, finding cadets already inside. A wide glass bridge carried them over the Nivror Solar System below, summoning the memory of the Star Deck's Tranquility Chamber with the not-so-tranquil Dalex creature. The bridge glowed blue and led directly to a large circular pad. The other cadets huddled around an instructor standing beside a small craft. Its design was sleek and angled, as if built for speed and maneuverability.

Conor instinctively looked for weapons—large guns or missiles—to show it meant business. He contained his disappointment when he couldn't find any. That didn't mean they weren't actually there. He was learning that just because he couldn't see something didn't mean it didn't exist. This place came with a bucket full of surprises.

The new instructor, dressed in the blue-and-gold Federation flight suit, paused his lecture and walked over to the bridge where it met the pad. "Welcome, Cadets. My name's Nicet Blatori, and I'll be your spectacular Piloting instructor. We're glad to have you. The Chief gave me the go-ahead, so I already had my assistants pull extra vehicles from the garage. Come join us. I'll check your registrations once we separate for the cockpit introduction." The infectious energy the instructor exuded made him appear much younger than any of the others Conor had met thus far. Then again, who wouldn't sweat adrenaline hanging around sleek fighter crafts all day?

"We were just going over some of the nomenclature of the VR-9. It's better known as the Whiplash, and you guys will learn how it got that name soon enough," he said with a wide smile. "I can see you're all tired of listening to me talk." Nicet Blatori cupped his hand to his mouth to feign a whisper. "Especially coming from Fivor Yew's class." He then straightened up and dropped his hand, showing another wide smile. "Now, has anyone ever piloted a Whiplash before?" He looked around at all the recruits and didn't see anyone step forward. "Good. It's against the Federation Code without proper training and certification. That was a trick question. Buuuut, my young friends, that is exactly why you're here. I'm gonna teach you the good stuff."

Instructor Blatori kept talking, but Conor couldn't keep from looking back and forth between the instructor and the ship on his left. His hands began to tremble in anticipation of climbing inside and flying it. He shifted close enough to reach up and touch the wing. His fingertips traced the polished metal around the wing fin, imagining it cutting through air and space with tight precision. His daydream entranced him so much he didn't even realize the instructor was speaking to him until he heard some laughter from the recruits.

He dropped his arm and placed it behind his back. "I'm sorry. I didn't hear you."

"Don't worry about it," Nicet Blatori said with a grin. "They are beautiful ships. Just wait until you're flying. Buuuut, you guys are going to have to wait. We can't start you off with dessert first." He then depressed a switch in his hand, and the galaxy faded into the open-plains landscape of northern Jopal. The walkway bridge hadn't been suspended at all. The floor panels around it opened for twenty land vehicles to rise up from the under-garage.

Despite the impressive presentation, Conor and some of the others had to fight back a degree of disappointment. They wouldn't be airborne today. Nevertheless, these land traversals still looked pretty fun. The machines rested on the edges of four wheels, or discs. The open top displayed two seats with a slight forward tilt, one each for the operator and the passenger.

The instructor moved to the closest one and placed his hand on one of the front discs. It reached waist-high, looked thick, and was lined with interlinked hexagonal pads. "First, we will introduce you to the Spectre. It's primarily land-based but does not create contact with it. Due to its hovering aspect, you will also have no problem traversing small, shallow bodies of water so long as you keep up your speed. And if it's speed you're craving, then we'll make sure you get your fix.

"You've all been selected for Piloting. Not everyone is chosen, so I guess you're special." The recruits matched his smile. "Go ahead, look around. Not everyone is here. They've been pushed into infantry-insertion, artillery, technical support, or other courses. But you, my friends, get to be pilots. This course is reserved for Second-Circuits and above, so for some of you, this is your first time in the piloting course this go-around. As such, we need to make sure you have the level of awareness and aptitude of handling our vehicles before we send you out into space and maybe get yourself killed. So, no more frowning at the fact that I didn't stick you right into the cockpit of the Whiplash. Not everyone will be cut out for it. Of course, that doesn't mean we can't get you tearing apart some territory closer to the ground. At least we won't have to worry about you falling out of the sky when you screw up."

He moved around the two-person vehicle, slapping the electric-blue side panel. "This here is constructed from carbon-sivix so it can take a beating, because when you're moving at 220 GUMs per hour, you'll be dependent on this little beauty to hold itself together. Has anyone operated a Spectre before, other than my three-, four-, and five-term recruits?"

One hand raised. To no one's surprise, it was Tiera's. The instructor looked directly at her. "Of course, Cadet Welcos. No doubt you're pretty comfortable and confident in your abilities with this type of vehicle."

"Yes, sir. My uncle gifted me one. I've also flown the Whiplash once or twice." Nicet Blatori lost his smile for an instant. Then it came back again.

"Well, I'm not gonna question your uncle. Nope. Not me. Hopefully we can still furnish you with a few surprises, though," he said as he swiped the Spectre's mist screen. The vehicle's cyclonic engine came to a low roar, like a content jungle cat yawning after a full meal. The disc wheels pushed against the ground as they now glowed blue, causing it to raise up off the floor. He swiped again, and two guns extended out from its front fenders. "The military version has some . . . uh . . . modifications above and beyond the public version." Tiera lit up with a grin. "Yeah, I think you'll find plenty to fill your appetite in here."

# CHAPTER 18

**Hadak-5**
**Riptide Coves**

Makon stood at the open door, once again taking in the mess of the short, yet perilous trek over to the Kravii ship. He looked over to Shila. "You ready?"

She slid on the second sleeve shield, stretching the light fabric over her forearm up to her elbow. Then she closed both fists; the clutching movement engaging the push-button panel in her palms. This triggered the deployment of each device. A thin, lightweight panel sprung up from each sleeve, large enough to protect the head and shoulders from projectile bombardment.

"You believe these will deflect the debris?"

"They're strong enough to absorb a couple of Kravii bolt blasts, so I expect they'll do the trick," Makon answered. "Either way, we'll have to move quick." He bent down and activated both ankle cuffs with a pinch and a twist. They now glowed green around the protruding notch.

Shila did the same. "It feels like we're geared up for battle, not a 100-yard sprint across a field."

"But that field is nothing short of a warzone. Let's have at it." Makon's collapsible shields shot outward as he began the march across the wasteland. The wind's velocity worked to knock him over, but the plasma spikes linked through the ankle cuffs stabilized him. He reached out his right arm while guarding against the storm winds with the left. The raising of the hand activated the magnetic pull on the spike, tugging it free from the ground up to its notch in the bracelet. He could now move his leg forward, taking a step before lowering his hand and sending the spike back through the cuff and into the dry ground. He repeated the same measure with the left, taking another long, slow step.

After several steps, he checked on Shila. She handled the gear well, moving forward at a steady pace. He turned back just in time to duck behind his left shield as three shards the size of serving spoons pelted it. The granite met the shield and dissolved into its panel, protecting the wearer. Relief washed over him, granting him the confidence their shields would hold up in the environmental onslaught.

"Let's move faster," Makon said as he whipped his hands rapidly. The plasma spikes moved like machine pistons going up and down as they gripped and released the surface with precision. He soon reached the enclosure where the other ship had docked. The massive overhang blocked the wind and debris as if he were entering the eye of a hurricane. He reached out and touched the blue-purple ship, absorbing a deep breath and a moment of comfort.

He'd seen and destroyed plenty of the enemy's ships, but this one was a unique command-class battle cruiser—a definite rare find. Not only would this be a pleasure to explore, but it could be the key the Federation needed to understand the new cloaking program that had destroyed much of his capital city.

Excited, he started to move to the open landing platform to begin his exploration of the ship's internals, but then he stopped. Having been pulled into the moment, he'd forgotten his companion. He turned, suspecting she'd be at his back, or at least close behind, but he spotted her 50 yards away, on one knee, halfway between the two vessels. Shila's head was slumped down. He called to her, but the winds drowned out any other noise except the torrent swarming around her.

She looked dazed, visibly hurt in some way. Therefore, she couldn't see the extreme danger soaring toward her.

**The Academy**
**Piloting Pod**

The Spectre moved with alarming speed over the green hills, weaving through low-hanging trees and around odd masses of tubular vegetation rising from the ground, like undulating tentacles feeding on the air and wind. Seated directly behind the operator, feeling the surge of adrenaline rise with each sharp turn and burst of speed, Conor gripped the handlebars tight.

The Piloting instructor had paired him with an experienced Fourth-Circuit recruit, friendly and spirited—not to mention daring. His name was Adin. They'd met before, when Conor had almost punched him in the ascensor lift.

Adin's thrill-seeking was in full evidence as they raced forward, barreling down a steep hill toward a massive tree, its trunk twisted on itself. It stretched far above, with its breadth large enough to build a tree castle. It grew larger as it pressed into view, getting closer and larger with each passing moment. They would surely ram into it without an abrupt turn.

Conor's trust in Adin began to fade, until it disappeared entirely. The pilot showed no intention of turning to evade an impact with the immovable mass. "Watch out!" Conor yelled over the hum of the engine. This had no effect. His eyes slammed shut just before the devastating impact.

But there was no devastating crash, just the irritating buzz ringing out from the Spectre's dual consoles. Adin cut the wheel hard, and they banked to a stop. Conor opened his eyes and looked up. The tree still stood, but they were now directly behind it. "Wha . . . what happened?"

"We just scored a violation. That's the annoying alarm you hear right now with the red flashing screen in front of you," Adin said as he dismounted. "Can't get too many violations or they kick you out of class and send you off to work in the Muscle Rovers. But I wanted to show you there isn't anything to fear in here, unless, of course, you flip us. Try to avoid that. Now, switch places. It's your turn to operate."

Conor climbed out of his seat and moved over the hump into the front cockpit. The older recruit jumped into the rear position. "You remember the controls?"

"Yeah."

"Okay. So, now that I've removed any fear that might hold you back, I want you to get on it. Push your limits. It's the fastest way to learn and see if you deserve to be a pilot. Move fast. Just look forward and plan your path ahead of time. Let's go!" Conor fired up the engine. The sound of it roaring to life fed the thrill of the moment. "One more thing. Try not to hit anything. They'll blame me for the violations because I'm not supposed to let you operate yet."

"Go fast. No fear. Don't hit anything. Got it," Conor said as he moved the throttle knob with his right hand. They started to move faster than he thought they would. Once he adjusted to the speed, he knew they needed more, or else his passenger wouldn't be pleased.

The Spectre responded with precision to each micromovement of the controls. It twisted and turned through the hills with rampageous spirit and reckless abandon like a charging bull without a target. "Well done. You catch on quick," Adin's voice sounded in Conor's earpiece. "So, let's get a little more adventurous. I know you're up for it. Head over there, into the canyon."

Conor whipped the vehicle to the right, cutting around a bend where the landscape dipped into a valley tucked between twin cliffs. It zoomed over simulated rock and shale, past dusty boulders and dying, brittle trees that had mistakenly rooted in infertile soil. The path dipped and narrowed into the mouth of a cavern burrowed into the mountain. He hesitated but knew this was where his partner intended. His next words reiterated this. "You're gonna love this! The Gravity Groves. There's nothing like it."

The cavern enveloped them in darkness. It would've been heavy darkness if not for the blue glow from the consoles and the levitating discs. The light reflected off the crystallized walls, ceiling, and ground, making it look as if they were coasting through jagged ice. Conor pressed the top edge of the console, and bright white lights illuminated from the front, cutting deeper into the dark. He could now see objects ahead of them swaying slightly as if in a light underwater current.

They looked like green-orange organic columns with coiling roots stretching from both ends—one burrowing into the ground and the other in the ceiling. It looked like a forest of strange, branchless trees, unsure of whether they should root above or below. "Don't hit anything," Adin sounded in his ear. This enticed Conor to ease off the throttle as he cut the Spectre left around the first organic tree-thing. He felt the left side of the vehicle slipping. It began to lift.

"What's wrong with this thing?!" Conor exclaimed.

"It's the Gravity Groves, my friend. Looks like the pull is to the top today. It shifts!"

"What do I do?"

"Don't fight it, keep your speed up, and go with it." The Spectre pulled further to the left until they were now traveling along just above the jagged wall. They then moved back down the ground again in a clockwise move all the way up the opposite wall. As they moved around the cavern, up to the ceiling and back down again, Conor adjusted to the variation in the pulls. It looked like the cavern spun itself like a long, dark screw. This proved a peculiar and exhilarating challenge to traversing the cavern—not to mention he still had to evade the column trees as well. A bead of sweat trickled down his face, and he had to remind himself everything was just simulation.

That worked to ease his mind until he failed to factor in the next gravity pull enough to miss the next column. The Spectre's rear fender clipped the side of it, and they bounced off. They flew sideways, headed for a broadside collision with the next one. Conor throttled up, giving them enough thrust to jolt forward as he jammed the tiny steering wheel hard to the left. The instinctive maneuver moved them just past it on the right.

"Oh, I forgot to mention. These aren't simulations in here."

"You think?!" Conor shouted, still working them through the cavern, now with more anxiety. "Could've told me that sooner!"

"Good job, though. Just a little bit farther. Wait till we get to the exit—it's awesome."

Conor wasn't so sure about that anymore. All at once, the danger factor had crept up from a two or three to a solid ten. His grip instinctively tightened on the wheel.

They came to an upward bend in the cavern ahead. He negotiated the change in terrain and continued forward, weaving through the last of the columns as they pressed upward.

"You're going to want to really hit the thrust now. Give it all you got, or we won't make it all the way up," Adin said. Conor listened. He moved the throttle to full, feeling confident since there weren't any more obstacles in the way to crash into. The gravity mitigated the Spectre's speed, tugging them back down into the depths of the cavern. Conor fought it, but the vehicle handled easily, continuing its climb with building momentum.

The cavern carried them upward, now in a straight vertical. "Hold it steady, and touch the blue one on the left." Conor briefly looked over to the left of the console. A small triangular button glowed blue. He tapped it, and nothing happened. "Need to hit it twice." He tapped it a second time, and the engines lit up white with a new fuel source. The changeover propelled them forward with a breakneck push. The Spectre screamed upward toward a small opening ahead. This opening happened to be a narrow gap just wide enough to fit so long as they held the middle.

They squeezed through, shooting out the mountaintop as if spit between a giant's cracked teeth. They were now high above the pod, the galaxy's stars seemingly within reach just above. Conor enjoyed this sensation: the thrill of flying—open space all around with the rush of tremendous speed. He let up on the throttle as their trajectory now sent them downward. He then remembered this wasn't an aircraft. They weren't quite flying. They were falling.

"Keep us level, and guide us back down."

"Okay!" Conor shouted as he managed the vehicle into a downward glide.

"Remember, it's not an aircraft. Just a hover speeder, so it's seeking the ground."

"Got it," Conor replied. He worked the controls to keep them as level as possible, feeding it thrust as needed to avoid a dive bomb.

"Wooo! And try to enjoy it! After all, I just took you on your first flight lesson."

"Yeah. Enjoy it. Sure," Conor mumbled to himself. This required way too much sharp focus to even think about having fun. *Not dying* took precedence right now. The nose kept trying to dip, but the Spectre's steering didn't have an adjustment for altitude. Every nerve in his body told him this was a terrible idea.

The ground approached sooner than he thought it would—which was both a good thing and a bad one. The other recruits abandoned their vehicles and gathered near the instructor with craned necks, watching this soon-to-be-disastrous stunt. Conor's vehicle started to plummet faster, so he pulled back on the throttle even more.

"Don't totally cut the power. Dead engines are a bad thing," Adin said. Conor heard, but it took every bit of courage to resist completely cutting the thrust. "You're doing great. Try to land us on the main platform." Conor aimed for the far side of the platform away from the Whiplash and all the poor souls about to watch his spectacular crash. "Or not, I guess," Adin mumbled as they overshot the platform.

The Spectre bounced. Not something in its design. It couldn't quite handle the speed and the angle of approach, so it bounced, slamming its belly into the floor before rebounding. It bounced one more time, before the levitating discs caught up and held them aloft again.

Conor powered down the engines and began to breathe again as they slowed to a stop. But his companion told a different story. "Amazing! Woooo!" Adin exclaimed as he leapt off. He slapped Conor on the shoulder as the first-time pilot more cautiously exited, still unsure the ride was over. Adin grabbed him by both shoulders and looked down into his eyes. "You did it right. Don't let anyone tell you different. Could've had a better landing, but pretty nice for your first day."

"Thanks," Conor replied, his voice wavering.

"Seriously," Adin continued. "I've seen these things explode before. It's fantastic. Parts and discs flying everywhere. From what I see, everything's still intact aside from some dings and scratches underneath. Oh, yeah, and the rear panel had seen better days before you clipped that gravity branch. Don't worry, though, we'll just say it was already there."

That explanation would be a long shot. Especially since the instructor had already left the other students behind and was approaching them with a stern face and a walk filled with purpose. Conor braced for the upcoming disciplinary assault. Both boys now stood side by side. Nicet Blatori faced them and circled the two wannabe pilots like a hungry shark. He stopped with his back to the class and stared them down.

"Listen up. Whatever you hear me say next, I expect you to react as if I just told you you're getting kicked out of the Academy. Understood?"

"Yes, Instructor," the boys answered in unison.

"All right." His eyes squinted. "What you did was reckless, especially with a First-Circuit operator. That should not have happened, nor will it ever happen again. I could have you removed from this course and quite possibly the Academy program altogether. Furthermore, I'm not pleased about you banging up one of my babies.

"And last but not least, that was not very smart," Nicet Blatori said, lowering his voice, "but it was soooo very cool. I just have to say, Cadet Hawk, that was some amazing flying—or gliding. Whatever. You both did exactly what I've been pushing this program to do since I got here. Cadets need to find and push through their limits. After all, we're not training for a stroll in the gardens here. I'm going to be interested to see what you can do in the future. But, for the time being, I am not permitted to sanction it, so you'd both better be gentler with my machines, get out of here, and wipe those smiles off your faces."

He then made an exaggerated gesture to the exit. After dismissing the boys with as much feigned consternation as he could muster, the instructor adjusted his flight jacket, and marched back toward the other students. Class was over.

This would be a stressful session this time around based on how many of the other recruits had timidly handled their Spectres. *But at least that boy showed guts and great potential,*

Blatori thought, *so long as he didn't wreck all the vehicles along the way.*

**Hadak-5**
**Riptide Coves**

Makon didn't shout at her. He just moved. He raced against wind and time. It would be close. A boulder resembling the size and shape of an upside-down luxury sailboat tumbled in the air. And its path led right to the disoriented woman. Shila was resting on her knees, her head in her hands, oblivious to the danger barreling toward her.

He swung his arms and pumped his legs, hoping the pulse grounders could keep up. So far, so good. Riostovi technology seldom disappointed. However, despite his quickness, the wind pushed back at him, the resistance driving down his top speed. He needed to pick her up and carry her forward enough to avoid crushing death.

Makon reached her in just enough time to snatch her up and fling her free. He gripped underneath her left arm and tugged, but she didn't move. She slipped free, and Makon stumbled. Her left leg still showed grounded firmly in place by the ankle cuff. No time left to pull her free without the rock smashing her legs, so he dove forward, landing on top of her. He flexed his back muscles and braced for impact.

The massive rock struck him, knocking him flat as it careened off into the distance. Makon collapsed over his Elite as his world went black.

# CHAPTER 19

**The Academy**
**Imperial Visitor Wing**

A tap sounded at the portal. The oversized Jopali man set the 4-D handheld wisp screen down beside him on the plush bed and sat up. It was starting to get late, so a visitor didn't stir much enthusiasm. After all, the members of the Council or the fascinating Wilda Ti wouldn't come to visit at this hour. They hadn't even given him significant attention yet. It'd been nearly seven days since he got there and still no conference. Of course, they had seemingly bigger problems, what with the ongoing war and all, but the next morning would be different. They had agreed to gather in the High Chamber for his presentation.

Perhaps it would be good to move from the bed—the room. He wanted to get another visit in at the Observation Deck and look through the scope one more time before making his case. The darkening of the third sun was an anomaly, and it was not a matter for light discussion. Its fall would mean the extinction of life in Sector 14. The effect on Jopal and neighboring planets in Sector 3 wouldn't meet that drastic a consequence, at least not initially, but it would surely have negative effects on their way of life.

"Come on, Nov. It's me. Open up," spoke the muffled voice from outside the chamber. Novac Riv didn't need to hear the pitch to recognize the voice. He felt a warmth in his chest knowing she'd come to see him. Stand by him. Was it just the need for company or a familiar face? Or was it something more? When he opened the portal and saw her, he knew.

Kim was standing outside the portal; she popped up on her toes. She smiled broadly and wrapped him in a hug before he could even say "Hello." He hugged her back and received a kiss on the cheek in return. They finally pulled apart, and he felt a blush simmer into his cheeks. "What are you doing here?"

"What? You didn't get my message? I sent you a view," Kim said.

"No. That's odd. I never got one. I thought you were dead."

"Well, I'm not," Kim said with a spin. She faced him again, brimming with excited energy. "You know about the observatory though, right?" Novac nodded with a twinge of emotional pain stabbing the corner of his mouth, and Kim continued, "Not everything was destroyed! I managed to get what I could of our research. Plus, you have what you have."

"That's good."

"Still can't believe you didn't get my message. Either way, what did Wilda and the Overwatch Council say? I'm sure it was tough for them to wrap their minds around it. Except Wilda, she's a sharp one. But the others, who knows? Did they understand? Are they going to do anything? Are they sending an exploration team out to Sector 14 to get a closer look? Should we go, too? It's going to be a long trip, but we lost most everything and should probably go. Shouldn't we?" Kim couldn't contain her exuberance. Her thoughts churned into words as they slid down a chute connecting her brain to her mouth.

She continued at the same rapid pace. "How about you? Are you doing okay? I was concerned. You look hungry. Have you eaten? Come on! Tell me what they said. I bet they were impressed we discovered it. I mean, you, but I was there, too. We have a dying dwarf star which could become a black hole.

That's just crazy and bad altogether. What? Why are you looking at me like that?"

Novac patiently waited for her to finish her little rant. He'd grown accustomed to these moments. He raised his hands to her shoulders in an effort to settle her, almost hugging her. He wanted to, and she needed it, but he resisted.

Her agitation spilled from her lips again. "What are they going to do? The Federation. Can we stop it, or do we need to begin planetary evacuations? We can't save everyone. It's so sad. I mean, I've never been out that far into the Nivror, but that doesn't matter. Their planets will die. What about us? What do they want—" Novac acted out of raw instinct when he pressed his lips to hers. It was the best way to calm and quiet her. Kim melted into him, feeling comfort soak her like sliding into a warm bath. Her hand moved to the back of his head and held tight.

Time trickled to a slow-motion crawl until Novac pulled back and looked down into her eyes. "Everything will be fine. I'm just happy you're safe." He took both her hands and didn't move away. She could feel his breath on her face. "We'll work it out, Kim. I'm really glad you're here."

The emotional bath had soothed her enough to relax. "Me, too," she whispered.

Novac pulled away and walked over to a clear-glass desktop with large galaxy maps rolled on top of it. He picked one and swiped the others to the floor. He unrolled it and spread it across the glass. A quick tap on the bottom corner of the desk illuminated the chart and then projected it into a 4-D image filling the room.

"I want to check this here one more time tonight," he said while pointing to an area of the hologram. He walked around it, checking the image from different angles. "What do you see?"

"What did Wilda Ti and the Council say?" Kim asked, her brain still rooted in the prior one-way conversation too much to hear his question.

"Nothing. I'll get to that in a moment. Tell me what you see."

"Did you really just kiss me?" Kim's face flushed with warm exhilaration.

"Kim, focus."

"Okay. Okay. I see the eight moons of Graddoi. Way out in Sector 14."

"No, right here," Novak insisted, pointing to a space between two of the moons.

"Nothing," Kim said, stifling her irritation. She didn't care about the map. She wanted to hear how Wilda and the Council had responded to their discovery—or, at least, kiss him again.

"Exactly. Nothing."

"What do you mean?" Kim asked, moving to gather her bag and set it beside the bed.

"There's nothing there. But there is," Novac Riv said as he massaged his forehead.

"I'm confused."

"The map shows Graddoi and its eight moons. Just as it should. But that's not right."

Kim settled herself into the present moment, paying closer attention to what Novac was trying to explain. "Nov, you're not making sense."

"No doubt. It doesn't make any sense."

"What doesn't make sense?" Kim asked, her words laced with a frustrated tone.

"I think Graddoi has grown a ninth moon, right here," Novac said with two fingers wedged between the two moons on the static image.

"Not possible. You must have just seen a passing meteor or something."

"That's what I thought at first, too, but no. I've checked it multiple times each day. It's not moving.

"Come with me. I'm headed back up to the observatory. I'll show you."

"I'll go with you, but first, I'm starving. The trip here took so long because of the newly imposed security protocols. How about I go get us something to eat and then you can catch me up on your meeting before you show me this ninth mystery moon?"

"They haven't seen me yet. I mean, they have and put me up in this room, but Wilda hasn't had time yet."

"You're joking," Kim said with her hands pressed on her hips.

"Because of the war."

"I get that, but this is just as important as the war."

"Maybe more so," Novac replied. "But they don't see it that way."

"Nov, we will get them to see it," she said with her hands on his shoulders. "We have to. I'm going to run for some food, and then we will prep for your presentation. When is it?"

"Tomorrow morning."

"Then let's make sure we have it right. They're going to be hesitant to give it the necessary attention, and we need to make sure we get them to care." Kim moved to the portal. It swished open from the top down. She stepped out and then looked over her shoulder. "Which way to the food market?"

### Corridor Alpha

Conor reached out and patted Titan's head. After the extreme adventure in Piloting class, he decided he needed to visit his dog. She seemed happy to see him, too.

The Academy teetered between moments of uncanny discovery and sheer terror—with no in between. It became overwhelming at times, and Conor felt as out of place as the friendly beast beside him probably did. Even though his memory faltered, Conor remembered Titan enough and felt their bond. She definitely remembered him, and that gave him comfort.

They wandered without any true destination. He just didn't feel like going back to his room to close out the day just yet. He felt overstimulated and like he needed some time alone.

He held out another piece of dried beef, and Titan jumped to snatch it from his fingertips. Whatever kind of meat it was, she loved it. The market merchant said she would. She devoured the slice and danced a circle around him. Definitely still a puppy at heart—just a really big one.

They turned the corner, venturing into an area he hadn't seen before. The corridor narrowed to a soft, meandering pathway lined with bent trees on both sides. Their tops reached above, their branches entangling with the opposite, neighboring trees, forming an organic canopy. The whole thing was illuminated in a soothing blue and white.

A young woman with short, cropped hair approached in a hurry. She stared hesitantly at Titan as she got near and shuffled to the side. She flashed a quick smile and then continued on.

The dog had that effect on nearly everyone, and they had both grown accustomed to it. Apparently, Titan was something they hadn't seen before, so they all tended to fear her. Except Commander Welcos and Ari. They understood her as he did—a playful companion with divine might and a fluffy heart.

The canopy ended, but the pathway continued further. As usual, the ceiling was nonexistent, or at least seemingly so. The galaxy's stars glimmered high above. Tall lamplights now lit the way, giving off a dim glow. This area looked residential, though nothing like the cloud tower where they put the recruits. These rooms were more like individual suites separated by weaving pathways.

Contemporary huts with domed rooftops and castle-like masonry sprawled out in an organized maze resembling a regal community. Each castle-hut carried the same size and height, but no two matched identically. It portrayed elegant class and individuality without elevating one resident above another.

They moved slowly, taking in the wonder. The solitude of the moment accentuated the atmospheric majesty. Conor wished they'd move his room here, in one of the mini castles, all to himself. At least then he wouldn't have roommates. Byro seemed cool, but sometimes his enthusiasm became unnerving. And the other two—a technological wizard elf and a magical green-eyed, floating boy whose name was pronounced "kill" didn't feel like ideal companions.

Titan suddenly stopped and began to growl. What now? Her lips curled into a snarl, baring menacing fangs soaked in saliva. Conor stopped moving. This was new. He hadn't seen her like this, and it worried him. He reached down to soothe her with a pat on the head, but she ignored the gesture. The growl grew louder.

She sensed danger.

Conor looked ahead, but he didn't see anyone, or anything that might incite Titan's anger. He started to feel strange, though. A heaviness hit his chest and sunk down to his stomach. His head began to ache. He felt a weight; something unseen sinking him as if a heavy blanket had fallen across his shoulders.

He dropped to a knee, one hand still pressed against Titan to help him stabilize. It felt uncomfortable, but not quite overpowering. He didn't feel ill—it was more like a physical depression, as if the air itself had grown denser. It scared him. Why did it scare him? The reason came in a flashback of deep blackness.

He'd felt this before.

–✳–

A soft tap came to Novac Riv's portal. He stepped away from the charts and picked up his shoes before moving to the doorway. Kim had just left. She couldn't have possibly gotten the food already. She must've forgotten something.

He activated the panel with a smile and then bent down to fasten his shoes. "That was fast. What did you forget?" She didn't answer. "You must want another kiss." He finished adjusting his shoe and looked up before slipping on the other.

Cold eyes stared down at him. The tall, dark figure remained silent, cloaked in robes of the blackest smoke. Novac's eyes widened as they took in the horror.

The assassin moved faster than he could scream.

– ✳ –

Conor's mind flashed to an image of a ship. It wasn't like any of these he'd seen. Its design and systems were much more outdated than the Gregor Monolith, but it felt familiar. Normally it brought comfort, but this time it didn't. He felt the heaviness. The depression of an increase in gravity's pull.

A man's stern face. His hand reaching out to him before moving away. Then another flash. A woman. Worried but brave. He knew her—the one standing in the doorway of a room in a place far away in his mind.

They walked in darkness. Titan led the way. Blood streaks on the walls. They hid from something. Something unknown. Intruders. Trespassers on the ship. Something dangerous and terrifying.

The woman was now holding a rifle. She looked back once. Her sad eyes met his. She was leaving.

Enclosed in glass. Lying in a pod—a sleep pod. Titan in one next to him. Alone. No, not alone. Flashes of light from gunfire. Gray-reptilian-skinned warrior-monsters moving closer. Then quiet darkness.

The flashes were quick and immediate. They left as fast as they came. He steadied himself on Titan, but the dog suddenly bolted forward. Conor stumbled before stabilizing himself, and shook off the uneasiness. He called out to her, but she disappeared around the nearby bend. He followed the sound of her barking. The deep resonating roar guided him with ease.

Titan had stopped, her muscles tense and rigid. Her barking subsided. Low-pitched growls now took its place. She seemed determined, but hesitant. Conor caught up to her and placed his hand on her back. The lamps had all extinguished, casting the area in gray shadow.

What did she see? Something had spooked her. He didn't see anything, but he knew it was there. Nearby. He felt it. He remembered the feeling that accompanied the heaviness back on the ship—a feeling that brought terror along with it.

Then that terror revealed itself as it stepped out of the open portal just ahead. It looked like it had been cut out of the night. A dark, hooded form laced in swirling thick smoke. It turned toward its witnesses and flashed black, ragged teeth. If evil wore a face, Conor was now staring into its eyes.

Sedit-Kal moved to them in silence, undeterred by the beast others feared. Conor grabbed Titan's collar and tugged. The dog didn't budge. She stood fixated like a sentinel bound to protect her master from the encroaching demon. Conor tugged harder. "Come on, girl. No! Let's go!" His commands were frantic, swamped in fear.

Titan raised on her haunches, tail wagging stiff and slow. She bared her own teeth, matching her opponent with a display of menacing fangs. She snarled, and Conor paused. He'd never witnessed his dog illustrate such fierce aggression.

Sedit-Kal pressed forward, unfazed by the creature's poised attack. His hands appeared at his side, low, with palms open, as if beckoning the beast to strike. Titan obliged. She tore away from Conor's grip on her collar and raced forward. She lunged upward, high, toward the demon's face, jaw gaping wide to snatch and tear away flesh and jawbone.

Sedit-Kal moved with fluid speed, catching and redirecting Titan just before she could find her target. He flung her high and hard against the wall. The dog crashed with a thump and a crack. She shook her head and tried to stand but collapsed as her legs gave out.

"Titan!" Conor yelled. The demon shifted its eyes from the slumped beast back up to the boy. He snarled, but this time his curled lip showed a trace of malicious pleasure. He sunk back into the swirling smoke and moved again toward the easy prey.

Conor's instincts fired, instructing him to run. Get away and get help! He raced as fast as he could back down the pathway. He spotted the blue-lit canopy and sprinted there. As he crossed under the archway, the sparkling lights began to flicker. Then they went out, leaving him standing alone in darkness.

He stopped, now disoriented, unable to see anything in front or around him. Why did he always end up engulfed in darkness? His heartbeat quickened as fear began to inspire panic. He knew the demon was close—he could feel it—deep and paralyzing. Conor balled his fists and backed up slowly, unsure, though, if he was moving away from or closer to his pursuer. His breath shifted to quick bursts as the black swallowed him like a cold ocean. He wanted to just crouch down and disappear into the floor, but he knew the demon would find him, no matter what. His mind raced for solutions, avenues for escape, but the fear of savage death at the hands of the devil blurred his thinking.

Then in the whirlwind of stabbing despair, a subtle whisper of calm trickled into his mind. "Conor, don't fear the dark. Just go find the light." He put a face to the words as the fog of a defective memory burned away for a moment. His father. A man who'd taught him to rise above fear and embrace the unknown with curiosity.

Find the light. Sure. How could he find the light when there wasn't any freaking light?

As if willed by his father, it suddenly appeared in the tunnel. A sliver of red, slithering through the dark like a snake in night waters. Its undulating movement was mesmerizing: a streak of levitating light engulfed in a crimson haze. It got closer, and Conor wanted to latch onto it.

He started to reach out.

The glowing rope-light recoiled away from Conor's outstretched hand and twirled back into the sea of black. As it circled backward, its red hue betrayed its source, exposing the outline of its bearer standing at the tunnel opening.

Conor now recognized the red streak as a threat rather than a tool for escape. The fire whip lashed forward. It lunged for his face like an angry snake. He ducked as the whip kissed the air just above his head, licking the canopy wall behind him. Sparks erupted from its contact with the entwined metal and glass.

He darted backward as it came around for a second strike for his torso. The whip moved swiftly and relentlessly, keeping Conor on a desperate defense to evade contact with the liquid-hot weapon. He lost his balance and stumbled as he hopped backward to avoid the whip's low attack. He scrambled and pulled his legs in as the whip scored the floor, leaving a smoldering gash in the metal.

The light lashed to his left and then sharply to the right. Then it swirled overhead as if toying with him. He knew it could move too fast for him, especially now with him on the ground. It circled just above, preparing to strike its deathblow.

A new sound then cut through the eerie darkness. A scraping against metal. The scratching of claws on hard surface. The sound intensified as it moved closer with furious speed. Conor couldn't see the new threat but sensed he was its intended target.

It was on top of him now, still unseen. Something gripped his shirt collar tight, yanking him backward. Conor jettisoned back just as the whip lashed downward. It missed as he was dragged out of range like a plastic bag in an ocean riptide. He struggled to fight against the object pulling him, but they moved too fast together for him to plant a foot or hand to produce any resistance. He reached up past his shoulder to the mechanism of what had ensnared him.

He found the fur-covered jawbone, then a pointy ear. The feel of the rugged collar encircling the creature's neck confirmed his guess, and fear subsided into relief. He patted Titan's head and ceased resisting his companion's rescue effort.

They cleared the canopy and shot out of the Imperial Wing, away from the pursuer and into the light. Conor reached up and patted Titan. "That's good. Stop." The dog slowed to a trot before fully stopping. She released her master's collar and turned back to face the corridor they'd just escaped. She stood at the ready, poised for another round of combat.

Conor could sense the demon was still pursuing them. He could feel it heavy in his gut. He stood and looked for a quick place to hide. He noticed a portal nearby and swiped his pulsero against it without hesitation. And without reading the designator. It didn't matter where he was going just as long as it hid them from the evil in pursuit. Besides, he was just happy it opened for a change.

They ducked inside and then shut the portal behind them. Conor allowed himself to take a deep breath as he rested his back against the rock face. He waited and listened, hoping they hadn't been seen. With each passing moment, his hope for their escape grew.

He could feel the wide-open space of the new environment despite the dark. The sky glowed a deep crimson hue over the blackened rock landscape. Twin active volcanoes spewed lava down their slopes like rivers of fire. Even standing at the portal, Conor could feel the abrupt rise in temperature. The heat bit at his exposed flesh.

He'd never been here before, but his thoughts drifted back to a tall girl with slick skin and hard, coiled dreadlocked hair. This had to be Ari's home world, and she didn't recommend it as a rest spot.

Had he paused long enough to read the plaque, he would've seen the word "Tretch" and might have avoided trading one danger for another. Hopefully, Ari had overstated the danger of her home world, but the set of serpent eyes watching him intended to prove otherwise.

# CHAPTER 20

**The Academy**
**Tretch Pod**

What was that thing? It looked like something between a ghost and a monster. It moved like a ghost. He knew for sure he didn't want to see it again. It had been carrying the heaviness. The closer he got to the ghost, the stronger it felt. Fortunately, the sensation dissipated as he now surveyed the desolate landscape below.

Conor let the fear dissipate as he slid down to his butt. He rested his head in his hands and tried to calm down as the image of his pursuer continued to run through his mind. So far, it seemed as if they'd escaped, but he still didn't want to take the chance of opening the portal only to find it lingering in the corridor. He'd just wait here a little longer with Titan. Wait, where was the dog?

He got to his feet and looked around for Titan in the red dark. He wanted to call out to her, but then decided against it. Drawing attention to himself hadn't been working well for him so far. He took a few steps away from the rocky wall and realized he was standing at the top of a ridge. It overlooked cracked and blackened ground with rivulets of bright lava cutting through it like rain trails down a windshield. His feet shuffled back from the edge. It was a long way down.

Conor moved to the right, back along the rock wall hoping to bump into her. He resolved to call out in a loud whisper. Hopefully, Titan would come running because he didn't feel too thrilled about exploring Tretch right now. Ari's warnings about the perils of her home didn't make it sound very hospitable. If this place were so bad, why would they even replicate it at the Academy?

The sky above looked like rolling waves of fire clouds. Another volcano, the spewing geyser of wet lava declaring its active state. He soon wandered up to the twin posts of a suspension bridge formed of narrow perforated planks fastened together with cord. It descended at a slight angle to a plateau. His gut told him not to even think about stepping out onto it, and he was in total agreement with his gut.

Had Titan gone across the bridge? *Please, no.* Then his eye caught a slight movement confirming his fears. There was Titan, standing tall on the plateau ahead, her tail wagging enough to catch against the blood-red light. He called out to her in a harsh whisper, but she didn't react. He had to get closer. Conor placed his hand on the nearest post and rubbed his forehead with his other palm. He risked a step on the bridge. It swayed a bit under his weight, but it seemed sturdy enough. He reassured himself that it should be fine since Titan looked to have crossed without any problems.

His arms spread out to hold both parallel cords serving as handrails—mediocre barriers to a death drop. He risked both feet on the first plank. He bent his knees to test the sturdiness and debated jumping up and down to test it further—and then decided against it. What if it did break? How would he get to Titan? This thought gave him the surge of courage he needed. If he didn't get her, then she'd be stuck and lost alone in this firepit of a training pod.

His right foot found the next plank. Then the left joined it. He thought back to the Ascension obstacle course. This was kind of the same thing, except for the bubble gel and silicone slide to the bottom in case he fell. Hopefully, the bridge would hold, and he wouldn't need any of that. As his confidence in the walkway's craftsmanship began to build, so his stride began to lengthen.

Titan remained just ahead. Her tail stopped wagging and a low growl vibrated in her throat. Conor recognized this as a pretty bad sign. He couldn't tell what she saw, or heard, or smelled. Was it the black ghost, or something else? He kept moving toward her but slowed his pace. "Titan, come here," he whispered. He called again, this time in a louder tone. She still didn't budge.

Then he heard the thudding footsteps. They came from the plateau, moving upward toward the dog's defensive position. A pair of sharp, orange eyes pinned against a jagged black shape moved upward with each thundering footstep. The eyes moved up and up until towering high above Titan. The form now came into full view.

A Dragor. The devastator of Ari's home.

Interwoven scales, thick and jagged, coated its massive torso, and its oversized head sat between wide, muscled shoulders. Its two long arms extended just past two crooked legs, each the size of full-grown tree trunks. It slammed a four-taloned foot right in front of Titan and swiped both clawed hands across the ground in an X. It directed a retaliatory growl at the dog in an effort to terrify the bizarre new threat.

This didn't deter Titan. She stood her ground and roared a tremendous bark. The Dragor recoiled in surprise at this smaller beast's tenacity, but that just infuriated it more. It opened its jaws wide, revealing dagger-teeth the size of Conor's hand. It lowered its head and reeled back its neck, displaying a churning ball of flame resting at the back of its throat.

"Titan, look out!" Conor screamed. A spinning stream of flames shot out, drenching the plateau's corner with a wave of fire. Titan didn't anticipate the fire breath, but she moved too fast to get caught in it. She scooted to the side, causing the attack to miss its mark. The Dragor turned to the left, and, rather than try to catch the dog again with fire, it whipped one of its forearms at her. The blow struck Titan in the torso, sending her rolling and spinning in the black dust.

Without any plan of attack, Conor instinctively rushed forward in her defense. He had to get to her fast. However, a second stalking Dragor suddenly leaped onto the bridge behind him, launching him airborne. Conor landed on his stomach and quickly rolled over. The second monster now thumped across the bridge, moving ever closer with each lumbering step. The bridge's cords stressed under the initial impact and began to shred. Conor heard the tearing and clambered to reach the plateau before it either broke away or the creature bit him in half.

He couldn't reach it in time. The cords snapped and the planked walkway disappeared underneath them both. Conor flailed his arms, stretching for something to grab, but found nothing but air. The Dragor fell first, twisting and slashing to stop its plummet. Conor fell an instant later, both of them helpless to stop gravity's pull.

The Dragor smashed headfirst into the unforgiving rock. Its neck broke, and the rest of its body plopped lifeless with a loud boom. Conor fell slower than the monster, but it seemed fast enough. His legs hit first causing his knees to buckle and his chest to slap hard like a belly flop in a cold swimming pool.

He grimaced and rolled to his side. His chest felt like it'd been hit square in the ribs with a baseball bat. His first thought was "ouch." His second thought rested on the mystery of how he was still alive. The third thought made him jump back to his feet. He lay just several feet away from the monster's slack jaws. It didn't move, but Conor didn't want to wait around for it to spring back to life.

Hot lava rock now singed through his shoes as they burst into flames. He peeled them off and flung them away only to realize nothing protected his feet from the blistering surface.

He pranced away to keep the heat off his feet but realized the lava rock didn't burn. It felt warm, but not overly hot, like sun-drenched beach sand.

Conor couldn't help but look back up at the shattered bridge to reassess the height of the fall. The distance looked much too high to survive without wings or a parachute. He checked his body for blood and broken parts, but all things being considered, he felt okay.

Conor jolted with the sound of another roar as a splash of flames spilled over the edge of the cliff high above. One Dragor remained, and it was battling his Titan.

He sprinted around the mountainside to find an easier, faster way to the summit. He spotted a slope cut into one side of the jagged hill. Its steepness looked daunting but manageable. Conor hurdled a waist-high ridge and began his ascension. The pounding of his heart in his ears muffled the barks, roars, and intermittent fire spurts as he rushed upward.

The pathway stopped at a drop-off. It only led back down. He'd have to free-climb. He jumped to snag a chunk of rock sticking out like a hitchhiker's thumb. It was a short leap and an easy pull to climb on top.

He hesitated a moment but then collected his courage. The climb to the top would be the only way to save Titan. He took some comfort in the fact that he didn't need to climb a mountain—just a plateau. He could make it. He had to.

Conor dug his fingers at two opposing handholds and pulled himself up, one aft r another. His feet easily found plenty of places to push from. The rock was bumpy and riddled with pockmarks large enough for his fingers. He soon found a climbing rhythm as the fear of not reaching Titan in time replaced the fear of falling. The rock suddenly broke away under his right foot and Conor hung by a single handhold. He yelled out and looked down between his legs. A pang of fear pulsed in his mind as he spotted the ground far below. His fingers dug in tighter to the brittle rock as he swayed suspended by one hand.

Then a powerful revelation struck his mind like a spotlight in a dark room. Why was he afraid to fall? Hadn't he already fallen all the way from the top and landed on his feet . . . kind of? The fall wouldn't hurt him. He didn't know the reason. He just knew it wouldn't.

His muscles surged with the fuel of assurance, and this emboldened him. His climbing speed doubled as he grabbed whatever handhold he spotted, now moving with the dexterity of a tree lizard. He pushed himself, untired and driven. He looked down to the right and recognized another path leading to the plateau. He glanced back to the top and launched himself upward. He'd take the fastest route instead.

He soon reached the top edge and climbed to his feet. Titan lay on her side, her body pinned and crushed under the weight of the Dragor's foot. Its talons dug into the ground, locking her down. Conor cried out and dashed forward with the intensity of a falling meteor. The Dragor spotted him and snarled. Conor charged, wishing for a weapon to chop off its leg right at the knee, but he'd have to use the only weapon available—his body.

His shoulder lowered as he dove at the monster's ankle like a guided missile. The collision erupted with a resounding *snap* and an aching roar from the beast as it staggered back and toppled over. Conor rose up, hoping the crack he'd heard wasn't any of his own bones. He still felt strong as he turned to check on Titan. Surprisingly, the tenacious dog was already on her feet, poised for a counterattack.

The Dragor clumsily pressed to its feet using its long arms to push itself up. It was unable to rest steady on its left leg due to a freshly broken ankle, and Titan seized on its immobility to grab the easiest target. She lunged at the monster's tail, sinking her powerful fangs into the meaty flesh. The Dragor's scaled armor proved insufficient to protect against the bite as scales splintered off and flitted away like ice chips tossed in a spinning fan.

The Dragor roared again in agony, but it wasn't ready to accept defeat. It violently thrashed its tail but couldn't manage to shake the dog or lift her from the ground, lacking either the leverage or the power. It turned toward her and slashed Titan across the back with its extended claw. This took effect, and the dog released her grip.

They squared off again like two tired gladiators in a fight to the death. Conor wanted to uneven the odds. Blood was oozing from the Dragor's wounded leg, or more accurately, its foot. Conor looked over and found his weapon. Two of its talons had broken off and were rooted in the ground. They called to him like horned swords beckoning the chosen king to claim his destiny.

He rushed over to the nearest embedded talon, sliding along the broken shale and skidding to a stop just beside it. He wrapped his hands around it and yanked, hoping it wasn't as stubbornly impossible as the Harbinger's Bane axe. He breathed relief as it slid smoothly out of its dust sheath, a curved black dagger of savagery. It extended the length of his entire arm and took both hands to carry. He leveled it like a jousting lance and charged.

The Dragor spotted the boy with the stolen spear and swiped at him. Conor dodged and slipped on some broken gravel. He fell and immediately collected himself enough to scamper over and grab the talon-lance again. He hefted it up just in time to see the Dragor's dripping fangs looming overhead. There were too many teeth to count, but the Dragor obviously wanted to use them all.

Conor lunged forward with his weapon, but the monster had already pulled back. It hadn't wanted to eat him, at least not without cooking him first. The Dragor belched a wall of fire too massive for Conor to fully avoid. He planted the talon on its end and tucked as small as he could behind it. His eyes slammed shut as he buried his chin into his chest. The flames engulfed him, splitting around the vertical shield and carrying over him like an angry wave crashing on a weathered dock.

He couldn't get small enough to hide completely from the intense heat blast. It licked and shredded away his uniform sleeves up to the shoulder, and his pants disintegrated below the mid-thigh and around the hips. The fire burst was short, but it felt like broiling, slow-motion death.

Conor dropped to the ground once the flame faucet snuffed out. His arms and legs were charred; they ached as if the fire had siphoned all his energy directly out of his skin. Even his hair hadn't emerged unscathed. It was singed all over, and a wide streak of hair had been wiped clean away above his right ear.

The Dragor hadn't finished with him yet. It lingered over him, its eyes wide like a child who'd just been handed an ice cream cone covered in rainbow sprinkles. It moved closer, its tongue coating cracked teeth with a fresh coat of saliva. Orange eyes sparkled with the lust of a fresh kill.

But just as it whipped its head down to grab the seared snack, it jerked backward. Titan had its mangled leg in her maw and pulled the beast off balance with the power of a tow winch. The Dragor lost balance and stumbled to its knees. A shrill screech shot from its throat. It couldn't reach the nuisance yanking on its leg, so it turned back to the prey it could reach. It bit down toward the boy but found only rock and dust. Conor had moved.

He was now standing at the Dragor's right, just under its lanky arm. He lifted the curved lance up and drove it hard and deep into the beast's chest, piercing through scales and bone and lung. The creature recoiled in agony. It danced backward, toppling over the plateau's edge and pounding against the rock face over and over as it fell.

Conor limped over to ensure the battle was finished. Far below, the Dragor lay lifeless and contorted on its side. It didn't move, and this brought Conor some respite. Titan joined him at his side. Claw marks cascaded from the top of her back and down to her belly. They both wore the wounds from a challenging fight, but they'd somehow survived. One thing was certain: the creatures inhabiting these pods weren't simulation at all.

Considering himself lucky to have endured thus far, Conor felt ready to leave. There was just one problem—a significant one. The bridge leading to the exit had disintegrated, leaving just dangling cords. He didn't see any other way to get up to the portal on top of the ridge, unless he tried climbing, but he didn't have the strength for that right now. His arms felt like dead branches, and his skin looked like tree bark.

Looking out over the vastness of the Tretch pod, Conor wondered what else might want to put him on the menu. For now, he just wanted to lie down. But he couldn't do it up there—they were too exposed. "Let's get down," he muttered to Titan as he tugged her collar and started toward the best downward route. Fortunately, the Dragor's death drop had carved out enough patches of rock to navigate a way to the ground without climbing.

It took a little longer than anticipated, but Titan nudged him along until they finally reached the bottom. Conor snuck quietly past the dead Dragor just in case it wasn't as dead as it appeared to be. They wandered away into a small canyon, hoping there wouldn't be any more surprise attacks.

The volcano boomed in the distance, briefly drowning out the groans bellowing from the rock formations all around.

A bird screeched above them, and he looked up. No, not a bird. It resembled a giant bat, and it was circling with two companions. He needed to hide, find some sort of shelter.

Just ahead, he spotted a dark hole cut into the mountain. They moved to it and discovered it wasn't as deep of a cave as he'd hoped for. At least it would get them out of sight. After all, he had no idea if Dragors lived in caves and didn't want to stumble upon a lair. Why couldn't Planetary Studies have started with a discussion about Tretch instead?

This would be fine. It was a small, sheltered dent in the mountain as if a giant had dug out a boulder, broke it in half, and placed the parts just outside it. Conor ducked and crawled inside, placing his back against the wall. Titan moved inside to inspect it and then spun around to take a seat just at the entrance. She put herself on protective watch. Conor slumped his head, feeling grateful for his dog's new training regimen.

The wounded boy petted her back, being careful to avoid the bloody marks cut into her fur. "Good job, girl. You're the best," he whispered.

Then he slid down and passed out.

**Hadak-5**
**Riptide Coves**

"If you're done napping, there's something you should see," the calm voice sounded just above the Commander. Makon shut his eyes and opened them again, trying to regain his bearings. He turned to his side, propping himself up on an elbow. His surroundings were completely foreign—an interior dark and dominantly black save for the light spilling from the open doorway. The ceiling stretched high and looked spongy. Somehow it also appeared oddly familiar. "Come on, get up."

Makon looked up and saw Haviro's face. "How'd you get here?" the Commander asked as he reached out to the wall to help himself to his feet. The wall squished between his fingers and he yanked his hand away. "What the—? Oh, of course." Now he knew the place. The typical oozing walls and ceiling of the Kravii should've been expected.

"You went down after taking a giant rock to the back of the head. Should I even be surprised it didn't kill you?"

"Nope," Makon replied, rolling his head in a circle to chase away the dull ache.

"I figured. Knocked you cold, though."

"Hey, it was a big rock. I don't recommend you trying it." Makon looked around for Shila. He found her in the cockpit area, looking bewildered as she scanned a long column stretching from floor to ceiling. He placed a hand on her shoulder. "You okay?"

She turned to him. "Yes. Just a little shaken up back there. How about you?"

"Me? I'm good. I think I just needed a nap."

Shila smiled. "Thank you, Commander. You saved me."

"Don't mention it."

"Fine."

"No, I mean it. Don't mention it to the Vice Commander. I don't want Valitat yelling at me." Makon flashed a smile. "So, what do we have here?"

"I don't know. I'm trying to figure this thing out. I have no idea how to start it up. This is foreign technology. It's not as intuitive as our V-tech."

"Well, keep at it. We need to figure out what they have. Anything we can get on their cloaking, battle plans, or what they were even doing way out here in this desolate death trap."

"I'll let you know as soon as I do, but you should go talk to Haviro. He found something."

"All right, then," Makon said as he pulled himself back through the cockpit, being careful to stay away from the slime walls. He poked his head around the corner and found Haviro. "You have something?"

"Yes. Actually, two things. First, come follow me outside." Haviro activated the door and waited for it to descend. "Figured out how to work this door first just in case a rock shower decided to greet us in the alcove. So far, we look tucked away enough from the wind and stone." He moved down the gangplank and around to the nose of the ship.

Makon followed, but as soon as he reached it, he knew what the Elite wanted him to see. Haviro was standing in the midst of a graveyard. Kravii organic armor lay scattered and riveted in the dirt, most of it torn and mangled. It looked like a pack of ravenous animals had laid waste to the ship's entire crew, shredding the armor and devouring the host. "Beast attack?"

"Appears that way, but not likely. Their armor is much too tough for tooth and claw. Besides, what kind of animal could possibly live out here in this place? This had to be something else."

"Bandits, you think?" Makon asked.

"Don't see blaster or electric burns. Something cut through the armor clean. And if you hadn't noticed, where are the bodies? Or at least parts?"

"The wind might have carried them off, or decomposition."

"The winds don't reach inside this alcove very much, and they haven't been here long enough for decomp. You can tell by the minimal dust accumulation on the armor and the ship."

"Well, you've been at this longer than I have; tell me what you think," Makon said as he plucked a severed Kravii gauntlet from the dirt. It began to writhe in his hand, working its way around the back of the hand and sliding in between his fingers. He peeled it off, letting it fall to the ground, motionless. "Armor still works. Nasty stuff."

"You want to take some home?"

"I'll pass. It'll probably try and choke me in my sleep."

"Let me show you the other thing I found," Haviro said as he moved through the graveyard, cautious not to step too close to the armor in case it tried to grab his boot. They moved back into the ship, and Haviro walked to the gunner's bay. A staff was resting against the torpedo launcher. It was long and black, coming to a twisted U-shape at one end. Makon reached out for it. "Don't drop it when it starts wriggling. I think everything Kravii-made has a mind of its own. I found it out there with the other armor."

"I'm pretty certain this is a Battleborn staff," Makon said as he inspected the weapon.

"Yeah. Could be, I guess."

"You don't get it. The enemy doesn't award this on a whim. It means the owner is a battle-hardened warrior of the ultimate rank. It must belong to Utirot."

"He's a vicious one. You sure it's his?"

"It's my job to know, my friend. See the U-shape? Obviously, belongs to Utirot." Makon shrugged. "It also means that he wasn't traveling with just any squad of warriors."

"So outside are the remains of some pretty hefty guys," Haviro added.

"Exactly. It's pretty much the equivalent of something wiping out you and me, along with the rest of the Elites."

"Oh. That really doesn't make sense. It would take a massive army to do that, if I say so myself."

"Or something deadly. Something we haven't seen before. On the plus side, it took down Utirot for us. That's a good thing."

Haviro shifted his weight and scooted past the Commander. "In that case, I want to get off this planet. Anything strong enough to take out a Battleborn and his Knights is something I don't want to meet. I'm going to get an update on the repairs to the ship."

Makon studied the staff in his hands, not really listening. He planted it on the floor, leaning on it a bit as he swam in his thoughts. After pausing a long minute or two, he plucked the staff and moved back to the cockpit. "Where's Haviro?"

"He went to the other ship," Shila answered without looking over.

"There was a meeting here. It must've gone bad—at least for the Kravii. Any luck figuring out how to start this thing?"

"Nope. If we can't turn it on, we're at a total mission loss."

Makon ran his palm across the oddly placed vertical column resembling the mast of a sailing ship. Its surface felt rubberized, with grooved sections. This thing couldn't be just for decoration. At about waist level, it had two deep cuts narrowing itself down to a dark glass cylinder. He glanced at the staff in his hand. "Good news."

"What?" Shila asked.

"I think you just needed the key." He then leveled the staff and inserted the U-shaped end in the grooves around the glass tube. The cylinder glowed purple with a building hum as the column came to life. He pulled back the staff with a grin as the front dash illuminated with Kravii symbols, and the dark chamber filled with a purple light. The column then spun, unwinding into two halves of a massive screen. That, too, sparked alive—one side a galaxy map of their current position and the other a graphical collage of more symbols.

"Now we're cooking," Makon said as Shila ducked under the screens to stand beside him. "I don't suppose you read Kravii, do you?"

"Who doesn't?" she asked with a smirk.

**The Academy**
**Tretch Pod**

"Shhhhhh. It's okay. Don't go crazy." Titan's tail swung back and forth like a pendulum in overdrive at the sight of a friendly face, or at least the sight of something without fire breath. "We found you. Good job," the man continued with a whisper.

Conor opened his eyes to see two armored men crouched down just outside his hiding spot. It took him a second to register who they were. "Good morning, Cadet Hawk. You picked a strange place to take a nap. You remember me?"

"Elites," Conor mumbled.

"Indeed. Iopo Lex and Bradok," the Primo Officer replied.

"How'd you find me?"

"Your friendly little beast here has a tracker in her collar. You both went missing, and we were tasked to find you, so here we are. I do need to say, this was a bold choice for a place to explore."

"Uh . . . I wasn't exploring."

"Tretch is dangerous. Just like the real planet," Bradok added. He was standing now, armed with a rifle and seeking potential threats.

"Probably the most dangerous pod here. Well, other than Kravos. Only Fifth-terms are permitted, and, even then, only under troop supervision. I'm surprised you even have access," Iopo Lex said.

"Why is it even here, then?" Conor asked.

"We need to test you in the harshest environments. From the looks of things, you performed well. Survived a Dragor attack."

"Two. There were two of them."

"Bradok, this guy took down two. I'm impressed."

"Not the same," the muscled Elite replied. "The pulsero limits the effectiveness of their attacks. Slows them and shields the wearer."

"I would agree with that, but what if I showed you this?" Iopo Lex reached out for the boy's left arm and held it up. Conor hadn't noticed before. The pulsero was still wrapped around his wrist, but it had sustained heavy damage.

Conor thought for a second. "It must've broken from my fall from the bridge."

Bradok glanced at the pulsero and then turned back to the canyon. "Okay. Now I'm impressed."

"What do you mean you fell from the bridge?" Iopo Lex asked with a perplexed face. "That bridge? *The* bridge?"

"Yeah. A Dragor jumped on it, and it broke."

"Ha. Ha," Iopo Lex laughed. "Boy, you have a story to tell! Not here, though. We should get going. Dragors have already scavenged the fallen, and they'll likely circle back soon to find us once their hunger builds again. Come on, we'll get you a new suit. Looks like it got shredded."

"It was fire. I got burned."

"Woah. Fire bursts from those things are no joke. Where'd it burn you?"

"Everywhere. My arms and legs."

"Uh . . . you sure?" Iopo Lex asked, looking at him like he was making stuff up.

"Yeah, look—" Conor paused as he looked at his arms. The skin showed no trace of burns or even a char mark. The blackened skin had cleared away on his legs as well. "I swear I was burned. It hurt really bad. I . . . I couldn't even walk. Titan got hurt, too."

"She seems fine. Don't see any injuries." Conor sat up and crawled over to his dog. He dragged his hand in circles looking for the claw marks but couldn't find anything.

"I swear—I'm not lying."

"Relax, boy. I believe you. How do you feel?"

"I feel all right. Just really tired still."

Iopo Lex stood and moved to whisper in Bradok's ear so they couldn't be overheard. "We should inform the Commander about this."

Bradok sighed. "I'm willing to bet he already knows."

"Probably right." Iopo Lex stepped out into the canyon path. "Let's go. Stay quiet and low." Conor pushed up to his feet, which were still black, covered in ash and warm silt.

Bradok noticed the boy's bare feet. "Where are your boots? Don't tell me you came in here barefoot."

"My shoes caught fire, so I took 'em off."

"No doubt," Iopo Lex added. "You need the right boots in here. Being combat-ready always starts with the appropriate footwear. It's what I always say. Don't I, big guy?"

"Whatever you say. I don't listen to you most of the time," Bradok replied.

"Sure, you do. I'm the sunshine in your breakfast bowl. You good to carry him over the lava rock?"

Bradok looked down at Conor, sizing up the level of burden he'd impose. "I suppose."

"No. I don't need to be carried," Conor said as he fought off a quick dizzy spell and steadied himself. "The ground's not that hot. It doesn't burn."

The two Elites shared a bewildered glance, and Iopo Lex shook his head. "That sure sounds familiar."

Conor patted Titan and followed the two armored Elites back through the narrow valley toward the ridge. He felt grateful for the short distance to their destination. A bed and a quiet room seemed really nice right now. Dragors hadn't tracked them back to the ridge, but, looking up, Conor had no idea how they would get up without the bridge. He could manage the climb, but what about Titan? "Are we climbing up?"

"Kind of. Don't worry. You're with Elites now. We do it the fun way," Iopo Lex said as he scanned the ridgeline far above.

"You think they'll reach all the way to the top?" Bradok asked.

"They better. V-64 just upgraded them last year. If not, then she and I will have to chat."

Bradok flexed his eyebrows and looked down at Titan. "I guess you want me to carry this one."

"You know, I hadn't even considered it," Iopo Lex said, feigning surprise. "But now that you offer . . ."

"Of course, you didn't," Bradok said, absorbing the sarcasm. He then patted Titan on the head, reached down, and wrapped his right arm around her torso. "We're going up, my friend. Please don't bite my arm off." He then released the claw affixed to his left wrist, firing out a long cord straight up. The four metal fingers dug into the rock and held. The device then began retracting, slowly pulling them both upward. Bradok kept up the rhythm by pumping his legs off the cliff when necessary.

Iopo Lex waited until they reached the top before activating his claw. He then turned to Conor. "You sure you don't want to just jump up there?" Conor gave him a perplexed stare. "Never mind. Just climb on my back, and hold on. Oh, and remind me we need to get you a haircut. You look like you had a run-in with a wild animal or something."

# CHAPTER 21

**The Academy**
**Residential District**

Something plopped down on the foot of Conor's bed, landing on his legs. It didn't jolt him awake; it merely disturbed his slumber enough for him to open his eyes and roll over. He assumed it was one of his roommates—definitely Byro or V-23—but confusion set in when he recognized the face. Anibal, the mysterious guy who just seemed to show up out of nowhere.

"Get dressed," he said, pointing to the combat-training outfit neatly folded on his bed. "Let's go." Conor looked over, noticing his roommates still sleeping. He wiped the eye crust away and slowly sat up.

"Where are we going?"

"You're with me this morning. Hurry up, and meet me outside."

Conor stretched, feeling a little ache in his muscles from the Dragor battle the day before. He wondered if trouble awaited. The Elites had escorted him to his room in the afternoon, and he'd simply gone to bed. No one had spoken with him yet, so maybe Anibal was there to render discipline.

He grabbed the slick, long-sleeve shirt, pulling it up to his lap. Anibal wore his usual long black tunic. He stopped at the portal and turned with a smile. "By the way, nice haircut."

Conor instinctively ran his hand across the shaved parts of his head. The sides and back were now skin-close to mirror where the fire had burned away patches of hair. He left the top long and pulled front to back. A stimulator had been applied to condition the hair to permanently style in the manner Iopo Lex indicated. The cut looked aggressive, even tribal, and Conor hadn't decided yet if he truly liked the change. At least the Elites approved.

He hurried to get dressed so he didn't keep the Paladin waiting, a strange title for someone who hung around the Academy. Maybe today he'd finally ask the man what it meant.

As they left the recruit towers, he anticipated he'd hear about where they were going or that he should expect a demerit for going into the Tretch pod. This never happened. The only thing Anibal did was hand him a new pulsero and tell him he looked like a warrior now. Another haircut admirer.

They made their way through the marketplace, empty because everyone else got to enjoy their sleep. Anibal led him to The Forge, and his anxiety began to lift because this meant they weren't marching to face the CAL or a bunch of angry instructors. Actually, he didn't really know what it meant.

He first spotted the Freefall, recalling how miserably he did there. Then he remembered his recent climb in Tretch and thought he might do better next time. "You want to try it?" Anibal asked, noticing the boy studying the Ascension obstacle course.

"No, not really. Do I have to?"

Anibal smiled. "Not unless you want to. I've got something better. Follow me." Conor trailed him past the training huts and over to the range. The structure grew in size as they neared. Since he'd seen it only from a distance, he falsely assumed its actual size. The building stretched as wide as its height, like a quadruple-decker warehouse.

Conor moved to the tall portal marked by tinted glass. He'd wanted to explore inside this place since he'd first spotted it, so when Anibal moved away, he felt a ripple of disappointment.

The Paladin veered down an unseen path, disappearing out of view. Conor scurried away from the range in an effort to relocate his guide, spotting him again once he moved directly behind him. Another illusion. He paused to check out the curtain. On one side it appeared to be empty flooring and space extending far off into the distance. On the other, a winding pathway marked with ankle-high floating light pods meandering toward a secret alcove. The Academy loved to use these illusion screens. Hopefully, this one wouldn't lead into a monster's lair like on the Star Deck.

It didn't. Not even close. They stepped out onto a wide bridge, smooth and semi-translucent and outlined in black metal. Conor looked down between his feet and saw a river far below carving out a tropical jungle. "Is that real?" he asked.

"Jump and find out," Anibal answered back over his shoulder. At this point, his experience taught him that it could go either way. They could be walking on a massive bridge over a deep gorge, or it could be paneled flooring just below them. Curiosity got the better of him, and he had an idea.

Anibal sensed the distance growing between them. He stopped and turned to see the boy flat on his stomach and swinging his arm off the side. He chuckled. "Come on. You don't need to explore every remarkable thing you come across. It gets you into trouble you're not prepared for." Conor pushed back up to his feet. "If you must know, it is real, so don't fall."

They continued the length of the bridge up to an open tower extending high above. The arched gateway appeared large enough to pass a cruiser ship through without bumping the sides. Five other towers joined only by the same bridge circled around the center—a large round disc emitting a blue light. As they drew closer, the light became the mist particles ever-present in the Academy.

Anibal stopped at the edge of the circle and motioned for Conor to move onto it. "Please sit, Master Hawk." Conor stepped forward with apprehension, but it felt smooth and cool. Conor took a seat on the left, not really knowing what to expect but trusting him enough to know he wasn't currently in danger for a change. Anibal stepped forward and joined him.

"Welcome to my training temple. Built and fashioned per my specifications." The man then tapped his pulsero, and they both lifted off the disc.

"Woah," Conor breathed as they began to lift high. He followed Anibal's example and tucked his legs together to prevent them from dangling. Soon the lift ended. They stopped ascending, now suspended high in mid-air. Conor couldn't help but start to drift. He started to slowly circle around as the Paladin maintained a stable position.

"You'll learn to control that. Hopefully. This is where I take select students for advanced tactical training. It's not for everybody. I've trained other recruits, but many found it too rigorous."

"Like who?"

"You know the twins? I tried with them. They have the talent but lack the mind." Conor now circled around him to the right. "Look, I can't talk to you seriously with you doing that."

"Sorry, I can't help it," Conor said as he tried to swim back to the front. Anibal reached behind him and grabbed Conor's forearm. He then pulled him forward so they faced one another. He stifled a smile as he watched the boy struggle to hold still.

"Sorry." Conor slumped down and spread his hands to halt the drift hat had already started again.

"Just touch my knee if you can't balance."

"Balance?"

"Yes. It's balance. You have none. One must center themselves. It's all about inner balance, harmony within. Only then can you remain precisely where you intend to be."

"How?"

Anibal sighed. "If you learn it, you'd be the first. I can train you, but I can't teach you to learn, can't teach you to work. It requires effort and sacrifice." Conor reached out and tapped Anibal's knee to steady himself.

"What kind of training? Is it different than the normal Combatives?"

"Yes. You would continue with Combatives, but I will enhance your gifts."

"What gifts?" Conor asked.

"If you have to ask, then you aren't yet seeing. Tell me, Master Hawk, what have you seen?"

"What do you mean? I don't get it."

"Tell me of your experience."

"Here at the Academy, or in general?"

"All of it."

"I've only seen Jopal and the Academy—well, different parts of the Academy. It's all odd to me. Everything feels new. I don't know—different, I guess. It's hard for me to keep up. I keep making mistakes."

"That is true. You feel like everything is strange to you?"

"Yes," Conor said, steadying himself at Anibal's knee again. The man nodded.

"I think it's time to enlighten you on some things. Where are you from?"

"Jopal."

"Really? Where in Jopal? It's a big planet. Can you describe your home for me?"

"Uh . . . the southern part."

"You sure? Describe it." Conor paused, his eyes darting to the right and left as he struggled to remember. Anibal canted his head to the side. "Having trouble remembering your home?"

"No. I mean, yes. Commander Welcos told me I'd lost my memory. Said I can't remember because of a trauma."

"He's right, Master Hawk. But it's not Jopal you can't remember. The Commander found you and your animal on a broken spaceship. A spaceship not from this galaxy."

"How do you know?"

"Commander Welcos told me. Oh, and because I shot you with a bolt rifle." Anibal's eyes gleamed.

"What? I didn't get shot."

"Yes, you did. I don't miss. After the attack on Jopal, you appeared on a small hill wandering over to the fallen towers."

"I remember you there," Conor said, thinking back to the day.

"You remember something stinging you and then you rolling down the hill?"

"I think I tripped."

"No, you got blasted with a molt slug. Should've ripped a hole in your leg and cooked muscle right on through." Conor just looked up at him with wide eyes. "That didn't happen, did it?" Anibal asked.

"No." Conor tapped Anibal's knee again.

"So, now tell me what else you know about your gifts."

"Wait. You shot me?"

Anibal just shrugged. "I wanted to see for myself."

"See what?" Conor asked. "I don't have gifts. You mean, like superpowers?"

"Not quite, but go with it."

"I don't think I have any powers."

"Master Hawk, based on what you know about yourself, what would happen to you if I suddenly activated the gravity field right now?"

"I'd fall. We both would."

"Then what?"

"I don't know."

"Answer the question."

Conor hesitated a moment. Then he finally started to piece it together. "I would fall slower than you, I think." Anibal nodded and waited. "Then I would land on my feet or stomach or butt."

"Right. Would you be hurt?"

"I don't think so."

"Do you believe this to be normal?"

"I guess it's not."

"How about speed? You find yourself running pretty fast lately?"

"Yeah," Conor replied, feeling a mix of uneasiness and excitement at the thought of superpowers.

"I've seen it. You have gifts. Once you learn to use them, you will replace your clumsiness with ability and aptitude far superior to the rest of us."

"Why do I have powers . . . er, gifts?"

"It has something to do with your molecular structuring in relation to the dynamic physics of the Vesputi galaxy. The Elders understood it. They could explain it to you in a more technical and confusing way, but they aren't here anymore. You're stuck with me. So, I'll keep it simple. You run faster, jump higher, and are more resilient to physical damage than others. You heal quick. Remember the fire?"

"I still don't like fire. It hurts."

"You're not immortal, my friend, but you still healed quickly."

"I suppose. Why are you telling me now?"

Anibal looked away from his pupil for the first time. "That day in the Commander's palace. You and Tiera came back and saw me there."

"I remember."

Anibal nodded. "The Commander didn't want me to tell you. You'll have to ask him the reason."

"Why tell me now?"

"He's not here." A hint of apprehension displayed in his countenance. Anibal acted against orders. "He knew you weren't ready. You still aren't. But we're running out of time. There's something dangerous close and brewing, and after yesterday, Wilda Ti and I agreed your training must begin."

"I have been training, though."

"I mean your *true* training, Master Hawk."

"What did Commander Welcos say?"

"He can't be reached for some reason, but the Vice Commander, Valitat Bithos, consented."

Conor remembered the tall, attractive woman in the black and red from the Gregor Monolith. "How many people know about me?"

"Several. Keep it that way. At least for now." Anibal placed his hands on his knees. "Any questions?"

"Yes. Who are you? What is a Paladin? That's what you're called, right?"

Anibal nodded. "The Paladins are friends to the Federation, but we don't belong to it. We operate outside of any faction or organization to ensure universal balance. We are few, but we work to make a difference."

"Why are you here at the Academy? With me?"

Anibal smiled. "Wilda requests my assistance from time to time to assess certain cadets with high potential. But I'm here now because of you. The Commander summoned me the day he found you."

"What does that purple stripe on your back mean?"

"It's my rank. Starts with white then blue to purple to red. The color changes through achievement and experience to reflect one's mastery of self."

"Red's my favorite color. I'd want red."

"You'd definitely be a white, Master Hawk, but the red mark is the impossible goal. Only one has ever achieved its honor."

"Oh," Conor whispered, still holding on to the prospect of a red-line achievement.

"Any more questions?"

Conor thought for a second. "No. I guess not. Yeah. One more. How do I learn more about the abilities I have?"

Anibal looked up with just his eyes. He then leaned forward and smiled. "Good question." He tapped the pulsero twice, and suddenly Conor dropped. He yelped at first, feeling the sudden pull of gravity yank him downward. The fright of falling then yielded to thoughts of landing. He impacted the blue disc with both feet, absorbing the shock with bent knees. His arms shot out for balance and stability. He didn't break. He didn't even fall over.

In that moment, the fear of great heights morphed into possibility. A surge of confidence coursed through him like electric shockwaves. He looked up, and Anibal was still sitting, suspended high above. "Now what?" Conor called out.

"First lesson. It's simple. All you have to do is touch my shoulder." A series of golden transparent panels appeared from the five columns. They were substantially spaced apart and continued upward from the ground to the top like a spiral staircase for a small-footed giant.

He hesitated a moment, in case more instructions came, but Anibal's silence directed him to get moving. Conor ran to the closest, lowest panel and jumped. He caught the edge with his hands and pulled himself up. *Pretty good*, he thought. The next one would be more difficult since he didn't have a running start this time. He stepped forward and leaped, launching himself at the next column. Just as his fingers reached the panel, it disappeared, and he fell.

Off-balance and contorted, Conor dropped to the floor with a graceless thump. He got up, collected himself, and moved back to the low panel again. He raced forward and jumped to grab it, but as he reached out, it disappeared. He fell again. At least this time he wasn't as high when he crashed down, landing on his side.

He pushed himself to his feet and looked up. He couldn't tell if the Paladin even noticed him. Conor shook his head and decided to try again. He moved a few steps away and raced for the panel. This time, he reached it, grasping it with tense hands, but just before he could pull himself up, it faded away. The drop didn't faze him too much this time because he'd half-expected it. He landed on his feet, which was good, but now his frustration brewed over.

"No hands," Anibal shouted below.

"Ugh! Okay, no hands," Conor muttered. "How am I—? Never mind." Conor walked over to the left a greater distance to give himself a better running start. He raced forward faster and jumped higher than before. This time his flight path would land him right on top of the lowest panel, but that didn't happen. It vanished right under his feet, leaving him falling, landing, and standing on the ground again.

"No running," the mental terrorist of a teacher shouted again.

"What?! How am I supposed to reach it?"

"Jump higher."

Conor started second-guessing this advanced special training. He stood under the panel, studying it, wondering how he would jump that high without a running start. It glowed above, roughly the height of three grown men standing on top of each other's shoulders. His head shook. "I can't do it."

"Then you won't."

"It's impossible."

"So is mistaking a bullet for a bug sting."

He had a point. Couldn't argue that. Apparently, the teacher floating in the air believed he could do it. That must count for something. Conor crouched and swung his arms.

"Stop!"

Conor paused. "What?"

Anibal descended to the level of the first step. "Are you going to land on it?"

"I think so."

"Then don't do it. You're already on the path to failure. You need to *know* you're going to do it. Do you try to walk? Do you try to breathe? You don't think about it. You don't *try* it. You just do it. It happens. I can tell you over and over that I know you can do it, but it won't matter. It needs to grow from within yourself. Believe in your abilities. Believe in yourself. You jump. You land. There is no other possibility in your head."

Conor took a deep breath. He bent his knees and jumped. He went high, higher than he thought he would, but not high enough. His forehead reached only the panel's edge before he descended again.

"Try again. This time, actually jump with force."

Conor jumped again but missed. Again, again, and again, he jumped and fell. After the 11th attempt, he stopped and hung his head.

"Are you tired?" Anibal asked, his tone making the question more disparaging than inquisitive.

"No. I just don't know how I can possibly jump on top of that thing."

"That's the problem. You're jumping with just your legs. You haven't even visualized landing on the platform yet. If your mind can't see it, your body won't do it. Now sit."

"What? Why?"

"Sit down right there."

Conor plopped down on the floor, feeling like a child who'd just been reprimanded to stand in the corner. "Tuck your legs and calm down. Don't get upset with me. I'm not the one in your way." Conor took a deep breath and exhaled slowly. "Good. Frustration is like trying to do something while shackled to a mountain. Release it. Now close your eyes and picture it. The preparation before the jump. The tension in your muscles. The floor under your feet. The push upward. The weightlessness of flight. The target—not the panel itself but a spot high above it. You don't aim for where you want to go—you aim higher, farther than the intended target."

Conor opened his eyes. He looked up at the gold-lined panel. That thing mocked him, so he chose to ignore it this time. He surveyed the column, holding it instead, the sleek, cool metal pulsing with blue light and intricate runic designs. One design caught his attention—a diamond with lines extending from each of its points. It resembled the mark of the Federation. That's what he wanted. That would be his target. He would touch the diamond.

He sat longer, visualizing the leap and the slap of his outstretched palm against the column, his hand covering the mark. He felt ready, so he untucked his legs and slowly stood.

His eyes closed, leaving only the picture of the glowing diamond star imprinted on his mind. He contracted like a spring, pushing all his energy low. Then, in a reflexive instant, he sprang. He soared high, tearing through the gravitational pull as if it were nothing more than a brittle leaf. He opened his eyes but didn't see the panel. No matter—he just wanted to touch the diamond. He stretched out his hand, finding the symbol out of reach, and he only managed to slap the column on a lower spot before descending.

He landed flat, the ground still far below. His feet were resting on a smooth-edged square highlighted with a golden glow. The panel hadn't disappeared; it merely waited underneath him by the time he'd opened his eyes.

He beamed a smile as he looked across to his teacher. "Woohoo! I did it."

"Of course, you did," Anibal said, matching the boy's enthusiasm. A series of soft chimes sounded overhead. "Now you have only 14 more steps to go."

Conor's smile faded and his lips contorted as if he'd just sucked on a lemon.

"But that's for another day." Anibal deactivated the panels, and Conor dropped down. This time, he didn't mind so much.

The gravitational suspender released, and the Paladin stood next to his pupil. "Well done. I think you're catching on."

Conor reached out and tapped Anibal's shoulder. "Got you."

"Nice try. Doesn't count. We will try again tomorrow. Same time. Meet me here."

"Okay."

"Now, go. I believe you have Combatives next." Conor thanked him and then rushed off toward the bridge, feeling lighter, faster, and more powerful than he'd ever thought possible.

### The Forge

The early exercises ended, and the recruits had already divided into distinct groups. Some attended the range to work with sidearms and light rifles—good weapons for taking down pirates, beasts, and even a warlord platoon, but not heavy enough to stop a Kravii warrior. The heavier weapons were reserved for Third- through Fifth-Circuit cadets. Others worked on exercise mechanics, building strength and stamina with resistance inducers to isolate muscle groups or enhance flexibility.

Conor considered joining the group tackling the Ascension, but Byro talked him out of it. His friend didn't seem too keen on that sort of challenge today, so he relented. Instead, they decided to practice with melee weapons. A long row of distinct handheld instruments, some sharp and straight or jagged or curved, others blunt and solid. At first glance, they looked like swords, daggers, axes, hammers, spears, and sticks—but, by now, Conor knew each one always held a surprise effect. He walked the row of chests, briefly inspecting them like a window shopper in a luxury boutique.

A long-handled hammer caught his eye. It was double-sided with each head composed of three stacked segments. "What about this?" Conor asked, but then left it for something else that caught his eye. "No, let's train with this!" He brushed his fingers over the shaft of a thick-handled axe. It, too, was double-headed, sharp, and powerful enough to split metal. It looked massive and nothing short of savage.

"No. Those are too heavy for us. Save those for the big guys," Byro said.

"I bet they're really effective."

"Yeah, sure. That will definitely do heavy damage to some Kravii organic, but they'll snatch it away from you before you can finish your swing. Here, try this instead," Byro continued as he handed Conor a stick.

"A stick? What's this?"

"It's a Dysart Baton."

"What does it do?"

"You, uh, hit stuff with it."

"I mean, is that all?"

"Yeah."

"So out of all these fancy and wicked weapons, you want to train with a stick."

"No. It's a Dysart Baton."

"You frustrate me sometimes. Fine, then," Conor mumbled as he grabbed the stick from Byro's outstretched hand.

"Let's practice with sticks." He took it in his hand, wrapping his fingers around the soft handle. It felt extremely light and rather non-threatening when compared with everything else.

"Hold it a little lower," Byro offered as he led them over to the practice models. A black, faceless rubberman with rounded feet and hands stood lifeless off to the side of a cluster of similar forms. It was tall, thick, and long-armed. Byro reached out and tapped his pulsero against the model's torso. "Here, tap yours against it, too. This'll make it ours for the training."

Conor leaned in, distrusting it wouldn't try to swing at him, so he quickly flicked his wrist against it before stepping back. The model came to life, stepping outward and following Byro.

"Don't worry—it won't attack us. It just follows and moves so we have a moving target the size and shape of an opponent."

"Yeah. A slow and fat one," Conor mocked.

"Just go with it," Byro urged.

Conor stood off to the side and watched other students delivering attacks on other models. Now he noticed the practice models didn't actually attack, they just moved around at slow speeds. This training would be easy, though he did feel a tinge of jealousy watching three recruits attack theirs with swords and pulsing knives. He couldn't help but look at his stick again and feel a little thwarted.

They found a space on the training pad away from the others. Just then, one of the instructors swooped in. "Hellloooo, Cadets! Get some good swings in, because next, you're headed to the range for some sweet blasting!"

"We were just about to—"

"Oooooooo! Look at that. Good choice of weapons, fellas!" the instructor interrupted with way too much enthusiasm. Instructor Piopo was a tall Jopali with big hands and narrow head, almost a size too small for such a large frame. His squeaky voice made everything he said a little comical, but he somehow made the bleakness of battle seem fun. It was easy to see why the cadets heralded him as one of their favorite instructors.

Conor couldn't help but think back to his earlier advanced training in Anibal's temple. Despite Piopo's encouragement, the Combatives didn't seem to hold as much thrill anymore. "Yeah, we have sticks."

"Dysart Batons! So much more than just sticks. I looooove those!"

*Good for you*, Conor thought to himself. He checked the baton over again. A single solid piece with a dome tip. It didn't even have a sharp end for penetration. Remarkably unremarkable.

"Well, get to smacking this Kravii scum. Call me over if you need assistance." Instructor Piopo zoomed off on his levitating disc.

"He's the best," Byro said. "Okay, you go first. Just whack the model wherever you see a good spot. He moved behind Conor so the model would focus on him instead.

Conor gripped the baton with one hand and then decided on using two. If all he had was a stick, he might as well hit this stupid zombie-model hard. Conor moved to the side and saw an opening at the torso as the rubberman extended its arm. He took a deep step, wound up, and swung. The baton impacted, and "BOOM!" The model staggered from the blast.

"Hahahaha! I told you they were awesome!" Byro shouted.

Conor looked down at the baton. It appeared unchanged.

"The Dysart Baton. Its tip has a perpetual concussion cap. It isn't strong enough to crack their armor, but it will certainly wake 'em up!"

"There's an explosion every time you hit?"

"Yes, indeed." Byro grinned like the Cheshire cat.

Conor smiled. Then he ducked in on his opponent again. This time he used one hand, letting out a flurry of strikes to its legs, left arm, and torso, finishing on the head. Six blasts in total rocked the model as if he'd just dropped a cluster bomb on it. Maybe Combatives wouldn't be a waste after all.

"Hey, give me a turn," Byro said as he moved in to deliver strikes. The model took the abuse, its fortified flexible compound designed for extreme absorption. They took turns striking it, sometimes independently, other times together.

Conor moved in again for another swing, but the baton caught on something and came out of his hands. He stumbled through the remainder of the swing and caught himself just before falling. He turned around and saw the problem.

Cyril and Gavril of the infamous Collective.

"Nice stick, kid," Cyril said as he held it up high. "Might still be too much for you, though." He flung it away over his shoulder. "Maybe someday you'll graduate to adult weapons." He held up a large broadsword. "Nah, you're too puny for something like this."

Conor considered ignoring him and going over to retrieve the baton. He considered walking away altogether. But today he chose to do neither of those things. This would be an anti-bully moment.

He canted his head to the side. "You're right. That is a big sword. That's why I'm surprised you aren't having your brother help you lift it."

"Ha. Ha. Not only could I lift the sword, but I could lift you over my head and break your little body in half," Cyril said.

"Then there'd be two of me to make a fool out of you."

"Come on, guys. Just walk on, and leave us alone," Byro interjected. Gavril grabbed his shoulder and held him stationary. "And Conor, that's not really how it works . . . you know . . . getting ripped in two," his voice trailed off.

Cyril turned his sword upside down and tossed it over to his twin. Gavril snagged it out of the air and planted the tip on the mat. "I think you need a lesson, little hawk, in respecting your superiors."

Conor turned his head back and forth, appearing to look all around. "Sorry—don't see any superiors."

"This time your sister won't be here to save you."

"Good. She might try to stop me from making you cry." Conor's threatening words masked the fear he stifled. He was about to fight an older boy twice his size and far more skilled. Running fast and jumping high might not help him much at this moment.

Cyril charged like an enraged berserker. His right arm swung out wide, an effort to end the fight with one devastating punch. Conor moved left, ducked the arm, and slid in behind his opponent. He reached out to push him forward, but the trained fighter had better defenses than to allow that. Cyril spun around, deflecting his arms away with his right. He then wrapped his arm around Conor's neck and chest, yanking him off-balance. He kicked his right leg backward, sweeping out both of Conor's legs.

They both crashed down on the mat, Cyril landing on top of him. Cyril pinned him down under the weight of his chest. A thundering fist to the side of the face jarred the less-experienced fighter.

Conor tried to squirm free, but two more strikes to his jaw and nose rattled him.

Byro refused to watch the mismatched assault without helping. He drove an elbow into Gavril's gut, causing him to double over and release the grip on his shoulder. He then raced over and swung out a roundhouse kick to the bully's head. Cyril sat up and blocked it with a strong right forearm. He then released Conor's arm and used his left to pull Byro's exposed leg close. He punched him hard in the center of his stomach, flinging him backward over Conor's legs. Byro landed square on his back, sucking wind from the blow.

Conor turned to his side, since both arms were now free. His friend lay in a crumpled heap, writhing in pain. Conor's face flushed with anger. Tears of rage filled his eyes. He looked up at Cyril, feeling the adrenaline pump through his muscles like fuel feeding an engine. He reached up and grabbed him by the shirt collar yanking downward with tremendous force. Cyril's head struck the mat, and he flipped over onto his back.

The bully scrambled back to his feet, but his smaller opponent was waiting for him to turn around. Conor jumped up, lashing out with his knee right under Cyril's chin. He staggered backward, the room spinning in his head.

Conor dove forward, planting his shoulder into Cyril's midsection and driving him onto his back. This granted Conor a mounted position over his opponent's chest. He brought his right fist high to pummel Cyril's face but stopped.

The Collective member was already unconscious. Conor remained on top of him, sucking in deep breaths, still feeling the choke of rage. "Conor, watch out!" a girl's voice screamed from the other side of the mat. Tiera moved to the pad, but she'd never make it in time.

Gavril raced at Conor with the broadsword. He closed fast, taking two long steps and a mighty swing for the boy's head. Conor didn't duck. He instinctively brought his right arm up to his head, protecting his face and cupping his ear.

The sword struck his forearm with force and flexed without cutting skin. Conor absorbed the blow feeling like he'd been hit with rigid foam. He reached out and snatched the blade.

Conor stood up with the sword in hand. His red, wet eyes matched Gavril's. He then took the sword in both hands and snapped it over his knee, tossing down the pieces like dry tinder. Gavril backed away as if he'd just woken a sleeping demigod.

The other recruits gathered. The instructors stood quiet. Silence hung over the entire pod as everyone puzzled over what just happened.

Conor felt their stares. Felt their condemnation. Suddenly, he was plucked off the ground like a weed and dangled high above the floor. Before he could react with violence, he found himself staring into two large, kind eyes. “Fight is over, and you are still angry. Time to calm, little one.”

Conor couldn’t help but let the anger subside at the sight of the giant. Jip turned him away from the crowd. He set him down at a distance from the rest of the class and brushed a finger down his back to smooth out Conor’s crumpled shirt. He then took a knee and bent forward. “Good fight, but anger not good. Now, go. You must calm.”

Conor placed a hand on Jip’s finger and nodded. He then turned to exit but caught sight of the open weapon chests. He moved first and only to the axes, grabbing a double-sided one, supposedly too much for him to manage. He flipped it around in his palm and looked back to Gavril.

Conor stepped forward, raising the massive weapon over his head and then flinging it forward. It soared through the air as if shot from an artillery cannon.

The training model still meandered in circles trained on Byro’s pulsero. The flying axe smashed into its chest, burying deep, and propelling it backward off its feet. Several gasps expelled from the gathered recruits as they stared in shock and fear.

Conor simply turned and marched through the exit.

**Residential District**
**Recruit Towers**

The portal door cut away under the hot stress. It sparked and seared from top to bottom as the collapsed fire whip dragged downward. The cut piece flexed forward into the corridor, leaving a gap large enough for the assassin to pass.

Sedit-Kal sheathed the red whip and stepped inside the room. He stopped just inside, assessing the chamber for adversaries. Circular couches and four beds. His black-red eyes squinted at the near-side bed. It was overturned and covered by a thin sheet. Odd. He moved to it, dragging his claws across the sheet covering. It fell away, revealing nothing but a single pillow. No one present.

He could wait for the child witness to return or advance the mission. He chose the mission, but the boy must die.

His hand gripped a primitive beacon belonging to the former Kravii Lord Raider, Gilgorst. He activated it, watching it pulse a purple glow before tossing it high up on the floating cylinder.

The assassin knew the Kravii would be hunting him after he'd killed their beloved Battleborn Chief Utirot. They would follow the beacon, attack this place, and fuel the war within the Vesputi. This was the ultimate mission goal.

"Come," he hissed before fading into smoke.

# CHAPTER 22

**The Academy**
**Corridor Theta**

Conor trudged through the corridor, away from the Forge and away from everyone else. As his anger abated, embarrassment took its place. He decided to just head back to his room and linger in peace and quiet.

"Conor! Conor, wait!" a girl's voice called out. He continued on without turning, but the rapid patter of footsteps meant she was closing the distance.

"Go away. I don't want to talk to anyone." It didn't take him long to figure out who it was, and right now, he didn't want to deal with Tiera's snide attitude.

"Conor! Stop!" Her orders had no effect. "I'm on your side." That worked. The boy stopped walking, but still maintained defiance by refusing to turn around. She simply walked around to face him. "Hey, it's me. I didn't do anything to you."

"You brought me here. I hate this place," Conor said.

"No, I didn't."

"You and your uncle did."

"That was all him, his doing."

"Yeah, well. Still."

"Look, The Collective are just rotten people. I don't like them any more than you do."

"You're not much better."

"What are you even talking about?" Tiera asked, offended by the comment. "I've defended you." Conor rolled his eyes and turned to face the Administrative Wing. Tiera relented. "Maybe I haven't always treated you as nicely as I should've."

"Why not? What have I done to you?" Conor asked.

"Nothing."

"See, exactly. That's what I mean. Your people are just naturally cruel. You've never liked me since the day we met, so why are you even here right now?" Conor began walking again, leaving Tiera behind.

She stood silent for a moment, toying with the words to truly match her thoughts. She decided to speak the truth. "I'm jealous."

Conor stopped and turned around. "Jealous?"

Tiera moved close to him again. She reached out and touched his arm. Turning it over. "No mark."

Conor pulled away. "So what?"

"So, you blocked a broadsword swing with your arm, from Gavril, of all people. You don't even have a scratch. Then you snatched it away and broke it in half!"

"It wasn't a real sword."

"What are you talking about, Conor? Of course, it's real. We don't train with toys."

"Well, it didn't feel real."

"The only thing here that isn't real is *you*."

Conor recoiled with a face of bewilderment.

"Yes, you. And that's why I'm jealous."

"Why would the amazing Tiera be jealous of me? You're the niece of the great Supreme Commander Welcos," he uttered in a tone coated in sarcasm.

"And you're his adopted son. I've seen the way he looks at you. I've even had to listen to Ari talk about how cute you are every single night."

"Wait . . . what?"

"I shouldn't have said that. Forget I did. She'll kill me," Tiera spat out rapidly. Conor couldn't help but smile. "Don't get arrogant. Apparently, she's attracted to dorks."

"Thanks."

"And after today, everyone's going to talk about Conor Hawk," she said with a sneer. "You can do things the rest of us can't. You're just still clumsy, but Anibal will fix that. I know it. Do you have any idea how long I've wanted him to train me?"

"You know about that?"

"Of course, I do. I'm the niece of the great Supreme Commander," she added with a smirk.

"Do you know?" Conor asked.

"Know what?"

"About me. About where I'm from."

"I know my uncle didn't find you in Jopal."

"No, he didn't. I'm not even from this galaxy."

Tiera nodded, unsurprised by the confession. "I also know you can do things I've seen only one other person do."

"It doesn't mean you get to treat me like garbage."

"You're right. I'll stop," Tiera said.

Conor looked at her sideways.

"I'll try. But you gotta promise not to throw any more axes at people."

"Fine, but for the record, I threw it at the training model."

"You could've missed and taken someone's head off."

"I know. It was stupid. I was mad."

"Uncle told you not to lose your temper. He knew you'd be dangerous."

"I'm not dangerous." Tiera looked at him sideways. "Ugh," he breathed. "Fine. Good point," Conor added with a sigh.

"Where are you going?" she asked, changing the subject.

"My room."

"This isn't the way."

"I changed my mind. I was going to see the CAL and ask to leave."

"Don't do that. Where would you even go?"

Conor shrugged.

"Can I say something without you getting the wrong idea?"

He shrugged again.

"I like your hair design."

Conor chuckled. "Thanks. I'll make sure I don't get the wrong idea."

"She likes it, too."

"Who?"

Tiera simply smiled and shook her head.

Just ahead, they heard some commotion and a distraught woman's voice. Something was happening, and they shared the same curiosity. They turned the corner and spotted an unfamiliar man standing next to Wilda Ti and two Council members. Two armed soldiers flanked the group.

The strange man with them wasn't wearing a uniform, and he clearly didn't look Jopali. He loomed a head taller than the others; he had dark-lined eyes and a russet brown complexion. He was also dressed differently—completely. The white suit gleamed against the Academy's dark scheme, and the black flat cap accentuated his peculiarity. "Who's that guy?" Conor whispered as they tucked behind a column just out of view.

"That's an Investigative."

"What does that mean?"

"He's from Digor-Yi."

"What's Digory?"

"No, Digor-Yi. Two words. Shhhhh. I can't hear with you talking," Tiera said in one of her customary whisper shouts.

"What is it?" Conor asked as quietly as he could.

"A tiny planet in Sector 4 near Wildora."

Conor supposed Tiera believed that would mean something to him. He still didn't have a clue as to what she was talking about.

Fortunately, she couldn't contain her excitement and needed to explain more. "If an Investigative is here, that means something happened. Something significant. I can't hear, though. We need to get closer."

The tall Investigative turned in their direction, and Conor pulled Tiera back behind cover. He didn't see them. He just took a few steps away from the conference room out into the corridor. When he moved, Conor noticed a seventh person in the group.

A short, dark-haired woman slouched beside them. She appeared to be the focus of the Investigative's attention. Visibly upset and frightened, she looked familiar. Not a recruit or an instructor. She was a civilian—a visitor. It was the woman who had hurried by him and Titan under the blue-light canopy. She'd been so much more cheerful the first time.

The two soldiers grabbed onto her arms, and she slumped low, dropping her weight with loud sobs.

"Oh, I wonder what she did," Tiera whispered.

Conor didn't hear her as his thoughts scanned the memories of that night—the woman, Dragors, Titan, . . . and the ghost demon. It had to be related!

Without really thinking things through, Conor found himself stepping around Tiera and walking down the center of the corridor.

"What are you doing?!" Too late now. They'd definitely spotted the impulsive boy, so she threw up her hands and followed.

"Wait!" Conor shouted.

Wilda Ti turned to face the intrusion and stepped toward the boy. "Cadets, return to your courses. This is administrative business."

"No," Conor said with bold defiance. "Not until you hear what I have to say. You're making a mistake."

"I won't speak it twice. Discipline will be leveled against you both."

Tiera pulled back on Conor's shoulder, but he shrugged her hand away.

Wilda Ti sparked at the boy's rebellion. "I will remove you my—" She froze upon recognizing the cadets—the Supreme Commander's children. The initial shock faded, and she let patience trickle in. A light touch glanced her arm as the Investigative moved to her side.

"Let's hear him. I'm intrigued. He seems passionate," the Investigative said in a soothing tone. He waited for the cadets to finish their approach.

"Cadet Hawk, I will let you speak your mind out of regard for your sponsor," Wilda Ti offered.

"Thank you, Chief. I don't know this woman, but—" Conor started before being cut short.

"Then why are you here proclaiming her innocence?" a hefty councilwoman asked.

"Let him finish. Continue," the Investigative offered in a deep-toned accent.

Conor moved forward to face Kim. "You remember me? I was walking with my dog . . . uh, beast. He frightened you a little."

She nodded.

Conor then turned to look up at the Investigative since he appeared to be the most interested in listening to him.

"Is that all?" the tall, lanky man from Digor-Yi asked.

"I don't know what happened, but I would bet it had something to do with the Imperial Visitor Wing." That comment captured everyone's attention.

"Why would you believe that?"

"Because I felt something. It made me sick, like one of those machines," Conor turned to Tiera. "What's it called?"

"Spectre," she added.

"No. Other one with the wheels and the Crestadon."

"Rumbler?" Tiera offered but more like a question. What was he getting at?

"Yeah. It felt like a Rumbler parked itself on my chest."

"That doesn't tell us much, Cadet," Wilda Ti said.

Tiera then stepped forward. "Someone died."

"And who might you be?" the Investigative asked.

"I'm Tiera Welcos."

The Investigative turned to Wilda Ti with an inquisitive expression. "Is this—?"

Wilda intercepted his question with an anticipatory nod. "Yes, the Supreme Commander's niece."

"That's not the connection I'm referring to." The Investigative stepped closer to Tiera and bent forward toward her, studying her facial features. He then stood full again. "Very well, Cadet Tiera Welcos. I'm Sandor Leo, Investigative First Class. Tell me how you know there's been a killing."

"I didn't, but you just told me."

Sandor smiled. "Glad you caught that. Go on."

"It's simple. First, you're here. That means something big happened. First Class Investigatives are rare. Second, this woman is distraught. She lost someone dear to her."

"How do you know? People cry when they get detained."

"She was crying before that. Besides, Conor spotted her leaving the Visitor Wing. She didn't come alone. That person's now dead. And you accuse her because she was the last to see them."

"Very good, Cadet Welcos. I like the way you think. Yes, there's been a killing, but right now, this woman is our main suspect. At least until we prove otherwise."

"It wasn't her," Conor interjected.

"Hmmmm. She happened to be the only one accessing the victim's room."

"Not true. I saw it."

"What did you see?" Wilda Ti asked.

"A ghost. Smoke. It was all black and . . . evil."

"That sounds ridiculous," the councilwoman added.

"I know it does. But it chased me. That's why I hid in the Tretch pod."

"Oh," Wilda Ti said as she moved closer to Conor. "Something must have scared you, then. I heard about your time in Tretch, and I'm glad you're safe."

"I'm not safe. None of us are," Conor said with exasperation. "Not while that thing is out there."

Sandor Leo placed his palms together and stepped closer to Tiera. "Here's what we will do. With your permission, Chief Wilda Ti, I will go to the victim's lodging and inspect the body along with the sleep chamber."

"I'll have someone direct you there," Wilda Ti replied.

"No need. I have *her*," Sandor said, signaling toward Tiera.

"She's just a cadet. She can't."

"Yes, she can. This is my investigation, and she'll accompany me."

"Very well. It's hard to argue with your choice. If there are any concerns, please let me know. It may be your investigation, but it's my Academy. And Tiera, you do us proud," Wilda Ti said with the swelling pride of a doting grandmother.

Tiera beamed with excitement. Tagging along with an Investigative had been a lifelong dream. "And as for you, Cadet Hawk, why not return to your courses? I will personally ensure your and everyone's safety."

Conor bit his lip to avoid saying anything harsh. Obviously, they didn't care for his warning. Sensing his frustration, Wilda added, "We will find the killer, and if there's a threat on base, we will capture and eradicate."

## Imperial Visitor Wing

Tiera directed Sandor Leo to the visitor wing with a quick pace. His long legs easily matched her hurried gait. "This is it," she said. "I imagine you know the chamber."

"My best guess would be that one marked off with the security bubble."

"Right. So, what do we have?" she asked.

"Let's go see."

Tiera reached the opaque bubble first. It billowed out around the entryway, consuming a portion of the pathway as well. She waited for whatever Sandor needed to do to remove the thing, but he paused in the corridor, standing still and calm. After a few long seconds passed, Tiera realized he wanted her to retreat and join him.

"Cadet Welcos, do not rush into an event. Study the entirety first. Observe all. What do you see?"

Tiera glanced around, knowing she'd missed something as she had hurried toward the security bubble. She spotted it. How could she not have noticed? A large indentation into the metallic wall as if it'd been pounded in with a sledgehammer. "This," she said, brushing her fingertips along the rim of the cratered metal.

"Good. You think it may be relevant?" Sandor asked.

"I think so."

"I concur. Anything else?"

Clearly, the Investigative had already observed something more. Tiera rose to her tiptoes and leaned in close. She studied the broken wall as intently as she could. Then she noticed it, wedged in between the folded metal. She leaned closer and pinched her fingers to remove the coarse fibers. She held it close, inspecting it, rubbing it between her fingers. She recognized it.

"What have you found, Cadet?"

"Animal fur."

"Correct," Sandor replied. "Could it be a considerable beast caused this attack?"

"No," Tiera replied with defiant confidence.

"Interesting. What brings you to such a conclusion?"

"Well, maybe a beast caused it. I don't know. But it wasn't this beast."

"Go on," Sandor urged.

"I know this fur. It belongs to Conor's animal. She is strong, but friendly and obedient. It looks like she was attacked."

"Interesting. It must be a powerful creature, indeed, to inflict such damage to this edifice."

"You have no idea," Tiera said, dropping the fur.

"Very well. The boy advised that he and his beast were present at this location. The evidence may confirm this. Let us continue," Sandor said as he now moved to the round panel on the security bubble, placing his palm against it. The bubble dissolved into gold mist, swirling at first and then draining into the panel. Sandor tucked it into his pocket with a wink. "Investigatives enjoy universal case clearance."

Tiera smiled, but this faded once she eyed the body lying face up in the portal way.

A flimsy foam linen covered the body, so she couldn't observe much. At least until Sandor pulled it free. Tiera stared into the face of an older Jopali man, bald with slight girth around the exposed waist and chest. His eyes were closed, and his mouth had frozen slightly ajar.

"Don't be concerned about disturbing the body. He's been repositioned after the recording and structural analysis. This is Novac Riv, Lead Stellar Observer of the Mertio Observatory.

What do you see, Cadet?" Tiera covered her nose and mouth as a stale odor pricked her nostrils. "Here, this'll help with that," he said as he tossed three small cubes into the air. They hovered and circled above the body. "I've grown accustomed to the smell of decomposition, but the scent cubes will clear and refresh the air a bit." He then leaned down and cupped a hand to his mouth. "If I'm honest, you Jopali smell the harshest," he said with a shrug. "Must be your diet."

Tiera pulled her hand away from her face and risked an unfiltered breath. The air had already freshened enough to focus on something other than holding back vomit.

"So, was the death natural, accidental, or deliberate? Thoughts?" Sandor plainly asked.

What a trivial question. Sandor was testing her. "The four deep lacerations from collarbone to belly would indicate deliberation. The one across the neck did the most lethal damage."

"Good. Agreed. What else?"

"Did the report list any other injury?"

"Good question. No, it did not."

"Okay, then. He died from a single slash with a sharp, curved weapon."

"Hmmmm," Sandor said with a finger raised to his temple, mostly to mask his smile. "There are four lacerations there. Explain how it could be a single slash."

Tiera hesitated, not wanting to disappoint him, but then her natural confidence took shape. "The killer couldn't have slashed him four times without him moving. And I bet . . ." Tiera reached down and pulled the flaps of Novac's robes over his chest. "There, the gashes in the fabric match completely. He didn't put up much of a fight."

"Why not?"

"Surprise. It was too sudden."

"Any idea on the weapon? You said you think it was curved."

"I think so. The wounds look deep from top to bottom, as if the blade got under the flesh and tore downward. A straight blade wouldn't do that."

"Yes, it would. If the killer stabbed first and cut down." He tested her again. She was right, though. He just wanted to hear if she knew why she was right.

She didn't disappoint. Tiera knelt down and pointed to the bottom four marks just below Novac's belly button. "Right here. The skin is folded over from being pulled. Only a curved weapon does that."

Sandor nodded. "She taught you well."

Tiera flashed a sad smile. "I studied lots of my mother's cases. Sometimes, when she wasn't looking."

"We never met, but I knew of her—your mother. The only Jopali Investigative in the history of the program."

"I've always wanted to follow in her steps," Tiera replied, her sadness rebounding into pride.

"You show promise. That day may come, Cadet Welcos."

"Thank you." Tiera stood up with a blush in her cheeks and walked away from Novac's corpse, deeper into the room. Interstellar charts littered the floor. Toppled travel bags were crowded beside the bed, unopened. For the most part, the chamber appeared orderly and undisturbed. "Now that I've passed your test, will you tell me?"

"Tell you?" Sandor chuckled. "Oh, you mean, that the woman named Kim didn't kill Novac Riv, and that boy you were with could be telling the truth."

"Conor wouldn't lie. He's strange, but he's . . ." She searched for the right word. "Good. He's good." That seemed to fit right. "I have a question, though. If you don't think Kim killed him, then why treat her as a suspect?"

"I didn't want to incite panic. Wilda Ti and the others will feel better with an easy explanation. But this is not easy. Not in the least. I fear this is bigger than one death, and Kim is in significant danger."

### Hadak-5
### Outer Orbit

Three large masses appeared on the overhead mist panel. "Please tell me that's not what I think it is," Valitat Bithos uttered.

"Kravii warships, Vice Commander!"

"Damn their cloaking!" The ships should've been tracked much sooner. "Prepare for engagement! Ready torpedo launchers and heavy guns." The three gunships were half the size of the Gregor Monolith, but each one contained the appropriate firepower to take it down. "When they're in range, fire. Do not let them close enough to flank us." Valitat paced around the bridge. Makon and she had shared plenty of firefights, though three warships would be a fair match. She couldn't stifle her agitation because the ensuing battle didn't outweigh her greatest concern.

"Stay on the communicator. Advise if you get any word from down below," she ordered. She had troops grounded below, one of them being the Commander. This spiked her anxiety. If they needed to retreat at some point, that option would not be available to her—she wouldn't think of abandoning her troops below. Were they even still alive?

The answer came through the front airscreen. The second warship deployed three troop carriers. They coasted away from the mother ship and paused while adjusting trajectory. She felt a twinge of relief at the sight. Makon had to still be alive. Then the feeling adjusted back to anxiety. "Fire on those carriers. Now!"

"Torpedoes away," the gunner said as he unleashed a barrage of hull-busters. They watched with anticipatory tension as the torpedoes zoomed toward the targets. The lead warship turned hard to starboard, creating a shield for the troop carriers. It intercepted nine of the ten torpedoes, absorbing the devastation along its bow and forward port side.

A series of rapid explosions rocked the ship, with devastating effect. The tenth torpedo swung too wide and missed all targets. It carried off into the atmosphere exploding upon entry. The sacrificial move protected the troop carriers at the cost of the warship. A significant cost. "They're more interested in what's down there than they are with us," Valitat uttered. What was so important? What did Makon find down there in the Riptide Coves?

The troop carriers finished their maneuvers and accelerated into the Hadak-5 atmosphere. "Commander, we lost the carriers. They made atmospheric entry."

"Nothing we can do now. They'll be disappointed when they come face to face with our Elites. All we can do is clear a path for their return. Finish off the lead warship."

"Torpedoes?" the gunner asked, his fingertips poised just above the trigger.

"No. Molt canisters. Tear it apart from the inside out." The second warship maneuvered around the lead ship's stern and sent the Gregor an unfriendly reply, its forward guns pounding out a series of hot missiles. "Here it comes," Valitat warned.

"Brace for impact!" the Primo Engineer shouted from just below the commander bridge. The purple warheads riddled the bow of the Federation's prize with a multitude of explosions but luckily no breach.

"Come on. You guys should know better than that. It's going to take more than that to rattle this beast. Have we released the canisters yet?"

"Away, Commander."

Valitat watched the seven projectiles topple at slow speed and strike the weakened warship along its port. They exploded, releasing liquid heat, melting away the external shielding and oozing inside the cracks and holes like volcanic lava slithering across the countryside. The material held a perpetual burn, impossible to contain once ignited, and just as hard to extinguish. Since the canisters had to be lobbed rather than launched to prevent in-flight ignition, they were best used for weakened craft without the ability to dodge or intercept them with gunfire.

Valitat's tactical decision proved astute. The warship began to dissolve as small fires sparked and grew into a rolling inferno. One down.

"Lead ship has released Sprawlers!" the Primo Engineer yelled.

"Figures." At least thirty small fighter craft launched from the starboard docks on the warship's protected side. The Kravii fighters flew in tight formation, resembling a high-speed swarm. Valitat activated the intercom. "Guns active. Go hot." She then turned to the Primo Engineer. "And you need to stop shouting. No need for all that."

"Apologies, Commander," he said as he slunk back down in his seat. "Should we release the Whiplash fighters?"

"Not yet. I want to be free to make a hasty escape once the Commander returns."

"Copy," the engineer replied in a hushed tone. "Guns it is, then."

"Come on, Makon," Valitat said in a hushed voice. "What are you doing down there?"

### Hadak-5
### Riptide Coves

"Try that one. The one with the picture of the tent with the squiggly lines."

"Commander, let me do this," Shila urged.

"Just try it."

"That symbol means 'inspection.'"

"Well . . ."

Shila tapped the pictogram, and holographic images of the craft emerged. "See. It's just inspection views of vehicle maintenance." She closed the display and paused. "We've been at this for a while—maybe what we're looking for just isn't here."

Makon dropped his hands in frustration. There had to be something useful regarding the Kravii's new cloaking capabilities, but the file search proved a bust. He paced around the dark interior. "Come on, think," he muttered.

"We've been through most of the files. There's nothing."

"Maybe we just need to figure out how to activate and then reverse-engineer it. I'm sure the Riostovi engineers can duplicate it and get us some new detection tech."

"That's fine, Commander. We can activate it, but how does that help us out here?"

"Good point," Makon said as he stared outside at the whipping winds. "Wait. Hold on. Do we really think the Kravii developed advanced cloaking before we could?"

"It looks that way."

"Nooooo. These clan people are fierce warriors, but everything they have, from their weaponry to aircraft, has been either borrowed or stolen and then modified."

"Someone gave it to them?"

"Exactly. And maybe we've been sitting right on top of it this whole time. Can you access on-board visual recordings?"

"Oh, yes. Found that one a long time ago."

"Good. Pull it up. Let's see who Utirot met way out here in the middle of nowhere."

Shila flipped through the pictograms and soon highlighted the recordings. "Got it."

"Just activate the last one. Let's see who's been helping them."

The archived footage materialized on the overhead screen, providing a forward view just below the ship's nose. At first, Makon thought it was inactive or blocked. They could see only deep black matched with the sound of a loud roar. Then he realized it was just the howling wind. "Scan ahead." The image remained unchanged in fast-forward motion. Then purple streaks and blue lights flashed. "Hold. There," he said, pointing at the lights.

"They lit their armor. Don't see what for, though." They continued watching as the ultraviolet flashes jerked around and then fell away. More flashes of blue from their *Kralanzas*. "They're firing at something, but I can't make out what it is. Looks like there's only a few Knights left." Once again, the purple lights began to fall away. "What is that?"

"I can't tell," Shila said, staring more keenly. They watched flashes of red attack the purple-lit warriors like an airborne snake, striking and recoiling. "I don't know."

Makon moved the images backward and then played it again. He paused on an image with the red light extended and wrapped around what looked like an arm. "It's a weapon. Maybe tracer rounds."

"It moves like a whip, but only if the whip itself were alive," Shila offered.

"You might be right. I hope you're not."

"Why? What does it mean, Commander?"

A distant memory stabbed at Makon. He remembered standing at the helm of a battle-class smuggler ship. Darker times. Fun times. Before the Federation latched onto him and altered his life path.

A luxury cruise vessel off orbit of Iosa, the paradise for vacationing princes and global ambassadors. It was supposed to be a smooth snatch-and-grab. Liberate the vessel of any desirable cargo and the passengers of their valuables.

However, instead of fat bureaucrats and lazy princesses lounging by the waterfall ponds and exchanging snobby banter in the stellar tunnels, the Windevil crew found a decimated security force and passengers cowering in corners or scurrying in a panicked frenzy. The mission parameters had suddenly changed. Against the majority opinion of his crew to just leave, Makon insisted they stay to assess and eradicate the threat. They could then still collect valuables and supplies so the mission wouldn't be a total loss. Besides, Windevil never turned from a fight.

But it was worse than a total loss. Expecting other pirate renegades or a Kravii invasion, they found a more compelling enemy. Scaley, hulking beasts armed with sophisticated weapons of destructive effect beat them back with ease. The foreign troops blasted through his crew stealing away with more than a few important dignitaries before securing their escape with a well-placed gravity bomb.

Makon had escaped with only two other crewmates before the ship imploded into oblivion. But before they departed, he saw him. The leader. A young, pale-faced demon with crimson eyes wearing a hooded robe of deep black. It lashed out with a whip—red flashes swirling, striking, and killing anything it touched. It looked alive, like an extension of the handler.

That was a first for the intrepid Windevil. The first time he'd felt fear. The first time he'd fled.

Makon's mind pulled back to the present. "I've seen that weapon before. In a life long past."

"So, how bad is it? Worse than the Kravii?" Makon just looked at Shila with concern etched into his countenance.

"Oh," she uttered under her breath. She'd never witnessed that look in her Commander's eyes.

Suddenly, Haviro and the two other Elites bounded into the Kravii ship. "We have visitors!" Haviro exclaimed as he pointed outside. Makon stepped from underneath the open door and spotted three inbound troop carriers, each one likely holding dozens of warriors.

"That's not good," Makon said. The trailing carrier spun sideways in the wind riptide. Three huge rocks pounded into the hull, pulverizing it enough to shake it off course and send it spiraling downward into a fiery explosion. Makon shrugged. "Well, at least that's good." He turned back to Haviro. "Good news. Only two carriers left." He held out his hand and a pulse rifle was pushed into his open palm. "You guys get the ship fixed and ready for flight yet?"

"Not quite. Still having trouble routing power to the instrument panel," one of the Elites responded.

"We pretty much need it to be ready already," Makon replied.

"We got the guns operational at least." Just then the lead Kravii carrier fired two short-range torpedoes and the Federation Tidal erupted in a catastrophic mess of fire, smoke and sprawling debris. Makon squinted and pursed his lips, exchanging silent glances with his Elites. Haviro shrugged.

"Well, I kinda preferred Plan B anyway," Makon said.

"Do you have a Plan B?" Shila chimed in.

Makon cocked the firearm and stepped behind cover, unleashing a barrage of hot pulses at the closest Kravii ship. The other Elites took positions and followed suit, pumping as much firepower as they could muster to deter the ship from releasing its treacherous cargo.

The belly of the carrier opened, spitting large orbs down to the surface below. They fell like boulder hail, round bubbles filled with demon spawn.

# CHAPTER 23

**The Academy**
**Mess Pod**

The salty meat melted away as he chewed. He hadn't tried the rordrav meat before, but the vendor's recommendation didn't disappoint. Conor had no clue what a rordrav looked like, but he knew they were tasty.

The Mess Pod wasn't empty. Instructors, security officers, and other Academy workers milled about conversing or grabbing a quick bite. However, the other cadets remained in their assigned courses. This suited him just fine. After the embarrassment during Combatives and then being dismissed so readily by Wilda Ti, he wasn't in the mood to see anyone.

If only V-23 had known this, maybe he wouldn't have come bouncing over to Conor's secluded table and plopped himself right next to him. The little alien elf sat down, folded his hands, and beamed a giant smile.

Conor took a couple of bites in silence without looking at him. The little guy shifted back in his seat. The excitement brimmed inside him so intensely that Conor could feel it. The Riostovi seemed like he was about to pop with a scream.

Conor sighed and lifted another morsel to his mouth. "Go ahead. I know you're dying to tell me something," he mumbled as he chewed.

V-23 bolted up in his seat. "Yesssss! I have something to shooooow you."

"What is it?"

"I show you."

"Then show me."

V-23 looked around. The dining pod had too many people around. They could see. He didn't want them to see. That wouldn't be good at all. "Nope. Nope. We can't show here."

Conor sighed again, not making any effort to hide his lack of enthusiasm right now. He moved the rest of the food around on his plate and looked down at his jittery companion for the first time. He offered only an involuntary eye roll, but V-23's smile finally found its mark. Conor broke his depressed state with a slight chuckle. "Fine," he said, pushing the plate away. "Let's go see what's got you so excited."

### Imperial Visitor Wing

Sandor Leo's tall form loomed over the nautical charts. Tiera stood watching him, wondering what was streaming through the mind of the mysterious Investigative from tiny Digor-Yi. While he had always maintained a quietly analytical composition by nature, perhaps he had simply paused in thought for dramatic effect. He finally spoke. "It all fits."

"What does?" Tiera asked.

"This Jopali man's visit to see Wilda Ti and the Overwatch Council. Then his death. Your young friend's account of the phantom assassin. It's something unseen or known in my time—a foreign creature. Perhaps not from here."

"From where, then?"

Sandor shook his head. "Don't know. And then the sudden attack on Jopal."

"The Kravii," Tiera uttered, flashing back to the falling pods filled with warriors and the countless Sprawlers laying waste to her home city.

"They are linked."

"Really? How?"

"I've been told Commander Welcos is working on that," Sandor replied. "He just doesn't realize it."

"My uncle? No, he's making preparations for our counterattack."

"Perhaps. But he's also investigating the new cloaking tech that somehow mysteriously fell into the hands of the Kravii."

Her thoughts darted back to the attack on Jopal again. "They used it to avoid our atmospheric detection and defenses. So much was destroyed before we could stop them."

"Yes. Anything in particular targeted?" Whether he already knew the answer or was just having Tiera put together the pieces remained uncertain to her. She took the bait anyway.

"The Towers of Prudence were destroyed. The Elders all wiped out."

Sandor nodded. "Anything else in particular?"

Tiera thought for a moment and remembered the flash explosion. "The Mertio Observatory." The Investigative nodded again. "So, the Observatory was destroyed along with everyone inside except the Lead Stellar Observer. But he escaped only to be assassinated."

"And do you know the name of his assistant?"

"Kim." Tiera now realized why she would still be in danger.

"The Mertio Observatory is one of only two observation decks powerful enough to see it," Sandor Leo said.

"See what?"

"To quote the Jopali woman, Kim, 'Powerful enough to see the darkening of the suns.'" Sandor shared an ominous glance with his astute pupil. "There's one more thing. Guess where the other observation deck is located."

Tiera felt her stomach drop as if the floor had fallen out from under her. "The Academy," she whispered.

"Which means we're all in grave danger."

He let the weight of the words distill on her before sharing the next realization, but she'd already moved ahead of him. "It also means the assassin is still here," Tiera added.

Piercing alarms suddenly blared overhead. The signal was distinctive and powerful, having been designed to announce one thing.

Attack.

## Observation Deck

Conor trailed V-23 as he led them to the observatory. As expected, the ceiling opened to the stars. Discrete workspaces equidistantly spaced in two crescent-moon rows faced the observation deck. The deck held the monstrous telescopic view projector, which flashed an image on the mist screens surrounding it. The screens weren't active right now, but it didn't matter. That's not why they were there.

Conor looked around to ensure the deck was empty. "No one's here. What's so important to show me?"

V-23 jumped up and shot him a big smile. He then dug his hand into the small satchel at his side, pulling out a sphere larger than his tiny hand. He balanced it in his palm and stared at it with a grin before looking up at Conor.

The boy was visibly less enthused. "V, I've seen that before. Didn't I buy it for you?"

"No, you bought the Nova Bulb." The smile faded. "This . . . this is an Astral Orb. The bulb sits inside it. It's all fixed."

"Good job. You fixed it. What's so special about it?"

"Oh. Oh. Oh. It's outlawed."

"Outlawed? Like it's against the law for you to have?"

"Yep."

"Why?"

V-23 held it out toward Conor, who instinctively took a step back. "You hold it on its side and then turn the top toward you and the bottom away like this."

"Don't do it!"

"No. No. No. Too dangerous." V-23 moved the Orb down.

"Why is it so dangerous? What does it do?"

"The Astral Orb gives off the light of a star. Can be seen from space. Blinds unprotected eyes." V-23 looked down. "They blinded too many Federation heroes, so now the only ones left are deactivated or locked away. All, but this one."

"Well, put it away then, and don't get caught with it."

"I fix it for *you*," he said as he offered it to Conor. "A gift."

"Why don't you just hold onto it for now? I'd like to keep my eyes from burning out of my skull." V-23 retracted his gift with a hint of sadness. Conor perceived his friend's disappointment and placed a hand on his shoulder.

"Thank you, V. I know who to come to when the lights go out."

Loud sirens blared overhead, the sound both thumping and piercing.

"What's that for?!" Conor shouted. V-23 moved away from the telescope, taking rapid short steps backward with his head craned up to the stars. But he wasn't looking at the stars. They were being blotted out by the numerous Kravii warships, cruisers, and fighters floating in space just above.

"It means trouble, Master Hawk. Lots of really bad trouble."

### Recruit Towers

The portal fell away, and Tiera bolted through the open doorway like a guided missile straight toward the Infinity Chest flanking her bed. It opened at her first touch, and she sifted through the contents display. She first selected a choice uniform—combat fit—and flung it on her bed.

"Are we seriously under attack?" The question came from Ari, standing across the room, rooted by fear or uncertainty, or both.

"That's the only thing it can be," Tiera said as she stripped off her current outfit and dragged on her combat uniform. She adjusted the sleeves and smoothed out the legs before tapping the display again and reaching into the chest.

"Where are you going? Shouldn't we stay here until they mobilize us somewhere?"

Tiera snatched the item from the chest and unfastened her pulsero. She replaced it with the new one from her secret inventory.

"What's that?"

"Just something my uncle gave me in case of emergency."

"What does it do?"

"Lots of things." Tiera then glanced up at her friend. "Well, you coming?"

"Where?"

"There's something I need to check out. Has to do with the killing."

"Killing? There was a killing?!" Ari shouted.

"Yeah, but we have bigger problems right now. And I think the killing's connected to those bigger problems, so, suit up, and let's go." Ari finally jolted from her fixed position and pulled out her combat uniform. Tiera didn't feel in much of a mood to wait, so she was already standing in the open portal while the Tretchian girl changed out. Just before she could tell her to hurry up, she remembered something, almost forgetting it in her haste.

Tiera marched back to her bedside and reached in the chest for one more thing—her *Paraeo* batons. She fastened the double holster around her waist and slid both batons into the X-shaped holders at the small of her back. Now she was ready.

She moved out of the room and into the corridor, with Ari right beside her. Other recruits scattered around, some dressed and ready for combative defense, and others unsure of what to do. Tiera just increased her pace and paid them little attention. They reached the ascensor lift and shot down to the base of the towers. As soon as they reached the bottom, an agitated boy accosted them.

"Hey, Tiera!"

"What, Byro?" Tiera blurted out, her words laced with irritation. She moved to the edge and held her pulsero up to the nearby post. The post illuminated, and a glowing orb encircled her wrist. Ari stepped beside her and did the same.

"Have you seen Conor?" Byro asked.

"Nope."

"Where are you going?"

"I've got something to do," she replied.

"Looks urgent. And you both look ready for battle."

"You should be, too," Tiera said, eyeing him up and down.

Byro looked over his casual attire and knew she was right, but this wasn't the time to worry about what outfit to wear. "Can I come with you?"

"Of course," Ari interjected as she stepped off the edge.

"Yeah, whatever," Tiera mumbled as she jumped off. Byro leaned over and watched the girls zoom downward at a diagonal as if attached to some unseen wire. They landed on the launchpad and started to hurry off. He raised his arm for the orb to take him, knowing he'd probably need to chase after them in order to keep up.

Overhead the sirens continued to blare.

They reached the main corridor, and security personnel nearly trampled them as they raced with pulse rifles to the main loading dock. This confirmed the presence of an imminent threat. The sense of danger electrified the air and injected a surge of urgency into Tiera's steps.

They raced to the entry dock, where the pounding sound of Concussion Cannons and Rage Missiles drowned out the wail of the sirens. Byro looked up as a barrage of six large, blue-flamed pulses shot from the three cannons mounted to the exterior just above them. Through the transparent loading dock, he observed the bow of a single Kravii warship. Was this the only one? He hoped so.

Tiera began running away again with Ari in tow. Byro started after them, but stopped, hesitating. Had the docking port always been transparent? Federation soldiers flooded the bay, setting up temporary barricades and hunkering down with their weapons readied. He quickly found himself in a place he didn't want to be, at least without being armed.

Byro took off after Tiera and Ari, finally catching up to them as they rushed into the observation deck. He spotted the girls moving toward the telescopic-view projector positioned on an octagonal deck above the rest of the room. Another boy and his V-Tech companion stood by the projector, both staring up at the stars. He felt relief in spotting his roommates, but the sight of what moved above them annihilated this comfort in an instant.

He counted no less than four Kravii warships lingering above the Academy, each one spitting out small fighter ships that buzzed around like insects cut from a rotten carcass. They battled against the Federation fleet above. A squadron of Whiplash fighters expelled from the massive Federation carrier engaged the smaller fighters while firing on the warships with their molt bombs. It seemed to be an even battle, what with the Academy defenses supporting the assisting fleet.

Byro placed his hand on Conor's shoulder. "Been looking for you." Conor glanced over to his friend and then turned back to the space battle. Tiera activated the projector along with one of the screen displays. It came to life with light as the power surged through the scope.

"What are you doing?" Conor asked.

"Need to check something. And I bet it's already dialed in to exactly what I'm looking for," Tiera replied. She stepped back to the screen and waited for the image to emerge. An orange sphere laced in black spots showed on the screen. A sun normally bright hot yellow and orange now appeared charred as if it were fire-soaked and dipped in water to cool. The tag on the upper right corner of the screen read: Tiptokon III. "Look," she whispered. The others joined her at the display.

"Is that normal?" Ari asked.

"No. It's not normal at all."

"What's happening to your sun? Er, I mean the sun? That thing there." Conor asked, correcting his slip of the tongue.

"It's burning out," Tiera answered.

"Should that be happening?" Ari asked.

"I don't think so," V-23 responded. "At least not for a few hundred million more years."

"We're under attack," Tiera said.

"Yeah. There's no doubt about that," Byro said while looking up.

"No," V-23 said as he moved closer to the screen and propped himself up on the stool. "She's right. This shading isn't natural. That sun is being extinguished."

"How? Why?" Byro asked, his eyes still glued on the battle spectacle above.

"I don't know," Tiera responded. "But we have even bigger problems right now." She stepped back and looked up as two troop carriers eclipsed the projector, moving silently overhead. The ships drifted so close she could see the Kravii markings on their underbellies.

"Oh, no," Byro gasped. The Federation carrier, riddled with flame pockets, suddenly burst into rings of light as it quietly disintegrated into shrapnel. The concussion wave pushed out to the Academy, shaking the sphere and knocking the cadets off balance.

"What do we do?" Ari asked.

Tiera looked at her friends and stifled her fear as much as she could. "We do what we've been trained to do. We handle the incoming problem."

Byro thought back to the Entry Bay and the transparent dock with all the soldiers positioned to defend it. The bay portal wasn't transparent at all. It was open and ready to receive visitors. "We need to get to the Loading Dock. That's where they're inserting."

Conor stepped off the upper deck and began to move slowly to the exit. He reached the open doorway as Byro called out to him. "Conor, what are you going to do?"

He paused a moment, weighing how to put into words his unwillingness to tolerate any more bullies. He bit back the fear of death and uncertainty, replacing it with courage, brewing anger, and his newfound weapon—self-belief. "I've been in a bad mood today, so I'm going to show them what happens when I get angry."

**Hadak-5**
**Riptide Coves**

Blue-purple charge blasts soaked the doorframe of the Kravii fighter just above Makon's head. He returned fire on the warrior troops as they took cover behind rock formations and encroached further on their position. Three rockets from the enemy carrier pummeled the top of their stationary spacecraft, knocking two of the Elites to the floor. One began to stand and caught a blast to the chest, scorching through his lifesuit and chest cavity.

Makon reached out and pulled his lifeless body back inside before reengaging. He fired a barrage at one of the warriors as he poked out from behind the rock cluster. Its shoulder, neck, and head were the target, but just before the blasts hit their mark, the organic armor slithered to protect, reinforcing the areas of the incoming threat. Makon's rifle blasts knocked the warrior off balance, but the reinforced armor rendered the attack ineffective.

"Man, I hate their armor!" Makon yelled in frustration. The second carrier dropped its payload, showering fifteen pods to reinforce the other warriors. "Shila, get us airborne now."

She manipulated the controls, firing up the thrusters. "I'll do you one better," she said as she charged the cannons. "Shoot at me, will you? Let's see how you like it." Three depressed cannons pushed up from their discreet housing and adjusted to fix on the intended target. Shila tapped the screen, launching a wave of purple bolts at the carrier.

The Kravii ship cut left to dodge the attack but took heavy damage on its bow and port side, pushing it high and away, just in time to receive devastating impact from the cyclonic rock. Merciless granite bombarded its front as if they had just moved into an asteroid field. The carrier erupted and spiraled downward in a fiery mess, exploding on the terrain behind the warriors.

The second carrier responded with torpedoes, catching Makon's hijacked craft with unwelcomed damage. The ground warriors seized on the opportunity to blitz and converge on their vulnerable position. "Take off, now!" Makon yelled as he observed the troop mobilization.

"Okay! Okay!" Shila yelled as she engaged the thrusters and yanked on the steering column. The ship lifted and cut to the left, pulling slightly away from the outcropping. They still weren't yet high enough to avoid the Kravii, hellbent on preventing their escape. Three warriors leaped up to the open gangplank and lashed out at the Commander and his Elites still in harm's way. Makon fought with two of them, avoiding the first Lanza blast that overshot high into the cabin. He wrenched the weapon from the warrior, tossing it away before placing the muzzle of his weapon at the warrior's head and pulling the trigger. Multiple blasts pounded at the gathered armor wrapping its skull and face. The rounds didn't pierce, but they pounded hard enough to significantly disorient the warrior. Makon followed with a stomp kick to his stomach launching him far off into the swirling winds.

The second warrior smashed the rifle from Makon's hands and swiped a jagged sword toward his throat. The Commander ducked and countered with a vicious kick to the back of his leg. The Kravii twisted from the devastating blow and dropped down to one knee. He then found a secondary target.

Haviro and the other Elite were fighting with the third Kravii. The warrior's skilled attacks with the *Kralanza* proved too vicious and calculated for Haviro to retrieve the Vulcan Bo dangling from his belt. He struck the warrior in the head, but the armor easily defeated his punch. He then grabbed the Lanza, hoping to wrench it free and turn it against his opponent. The struggle gave the other Elite an opportunity to seize his own Bo, but just as he palmed it, an unexpected sword skewered him through spine and chest. He dropped, bouncing off the gangplank before toppling to the ground far below.

Makon watched his soldier fall and surged with rage. He grabbed the kneeling Kravii by the head and lifted him high. With his free hand, he tore away the organic armor around his throat and squeezed. The warrior flailed at the crushing arm but couldn't break the grip. Makon placed his other hand on the top of its head and pulled backward, snapping the warrior's neck. He let the body fall limp with nothing more than a grimace on his face.

Makon then turned to the final warrior fighting with Haviro over the Lanza. He struck the Kravii in the back with a fist laced with tremendous power. The warrior winced in pain, relaxing his grip on the weapon enough to yield it to Haviro.

The Elite twisted it away, spun it, and drove it forward into the enemy's belly, impaling him with enough force to defeat the armor and penetrate flesh and bone. The Kravii dropped to his knees with a squelch, and Haviro nudged him off the craft to finish his death on the rock surface below.

Makon and Haviro shifted back from the portal as Shila tapped the closing panel.

The Kravii stealth cruiser pushed through the riptide winds, evading a final torpedo barrage from the remaining troop carrier. The Lanza bursts from the warriors below peppered the underside of their craft, but this feeble firepower couldn't prevent the ship's escape.

### The Academy
### Control Center

Wilda Ti slammed her fist on the control panel. The portal interceptor missiles still wouldn't engage. The Academy's number-one defense had failed, leaving the door wide open for the Kravii fleet's assault. "Someone please get this thing to work!" she shouted at the two Federation technicians still working feverishly on the sphere's defenses.

"Cannons are operational and inflicting concerted attacks on the warships," the nearest technician responded.

"Well, they're not going to do much. We need our missiles operational," Wilda Ti replied.

"Good news, CAL," the other technician with short-cropped, red hair blurted out with too jolly of a tone to fit the present situation.

"Go with it."

"The warships have ceased heavy fire on the sphere."

"No, that's not good news. That means they're inserting. Aim for those troop carriers and take out as many fighters as you can. Forget the warships."

The portal to the control room slid down, and an unexpected face ducked under the entry as he glided into the room. Wilda Ti turned to glance over at him before bringing her fist up to smash the mist screen again.

"Don't do that," the man from Digor-Yi said in a soft tone.

Wilda halted her violence on the control panel and glared at him. "What are you doing here, Sandor? Shouldn't you be out investigating or meditating somewhere?"

"No. I shouldn't. I wish to observe the security views."

"If you haven't noticed, this is a pretty bad time."

"Why is that?"

"What do you mean, 'why'?" Wilda couldn't help but coat her words with exasperated frustration. "Perhaps because the Kravii are trying to destroy us."

"This is not new."

"True, but . . . look, I don't have time for this right now. Our defense systems are pretty jammed up."

"You should stop bashing them. That won't work. After all, I reason they've been sabotaged."

Wilda's first instinct was to refute the claim as preposterous, but then she paused and let the possibility soak in. "How? . . . Who?"

"Our mystery assassin."

### Entry Dock

The Kravii troop carrier absorbed a mediocre amount of small-arms fire as it cruised into the Entry Bay. The assembled Federation security force housed at the Academy did its best to thwart the landing, but the internal defenses weren't designed to hold off an invasion of this size. The enemy carrier's pulse cannons riddled the troops huddled behind their improvised barriers, effectively carving a zone for its pod deployment.

A hailstorm of thirty pods descended on the deck, rolled forward, and then burst like lethal popcorn, inserting the first warrior platoon into the firefight. The carrier finished its barrage of cannon fire and then moved away, granting space for the next trailing ship. As it pulled away from the sphere, it fell into range of Wilda Ti's team. They punished the vessel moments after delivering its payload, ripping it apart with hot destruction. A small victory, but a little too late.

Conor and Tiera entered the bay first, followed by Ari, Byro, and V-23. They couldn't help but marvel at the sight. Uniformed soldiers battled lithe warriors in an intense firefight, green rifle bursts sprayed the aggressors as they dodged and swayed, inching forward with retaliatory blue shockwaves from their *Kralanzas*. A docked Federation frigate lay toppled on its side, scorched with a gaping hole torn in its side. The rubble of two Whiplash fighters flanked it, both blackened and still alight with fire.

Conor didn't know where to go, but as Lanza blasts hit the wall right next to him, he knew standing there was the last place he should be. He dashed to a nearby barricade and hunkered down as his companions huddled beside him. He hesitated. Should they flee or fight?

Tiera answered this question. "We need weapons."

Indeed, they did. The Kravii seemed to effortlessly advance through the Federation security, slowly encroaching on their position at the rear of the hangar. Conor risked a glance around the barricade's edge and spotted three Kravii warriors just a short distance away.

They tore into a few security soldiers with multiple Lanza bursts before leveling one with a downward slash from shoulder to hip bone. They impaled another soldier. As the warrior let the soldier slide off the tip of its lance, she spotted Conor peeking out. They caught eyes, and Conor ducked back behind cover.

He'd been here before. The training simulator in the Gregor Monolith. He recalled the dread he felt then of gruesome death by a fabricated monster. He glanced at his friends and saw it in their faces. He steadied himself. This time he wouldn't cave to that same fear.

He stood to face the three warriors, only to sense a little discouragement when he now spotted five. *Do these things just multiply?* The closest one leveled its Lanza and shot a charge directly at Conor's chest. He watched the crackling power surge toward him and side-stepped. Another came roaring toward his head. He ducked.

The warriors moved in a wedge formation, the first three all leveling their Lanzas at the slippery target. A hooded shadow now moved behind them. Conor saw it, but the warriors were too fixated on him to notice sweeping death.

Anibal pulled his gold-hued dagger and slithered in between the two rear warriors, slashing high and low as he attacked with chaotic precision. The blade cut through the organic armor with devastating ease, leaving both Kravii crippled and dying in pools of black blood.

The forward three warriors alerted to the new attacker and spun their attention away from Conor. He seized upon the opportunity to leap over the barricade and join his mentor in the fight.

A Kravii warrior proved its namesake for fear in battle when it deflected Anibal's strike and countered with the lance's shaft, delivering a crushing blow to the attacker's face. Anibal stumbled back as another warrior hit him with a downward blow across his shoulder blades. The Paladin spun away to gain some distance and gather his wits, but the third warrior joined the concerted attack, leveling his lance for a thrust into Anibal's chest cavity.

He lurched the weapon forward, but it halted in mid-thrust—caught on something. He looked down to see the small boy holding the Lanza in his right hand. The warrior snarled at him. Conor looked up and shook his head. Before the warrior could wrench the weapon away, Conor chopped down his left hand on the elongated shaft, snapping it in half like a brittle icicle. Seizing upon the warrior's shock, he then snatched away the forward piece of the lance, turned it around, and drove it into the beast's belly. Apparently, the organic armor didn't perform too well against a Kravii's own weapons.

The warrior reeled backward in time to receive a spinning *Paraeo* baton to the side of the head. She tumbled off balance and leaned forward—her head in perfect position for Conor to seize. He wrapped his hands around the back of the Kravii head, feeling the organics move underneath his fingers, reinforcing to protect the area. This mechanical mistake left the warrior's face exposed. Conor leaped backward driving the enemy's contorted face hard down to the floor, the impact splintering skin and bone.

Anibal now gripped his dagger's hilt with two hands, giving it a subtle twist. The blade grew in length, doubling in size. He stretched out the sword to the remaining warriors as its golden hue swirled like liquid smoke lacing the blade's edge.

This didn't deter the nearest warrior. He lashed out with the Lanza, striking down, clanging with the sword and then slashing backward to catch his opponent's neck. Anibal dodged and countered by blocking the lance before the warrior could bring it back into attack, and then slashed through the Kravii's neck. Knowing this to be a lethal strike, he turned to the second warrior, spinning around to evade a leveled charge blast that splashed against the wall. He slashed for the claws holding the weapon and then ducked behind, attacking the inner thigh and groin with an upward swipe before cleaving the head in one final blow.

The brief pause in hand-to-hand combat afforded them the disappointment from observing the second carrier dispel its warrior troop. This one dropped even more warriors than the first. Fifty pods spilled out like a shattered jar of marbles. Each one burst into action with a determined fighter spewing Lanza blasts at the remaining soldiers.

The Kravii now swarmed the loading bay, some moving into other areas to take over the Control Center, and others splintering into tactical assault groups, inserting into the nearby auditorium and corridors. The majority gathered around the newly arrived Battleborn Chief with her customary battle staff. The staff resembled the one Utirot wielded, except a jagged "S" topped it—the marker of the owner's name. She shouted orders of some kind, causing the warriors to form two crescent-shaped lines around her position. Two forward assault teams of eight warriors then moved out from behind the lines to sweep up any remaining Federation resistance. The Chief had just claimed the Entry Bay as her territory.

Anibal scanned the faces of the young cadets and then fixed on Conor. "Run."

# CHAPTER 24

**Hadak-5 Orbit**
**Gregor Monolith**

The Gregor Monolith pummeled the second warship, punishing it for even thinking about engaging in combat. It came apart—little chunks at first, followed by its hull splitting in three and drifting apart quietly into the void of space.

"Take that, you bastards," Valitat uttered.

"Nicely done, Vice Commander. Only one left," the Jetson advised.

"No. Leave it. We don't have time." Valitat Bithos stared over at the display depicting the only available image of the surface of Hadak-5. Flames blanketed the wreckage of the Federation Tidal ship. She feared the worst but hoped for the best. However, the best right now would mean desertion of the Commander and a later return. Hopefully, she wouldn't be returning to collect just corpses. "Prepare for rapid departure."

"Copy, VC. Are we sure we want to leave the Commander down there?"

"We have to answer the Academy's distress call. We have no choice, with or without the Commander," the Vice Commander replied.

"Copy. Moving to divert," the pilot said as he engaged the starboard engines, adding thrust to turn the ship away from the last remaining warship.

"VC, we are still engaging Kravii Sprawlers," one of the gunners offered.

"Stick them with the guns. Once we hit the accelerator, we'll leave them far behind."

The gunners unleashed on the remaining fighters as the Gregor made its turn. One larger ship closed on their position, avoiding the pulse weapons. It moved closer but hadn't fired. The gunner paused, lining up his shot. He had it on lock, about to serve up a hefty barrage when a familiar voice sounded loud overhead.

"We would appreciate you refrain from firing on us, and just let us board already," Commander Makon Welcos said with a sigh over the communicator. "I know what you're doing there, Yito. Don't you pull that trigger." The gunner relaxed his grip and smiled. He then alerted Valitat of their Commander's return.

Valitat met Makon personally as soon as they docked and disembarked. "I see you brought a prize with you. Nice ship."

"Shila's a pretty good Kravii pilot," Makon replied. "Let's keep her around. Unfortunately, we lost two Elites—Hage and Rioso. We must render a proper tribute by wiping out the rest of these Kravii and retrieving Rioso's body for proper burial."

"I'm sorry, Commander," Valitat started, using his proper title in front of the nearby crew, "but we will have to delay that. There's been a distress call from the Academy."

"What type of distress call?"

"Full assault."

Makon felt the ache of anxiety punch his gut. He dropped his gear and headed straight for the bridge. "Why are you still here?"

"We were just leaving."

"I noticed. But you should've left immediately upon receipt."

Valitat understood his frustration, but he'd have to get over it. She didn't need to state the obvious—that she couldn't just leave him to die on a deserted planet. She chose instead to let the conversation die and the Commander get to work. He stepped up to the bridge and, without hesitation, barked, "Course set for Sector 3—the Federation Academy."

"Copy, Commander. I'm already on it," the pilot stated.

"Give it full accelerator. Get us there now. And I mean move this thing faster than it's ever flown before."

**The Academy**
**Main Deck**

Five Kravii warriors moved swiftly down the corridor, breaking off from the main contingent to seek out the source of the activated transponder beacon. Their course pinpointed the Residential District, more specifically, the Recruit Towers, as their mission destination. Their course had been uncontested as the majority of the Federation security force concentrated in the Entry Bay—territory now maintained by their Battleborn Chief, Sveta.

Finally, an opponent met them at the other end of the corridor. He would become the object of their bloodlust. This Jopali man stood against them in defiance to their dominance. He was of shorter stature than the average Kravii, but muscle mass more than made up for what he lacked in height. He moved slowly toward them, curiously unintimidated by their presence, holding a large gun, leveled at his hip. It looked aggressive. No matter. The Kravii still held the firepower advantage.

The warriors pointed their Lanzas and fired a barrage of charged blasts. The Jopali suddenly deployed an expandable shield wrapped around his forearm, absorbing the two shots that happened to be on target. Another soldier, lean and formed, stepped around from behind the burly man. The Kravii recognized his uniform. These weren't ordinary Federation soldiers. They were Elites.

This fight just got interesting. Bradok smiled. "Now it's my turn." He squeezed the trigger on the Cyclon—the massive barrel spun, spitting out hot molt charges like a torrent of Dragor fire. The first three Kravii took the brunt of the assault, their organic armor failing to reorganize to deflect enough of the bombardment. The molt rounds tore through the armor coating blue-black flesh, burning through bone and organs. The three warriors were reduced to smoldering corpses and fell. The other two spun and ran alongside the walls, digging claws into the metal to resist gravity's pull. They avoided Bradok's firepower, closing fast on the Elites.

Iopo Lex stepped forward, drawing his Vulcan Bo. He twisted its center, causing it to fully extend and begin its spin. The coils reddened, sending a message of hot malice to anyone who might be tempted to come close. The Kravii remained undeterred.

Iopo moved to the first target, sweeping high to catch the demon as it traversed along the wall. The Kravii anticipated the attack and pushed away, flipping off the wall and landing beside the Elite. It slashed toward Iopo, but he dodged. Their weapons met in a clash, each one going for a destabilizing blow.

Iopo pulled away and lashed the Bo forward again; it was deflected, so he brought the other end forward in an overhead strike. The warrior blocked, but the Elite's attacks became quicker and fiercer, demonstrating Iopo Lex's mastery of the Bo. He caught the Kravii at the base of the neck, the coils tearing through the armor like wet paper. He followed with a vicious kick to the inner thigh before sweeping the non-coiled end in a horizontal slash to the side of the Kravii's face.

Staggering, and too dazed to react, the warrior left his chest exposed long enough for Iopo's next strike. He thrust the Bo forward, allowing the weapon to burrow deep, clean through to the other side. He then pulled the weapon and watched the warrior fall dead.

Bradok repelled the other warrior's lance blow with his Cyclon. He dodged a piercing thrust and tried to push off to gain some distance to fire the weapon, but the warrior's attacks pressed. He couldn't get space, so he did the opposite. He dropped the rotary cannon and closed in, grabbing the Lanza with one hand and wrapping his other arm around the enemy's waist. He shifted his grip from the Lanza to the Kravii's wrist and thrust his weight forward, kicking out his near leg.

The warrior lost his grip on the floor and tumbled through the air, landing hard on his back. The Elite behemoth delivered two punches to the Kravii's head and then dropped a knee across the enemy's belly. The warrior struggled to remove the weight, still clutching the Lanza, but the long weapon proved a disadvantage at this close distance.

Bradok reached for his holstered sidearm, drew it out, and fired four times at the Kravii's head. The rounds splintered the organic armor, sending chunks of it flying. Bradok stood and turned to Iopo Lex, giving him a nod. "Their armor ain't so tough."

"Um," Iopo replied while pointing to the ground behind his companion.

Bradok looked back and observed the Kravii turning its head in an attempt to get up. The stout Elite sighed. "Come on," he muttered in disappointment. He wrenched the Lanza from the Kravii's clawed hands, turned it over, and drove it hard into the warrior's chest. The savage warrior gasped once just before its life left its body. Bradok hesitated a moment to ensure that the lance blow had done the trick.

"You through?" Iopo asked.

"Think so. These things are tough to kill."

"Yeah, so are we. Let's move." Iopo retracted the Bo and moved down the corridor.

"Don't worry. I'm not leaving you, sweetie," Bradok uttered as he gathered up the Cyclon.

### The Academy
### Control Center

"Here they come," Wilda Ti uttered. Heavy Lanza blasts pounded on the closed portal to the Control Center. She drew her pistol and stepped back, taking a stand beside the two technicians with their raised sidearms.

"I assume there's no other way out," Sandor Leo said as he stepped to the side of the portal.

"No, there isn't. We're trapped."

"Well, then," Sandor whispered as he pulled a pair of black gloves from his pocket. He slid his fingers tight into each one and tapped a tiny panel embedded at the wrist. A surge of black energy coursed from the palm out to his fingertips.

The Kravii managed to break apart the right side of the door, pressing their entry.

"Do you need a weapon?" Wilda asked as she holstered her sidearm and grabbed a plasma rifle from the cabinet. She then palmed two orb grenades.

Sandor didn't reply. He just mimicked a smile.

One of the technicians fired at the first Kravii head poking past the threshold. The pulses pushed the female warrior back, but the organic armor deflected any damage. Two sets of Kravii claws now pulled the portal back, bending it far enough for entry.

"Remember the armor. Concentrate your fire!" Wilda Ti shouted.

The first Kravii stepped into the room and pumped charge rounds at its huddled prey only to receive a bombardment of plasma fire from two sidearms and a rifle. The rounds disoriented her armor, exposing anatomical weakness along the torso. She fell dead, but not before her comrade entered and punished one of the technicians with a blast to the side of the head.

Wilda Ti spotted at least five other warriors anxious to get to them. She and the remaining technician fired mercilessly at the one to the right, but two others snaked past on the left. They were greeted with fierce hand-to-hand combat by a lanky Investigative from Digor-Yi. He matched them in height, but lacked the sinewy muscle, ferocity, and honed aggression of even the lowest of Kravii warriors. Which is why the focused power from the first of Sandor's punches erupted with such surprise. His gloved fist pounded into the side of the warrior's head with such force it knocked him unconscious. The combatant staggered and collapsed as his knees buckled.

Sandor yanked on the Lanza of the next warrior and squeezed his fingers tight. A shockwave rippled through the weapon up to the bearer's claws, causing the warrior to shudder from the vibration. Sandor then stepped forward and landed a palm strike on his center chest. The armor caved inward from the impact and sent him barreling into the two warriors behind.

Wilda refocused her fire at the weakened warrior's exposed chest. Three down. Only now there were more than five warriors. Wilda did a quick count of at least eight. They couldn't survive an onslaught of *Kralanza* charges if all fired together, and that's what they intended.

The Kravii had torn the portal completely away from its housing. Sandor didn't appreciate the overwhelming exposure to their ranged weapons. He turned back to Wilda Ti. "Use the orb grenades."

"They're too close."

"Not yet. Grant me a moment." Sandor then bent down and picked up the unconscious warrior. He hefted the creature high over his head and launched him forward at the encroaching Kravii like a sideways tree log. The limp warrior crashed into the firing squad, knocking three over and pushing the others back. Before he could turn his head, two pulsing orbs soared past Sandor's ear, landing at the Kravii feet. The orbs plopped to the ground as if landing in honey before lifting back into the air with a click. Sandor knew what would happen next, so he spun backward and tucked his head.

The orbs activated with a *whoosh*, sending out a paralyzing wave, encircling the Kravii and creeping past the portal. The wave then collapsed on itself, crushing everything within its reach, reducing it to wet, mangled rubble. Gravity grenades never produced a pretty sight.

Wilda Ti stood up from behind the table she'd overturned for cover. She checked the fallen technician to determine if his injuries were fatal but was met with disappointment. Her fingers brushed down to close his eyes before gathering status reports from the other two survivors. The female tech nodded. Sandor peeked his head out into the corridor to assess for more attackers. He glanced down at the heap of bone, teeth, and armor, and uttered, "Messy business," before popping back inside the Control Room.

He deactivated his gloves and moved back to the mist screen. Fortunately, it had suffered only minimal damage from the charge blasts. "Now let's see those security views."

Wilda Ti and the technician obliged the Investigative's request despite their shared belief that this wasn't the best time for an investigation. They huddled around the screen as the tech collected herself and accessed the view projectors. A checkerboard of images pushed upward from the screen.

The first displayed the present battle for the loading dock. The Kravii had overrun the area, with only a smattering of

Federation security force remaining. They stared at the image in cold silence until Sandor shifted it aside. "First things first."

Wilda Ti canted her head and glared up at him, not understanding how past views were more urgent than the current invasion. Sandor flipped through the images looking for the luxurious Imperial Wing, but something else caught his eye. It took him a moment to process it. He swiped the image back and leaned downward, studying it.

The Infirmary. The image showed a darkened room; only the blue hue from the emergency backup bulbs embedded in the ceiling and floors cast a picture. "What?" Wilda Ti asked.

"Did you have the Jopali observer called 'Kim' transferred to the Infirmary?" Sandor replied.

"Yes. She is under guard."

"Not for long." He pointed to black smoke rising up from the floor like a totem of doom.

Wilda Ti bent forward. "What is that?"

"That is darkness in its purest form." He paused and then noticed movement on the next screen. He swiped to the left. Four cadets, trailed by a tiny V-Tech, entered the view just outside the Infirmary pod. "And they are in pure danger."

### Main Entry Bay

Anibal had to take cover to avoid being carved to pieces by the onslaught of electrified charges sent downrange from the Kravii position. He didn't have a ranged weapon to retaliate, and the few remaining soldiers who exchanged fire were being eliminated with relative ease.

He watched as Conor and the others rushed away down the nearest corridor. It wouldn't lead them away from danger, but at least it would take them away from the majority of the enemy troops. Besides, the Infirmary would be a decent place for them to hide out until Federation reinforcements arrived. If they ever did arrive in time.

A rapid sequence of charge blasts peppered the top and side of the barricade, tearing a chunk of it away. Those reinforcements needed to come fast. And on a more critical note, the Paladin knew he had to find some better cover.

He scanned the environment and observed a conical pillar utilized for housing mechanical repair equipment. It should be able to withstand the enemy's firepower better than whatever remained of this dilapidated barricade. Only one problem. He would have to leave cover and move toward the enemy to get to it.

More blasts rocked the barricade, several of which would've cut him through if he hadn't been low enough—belly low. He waited for a hesitation in the barrage and then pushed up from his stomach to feet in one movement. He leaped over the shredded wall, picked up a *Kralanza* and dashed to the right, pumping out three bursts of electric lightning as he slid in behind the pillar.

The satisfaction of achieving the maneuver proved short-lived. The Kravii seemed unimpressed, perhaps even inspired by his movement. They aggressed, converging on his position. Every time he peeked around to fire back at them, they greeted him with a hail of crackling blue fire. Several fanned out to the right in a flanking attempt. The warriors moved tactically, avoiding every one of Anibal's shots. Their lifelong training reflected in their expertise in ranged warfare tactics.

He sank low to create a smaller target, trapped with the inability to close ground quickly enough to instigate melee combat. Nowhere to go and no one for backup. Or so he thought.

The whir of a high-velocity Cyclon precipitated the rain of chaos about to befall the Kravii. Bradok pushed forward slowly as his weapon of heavy destruction cut through the three flanking Kravii as punishment for trying to take out the noble Paladin.

The two Elites granted Anibal the reprieve he needed to return fire. The Kravii began to fall or retreat back to take cover themselves. Even the Battleborn Chief took notice. She didn't appreciate this new resistance, and Elites were her specialty. Chief Sveta made a call for reinforcements of her own, knowing her enemies would soon regret their resistance.

### Infirmary

Conor didn't like leaving his mentor alone in a warzone filled with Kravii killers, but Anibal insisted they flee to another area where the enemy didn't have such a concentration of forces. "Where are we?" Conor blurted out, not recognizing the darkened corridor.

"This is the medical wing," Ari replied. "Guess it's a good thing you haven't been here."

"Seems pretty dark," Byro offered. "That's not normal. What happened to the lights?"

"Must have something to do with the attack," Ari replied. "Come on. We can hide out in here." She activated the portal with her pulsero, and the group ducked inside the main room.

Three sensing-treatment pods were lined up along its center. The domed pods were utilized for more critical medical procedures like trauma or disease eradication. Recovery beds lined the walls, along with assorted medical devices. The beds lay empty, but the room wasn't.

Tiera and Conor recognized the woman seated in the chair. She exhaled a sigh of relief to see them instead of Kravii infantry despite the two security guards by her side. "What's it like out there?" one of the guards said, stepping toward the cadets.

"It's bad," Tiera responded. "A full invasion."

"Why invade the Academy?" Kim asked, standing up and moving with the guard.

"Not entirely sure, but I think it has something to do with you," Tiera replied.

"Me?" Kim asked. Her hand instinctively moved to her mouth as a tingling sensation of trepidation swept her. "What did I do?"

"Don't think you did anything. I think it has to do with what you discovered. You and the other guy."

"Novac," Kim gasped. His name escaped in a hushed breath, but she felt its weight as it left her lips. She turned away to stifle the tears and mask her pain from the children. "Why would the Kravii want me?"

"We don't know, but they're here for something."

"Yeah, to kill us," Byro quipped.

"*They* don't want you. Something . . . else . . . does," Conor said, his words escaping slower as he noticed black smoke pushing up from the floor of the darkened room. He immediately knew what it meant. He'd seen it before, and he felt it now: a deep pull, as if the air was starting to press against him.

"What is after me?" Kim asked.

"That," Conor spoke with his finger extended toward the smoke. Kim turned to face it, taking three instinctive steps backward. The guard stood firm, leveling his rifle at the mystical danger.

A dark, cloaked figure emerged encircled by a spiral of crimson light. Conor hurried to Kim, latching onto her arm. He planted his feet and pulled her away just as the red light lashed out, missing just past her head. The whip moved again, this time licking the weapon and the guard holding it. Both targets split apart with searing heat.

Conor backed away with the others. He shielded Kim and V-23 from the threat but felt an overwhelming need to run. The remaining guard fired at the smoky figure, but the fire whip had already ensnared her. It snaked around her weapon, up her arm, and around her neck. The whip sparked brighter, and the guard split into pieces as if she'd been put into a hot dicer.

The smoke faded from the figure as it turned to face Kim and the cadets. Conor finally got a good look at the assassin named Sedit-Kal. He stood tall and slender, but his body remained cloaked by full robes. The hood draped a shadow over a coal-black face with deep cracks lining the skin like etched scars. His red eyes, two portals displaying only malice and pain, scanned them as if they were trapped rodents.

The fire whip coiled back around the assassin before retracting back to its master and disappearing from view. The cadets slowly stepped back from the mysterious creature. They needed to flee quickly, but the portal behind them had already been shut. At that moment, Byro really regretted shutting the door.

Sedit-Kal slowly stretched forth his arms, curling his claws inward. A gray mist began to spray forth and swirl, moving outward.

# CHAPTER 25

**The Academy**
**Outer Orbit Perimeter**

The Federation Craft Carrier split in half, riddled with explosive destruction. The front of the ship tore away, falling at a 90-degree angle into the void of space. The last of the Federation frigates ruptured nearby. The concussion emitting from the explosion pulverized the raised command deck of what remained of the Craft Carrier.

A handful of Federation Whiplash fighters persisted in what would be the last stand of the Academy's defense. Wilda Ti and her technician stood at the controls managing the struggling cannons in an effort to hold off the four warships and swarming Kravii Sprawlers.

If only the interceptor missiles hadn't been deactivated. Then she could at least take down one or two of the warships before the Academy fell. And at this point, a full invasion and capture seemed imminent. Based on the directed fire still being unleashed on the Academy defenses, she couldn't tell if the enemy intended to blast the sphere into oblivion, or if they wanted to just invade and kill them all more personally. One thing had been made clear over the many years of their ongoing war with the Kravii—they seldom took prisoners. They seemed to prefer trophies over survivors.

Sandor Leo stood at the open portal, looking for a secondary assault. Soon the Battleborn Chief would send another platoon. However, according to the screen displaying the footage of the Entry Bay, she seemed more preoccupied with the two misfit Elites holding out against her complete victory. Their resistance proved heroic, if not futile.

### Entry Bay

Bradok continued to mow down the enemy, sending two more to an early death before they could make it to cover. Despite being overmatched, they seemed to be holding back the Kravii for the moment. The insurgents stopped their aggressive assault, choosing to instead exchange fire from a greater distance down the length of the long, wide bay. Of course, the enemy was anything but foolish, and Iopo Lex determined they'd realized the same thing he had about his comrade's devastating weapon.

"Getting low on ammo, my friend," Bradok said as he released the trigger, ending the horizontal hailstorm of hot rounds. Iopo Lex surveyed the battlefield. Anibal hunkered down to his right. He and Bradok held a weak position, while the Kravii occupied a much more fortified place near the entry. Even now, two docked Kravii Sprawlers provided an effective screen from Bradok's Cyclon. It was only a matter of time before the Battleborn would send forth her next wave to converge and squash their meager resistance.

"Isn't this supposed to be a recruit-training center?" Bradok said as he performed a round count on his weapon.

"It sure is," Iopo replied.

"Then where are they?"

"Not much they could do if unarmed."

"Well, next time, let's get these kids some weapons."

"Sure, my friend. Next time," Iopo Lex said. Out of nowhere, Bradok yelled in pain. Iopo spun forward assuming he'd been hit with a Lanza bolt, but the Kravii weren't firing on their position. Bradok dropped down on one knee, blood spilling from an open wound to the back of his leg. Another invisible slash opened up a gaping wound across his abdomen. The bloody injuries appeared to come from thin air. The large Elite dropped his weapon and held pressure on his belly. "Slayers," he muttered.

"Where?" Iopo Lex spun the coils of his Vulcan Bo. The Kravii Slayer was a special class of warrior, designed for lethal stealth engagements. It was odd to find them on this battlefield. "Can you see them? How many?"

"Don't know." Bradok grimaced as blood trickled through his fingers. They both searched around but couldn't see their cloaked attacker. "But this is definitely from a Slayer blade."

Bradok was right. The Slayer carried two curved blades shaped like crescent moons with additional sharpened metal bent in a half-circle over the hilt. This made the weapon effective for slashing, no matter the position or attack trajectory.

Iopo Lex looked high and low. He knew Slayers to be extremely agile and rumored to strike from unexpected locations. "Why can't we see them?"

A Kravii Slayer crouched silently on the barricade just in front of the two Elites. They huddled close enough to bite. He brought both blades up and out, ready to chop off the head of the smaller soldier just below. He relished the moment—an undetected predator versus unsuspecting prey. The other two members of his hunting party split up; one stalked the man with the sword in the corner while the other hovered over the larger, wounded man, bleeding on his knees.

### Infirmary

The gray mist pouring from Sedit-Kal's claws churned, filling the space between the assassin and the cadets. They backed up as far as they could until the wall behind them halted any further retreat. The mist swirled and then shot toward them, seeking to enter bodies through eyes, ears, nose, and mouth like a parasitic cloud of death. It swept first toward Conor and Tiera, the two bravest standing out in front in defense of the others.

Just before it drove upward into Conor's nostrils to infest and shred his brain, it stopped; halted by some invisible forcefield. The mist churned against the invisible wall which then began to gather and constrict. It concentrated into a ball and rose up and away from them. Conor looked to the wraith-assassin. His eyes squinted in a look of bewilderment. This wasn't Sedit-Kal's doing.

They all learned the cause of the attack's failure as a small, hooded figure floated into the room with his legs crossed in midair, and a hood shrouding his dark-crimson face. Conor and Byro had never been happier to see their mystical little friend than right now.

Keil finished balling the mist into an invisible orb and with a flick of the hand sent it hurtling above through the ceiling. He kept his keen green eyes fixed on the silent assassin and spoke in his scratchy voice. "I've been looking for you."

Sedit-Kal remained unthreatened and undeterred by his new challenger. The fire whip materialized in his clawed hand and began to glow and coil. Keil turned to the recruits below him and brought his palm downward. The portal door crumpled to the floor like a damp towel. "Go," he hissed. Ari, Kim, and V-23 dashed through the opening. They didn't have to be told twice.

The other three wanted to stay and help but felt it wouldn't be a good idea when Keil started trembling. His hands balled into fists, and the beds and equipment in the room began to shake and rattle. Sedit-Kal dug in against the building force, pulling him forward.

Byro grabbed Tiera and Conor, pulling them fast out of the Infirmary. "Come on. You don't want to be around for this." He exited and poked his head back in, looking up at his roommate. "Give it to him!" Keil grimaced, displaying fierce intensity. "Woah," Byro gasped. "I'm outta here."

Sedit-Kal couldn't resist the force drawing him toward the center of the room. He stumbled into a treatment pod as they clustered together. The beds skittered forward, banging into each other as the equipment containers toppled and spun. Everything in the room pulled toward Keil as if he were a powerful magnet. His fists slowly drew closer together, shaking with concentrated energy. His legs dropped, still suspended in the air, his fists pulled inward to his chest, nearly touching, as if compressing a coiled spring.

Then, in a sudden movement, Keil thrust his arms outward with a scream. Everything exploded outward, splashing against the walls. Beds dismantled from the crushing force, twisting and tangling metal and shredding fabric. The treatment pods smashed, split, and shattered. It looked like the aftermath of a tornado's wrath.

Keil descended to the ground, winded, and spent from the exertion. That was the first he'd ever attempted a maneuver of that magnitude, and now he felt its exhaustive toll. At least it appeared effective. He looked around for the assassin, but it had left no trace. Had he escaped somehow?

Keil turned to leave, but his legs buckled. He collapsed to the floor, lacking the strength to hold himself up. A hand grabbed his shoulder, lifting him upward. Expecting to stare into the face of his killer, he instead found that of his friend. "I got you. Come on," Byro said as he hoisted him up, noticing that he was even lighter than he thought he'd be.

"Told you to go," Keil said with a raspy voice.

"That's not what friends do. Don't get me wrong—I got out when it looked like you were about to explode, but I had to come back." Keil gasped and went limp over Byro's shoulder. "Nice job, by the way."

Byro carried the mystic into the corridor and hurried to catch up with the rest of the waiting group. "Did he kill it?" Tiera asked.

"Don't know," Byro replied. "Didn't see it in there, but you should see what Keil did to the Infirmary. Remind me not to get on his bad side."

"Whatever that dark mist was, I know he saved us from it," Tiera said.

"It's not dead," Conor whispered.

"How do you know?" Tiera asked.

"I can still feel him."

"I feel it, too," Keil whispered. "Been tracking it since it entered our room."

"That's not good," Ari said. "Let's keep moving."

Keil tapped on Byro's shoulder and motioned to be put down. He found his footing and paused to gather more stability. Byro watched with outstretched hands to make sure the little guy didn't collapse again. Keil reassured him with a nod.

Conor led them back down the corridor without much of an idea of where to go. They came to a crossroads, one way leading back to the bay—not a good idea—and the others leading to the various training pods. They hesitated, trying to decide which way to go. Then they noticed the three bodies scattered across the floor to the left. Two were cadets, the other an instructor. They rushed over, hoping they could still be saved.

"It's Piloting Instructor Nicet Blatori," Byro said with a gasp. The wounds to his upper body and the lifeless color in his face showed he was beyond rescue.

"I know this girl," Ari said as she rolled one of the cadets onto her back. She checked her for signs of life but found none. "She was so sweet. A First-Circuit." Her words choked in her throat. Conor moved to Ari and rested a comforting hand on her back.

"They're all dead," Tiera uttered.

Ari stood and wiped away the tears. "I think we should go back to Residential. We can just hide out in the Towers and protect the others."

"No," Keil whispered. "The Kravii will go there if they haven't already. I found . . . a beacon . . . active . . . in our domicile." His words became more labored in his weakened state.

"We'd just be sitting targets once they got there, anyway," Tiera offered. We need to get to the Armory."

"That's back through the Entry Bay. We'd never make it through there," Byro said.

Conor thought for a moment. "How about the Forge?" he asked, his thoughts turning to the collection of axes and swords. "We could hold up in there and make a sta—"

His words cut out from several lightning cracks fired from the Kravii, now rushing toward them, cutting them off from both the Forge and the Residential District. Conor swooped up V-23 and pushed Kim and Ari toward the nearest exit—back to the Entry Bay.

Byro scooped up Keil and ran with Tiera toward the Mess Hall, right into more waiting Kravii, cutting them off from the others. Byro bumped into the first warrior and fell down, dropping Keil. The mystic coasted to the floor while Byro tumbled over just fast enough to avoid the swiping lance. He scrambled away from the first attack, but Tiera wasn't as lucky.

A Kravii grabbed her under the arm and tossed her like fodder against the wall. She caught her breath and reached behind her back, pulling the *Paraeo* batons just in time to catch the heavy double-edged blade as it drove downward toward her head. Her hands spread apart as she spun to the side, avoiding the finishing strike. The lance hit the floor, but the Kravii caught the rebound, expertly bringing it back into position for a follow-up attack.

Tiera dashed to her right, leaping over the low sweep aimed at her legs. She doubled forward into a front flip, landing on both feet and rolling forward to create more distance. She turned to the side as she completed her roll and flung both batons at the warrior. They spun clockwise as they soared in the air, finding their marks at the shoulder and side of the head.

The blows rattled the warrior but left him otherwise uninjured from the blunt-force attack. He stepped forward to assault the girl again but stopped suddenly. He dropped the Lanza, bringing both claws up to his head. The other warrior did the same. Byro seized on the opportunity to slide away beside Tiera.

The warriors squelched and writhed as their armor slowly compressed, digging into flesh as it caved into their skulls, as if the organic armor had turned against its wearer. The organic armor wasn't malfunctioning; an unseen force was manipulating it to cause the lethal affliction. Keil stood still and silent nearby, his hands slowly curling into fists. The Kravii armor contorted and twisted, collapsing in on the helpless warriors, under the metaphysical command of its new master.

The warriors fell dead, the life squeezed from them. A sudden crack from a third Lanza clipped Keil at the hip, knocking him against the wall. The blast stunned him, leaving him incapacitated—an easy victim for the Kravii aggressor's lance. She took two steps forward and thrust down at the robed child, expecting to gore him through. Keil spread out his limbs in an X at the last second fading into a particle image through the wall at his back. The Lanza struck solid metal and reverberated.

Tiera turned to Byro, a stunned look on her face. "You know he could do that?"

"Nope. Cool trick," Byro said, grabbing her hand and pulling her away with him. They ran down the corridor, away from the remaining warrior, who was still confused by the disappearing boy and the crushed corpses of her fallen squad.

"Where are we going?" Tiera asked, seeing they had made a successful retreat.

"In here. I have an idea," Byro said as he swiped his pulsero on the portal to the Piloting Pod.

"Oh, yes." Tiera managed her first smile since the world had begun falling apart.

They rushed across the bridge leading to the center landing platform. Byro jumped onto the Spectre and fired it up. The sound of the thrusters spiked his adrenaline with confidence. "If we don't have weapons, at least we'll have a vehicle," he said to the girl standing beside the chariot.

She just smiled and leaned forward, touching her own pulsero against the control panel. The screen turned from blue to red, indicating its weapon systems had just been activated. "Who says we don't have weapons?"

"Oh, boy. I like you. Get on."

Tiera hesitated, looking to her left. "Nah. I have a better idea."

### Entry Bay

Conor found himself back at the Entry Bay, but it looked more like a battlefield than a loading dock for incoming vessels. Actually, it looked more like he'd just crossed behind enemy lines. The Kravii had taken over.

Two assault groups moved down the wide expanse in his direction while two curved lines of warriors slowly pushed inward from the dock. Several Kravii fighters had also landed inside. Clearly, the enemy now claimed the Academy as their own.

Ari, V-23, and Kim joined him as they surveyed the predicament.

Conor spotted Anibal up to the right, crouched down behind a maintenance tower and holding a Kravii weapon. The two Elites who'd rescued him from the Tretch pod hunkered down just ahead. The big one looked injured. No one was moving, as if they'd been frozen in ice.

The Kravii Slayer stood poised above its prey, ready to slash out for an easy kill. Iopo Lex couldn't spot the attackers. They could be anywhere. Good thing he'd been outfitted as an Elite. Bad thing for the Slayer.

"Optic. Heat," he whispered. The optical lens embedded over his right eye switched its perspective to infrared, designed to detect heat signatures. In an instant, he spotted the dark image laced in a crimson hue just above him. He flung himself backward just in time to miss the cloaked swords crisscrossing over his head. They sliced through several strands of hair as he dropped below their target. He thrust the Vulcan Bo upward into the bowels of the Slayer before crashing to his back. The coils ripped through his belly and groin, splitting everything apart wide with an incapacitating mortal wound.

Iopo instinctively looked around for other assailants. "Left shoulder!" he shouted to his kneeling friend. Without any hesitation, Bradok reached over his shoulder and grabbed at the air. His massive hand found a thin throat coated in slithering armor. He squeezed hard. Knowing the Slayer was still holding devastating blades, he stretched his left arm in a wide, sweeping move, hoping to catch his opponent between his slender legs. He heaved under his crotch, flipping the creature onto his back with a thud. He collapsed his weight on top of the Slayer and felt for the head. After delivering a pounding of elbows, Bradok wrapped his good leg around the Slayer's head and shifted his weight to his belly. The force from his leg extending backward snapped the neck. He couldn't see it, but he definitely heard the crack.

Iopo got to his feet and scanned the area. He spotted the third Slayer, creeping along behind Anibal like a silent serpent on an unsuspecting mouse. "Anibal! Behind you. Low right!"

But the Paladin was anything but a defenseless rodent. He moved with blinding speed as he planted the tip of the Lanza into the ground and kicked himself vertically into the air, his body and legs fully taut, as if he'd become an extension of the spear. He then flipped backward, yanking the long-weapon with him. He landed soft and smooth, spinning it once and driving it downwards, impaling the creature straight through the spinal column. He'd driven the blade so forcefully, it entrenched itself into the metallic flooring as if pinning the Slayer to an insect collector's corkboard.

The small victory against the Slayers proved short-lived. The Kravii horde aggressed toward their position with renewed vigor. Iopo Lex helped Bradok to his feet, handing him the heavy Cyclon. "Make your shots count."

"I'll try. This thing likes to spray, so we'll have to let them get closer," Bradok said as he lifted the weapon, resting the barrel on the top of the barricade.

"Oh, I don't like that. What I wouldn't give for some artillery right now," Iopo Lex said.

"I hear you," Bradok replied.

The Kravii stalked forward, keeping the pathetic resistance pinned down with relative ease. Iopo Lex felt a tap at his knee. He looked over and spotted Conor crouched next to him. "What are you doing here?" He then noticed a woman, a girl, and even a tiny V-Tech. "Oh, great. You even brought your friends.

This isn't the kind of party you want an invitation to. Why don't you go find wherever the other recruits are hiding out?"

"We ran into some trouble. Believe me, we didn't intend to come back," Ari replied.

"All right," Iopo Lex said as he glanced over his shoulder. "Let's try to retreat back the way you came. When I give the word, I need all of you to run down that corridor there. Stay low. The big guy will lay down cover fire for us. Move when I tell you, and move fast."

A charge blast suddenly caught Bradok in the lower back. He tumbled forward, slamming his chest against the barricade. Iopo Lex crouched down and spun around. Ten warriors moved to their position from behind, sealing off their retreat.

"We're pinned down! You okay?!" Iopo Lex shouted. Bradok gathered himself best he could. He sank down to his butt, his back pressed against the barricade with the Cyclon held loosely in his lap.

"Not so good, boss. That one did some real damage."

"Hang in there! If we don't think of something fast, we'll all be joining you real soon."

The Lanza blasts bombarded their meager position from both sides. Ari kicked her legs out wide to avoid catching a bolt right where she sat. "I hate this!" she yelled. V-23 cowered behind Conor and Kim. They couldn't move. Any attempt at flight or re-positioning would incur a flurry of firepower, like trying to avoid raindrops in a thunderstorm.

Suddenly, a loud explosion erupted behind the new Kravii contingent, followed by some banging, clanging, and grinding. The warriors turned to see the cause of the commotion and were swept aside by a soaring Whiplash, awkwardly carving its way down the corridor. Tiera didn't have much room to fly the fighter, and, in this moment, she realized she needed more practice behind the controls. However, she did find the cannons, and she knew how to work those well enough.

The Kravii scrambled as she strafed the battlefield with high-caliber rounds. The Whiplash flew straight toward her friends and she pulled up just in time to coast overhead. She worked the controls trying to avoid the walls and get more of the enemy in the way of her forward guns.

She breathed a sigh of relief once she'd reached inside the bay. The Kravii were numerous, but at least she now had plenty of room for flight maneuvers.

"Oh, yeah! That's what we needed!" Then Iopo noticed the Whiplash wasn't the only thing Tiera had brought with her. A Spectre zoomed forward with furious guns blazing, flanked by armed cadets, Combatives Instructors Piopo and Nalinia Haz, and even a giant.

Jip charged onto the battlefield with the collective speed and fury of a meteor catapulted from a medieval trebuchet. His snarled mouth flashed teeth resilient enough to snap through tree limbs. A dollop of saliva trickled off his lips as he roared with the vengeance of 100 Wildorian ancestors.

His feet produced thunderclaps as they trampled forward toward the enemy—none of which reached any higher than his midsection. He powered through the three charge bolts pounding against his chest and shoulder. Only a cannon could've stopped his enraged charge, and the Kravii didn't have one handy.

Jip bent forward, unleashing a backhand that launched two warriors airborne against the upper sections of the wall. They suffered three crippling strikes—one from his hand, another from smacking into the wall like soft fruit, and the other from gravity's unforgiving pull back homeward to the metallic flooring. He grabbed another as it turned to run. This warrior became a twisting missile hurled straight at the Battleborn Chief. Sveta managed to dodge the flailing warrior and turned to watch as he spiraled off through the vacuum veil and into open space.

Other recruits engaged in the firefight, having procured weapons from the Forge. Conor smiled. He wasn't the only one with great ideas. Two of the larger recruits slid into position beside him by the barricade—one a girl and the other a boy. He'd never thought seeing the Collective would ever be a happy moment.

Cyril glanced down at him. They locked eyes, and Cyril nodded. Conor understood. Their rivalry would matter tomorrow. Today they were united. The Collective twin then stood and fired several plasma bursts before moving to the next available cover. The female twin followed him, joining her sister beside Anibal. Conor tried to remember her name, but it didn't really matter. In this moment, he was just glad they were on his side.

Tiera hadn't really given enough thought to the amount of damage her craft would be able to endure from the Kravii weapons. A large object in a confined space made for an easy target. A sudden crash to the rear rattled the ship off-kilter. At first, she thought she'd been rammed by another ship, but the rear viewport let her know the Kravii had brought some heavy artillery. The second shot blowing apart her rear starboard thruster just confirmed it.

The battleground inside the Academy Entry Bay raged with such intensity, they'd hardly noticed the lighting had been extinguished. The newly dark environment offered the invaders the home-field advantage. They thrived in shadow.

"Having a hard time tracking these things now! They cut the lights!" Iopo Lex yelled. "Remind me to talk to Wilda about better emergency lighting. Why blue, anyway?"

"It wasn't them," Conor whispered, looking around for signs of the assassin. He spotted Anibal fighting close-range with two warriors, his back to the wall. The Collective formed their own squad, shooting down one warrior at a time to defeat the armor. They'd spent some time training this tactical scenario, but there were too many Kravii—and too few of them.

He felt the pulling weight of the assassin's presence. It was in the bay. Somewhere. Why would it come to the battlefield? Conor kept looking around and spotted Kim curled up next to Bradok, seeking the best protection available. Her face was masked with anxious fear.

Then Conor realized why the assassin was here. It wanted her. He reached over to Kim. "Come on. We gotta go!"

"That's not a bad idea, boy," Bradok said. "Get her out of here—and you, too."

Conor scrambled up next to Kim, grabbing her hand. "It's here," he whispered. She nodded, knowing exactly what he meant as the color flushed from her cheeks.

They crawled low, doing their very best to avoid getting clipped by Lanza bolts. Conor had no clue where to take her, but there had to be some place—any place—better than this. They scrambled over to the wall, hoping to make a small target and go unnoticed in their escape. They didn't.

Two Kravii spotted them and stalked in close for a sudden attack. The warrior jumped high, landing on Conor's back, its weight pressing him flat to the floor. The second one snared Kim's ankle and lifted her up. She screamed as she dangled upside down.

Conor squirmed under the Kravii's talons, struggling to free himself by slipping out. This strategy failed. He decided on another. He placed both hands under his chest in a pushup position, and then he exploded upwards to drive the warrior off-balance. The maneuver worked better than he thought it would. The Kravii stumbled off him and dropped to the ground. Then his head separated from his neck. Strange. Did he do that?

He got to his feet and saw the other warrior drop Kim, a severed arm still holding her ankle. It, too, fell victim to the cataclysmic effects of Sedit-Kal's indiscriminate malice.

Kim pried the lifeless claw off her leg and scampered back to the wall, creating as much distance from her pursuer as possible. The assassin stood over the cadet and the woman, intent on not letting either get away again.

The wall above them suddenly cracked apart, exploding into flying shrapnel as cannon blasts pitted deep holes into the metal. Sedit-Kal spun and shot his head to the right in time to see the Whiplash soar toward them. Tiera reduced speed and pulled back and to the left to avoid another claustrophobic voyage down the corridor. The damage done by the enemy cannons made her sharp turn extremely difficult.

Sedit-Kal plucked a *Kralanza* off the ground and moved back into Tiera's path. He took three bounding steps and leaped high into the air hurling the weapon straight into the Whiplash's cockpit. Tiera ducked to avoid being impaled by the sharp missile, but the attack achieved its purpose. The spacecraft toppled downward, bounced off a wall, did a belly flop, and spun as it skidded to a stop, awkwardly propped up against one of the barricades.

Byro witnessed the collision and maneuvered the Spectre over to check on Tiera. The machine zoomed into a hover skid next to the cockpit, and he stood up, trying to get a view inside. The pilot slipped out of the safety harness and clambered out. "You okay?"

"Could be better," Tiera said with a look of exasperation.

Luckily, the collision had pushed the Kravii back, but not for long. "Hurry! Get on," Byro yelled.

Tiera gathered her balance and looked around. She couldn't see much past the right wing due to its perpendicular position to the ground. She pictured the swarm of warriors closing in. The threat proved more worrisome down below than above, up in the fighter. She threw her leg over the Spectre, joining Byro in the forward seat. He hadn't expected this and flashed an unexpected smile, given the dire circumstances. Byro engaged the throttle and sliced to the right. He had more passengers to collect.

Ari climbed into the Spectre's rear seat and pulled V-23 up to her lap. The machine had been designed for two riders, but this one was destined to hold many more than that. "Everyone get on! We'll hold them back," Iopo Lex said as he helped Kim up behind the Tretchian with the flowing dreadlocks.

Conor moved to the rear-engine casing and paused. He turned back, observing the Kravii closing in again. Bradok's Cyclon held them back as best he could, firing sporadically in an effort to conserve the dwindling ammunition. The Kravii swarmed to overrun them. "Go," Iopo Lex said in a calm, soft voice, his hand resting on Conor's shoulder.

"But—"

"No, Master Hawk. I gave a promise to your father—my Commander. Protecting you is more than an obligation; it's been an honor. I doubted at first, but now I see in you what he sees. Now, go!"

Conor hopped on the Spectre, facing backward. He could see the horde closing in just over Iopo Lex's shoulder. The Elite exuded serene composure as death crept slowly behind him. "And one more thing for you, Master Hawk." Conor looked into the intrepid warrior's eyes. "Rise," Iopo said with a slight smirk.

"As one," Conor whispered.

The Spectre lurched forward but then stopped. Conor first assumed they had too much weight, but Byro declared the issue. "Uh, we have a huge problem here!"

Conor propped himself up and looked behind him to the front. There the assassin stood, cloaked in shadow trailing wisps of smoke. His fire whip curled hot at his feet.

Primo Officer Lex spotted him, his eyes narrowing to fierce slits. He needed to secure the cadets' escape. He raised the Vulcan Bo up to shoulder height, just before charging at the mystical enemy. "Aaaaaah! You're mine!"

Byro released two shots at Sedit-Kal, but he evaded, moving alongside them and clashing with the man holding the long staff. Iopo Lex expertly swiped high for a sweeping slash at Sedit-Kal's head. The assassin flinched backward, making him miss the target. The backhanded downward attack was also easily avoided. The Bo then thrust forward in a penetration move, but the assassin effortlessly dodged that as well. The Elite continued to work to land a targeted strike, but his opponent made him feel like it was a sparring session between a student and the master.

He tried again with a thrust, this time curving the spinning coils in an arch to the left and then back to the right. Sedit-Kal evaded, as if Lex's attacks were either telegraphed or just too slow. Iopo Lex tried next for a lower target, slashing from right to left across the midsection. The assassin moved away. He stepped back and then sprung forward, ending up alongside the Elite's right. Iopo sidestepped and attempted an overhead strike.

Sedit-Kal caught the Vulcan Bo, his hand wrapping around the hot coils. The contact should've liquefied the enemy's hand, but, to Iopo's shock, the coils began to slow and grind to a halt in the assassin's grasp. They ceased to glow as if they'd been covered in some invisible tar. Iopo Lex felt the end of his weapon get extremely heavy as if it'd been coated with the density of liquid mercury. He could no longer lift it, knowing that the weapon now belonged to his enemy.

Sedit-Kal sneered and let the Bo fall. It landed on the ground with a thump as Iopo Lex still held the shaft, entirely unable to lift it again. The assassin then drove his hand into the combatant's chest, stabbing him in five places with a hidden multi-bladed claw.

Iopo Lex felt the strength leave him as his breath failed. He slumped forward, holding onto the assassin's wrist as he was lifted off he floor.

"Go! Go! Go! Go! Go! Please go!" Ari shouted, not wanting to face the same brutal fate. Byro engaged the thrusters and tore off down the corridor. As the Spectre lumbered along under diminished power, Conor watched the Primo Officer slump to the ground in fatal defeat.

Bradok's weapon spun dry on an empty chamber. He dropped the spinning cannon and fought off the swarming Kravii with everything his tattered body could muster. He fought bravely until he was finally brought down with three Lanzas impaled through his muscled torso.

Sedit-Kal turned from the fallen hero. He moved toward the fleeing Spectre, his steps generating smoky trails. Conor watched as the distance grew. The assassin engulfed himself in smoke and then vanished.

"Is it still behind us?" Tiera asked.

"We don't see it," Ari replied.

"It's still coming," Conor offered, knowing the assassin wouldn't quit until it had eliminated Kim.

"Go faster," Ari ordered.

"I'm trying, but you all weigh too much. This thing is hard to control." Byro struggled to give the machine enough power while negotiating the turn. They fishtailed too wide, clipping the rear fender against the wall. Byro's move almost flung Conor from the vehicle, but he held on and spotted the path ahead. An idea sparked.

"Go that way!" Conor shouted to the Spectre operator.

"Where? Up there?"

"Yeah. Go to the Star Deck."

"Why?" Byro asked, nevertheless engaging the throttle toward the spiral. "There's nothing up there!"

"I have an idea."

"Better be a good one. That's a dead end."

"Exactly."

The Spectre took the path up the spiral. It survived the first turn upward but lacked the maneuverability to negotiate the next one. They turned sideways, and the power faded. Byro gave it thrust, but the engine cut out. "We lost power," Byro said, jostling the controls to no avail.

"Maybe because you crashed into so many walls," Tiera whispered in his ear.

"It doesn't matter," Conor said, leaping off the vehicle. "Let's go! We need to get to the top." He reached over and lifted V-23 off the machine before setting him down. He then bent down and held him by the shoulders. "You doing okay?" The tiny V-Tech nodded. "Good. I need something from you."

"What are you going to do?"

"Whatever I have to."

# CHAPTER 26

**The Academy
Control Room**

Wilda Ti watched in dismay as the Kravii decimated the remainder of the Federation protection fleet. Many of the Academy cannons had also been destroyed after their final battleship had gone down. The only hope seemed to be a rigorous interior defense against the invasion, but that, too, didn't appear feasible.

The screen to the right displayed the main battlefield. She swelled with a mother's pride with the valiant charge of her cadets. She watched as Jip, the Collective, Anibal, and a small contingent of Fourth- and Fifth-Circuit cadets applied their training to their utmost ability. But it was bittersweet. Many of the recruits were either still in hiding elsewhere or had fallen on the battleground. Her heart broke at the sight of the lifeless youth scattered around the bay from the merciless surprise attack.

The Battleborn Chief employed devastatingly vicious tactics. No wonder she'd been selected for this specific insertion. To make matters worse, another troop carrier had just landed inside the bay, reinforcing her platoon. Sveta now had more than enough warriors to secure her inevitable victory.

The Battleborn spotted a group of six young Federation warriors aggressing on her position. She decided to greet them personally.

The Collective concentrated their fire, pulverizing another Kravii combatant. Once he fell, they turned to the next in systematic fashion. They were joined by two other cadets, who assisted them with distractive cover fire.

Cyril appreciated the help. "Sweep those there while we take down this one!" he said to Adin, who immediately obliged with a vicious series of automatic blasts. Their tactics proved effective in killing another warrior while keeping the counter-fire to a minimum, but they failed to notice the lethal threat stalking from above.

Sveta scurried along the wall, high above her target, digging in razor claws for her anti-gravity traversal. She clutched her S-Staff in tight with her right hand while relying on her feet and left claw to dig into the wall. She now found herself perched above the group of Federation cadets. The tall, brown-haired boy pounded another round of firepower at her troops, and she pushed off. She flew through the air downward, her staff raised high above her head.

Adin never saw the blow that struck him. The staff crashed hard on top of his head, shattering his neck vertebrae and leaving him limp in death. The Battleborn stepped on his lifeless body as she turned to the twins. Rayna leveled her rifle at the assailant, but Sveta knocked it away with a swipe of her staff. The Battleborn slammed the butt-end of her staff into Gavril's chest and then fired an electric bolt into Rayna's shoulder. The female Collective cried out as she was flung backward.

Several rounds pelted Sveta's upper torso, but they failed to penetrate the organic armor. Danica yelled a scream of fury as she tracked up to the Battleborn's head. She simply shook off the nuisance and grabbed the cadet by the neck, hoisting her up. Danica wriggled, pulling at the claws squeezing her throat. She could feel the air being crushed out of her.

Cyril moved in from behind the Battleborn and cracked her on the back of the knee with his rifle. It had little effect other than inviting a powerful kick to his face. He stumbled backward as blood spouted from his nose. His head swirled in a blur as Gavril spun around him to re-engage in the fight. He began to fire on the formidable Kravii, but she shifted, bringing Danica in between them as a shield. He moved off the trigger and instead bashed the gun against the arm holding the girl.

Sveta's grip didn't break. She brought the staff around with blinding speed, smacking Gavril on the side of the head. He staggered. Then she leveled the weapon and fired, catching him in the hip. The blast spun the Collective recruit to the ground, causing him to collapse face down. She fired on another cadet nearby—the bolt searing the boy through the chest.

Still holding Danica up high, the cadet now nearly suffocated, the Battleborn surveyed her immediate area. Satisfied in her neutralization of the group of nuisance fighters, she nonchalantly brought the S-Staff under Danica's chin. She fired once and let the dead girl fall.

"CAL," the female technician said, her voice piercing the silence.

Wilda Ti didn't answer right away, having witnessed a malicious slaughter of some of her best cadets, captured in gut-wrenching clarity on the wisp screen.

"Wilda Ti!" the tech called out, hoping to break her leader's trance.

The CAL jolted back to the moment. "What? Yes, go ahead."

"We have a problem."

"Yes. I know." Wilda Ti fought back the wave of grief consuming her. "We've plenty enough problems."

"I agree, but this looks like a really bad one."

Wilda Ti switched over to the technician's screen, and then she spotted it. In the top section, space began to fold inward like the sides of a box bending in on itself. This meant one thing—a very, very large ship. She watched in anticipatory horror for what the Kravii were bringing forth now. The nose of the vessel peeked through the bending tunnel, and immediately six large torpedoes soared outward, trailing blue flames of destruction.

"Brace for impact! This is going to hurt," Wilda shouted.

The torpedoes raced from the unseen goliath ship toward the Academy. They moved too fast to intercept with the remaining cannons as a countermeasure. "Looks like they're planning to blow us apart entirely, Chief," the tech uttered calmly, as if accepting her dire fate.

Wilda Ti didn't respond. Her face paled as impending doom raced toward them. Then she noticed something strange. "Wait. Look," she said, placing a finger to the screen. The torpedoes veered to the left straight toward the Kravii warship. Five of the missiles found their mark, impacting the ship's hull. Two of this type of weapon would've done the trick. Five proved overkill. The ship ruptured in a fantastic explosion, ensuring no survivors or salvageable material.

A familiar voice then sounded overhead on the radio intercom. "Wilda Ti?"

"Go ahead," she replied, recognizing the voice, as a tingling sensation washed over her.

"Wilda, would you be so kind as to play a song for me?"

Tears now welled in her eyes. "Yes, indeed," she said with a half-smile. She brushed away several involuntary tears of joy as she glanced over to the tech, who also beamed with the same gratitude. She was already sifting through the playlist. "You have no idea how happy we are to see you. We're getting destroyed and barely hanging on here. We badly need your help."

"That's why I'm here," Makon Welcos replied.

"Any requests?" Wilda Ti asked.

"You know what I like."

Sandor Leo wore a perturbed look. "Music?" he asked. "That is the request? Who is this speaking to us?"

"Oh, you haven't met the Supreme Commander yet, have you?" She laughed. "He can be eccentric at times, but damn, is he good in a fight."

"Hmmmm. Well, musical tunes or not, I don't know if one Jopali and one ship will make much difference."

"Sandor Leo, keep watching that screen. You haven't seen the ship yet."

The Gregor Monolith creeped out of the wormhole like the mythical Kraken leaving its underwater lair. If the Kravii star fleet hadn't noticed it before, they certainly did now. It moved with the power and elegance worthy of the Federation's flagship. There was only one Gregor Monolith. And there was only one Supreme Commander Welcos.

Makon Welcos tapped the Vice Commander on the shoulder. Valitat turned a sideways glance. He was dressed in his lightweight combat suit under his favorite dark crimson robes. In this light it took on a shade of black. In the right light, it gave off a red hue—a declaration of the presence of a war-proven leader of the highest status. "We're going in."

"Of course, you are. You always get all the fun," Valitat said.

"Nonsense. Look at all that out there for you to play with," Makon said with a sweeping arm toward the windscreen displaying the abundance of Kravii opponents. "Come on. I know you'll have fun." He moved off the command deck at a quick pace. "Be sure to demolish every last ship."

"Will do with pleasure," Valitat said, turning back to the control deck. She placed both her palms on the raised counter like an emperor surveying her domain. "You heard the Commander. Rain down fire!"

Makon stepped into the teleport chamber. Ten of the fifteen available dark discs held an Elite, each one anxious to get into battle. "There will be no survivors from your wrath, my friends. Do us proud. And show everyone why you were chosen as an Elite. Rise!"

"As one!" the Elites shouted in unison with a raised fist.

Makon stepped onto his designated dark disc and turned around. The air around them grew in density as they were pulled through the harnessed power and mystery of their concentrated black holes.

### Star Deck

The smoke encompassing the assassin dissipated. He took several slow steps away from the ascending spiral leading him to the cavernous Star Deck. The universe opened up with the sensation of walking unfettered in space. Unseen walls, floor, or ceiling poured the majesty of endless void all around. The chamber offered the appeal of oneness with the stars, the appeal of being truly alone.

But Sedit-Kal wasn't alone.

Conor stood a short distance away, facing off against the demon in an act that mixed bravery and foolishness. His hands trembled. His heart pounded like war drums. He balled his hands into fists to keep them from trembling.

What was he thinking? This wraith could do things that weren't humanly possible. It killed Iopo Lex as if he were just a plaything. His mind flooded with the thoughts of flight. Anything that would get him out of this very moment.

The fire whip flashed and began to writhe as if it had a mind of its own. The assassin took several steps toward his next victim. Conor watched the red trails as the whip worked its way around its master and then slithered outward, creeping closer to its prey.

The fight with the Dragor. The Ascension. The Collective. Anibal's training temple. The encounters with the Kravii. His mind flashed to all of his recent challenges. Each one impossibly difficult. Each one somehow a victory.

Well, maybe not the Ascension course, but he'd have to give that one another go. He took down a Dragor! No, two Dragors—kind of. He could do this. One last challenge. If not for him, then for them—his friends. For Iopo Lex.

Conor took a deep breath and clenched his teeth. He unplugged the fountain of courage and began to let it turn to something else—something powerful when unshackled.

*Don't get angry*, Makon Welcos had cautioned him. No, Commander, this was a perfect time to get angry. Really angry.

Conor's face turned to a mask of spite. He yelled out a war cry and dashed forward, intent on breaking his enemy with his bare hands. The assassin stopped and assumed a fighting stance. The aggressing adversary was unexpected. Bold. Reckless.

Conor lessened the gap between them, rapidly closing the distance. The whip lashed out like a serpent's tongue. He ducked under its effort to lick his face. It came back again, this time striking at his legs. He dove over it, rolling into a somersault and bounding back up to his feet. He bent backward, watching it slice through the air above his head. Another miss.

It didn't seem to move that fast. He just didn't want it to touch him. He'd seen the whip cut through bone and metal. It had to be very hot. Hot. How hot? Dragor monster fire hot? In that moment, a crazy thought pierced his mind. *There was only one way to find out.*

Conor stopped moving and stood facing his opponent. The whip swirled through the air. Conor ignored it. He just watched the assassin as he twirled it. It snapped at him like a lunging asp. Conor still didn't move. He let it come.

He blocked the strike with his forearm. The whip wrapped around his muscle. Its heat singed his skin, tattooing the flesh with three deep lines. It stung, but it didn't cripple.

Conor looked at his arm and the alien weapon working to eat it away. He let it struggle and turned back to the assassin. Then he saw it.

Sedit-Kal gave away a look of bewilderment. He yanked on the weapon to recall it back to him, but the boy refused to let it go. He twisted his arm around the whip, gathering more of its length onto his forearm. He fought against the searing heat and the urge to get it off him, but the pain was tolerable, and the uncertainty in his enemy's countenance made it all worthwhile.

He reached forward and wrapped his right hand around the glowing material, feeling it singe the pads of his fingers and palm. He grimaced and yanked backward. The force of Conor's pull jerked the weapon from Sedit-Kal's hand. The whip extinguished and instantly cooled. Conor untwisted it from his arm and flung it behind him.

The assassin had lost his prized weapon and didn't appreciate the humiliation that came with it. He vowed to show he wasn't defeated in the slightest.

Sedit-Kal flashed two rows of jagged teeth and dropped his hands into view. He walked forward as long, sharp claws slid out from his extended fingers.

### Entry Bay

Synthesized orchestral music thundered overhead. The Kravii paused at the irksome noise but refused to be distracted from their mission. The Battleborn Chief scoffed at the enemy's meager attempt to somehow thwart their dominance on this battlefield with a displeasing melody. Their pathetic weapon failed.

She couldn't have known the Federation's ultimate weapon was already en route.

Makon materialized like a phantom, flanked by ten of the best warriors in the Vesputi Galaxy. The drumbeat pounded throughout the bay. The Supreme Commander smirked and nodded his head slow to the beat. Vulcan Bo's ignited and spun all around him. Makon flashed twin blades similar to Anibal's sword, but with red mist trails running through the blackened metal. With so many targets spread out before his eyes, he could hardly resist the urge to engage. But that's not what he wanted, so he waited.

It took only another moment to be noticed. A Kravii warrior bent forward and screeched at the line of Elite destruction poised to lay waste to the invaders. The Battleborn turned, spotting the new opposition. There it was. Her dark eyes flashed a spark of fear upon recognizing she was now standing on the same field of battle as the Unfallen, fittingly dressed in his robes of conquest.

The Unfallen would fall today. This conquest belonged to her. Sveta gave the command for attack, and her warriors turned to intercept the Elites as they raced forward. Makon outran them all with ease. He moved with blazing speed, whipping the swords in a treacherous cyclone that cut down the first two warriors brazen enough to cross his path.

Makon moved without hesitation or fear of being struck. Most couldn't touch him. The one that did, felt his weapon rebound off the Commander's biceps without leaving more than a scratch. He received a stomp kick in his groin for the effort. The kick struck him like a bomb, destroying his pelvis and propelling him backward into the docked ship. He lay in a crippled heap against the landing pilon, still conscious enough to watch his comrades receive a much worse fate.

The storm of Vulcan Bo's ripped through the Kravii lines alongside the Commander, carving a path to the Battleborn like a turbine in wet snow. Makon finished cutting down another warrior and turned to face two more. They suddenly vanished as one of the barricades flew through the air, bowling into them like twigs against a toppling boulder. Makon looked for the pitcher, knowing the Kravii were enduring the wrath of a very angry giant. Jip met his glance and offered a shrug in return.

Makon seized the moment to appreciate the music again. He adopted the rhythm as he continued the fight, slashing through the last two of the Battleborn's guards. He stopped and crossed his swords, a gesture to offer the opportunity for surrender. He knew she wouldn't accept it. The Kravii fought to the death.

Sveta slammed down the end of her S-Staff in clear refusal. Makon rolled his neck and flashed a smile. This fight would be her last.

### Star Deck

The assassin's claws extended the length of Conor's forearm and ripped through the air with lethal intention. The boy moved fast, making Sedit-Kal miss with the first three strikes. Conor blocked the assassin's backward slash at the elbow and retaliated with a low kick, aiming for the back of the knee. But the assassin proved both quick and skillful in anticipating attack response. He lifted his leg, forcing the boy to miss. That's when he finally caught him.

The claws came back around Conor's arm slicing down across his shoulder and triceps. Sedit-Kal followed with another expertly timed strike from left to right, tearing through Conor's shirt, and leaving four gashes across his chest.

Hot pain stung Conor off-balance. He bent forward for an instant but then felt himself forced downward to his knee. The assassin smacked Conor in the nose and then drove him backward, pinning him to the floor with a heavy, gnarled foot. Sedit-Kal bent low and raised his arm high, jostling the claws back and forth like wind chimes just above the boy's dazed face. The claws dangled above Conor's chin and neckline.

Just before jabbing downward, the assassin paused. He moved his hand slightly to the right to catch the silly rod soaring toward him. He caught it and glanced up at the sender. Tiera stood in full view, having moved away from behind the optical mirage. She was joined by her other intrepid mates, including Kim.

Sedit-Kal spotted his main target and smirked. The baton snapped like brittle candy in his palm, and he let the shards topple onto the child beneath him. The creature now spotted more desirable prey, and this boy under him proved nothing more than an intriguing nuisance.

The foot pressing into Conor's belly lifted, granting him a moment of relief. But the assassin didn't intend release or reprieve. In a flash, the claws extended and thrust downward into Conor's chest.

Conor flattened out to the floor with a scream, feeling the sharp points dig into his skin. Sedit-Kal's face changed from malice to confusion. He turned to look down at his victim. Why hadn't his claws penetrated? Rather than feeling the satisfying infiltration of flesh, bone, and internal organs, he was rattled by disappointment. The claws had pierced only slightly into the skin, like a sword thrust into snow only to be repulsed by a sheet of ice beneath.

Conor moved to raise up, but the assassin tried again, goring the boy once more with double the force. The same result. The confusion turning into frustration, Sedit-Kal gripped him by the pierced shirt and flung him away, toward the emptiness of space. Then he stood full and moved to his next and ultimate kill.

Conor slid across the starry floor until finally slamming against the invisible wall. The collision didn't feel good, but thank God for invisible walls. His chest and arm hurt, more of an ache than anything else. He pushed up to his knees and saw the blood pooling from the slices down his right arm. The warm rivulets of blood trickling down his chest cut red streaks into what was left of his shirt. It looked bad, but it didn't feel too bad. He'd been through worse. Besides, he knew it would heal quicker than it realistically should.

The wraith moved toward his friends. Byro and Tiera faced off against the assassin, with the others slightly behind. All they had for defense between them was a single *Paraeo* baton, and Sedit-Kal had already illustrated how ineffective that would be against him.

Conor's heart filled with dread and urgency. He knew the swiftness with which the assassin could kill. He had to do something.

Move.

Now.

Fast.

He got to his feet, fighting against the ache. He didn't have an attack strategy. He didn't have a weapon. All he had was a mixed cocktail of fear and rage surging through his core. He tucked his head and ran. He ran faster than he ever had before.

Conor moved so quickly, Sedit-Kal never even heard the freight train bearing down on him with the fury of a lost boy fighting for the closest thing he had to a family. Conor lowered his shoulder, crashing soundly into the assassin with a deafening crack. Sedit-Kal flew forward as if he were spring-loaded, landing face first with a mouthful of stars.

Conor got to his feet first. He glanced over to Tiera but didn't really look at her. He had unfinished business. Sedit-Kal climbed to his feet, unknowingly in the perfect position for what the boy had planned at the onset of their duel.

Conor yelled and charged forward again, leaping into the air and bringing down a thunderous punch to the back of the assassin's head. Sedit-Kal reeled from the nasty blow. Before he could defend himself, Conor scooped him up in both arms and dashed forward, straight into the open portal leading into the dark depths of the hidden cavern, seeking another meeting with what lurked inside.

### Academy Orbit

"All away, Vice Commander," the engineer said, confirming the release of the Gregor Monolith's internal fleet of Whiplash fighters.

"Good. Sweep them away," Valitat Bithos replied. The Federation fighters pursued the Kravii crafts, matching their opponent's swarm with fewer numbers but advanced skill and flight weaponry. It might have been an even battle, but the Monolith had no intention of that. She unleashed her guns on the enemy, taking down fighters with explosive precision.

"Another down."

"Very good," Valitat said as she watched another Kravii warship burn and fall away from its flight path. "Punish that troop carrier, too." It was likely empty as it had already disembarked from the Academy's entry port, but she endeavored to wreak retribution on everything within sight.

The Monolith still took some pesky fire from the largest ship remaining—the fleet carrier. Its large cannons stood to inflict the most damage on the Federation prize. At least it had turned its focus on them, away from the Academy sphere. "I want that one," she said.

"Yes, Commander. Unfortunately, the Kravii fighters have been defending it. They move into the path of our torpedoes every time."

Valitat nodded. Soldiers protecting their queen. The only way to end this battle would be to tear that ship apart. "Deploy the Dragor Kiss."

"Uh, Commander, I believe we are too close in proximity for that weapon."

"Well, the other option is to ram it. We don't have an endless supply of torpedoes and—" The quake generated from another cannon bombardment cut her off. She braced against the console as the lights flickered in the cabin. "And I'm tired of that nonsense. Anyone in favor of a good old-fashioned ramming?" She waited for an affirmative response. A hand went up from the navigator down below. Valitat canted her head and waited. A female's hand reached out and slowly pulled the navigator's arm back down. The new guy would soon catch on.

"All right. All in favor. Fire the Kiss."

"Charging," the Chief Gunner advised. The screen in front of him displayed a spinning concentric circle of dashes indicating the heating of the massive torpedo. It had to be housed in a dormant state, otherwise it would tear through its chute and melt through the rest of the ship. And that was even pre-detonation. The circles collided on the screen, forming a single red flashing dot. "Ready."

"Fire," Valitat ordered. The Dragor Kiss needed to be deployed immediately upon activation. It would continue to heat during its flight, reaching critical mass prior to impact. Critical mass meant the point of no return. Nothing could stop its devastation.

The Kiss soared out of the chute, a silent seeker of unyielding chaos. A Kravii fighter moved in its path to intercept and disintegrated like a snowflake in a blowtorch's flame. Several other brave warriors attempted the same but met only a flash of failure.

Valitat pulled herself from the mesmerizing display. She badly wanted to watch the spectacular weapon burn its way through the enemy like an unstoppable comet streaking through space on its determined collision course, but she didn't have that luxury. They were flying too close for comfort and would face devastating percussive damage once the Kiss detonated.

"All thrusters reverse. Full power!" She gave the command, and the pilot immediately engaged the negative engines. He'd already been poised for the order, being experienced enough to know they remained in range of the weapon's effects.

The Gregor Monolith lurched backward, driving fast through space. The Whiplash fighters had already been alerted by the Comms tech and retreated to a far distance. The Monolith needed to catch up.

The Dragor Kiss struck the carrier's oversight tower with a bright yellow flash, causing it to buckle from the impact, but that didn't last. As it crumbled, intense heat disintegrated any rubble until particlizing the whole of the ship. A percussive wave surged outward, as if a star had randomly exploded, its ring vaporizing any fighters unlucky enough to be within range.

The Monolith continued its furious retreat. Hopefully, they would be far enough away to escape the brunt of its crushing force. Valitat planted her feet and held firm to the console. They were about to find out.

The surge hit the ship, trying to spin it like a coin flicked in the air. The pilot fought to absorb the wave and counter its urge to flip them. He couldn't control the spin, but that wasn't a priority—the Monolith wasn't designed to fly upside down. The ship's bow rose high to an almost vertical axis. He felt her wanting to just give in and go over. "No, you don't. Don't you dare," the pilot muttered as he fought harder to level them out. He poured on the thruster energy as sweat trickled down his cheeks.

The Monolith finally changed its mind and tipped back downward. They leveled out as anyone standing on the deck crashed back down to the floor. Valitat picked herself up and straightened out. "Well done." She chuckled. "I guess I'll sit down for that move next time."

She looked through the windscreen and brought up the enhanced displays. The weapon's effects had been cataclysmic on the enemy fleet. Only a few scattered fighters remained, and they had taken to retreat alongside the last warship.

"Shall we give chase, Commander?"

Valitat thought for a moment, recalling Makon's order to eliminate everything. "It's tempting, but let's assess our damages and regroup. However, I do think we should send them away with a parting gift. Fire off a few Chaser torpedoes to say, *Thanks for playing.*"

### Entry Bay

Makon Welcos evaded Sveta's first attacks, ducking and spinning away from the S-Staff. He hadn't struck yet, choosing instead to study her techniques. He relished the rare opportunity for hand-to-hand combat with a Battleborn. Her moves were swift and calculated, yet efficient and force-generating. She left no doubt about her expertise with the staff, and therefore most likely with other weapons as well. But it came time to see how well she handled a fight without a weapon.

Makon kicked his right foot low toward her inner thigh. She avoided it, so he followed with a lunging kick aimed at her midsection. She evaded this, too, but that was intentional. It set him up for the move he wanted. His right foot came down and touched the floor; then, as if he'd landed on a trampoline, he leaped upward, spinning around in mid-air. The heel of his right boot whipped around, cracking against the side of her head. He landed smoothly. She toppled over.

The Supreme Commander looked down at her. Time to take away her weapon. He deactivated his swords, reducing them to daggers; then he slid them back into the sheaths in the front of his belt. He knelt down, grabbed her wrist holding onto the staff, and wrenched it over. The torque from the technique flopped the Battleborn onto her back. She relinquished the weapon, but she wasn't through with the fight yet.

She kicked up at him twice, and Makon deflected these with the staff. Her kicks were meant to grant her space only to get to her feet. She checked her wrist. It hung limp as the organic armor had twisted and snapped away, unable to defend the wearer against the force applied. The pain extracted nothing more than a grunt. She'd fought with injury before.

The Battleborn attacked the Unfallen, lashing out with blazing strikes. Had Makon moved slower, he might've been caught with one of the punches or the unseen jagged dagger aimed for his neck. *So, the loss of the staff didn't mean a deficiency in available weapons,* Makon thought. Her melee combat skills impressed him, matching that of most of his Elites. She would be able to down one or two of them in close combat for sure.

She stabbed her blade out toward his head. Makon sidestepped to the left, blocking the strike with his right forearm. His left hand came down on Sveta's outstretched arm, nudging it downward, just before his right fist slammed against her face. He added a flurry of punches to disorient her further. If not for the armor, her orbital bones and her jawbone would've been pulverized from the onslaught.

Sveta staggered. Makon grabbed her arm with his left hand and guided his right around her waist, pulling her close. She stood a bit taller than him, so he wrenched her forward before releasing her arm. His left hand then slammed against the back of her head, yanking her forward as he lifted her at the waist. She flipped over, landing hard on her back.

Makon then took this moment to scan around him.

The Elites assisted the recruits known as the Collective and others, including the not-so gentle giant. Haviro and Shila cut down a warrior as they fought in conjunction with each other. It seemed they'd become efficient battle partners.

Most of the Kravii warriors now lay defeated, returning the battlefield to the Federation, but the damage had been done. Academy security officers peppered the battlefield with their bodies offered in the ultimate sacrifice. Numerous cadets and instructor staff had joined the fray in bold defiance of the invasion only to fall victim to their superior opponents. The sight of so many dead broke his heart.

Makon then spotted the Paladin. He'd stopped fighting, and this seemed odd. Anibal knelt over a body in the near distance. He caught a flash of the uniform. An Elite. A pang of anxiety stabbed him. He had to go. Training session with the Battleborn was over.

He picked Sveta up by the throat and lifted her off the ground. She lashed out for his face with a clawed hand. That strike missed, but she caught him in the ribs with her dagger. It pierced flesh but didn't drive deeper than a superficial puncture. Makon winced and flashed a grimace of disgust. That mistake would be her last.

With one hand on her neck and another around the arm, Makon took a shuffle-step toward the open bay. He twisted his body and then swung forward like a discus thrower. The Battleborn soared through the air with the velocity of a diving bird of prey, spinning like fan blades. With nothing around to obstruct her flight, she rocketed straight out the portal into space. The air crystallized in her lungs, and her lifeless body froze in rigor mortis, doomed to roam the void forever.

Makon turned back to the Paladin, crouching over his fallen soldier. He sprinted to them, ramming one of the remaining

Kravii warriors in his path. The warrior stumbled and greeted an Elite's lethal Vulcan Bo as he fell.

Makon reached Anibal and paused, placing a steady hand on his shoulder. Then he dropped down on both knees, his hand wrapping around the back of Iopo Lex's head. Anguish brimmed inside him as he held his Primo Officer's lifeless body in his arms. The loss twisted his guts. "No. No. No. Not you, my friend." His tear-swollen eyes caught sight of the fallen Bradok. His thoughts raced through images of instructors, cadets, soldiers, and friends. *How many have died? Why didn't I get here sooner?* Heartbreak stabbed him to the core unlike any weapon could.

He looked up and yelled, "Where are my children?!"

**Star Deck**
**Tranquility Chamber**

Darkness. Deep enough to consume oxygen.

Conor landed on top of the assassin as they crashed to the cold floor. He rolled to the side and moved to what he remembered to be the corner near the entrance. He felt for the wall's cool metal. Once he gained it, he planted his heel against the crease at the floor to maintain his bearing. He shut his eyes to encourage his other senses to become hypervigilant.

"I can feel you," Conor said. "I've felt you since you got here." He sensed the assassin getting up and moving, circling around for a hidden attack.

"Be afraid. I can *see* you. There is no light here for you." Sedit-Kal hissed.

"Wrong." Conor said as he dug into the small pouch at his hip, pulling the orb into his palm. He breathed deep, holding it now in both his hands. "I *am* the light," he whispered as he gave the Astral Orb a twist in opposing directions. He then tossed it away, high and deep into the room.

The orb ignited in a blinding flash of light. It stung Conor's eyes even through his eyelids and the forearm covering his face. The creature of darkness didn't fare so well. The light singed his flesh and scorched his eyes with blindness.

Then another loud screech pierced the silence. The Dalex monster felt the pain, too, dropping to the floor from the light blast. The loose hatch in the wall tore away, instigating a vacuum. It pulled at the creature, sucking it into the hole, beckoning it to join the galaxy's cold vastness.

But it didn't intend to go without a fight. Its tentacles reached out, grasping the nearest object to tether itself to. Sedit-Kal grunted as the first two tentacles tore into his legs. He fought against the pull, but the third wrapped itself around his head swallowing him like a thorny scarf.

The assassin lifted off his feet and glided toward the monster's gaping mouth. Sedit-Kal's dagger-like claws tore into the tentacle covering his mouth, but nothing could stop them both from being dragged into the abyss.

The vacuum sucked away the Dalex. Sedit-Kal slammed against the wall, his back being pulled by forces stronger than he could counter. He knew the mysterious boy remained, somehow resisting the power of space. Another tentacle reached out for desperate salvation, wrapping around the assassin's waist.

Sedit-Kal grimaced and hissed a single word. "*Vosis.*"

Then the assassin disappeared out the hatch into the galaxy's coffin.

Tiera and Byro moved to the open portal, neither foolish enough to venture inside. They saw a star-lined tunnel leading to a black backdrop. Something approached—a shadow moving among the stars.

V-23 tucked himself between them to get a look. He smiled and jerked upward. "Did it work, Master Hawk?"

Conor traversed the corridor, letting the power of confidence supersede all the exhaustion he felt. He exited and swiped his pulsero against the portal to let it close. He then knelt down and placed his hand on V-23's back. "It sure did, my friend. You're a wizard." He then raised up and surveyed the haggard faces of his own collective. "Who's up for kicking some Kravii butt out of our Academy?"

### Entry Bay

Four Elites hoisted their comrade up, carrying him to the Imperial Suites. Haviro and Shila led the way, each one resting Primo Officer Iopo Lex on their shoulder. He was celebrated in life for his service; he'd be revered in death with the regality of a warrior-hero. The Supreme Commander would see to that.

It took an extra two soldiers to manage Bradok, but he'd receive the same respect and treatment. Anibal stood by, knowing this ceremony was reserved only for those who'd earned the designation of an Elite. The Paladin traveled a different path, and the reward of his charge now approached in the near distance. He flashed a smile. "Commander—"

Makon looked up to see a small group of misfit warriors walking the corridor, led by a boy. The boy was almost unrecognizable. He moved with a swagger of confidence he'd known once before in a young man he'd almost forgotten, a younger version of himself.

Tiera moved up next to Conor, filled with the pride of knowing her uncle would be pleased with their courage. Makon slapped Anibal on the shoulder. "There they are. Look at them!" The Supreme Commander beamed. "That, my friend, is our future. And on this dark day, it looks bright. Didn't I tell you? Didn't I?"

"Yes, Makon. You certainly did."

Conor looked to his right and nodded to Byro. He then turned to Tiera. She looked back at him, and once again took him by surprise.

She smiled at him.

# CHAPTER 27

**The Academy**
**Conversation Lounge**

"I don't know how you can do the things you do, but I'm just glad you can."

"Don't," Tiera said.

"What? I'm just saying," Byro replied.

"You'll get him cocky."

"Nah," Conor said with a shake of his head. "Just some tricks I've learned."

"Well, I suppose we'll be headed home for a while," Ari said as she stroked the head of the dog on her lap. Titan's tail began to wag. "Oh, I see you like that girl, don't you?"

"She likes you," Conor offered. "But that shouldn't be a surprise, I guess. Most people do." Ari flashed him a smile with a pair of warm eyes.

"Sorry, guys. Hate to burst your comfort bubble, but we start training again tomorrow," Tiera said.

"Really?" Byro asked, quite disheartened.

"Yes, indeed. The training pods hadn't been affected by the battle. And in case you hadn't noticed, they need us."

"Well, I am up for training." Keil wandered in on two feet and actually eased down into the plush chair across from them. He had a bandage around his shoulder, and he winced at the pain from the point-blank Lanza blast still nagging his hip.

"Even you, Keil? You don't even train with us," Byro chirped. "What happened to you?"

"Don't transcend into another room unless you know what's there. Impaled by the thumb of the Commander's recruiting statue." He shook his head in shame. "I could use some skill improvements."

"I hate that statue," Tiera mumbled.

"Me, too," Keil replied.

They laughed until the chamber began to rumble as a thundering mass of energy approached. The cadets didn't move or jostle from their seats. "Hey, Jip," Byro said as the giant plopped himself down behind him, sliding down to rest on his elbow.

"Hellloooo. You all ready to train again tomorrow?" His question met with a smattering of eyerolls. "Well, I am. They've had me on cleanup duty the past two days, and I'd much rather be training."

"I'm good with that," Tiera remarked, "So long as we get to honor the fallen at the funeral sendoff."

"Then we'd better get moving," Byro added as he rose from the chair. "We didn't get dressed up in our ceremonial uniforms for nothing."

The group moved out of the lounge toward the Observation Deck. They traversed the corridors in silence as mournful soberness lingered in the air. Rows of Federation soldiers crowded the Entry Bay between two docked battle cruisers. They stood in strict formation, adorned in formal black-and-white tunics with elongated Impaler rifles slung across their backs. They posed as a massive security force assigned to guard the Academy in its weakened state of repair and grief.

As they passed the battalion, Conor noticed Byro making an exaggerated effort to scan the soldiers. "What are you looking for?" he asked.

"The Elites. I wanted to see them in their gold-trimmed white with Vulcan Bo's," Byro replied.

"They're all on Jopal to honor Primo Officer Iopo Lex, Bradok, and the other fallen Elites," Tiera interjected.

"How many died?" Byro asked, feeling the weight of the loss.

"My uncle said Hage and Rioso didn't make it off Hadak-5," Tiera answered.

"Four?" Byro asked with a gasp. "That's crazy."

"And sad," Ari added.

"Let's catch their send-off," Tiera said.

The group moved through the bay and over to the Observation Deck. Conor remembered the room with the giant telescopic viewer where V-23 first showed him the Astral Orb—the ultimate weapon he'd used to defeat the assassin. The Dalex creature did the rest. Conor definitely didn't mind having a V-Tech tag along after all.

This time numerous attendees crowded the spacious room. Administrators, cadets, workers, medics, merchants, and instructors milled about, speaking only in hushed whispers. Several huddled around the telescope's wisp screen. Conor recognized the slim woman with the short-cropped chestnut hair as she turned to face the rest of the group. Kim. She spoke up in a loud voice. "They're about to launch."

Conor turned to Byro. "What's going on?"

Byro leaned in while keeping his view fixed on the planet off in the distance. "You sure you don't know? Never seen a military funeral before?"

"Uh, no. I mean, maybe when I was younger, but I don't remember," Conor said, trying to hide the fact that, of course, he'd never seen a Jopali funeral before. But at that moment, the tiny lie seemed better than revealing the truth about being from a completely different galaxy. Besides, perhaps Byro would be smart enough to figure that one out on his own.

"Any moment, we'll see them launch the capsules containing the soldiers. They'll shoot through the clouds and atmosphere and then rupture," Byro whispered in an effort to demonstrate reverence for the occasion. "There they go," he added while pointing toward the blue-green planet in the distance.

They watched on the Jopali satellite screens as dozens of tiny orange explosions erupted on the surface, sending the encapsulated caskets into space. Once they entered Jopal's orbit, they ruptured in a fantastic display of light. Byro leaned into Conor again and whispered, "The blue and gold sparks are the dead Federation soldiers. When you see one followed by a giant red ring, then that means it was an Elite or dignitary—someone really important. There, see," Byro said while pointing again.

Conor watched as one of the capsules exploded in blue and gold followed by a wave of crimson pulsing outward in all directions. Three similar bursts followed.

"I hope to get the red ring when my time comes," Byro said, as if to himself, his words drowned out by rapid booms sounding out from under the room.

"What's going on?" Conor asked, as he felt the floor vibrate.

"The Academy is releasing our own dead now. They're being recognized for their own sacrifices," Byro replied.

Conor pulled away and stood silent, just watching the funeral tubes explode outside in spectacular fashion. As the casket tubes launched, animated holographic images of the deceased projected above, looming large above the crowd. Dozens of soldiers, instructors, and cadets materialized and moved in silent footage, a celebration of their essence and personality.

Conor recognized many of them: Tiera's friend, Yaoli, Combatives Instructor Nalinia Haz, and Piloting Instructor Nicet Blatori. He'd never get to see if Conor had improved on the Spectre. Their loss would be profound, but Conor felt deep, wrenching grief when Adin flashed. He spun with the same optimistic energy and joy Conor had felt with each encounter. Adin's hologram ended with a wide smile and a finger point, as if reminding everyone to enjoy life to its fullest despite the circumstances.

Adin faded into a female's image. Conor recognized the girl to be one of his enemies, Danica of the Collective. She swung a sword with tactical precision, and then the image changed to her firing a rifle with focused intensity. He watched as her hologram shifted to a different depiction of the bully who'd brought him so much frustration.

She now embraced her twin, both adorned in training uniforms. The hologram rotated to show her smiling face, a side of her most had never witnessed. In that moment, Conor even felt sorrow for her, or more so for her badly injured sister seated across the room and being consoled by battle-beaten Gavril and Cyril.

As the event simmered to a close, most attendees wandered out of the Observation Deck. Some lingered inside, reflecting on the fallen and gazing into the majesty of space as their particles dispersed among the stars. Tiera led the group back into the loading dock, where giant banners depicting portraits of the deceased unfurled all around.

Conor trailed behind. He patted the fearless Titan strutting beside him as they walked the corridors back to the Residential District. His thoughts rested on the departed—all the brave guardians of the Federation who would be immortalized in the halls and memories of every Jopali. Then a sudden ache formed in his chest as a strangely familiar image floated into his memory.

An ashen-haired man with glasses moved forward, wrapping his arms around the woman standing in front of him. He kissed her neck and she smiled, adjusting the bundle in her arms. Norman and Melina were their names—his parents. This time, she wasn't holding a rifle or piece of toast. It was a baby named Grayson—his little brother.

They, too, had sacrificed and fallen in battle. Conor let the grim realization settle in that he would never see them again. They wouldn't be honored with fireworks displays and banners. But he would honor them by remembering. Tears soaked his cheeks as more and more memories untangled.

Gone, but no longer forgotten.

**The Forge**
**Training Temple**

The next morning, Conor met Anibal at the bridge over the winding river. He still wondered about making the leap below into the crystal waters, but this meeting didn't include swim time. "You feeling better?" Anibal asked.

"I feel good," Conor answered.

Anibal looked at the boy's arm. "Was it this or the other one?" He checked the other arm but didn't see marks on either.

"That's the one."

"Unbelievable. Three measly days, and there isn't even a scratch on you."

"They were still there, kinda, yesterday."

"Nothing now," Anibal said. He sighed. "Your training will now truly begin. It will go far beyond what the other cadets receive. Tailored specifically to heighten and advance your abilities. You think you're ready?"

"I am."

"Good." Anibal began walking toward the training temple's looming towers. "Another thing. Your father, the Commander, will also be participating in your training regimen."

"Oh, okay."

"Yeah, well you have no idea, yet. You think the Academy is impressive or challenging—even this place here? Just wait for what Commander Welcos has in mind for you."

"Sounds like fun. I can handle it."

"Wow. Look at this boy with all the confidence now. We'll see if you deserve it." They reached the center disc pad, and Anibal activated it. "You ready to try this again? Get to the top and touch my shoulder."

"Got it."

Anibal centered himself on the pad and looked down at his pulsero. He tapped the button and began to levitate. As he ascended, he tucked his legs and tapped the bracelet again. The illuminated steps appeared all around the columns—the steppingstones of a giant, or of someone who could defy gravity's influence. He reached the top and looked down to give Conor the signal to begin his climb.

He sat puzzled. His head moved around, trying to figure out where the boy had gone. Did he bail out on training already? Without even trying? What a disappointment.

"Hey!" Conor's voice rang out. He hadn't left. Anibal spun around trying to find where his pupil was hiding. He still couldn't find him. "Look up," Conor urged.

Anibal craned his neck upward and spotted the boy holding onto the column like a champion on the winner's platform. Conor hadn't just traversed the apex of the steps, but he somehow reached the very pinnacle, where steps didn't exist. And he'd done it with blinding speed.

"What took you so long?" Conor asked with a bold grin.

"Ha. Ha. Fine, your teacher is impressed."

"Yeah?"

"A little," Anibal said, holding his fingers out to indicate a small pinch.

"Well, I do believe you said I need to tap your shoulder, right?"

"Don't you dare."

Conor shrugged. "Gotta finish the challenge."

"No. No. No."

Conor nodded with a smirk. Then he dove downward.

# EPILOGUE

**Jopal**
**Mertio, Capital City**
**Lesser Temple**

The encapsulated candles cast the darkened room in a warm glow. Shadows draped the edges of the round room, giving the occupants the sense of absolute secrecy and protection from prying observation.

Wilda Ti walked in unaccompanied, only to find she was the last to arrive. She recognized the faces gathered around the round table at the room's center. One face took her by surprise. "Elder Waan," she gasped. She felt for a chair and pulled it away, sliding into it with trained grace and composure. "You are thought to be dead."

"That I am not."

"What brings you out of hiding?"

The Elder spread his arms out. "What makes you believe I am not still? Wilda Ti nodded and then glanced over at Supreme Commander Welcos, seated next to Valitat Bithos, and then to Anibal. She could understand their presence, but such a meeting shouldn't involve the Paladin.

"Why have you decided on this group?" Wilda Ti asked.

"Ease your mind," Elder Waan offered. "I will reveal it to you. Each of you will play a significant role in what happens next. Is everyone set?" He looked to each of the four other attendees. Once he received a nod, he proceeded. "Very well. I do not intend to discuss our war with the Kravii. Though this is a matter always present in our minds and demands exacting strategic planning and action, there is another concern far more crucial. You know of what I speak?"

"The assassin," Makon offered.

"Yes, but there is more to it. The Chief Administrative Leader of our illustrious Academy knows."

Wilda Ti hesitated as she collected her memories of the battle, the assassin, the murder of Novac Riv, and her meeting with the Investigative, Sandor Leo. "The darkening of the sun."

"That indeed, Wilda Ti. What you should know is that this is not new. It has been done in other systems before. Our Nivror system within the Vesputi galaxy is not the first. It is merely the latest. We have a new enemy, one of which your cadets have met."

Makon rubbed his eyes. "My son met him and beat him."

"Yes, Commander. A feat, I fear, few others could accomplish. Unfortunately, more will come. And let us not forget, Master Conor Hawk is not truly your son. He is your fellow countryman as you share the same native home you once referred to as Earth."

"What do you believe Conor has to do with the enemy?" Makon asked, hoping to divert the conversation away from the memory of his home.

"Locked away in his troubled memory is the key. I believe he has met them before, and he will be critical in our path to understanding their purpose, and if we are fortunate, the defeat of their purpose."

"This new enemy has aligned with the Kravii," Makon added.

"No, they haven't," Anibal interjected. Makon and Wilda Ti turned to him, and he absorbed their glances of disbelief. "I watched the assassin kill them as swiftly as our own soldiers."

Makon remembered the discovery on Hadak-5. "You know, he's right. This enemy uses them for its own gains."

"This could be turned into an advantage," Elder Waan said in thought. "But, for now we need to learn more. We must have haste. I fear time will work against us."

"How should we proceed?" Wilda Ti asked.

"The boy must be trained and brought to remember his life—the events leading to his arrival. This will involve delving into the destruction of his ship."

"The four of us will work on it immediately," Makon said.

"Very well. We will meet again once we've studied our darkening star and you have an update on the boy."

"There is one other thing," Anibal said, bringing his hands forward on the table. "It could be nothing, but when he and I discussed his final fight with this assassin-thing, Conor mentioned something it said before being sucked into oblivion."

"What was it?" the Elder asked.

"'Vosis.' He didn't know what it meant, and I don't know what a 'Vosis' is."

"What is Vosis? I've never heard of it before," Makon said.

"Me, neither. Could be nothing," Wilda Ti said.

"True—it could be nothing. But it could also be everything." Elder Waan closed his eyes, pausing for a long moment in deep thought. "Friends, I hesitate to say this, but what if we are asking the wrong question?"

Makon stretched forward in his chair. "What would be the right question?"

Elder Waan opened his eyes wide. "*Who is Vosis*?"

**To Be Continued . . .**

# AUTHOR BIO

Jason Bradford grew up in Baltimore, Maryland, and now resides in Arizona with his wife and children. He earned a Bachelor of Arts in English and dedicated himself to a career in public service. Endeavoring to tap into his passion for creative storytelling, he set to work on his *Solar Ashes* series. Learn more and connect at Bradfordbooks.com or Solarashes.com.